R.ea

P9-EJZ-688

WHEN PASSION BEGINS

As their carriage rattled past Candlewick Street the duke leaned toward Frances to encircle her slender wrist with warm fingers. "In London, sweet Frances, the streets are named for great people or whatever is sold on them."

"And what do they sell on Love Lane, my Lord Duke of Richmond?" she asked solemnly.

Too late, she realized she had entered dangerous territory. His hand on her wrist gave a little tug that brought her mouth within inches of his. She stared at him as if suspended, mesmerized. When he took her lips, she willed herself to feel nothing.

But the kiss went breathlessly on, making her press up against him while his free hand brushed down the arch of her throat. She moaned helplessly as his mouth and the backs of his fingers stroked her throat, her shoulders, shoving the thin material on both sides slightly down to kiss the hollows under her collarbones.

She couldn't breathe, couldn't think—could only sense the unquenchable desire she felt for this one man. She found herself kissing him back with an intensity she could not explain, with a wantonness she had never fathomed in herself.

His face, so close to her, spun dizzily to match the swaying of the carriage. Perhaps they were flying now, high above London, sailing in the cloudless heavens like his ship adrift in rapturous seas. . . .

IRRESISTIBLE ROMANCE FROM ZEBRA!

MOONLIGHT ANGEL (1599, $3.75)
by Casey Stuart

Dashing Captain Damian Legare, seeing voluptuous Angelique, found his blood pounding in his veins. Though she had worshipped him before with a little girl's adoration, her desires now were those of a passionate woman. Submitting to his ardent caresses, she would surrender to one perfect night of unparalleled ecstasy and radiant rapture.

WAVES OF PASSION (1322, $3.50)
by Casey Stuart

Accused of killing her father, Alaina escaped by slipping aboard a ship to America. Vowing to find the real murderer, she instead found herself in the arms of Captain Justin Chandler—a pirate she could never love. But Justin, unaware of her innocent heart, caressed her luscious curves until there was no turning back from desire—from endless WAVES OF PASSION.

PASSION'S DREAM (1086, $3.50)
by Casey Stuart

Beautiful Morgan Fitzgerald, hating the Yankees for having murdered her parents and destroying everything she cherished, swore she'd kill every last one of them. Then she met Lieutenant Riordan. Though she tried to hate him, when he held her in his arms her lips longed for his fiery kisses, and her heart yearned for the Yankee's searing love!

RAPTURE'S CROWN (1570, $3.95)
by Karen Harper

As the King's favorite, blue-eyed Frances could have had anything, but she was mesmerized by the heated emerald gaze of Charles, Duke of Richmond. Previously faithful to their royal master, the two noble subjects now risked treason, submitting only to the rule of desire, the rule of RAPTURE'S CROWN.

ISLAND ECSTASY (1581, $3.75)
by Karen Harper

Lovely Jade Lotus, kidnapped from Canton by sea-roughened sailors, was left to die on a beach in the fragrant Hawaiian isles. Awakening in the arms of the handsome Don Bernardo, she found him a cruel master—whose slightest touch made her ache with desire. Their passion burning in the tropical nights, Jade craved that his moment of kindness in saving her could become a lifetime of love!

Available wherever paperbacks are sold, or order direct from the Publisher. Send cover price plus 50¢ per copy for mailing and handling to Zebra Books, 475 Park Avenue South, New York, N.Y. 10016. DO NOT SEND CASH.

RAPTURE'S CROWN

BY KAREN HARPER

ZEBRA BOOKS
KENSINGTON PUBLISHING CORP.

ZEBRA BOOKS

are published by

Kensington Publishing Corp.
475 Park Avenue South
New York, NY 10016

Copyright © 1985 by Karen Harper

All rights reserved. No part of this book may be reproduced
in any form or by any means without the prior written
consent of the Publisher, excepting brief quotes used in
reviews.

First printing: April 1985

Printed in the United States of America

*To my husband, Don,
for all the trips to England*

Prologue

The woman stretched her long limbs, luxuriating in her lover's fierce embrace. Each fiber of her being, each smooth curve of satin skin anticipated the next caress of his huge hands, enticing lips, and darting tongue.

She kissed him back fervently, swept away in the swirling tide of passion. Nothing on earth—nothing—was more wonderful than this precious moment when they melded their two beings ecstatically together. The other men who had wanted to possess her, first in France, then here at the bawdy, wild court of King Charles II who himself had pursued her for years hoping to lie where her beloved did even now—none of them mattered. This forbidden love, the treasonous crown of rapture they recklessly sought together was worth any price, any risk, if they should be found.

"My darling, my darling," she murmured as his powerful body quickened its demanding pace to match her own exalted soaring of the senses.

"Frances, I love you—always have. I've always desired you so desperately since that first day," he rasped hot against her flushed cheek as their love crested and spiraled back down from the shattering heaven of their fierce union.

They clung together in the warm little nest they had thrashed out in her mussed bed, the silence more sweet for the lurking dangers that surrounded them beyond the walls of their room. She studied his handsome profile etched by muted candleglow, cherishing their private, intimate moment they could lie naked together like this as if they had already garnered all their safe and sure tomorrows.

She ran her fingertips over his lips while he kissed them. His strong brow creased in a hint of a frown. "My sweet, you know I dare not stay or we might be discovered. The palace has eyes and tongues of its own. Damn, but one slip might ruin all our precious plans," he said low.

"Everyone's elsewhere and the evening's early," she protested in a velvet whisper.

He groaned, leaned quickly over her to press her down into the silk sheets, took her willing mouth fiercely once again, then rose to yank on his breeches beside the bed.

"Coward," she teased, and stretched while her lips and breasts still tingled deliciously from his last hurried caress.

"Coward nothing, my love. I'd just as soon lie with you in the middle of the Banquet Hall of the palace if I thought I'd still live long enough to be able to spirit you away as I intend. But until the time is ripe—soon—we'd best not be caught with our gazes linked,

let alone any other intriguing parts of our ana-
tomies."

They both laughed, and she reached for their half-
empty wine goblets and offered his to him. "Just a bit
more wine to cool your blood before you desert me
then?" she said. Her smile turned blatantly alluring
as he stared down at her with his trunkhose and shirt
dangling from his fingers. "Damn, but I want you so,
you little witch," he said and dropped the garments.
"Maybe just another minute then—or twenty—or
thirty—"

They laughed again while he sat, molten-eyed,
beside her on the bed and pulled her hard against him
so that each soft curve melded to his angular frame.
They clinked glasses once; then she watched him set
his down. His fingers lifted to ficker a pert nipple to
new enticing tautness while she held her breath and
felt the treacherous tickle of fluttering butterfly
wings deep in her stomach at his mere touch. He
drank from the goblet she lifted steadily to his lips so
he would not know how, with no effort at all, he
swamped her senses and made her go all shaky.

A deep, rumbling scream shattered the silence.
Frances, startled, looked up amazed. A string of
curses exploded at them, shredding their warm
cocoon of intimacy. Frances shrieked. The king
himself, his face livid, his mouth moving gro-
tesquely, his eyes white, came at them from a gaping
doorway!

The goblet in her hand flew upward, splashing her
naked breasts with ruby wine, splattering the guilty
sheets. She screamed again in shock and fear as her
lover thrust her behind him to protect her from the

9

infuriated king.

The worst! The worst had happened, her careening inner voice screeched at her. Seen, caught, taken by the king himself, who thought he owned her, who had forced her for so long to—

"Hell's gates, Frances!" King Charles roared. "I'll have your head for this!"

Her insides cartwheeled over. In her outrage and shock, she saw the scene as if through blurred window glass. She yanked the mottled sheet from the bed and wrapped it around her nakedness at which the king stared aghast, his mouth and eyes slits of fury. She came around the long side of the bed toward both men, now prepared to lunge at each other, and put herself between their twin towering heights. When she tried to speak, she was astounded—she had a voice.

"I'm sorry, sire, sorry that you are hurt, sorry you have come in here like this to find out," she brazened. She shook deep inside, but her voice was amazingly strong and steady. "I know it is a shock, but you must surely realize His Grace did not force me," she managed.

Her words jolted her as well as the king. She, Frances Stewart whose livelihood, well-being, even her very life perhaps, had always depended on King Charles and his powerful family, dared at last to defy him and be free. Freedom or enforcd whoredom in his bed—she saw the choice clearly now, after all this time she'd struggled so against him and other men, struggled to love and to find the courage to face the truth that she could dare to choose her love.

"Has there been a string of others?" King Charles

was demanding. "How many times has he had you these years I've been your royal footstool?"

In her panic and anger, the accusations blurred, clanged, crashed together in her brain.

"Hellish years of fawning like a jackass at your heels while you've scorned me!" the king's voice pierced the once quiet, dimly lighted room.

"No, I didn't scorn you!" she insisted. She saw her lover's body go stiff with rage; he looked as if he would dare to attack the king here in the palace with royal guards no doubt hovering outside waiting for their order to descend.

"I have admired you, sire, I appreciated you; but I love him!"

Her lover pulled her away and thrust his muscular body between her and the king to shield her. Unbidden, her mind careened back in time, past the many passionate and lustful encounters since it all began. And now, now when she had learned in life's molten crucible what she most desired, it was to be taken away and ruined!

"Guards!" the king shouted. The words echoed off the walls. "Guards!"

She clung to her lover; she murmured frenzied words—she was not sure what she was saying—as the room imploded with crimson-clad Yeoman Guards who dragged her beloved off. "Please, no—please—no. We've done nothing illegal and this is a reasonable king," she heard herself say to the stony-faced guards.

The door slammed. Feet shuffled away; lances and metal pikes clanked to distant nothingness. Wrapped in only a clinging sheet, she faced the demonic, black

11

rage of Charles Stuart, king of England.

His glittering obsidian eyes raked her once, up and down. Only a tiny space of six feet separated her from the onslaught which had come to shake the years of yearning to their very core.

How very far in time and space, she thought erratically, she had come to this ultimate confrontation that would decide her very fate. If she had only known that day in the gardens when she had experienced the first faint ripples of rapture that had led to this, she might not have dared so much. But yes, yes, for rapture's own crown of love, she would face anything.

She stood her ground. She lifted her chin, and her eyes met his unflinchingly. Yet she saw not his angry face, but in her mind's eye, the great, gray medieval French château and the peaceful gardens where it had all begun.

Part I

The Lovely Rose

Song

Go, lovely rose!
Tell her that wastes her time and me
That now she knows,
When I compare her to thee,
How sweet and fair she seems to be.

Tell her that's young,
And shuns to have her graces spied,
That hadst thou sprung
In deserts, where no men abide,
Though must have uncommended died.

Small is the worth
Of beauty from the light retired;
Bid her come forth,
Suffer herself to be desired,
And not blush so to be admired.

Then die! that she
The common fate of all things rare
May read in thee;
How small a part of time they share
That are so wondrous sweet and fair!

—Edmund Waller

Chapter One

The great, gray medieval French château of Saint-Germain-en-Laye was the only place the young Scottish-born Frances Theresa Stewart could yet call home. Just as her dear companion, the Princess Minette, who was of marriageable age herself, and as Frances' own younger sister Sophia and little brother Walter, the slender, tawny-haired daughter of the English queen's poor, dead Scottish doctor, knew Saint-Germain's terraces and courtyards and its vast array of chambers as well as had the original architects who had designed and constructed the vast royal palace for King Francis I more than a century before.

This clear, brisk September day began as calmly as any other, but when the girl looked back on it later, it was as indelibly painted in her memory as were the priceless, ebullient mythological scenes she had loved when she'd seen the fabulous artwork gracing the Palais Royal in Paris during her brief visits to the court of King Louis XIV.

This September day of 1660, only four months after King Charles II had gone home at the invitation of the English Parliament to reclaim his throne, was a wonderful day. In general, these four months of the Stuart restoration had bestowed more joy and visitors, more happy plans and good food, more new clothes and new-found pride upon the once-wretched band of royalist exiles than they had imagined possible during the depths of their long despair. Wonderful days at last, but heavens, this special one—the day she had really come alive. It was when she was certain she had become an adult, the day she had first glimpsed the truth hidden in her dear friend Minette's heart, the day she had first seen her mother clearly, and the first day she had ever met one of the two Charles Stuarts who were to so dominate her life.

The queen's retinue, including Frances' mother Sophia and the queen's ever-present escort Lord Henry Jermyn, sat under draped silken awnings arrayed like painted shells along the Grande Terrasse of Saint-Germain with its splendid view of rose gardens and gravel walks framed by the blue-green hunt forest beyond. Behind the royal entourage stretched the blond-gray stone, steep-roofed, pentagonal château. Beloved by earlier French monarchs, home once to Mary Queen of Scots, birthplace of the present young French King Louis XIV, Saint-Germain had now been the court of the Queen Mother, Henriette Maria, King Louis' aunt for almost fifteen years. But on this day, they all began to think about leaving this home Frances had loved since her memory began. They were going home to the England of the newly restored King Charles II.

16

The Princess Minette and Frances sat on the steps sloping down to the well-manicured and flagrantly blooming gardens, and watched the two younger Stewart children dash in and out of the tall, trimmed hedges with four of the queen's yelping spaniels at their heels.

Minette heaved a huge sigh that shook her delicate frame and twisted her fingers in her lap as she spoke. "I suppose, Frances, we should don a straw hat or vizard in this sun or our pink faces will scandalize the royal French or English court—whichever we find ourselves in first. A scandal to have sun color on pale skin such as ours. My friend Philippe would chain me in a dungeon for weeks if he saw me thus, and whatever would King Louis say?"

Frances laughed, her light voice chiming in over Minette's. "You fret too much of pleasing men," Frances scolded. "This king, that king, Duke Philippe, lord whoever. But then, mother says we have been fortunate to be somewhat in control of our doings here, without men like a pack of dogs snapping at us."

The distant yips and shouts of the cavorting dogs and children made them both smile at her choice of words.

"It's true, Your Grace! I vow, we have had visits from your brother King Charles until he went home to London in May to be king and the French King Louis always sends orders, but usually from a distance, except when we've been to Paris to be with him on rare occasions," Frances protested.

Her voice trailed off as she caught the wistful softening of her friend's delicate features framed by ringlets of pale blond hair. "Yes, my dear cousin, royal Louis," Minette said, and her blue eyes darted away over the vast panorama of lawns, roses, and lime trees to the deep forest. "Dearest Kind Louis, and then, there is his brother, Philippe, duke of Orleans . . ." she mused, half to herself.

The princess said no more as if the crisp September wind had snatched her thoughts away with her words, and in Frances' agile brain these new brush strokes of Minette's portrait illumined a certain realization. Minette, to whom Frances had served as companion and maid of honor nearly since she could remember, Minette who it was assumed would marry the stylish, foppish Philippe, young brother of King Louis—this delicate Minette who laughed and whispered and strolled privately away with the young newly married, twenty-three-year-old King Louis whenever they visited Paris—Minette dared to love Louis, not Philippe!

Frances felt her cheeks blush hot in the sun at the impact of the secret opened to her now. Mother would be angry at their sitting in the sun and at the knowledge the princess had found herself in such a trap set by a man, even if he was the king of one of the most powerful nations on the earth!

"Frances, you look angry again," Minette pouted prettily. "Let's call Sophia and Walter and go up in the shade before we both get summoned and scolded."

"I vow, they're all right, Your Grace. We can see them from the terrace." And then, as they stood and started up the path, Frances ventured, "King Louis' marriage to Maria Teresa last June—it will make

18

him happy, I am sure, aren't you? I know you thought of it for days after.''

The moment she spoke, she regretted the probe, for Minette turned to her uncharacteristically narrow-eyed and haughty-faced. "And how do you know that, little Frances? Of course, I hope he's happy with her, but we've all heard how it goes with such dynastic marriages. He's had mistresses before to seek his own pleasure and is likely to again, I suppose, though that's none of my concern. One of the saddest things about my dear mother being alone now without my father, the martyred king, all these years, is that they were really in love. My brother King Charles told me so last time he was here. Our father wrote him a letter once before—before he was martyred and it said, 'You, my dear son Charles, are the son of our love.' Isn't that beautiful? And since Charles was firstborn, it must have been so for the rest of us: Mary, James, Elizabeth, Anne, Henry, me—all of us. I think it's wonderful—something to strive for. I hope to love my husband that well or to grow into love over the years at least. What about yours?''

"Mine?''

"Your parents, gooseling! We have both lost our fathers though, I dare say, at least you can remember yours.''

"I was only six when he died, you know,'' Frances answered, furrowing her clear brow as fragmented pictures cut through her memory: father, big and calm, but strict. His large, capable hands caring for her when she had a fever and mother would not even come into the room, father's quiet voice shushing mother's shrill one.

"Of course, they were very in love too," Frances said, and colored again to realize that not only had she blatantly lied to Minette but that she had never really dared to think about it before. She silently said a prayer, either to allay the falsehood or the pain of what the truth must mean.

"I'm glad they were in love too," Minette whispered, and smiled so pensively it tore at Frances' young heart. "I suppose that is why after your father died, my mother and yours have been such fast companions."

Suddenly, Frances was smitten with the overwhelming need to change the subject. Thoughts of her parents together frightened her much more than the gnawing awareness that the princess must love Louis, the French king, and was likely to be hurt and trapped and scandalized, as mother always warned, by it all.

"Speaking of royal marriages and things like that," Frances said and plucked a handful of heady-scented boxwood leaves from the hedge they strolled by, "is there more word on King Charles's choice of a bride now that he is a restored king and thirty years of age already? Surely now, he will have so many to choose from, and he is so clever and tall and brave that I guess any lady would love him."

Minette's face lit with some new awareness as she studied her young friend's apparently guileless face. "Do you recall him so clearly from his few quick and rather heated visits to the queen then, gooseling, or have you hearkened to my great admiration for him?" Minette inquired.

"I do remember him a little from the last time he

was here. They did argue a bit, didn't they?" Frances drawled, unsure of why she had dared to begin this new topic. "But not the two of you—you got on famously, I vow."

"Indeed, we did despite how my Charles—the king, I mean—and mother scarcely spoke over the way he made decisions for all of us as he has ever since father's been martyred. The queen believes she would rule us all, of course, at least she did until the king was restored to London. Now, I think, our dear King Charles will see a much calmer Queen Mother when we all go to London to visit this winter. No more scolding perhaps, no more mother's orders to a grown man. That last series of rows you refer to was over what our brother James should do and the way the queen is rearing King Charles's son little Fitzroy."

Even as Minette spoke of the eleven-year-old illegitimate son of King Charles II and Lucy Walter, one of his several mistresses in exile, the boy, called James Croft, Fitzroy, was tossing carved and gilt chairs and footstools into the fountain on the terraced slope below their view. Like her royal mother, the Princess Minette laughed and smiled indulgently at his antic crashing of floating furniture together as though the pieces were warships at sea, while Frances, like her mother on that same subject, held her tongue and silently predicted the boy would be spoiled like a rotten egg and there would be no controlling his demands as a young man if the new king ever sent for his child to come home. And since the lad's mother, Lucy Walter, had been dead for a year and the king now had a new mistress

21

named Barbara Villiers and no queen, the little brat of a half-royal union might be sent for to England as well as the rest of them.

The girls joined their mothers and the queen's party under the gently rippling silk awnings and listened politely to the adult conversations which centered as usual around the English Restoration of the House of Stuart or the complicated machinations of the French Bourbon dynasty.

It was a varied collection, mostly women, seated about the fifty-one-year-old Henriette Maria. Her companions had remained part of her loyal retinue in wretched exile and now were being swept along into happier times. Still, Frances thought, the tiny, thin queen with her grayed, frizzled side locks of hair, narrow mouth, and pale brows had never lost her nervous, desperate look even after the good news came. Next to her own auburn-haired, mother, Sophia, the Queen Mother Henriette Maria didn't seem much of a scold, of course, but still a tenseness of personality, like a coiled clock spring waiting to snap, was there. Lord Henry Jermyn, sat at the queen's side, looking as sure and smug as any favored, privy advisor might, especially one who had begun his dubious career as a mere master of the queen's horse.

"Dear me, but Fitzroy is splattering his new silk waistcoat," the Queen Mother observed, and ever the bemused grandmother when it came to the raucous, impetuous boy, she merely smiled and went back to her original conversation.

Frances, more restive and less disciplined in court protocol and propriety than her friend the Princess

Minette, listened to the chatter but it bored her. Men might be treacherous and deceitful as mother had often said, but women could be dull and tedious unless they spoke of men or things in their vast world, she thought. Now surely, if father had been here today, or perhaps the martyred king, as Minette always called her father, or King Louis—or if the new King Charles were here—things would be better because Lord Jermyn only discussed interesting things with the queen in private if at all—

Frances was jolted from her reverie as her mother tapped her wrist smartly and whispered shrilly in her ear. "Frances, the other two have wandered off too far. I don't know why you can't keep a steady eye on them. We surely don't need them splashing about in some fountain like that wild knave Fitzroy. I swear, I can't even see either of them on the slopes or parterre down there, and if they've headed off toward the forest, I'll skin them!"

"But they weren't far off when the princess and I came back up here. I'll just walk down along the terrace a little distance to fetch them."

Relieved to have an excuse to be off on her own, Frances curtsied, though no one noticed, and hurried away before Minette might think to join her. How vibrant, how clearly brilliant the rose beds below looked, the ribbons of tall hedges, the gravel walks, and the lime trees clear to the edge of the forest, Frances marveled, exhilarated as always by privacy or temporary freedom. The sun felt warm and the breeze cool on her face as her pink silk skirts and layers of white petticoats rustled below the purple bodice laced up over her small, firm breasts. Her high-heeled shoes with their new, large purple bows crunched on the gravel as she walked along the vast stretch of the château grounds above which she had last seen Sophia and Walter. Annoyed because they were nowhere in sight, she went down a flight of steps to where the boy Fitzroy still amused himself at the expense of three waterlogged chairs; a floating, cracked footstool; and two very wet and unamused footmen.

James Crofts, Fitzroy, was undeniably handsome, tall and slender for his age even as his royal father had always been, and Frances noted just before he saw her that in him was the same eternally pent-up tension his grandmother Henriette Maria displayed.

"Want to play, Frances?" Fitzroy yelled at her much too loudly, and she prayed the women on the distant terrace would not hear. "I can send you to sea on one of these chairs; or else hike up those skirts, and we'll both wade in."

"I think not, sir. I am only looking for my brother and sister. Have you seen them?"

The boy's eyes went rudely over her before he turned back to the fountain, swept off his fine, wide-brimmed, plumed hat, and thrust it down into the foaming fountain to fill its crown with water. "They were making enough noise with some of the queen's bitch dogs earlier but haven't seen them lately," he shot back over his shoulder. "Gad, they're all right, I wager. Stay and play with me, I said."

"I can't. Mother sent me to fetch them back."

"Nasty, too good, and prissy, pretty Frances!" he exploded, and she knew her shock at his verbal attack showed on her face. "Not friendly to anyone but

24

Minette and the queen 'cause you have to be, are you, prissy Frances, Queen of Saint-Germain?"

Despite the staring footmen, he suddenly spun and rushed at her, his hat slopping water. She gasped, startled, and darted even as the wide-eyed boy heaved the water at her. She stepped back into the six-foot yew hedge behind, half turned, and got the slap of water on her neck, throat, and bosom above the lace ruffles and silk of the bodice which were instantly soaked.

"Oh, you vile, little wretch!" she sputtered before she could stop herself. "You awful brat. I don't give a rap whose son you are!" She moved a step toward him out of the hedge, her fists clenched.

He retreated quickly, almost sheepishly, to the fountain's rim as though she had slapped him, turned his back, and sent a half-submerged, ruined chair bashing into a cracked footstool. "If they saw us from the terrace, just tell them you're so sweet on me you wanted to play with me, Queen Frances," he dared to taunt without even looking back at her.

Hot embarrassment prickled her face at being so treated and at the smothered, bemused looks of the two avid-eyed footmen. Suddenly, she felt the scratches of hedge on her neck and arms, the tangled tatter and loose strands of her careful coiffure, her dampened silk bodice clinging cold to her small, high breasts. Appalled, she spun away out of their view, around the edge of the hedge, and ran toward the looming palace. She would have to hurry now to change her bodice, then return to find the children before her mother became alarmed. Someone might note the change of garment, but that would be preferable to having everyone think she either rollicked with that rotten rogue Fitzroy or called the new king's son vile names! She only hoped no one on the distant terrace had seen what happened and that the little wretch wouldn't tell later!

She broke into a full run around the last turn of hedge, racing toward a doorway into the château, and slammed full length into a tall, hard-muscled man. The impact jarred them both, but his big hands shot out to hold her carefully as he stumbled off balance, taking her down with him. Together, they half-sat, half-fell between two white rose trees into a bed of golden marigolds.

"Oh! Oh, sir, I—I am sorry."

She dared look at him, sprawled awkwardly beside her. She was tall, a full five and one half feet, but this man's arms, chest, and long legs went on forever.

"Damn, mistress!" his deep voice growled, but his face looked more surprised and amused than angry. He was not French. He had rapped out those words in perfectly fine London English with a hint of drawl, even as King Charles spoke. Green eyes under raven brows went briefly over her wet, disheveled form as he helped her stand and stood to brush himself off. His dark brown velvet breeches hid the dirt well enough, but his white boothose were smudged and his lace cravat and one of the fine cuffs draped elegantly from his green waistcoat showed streaks of rich garden loam and gold marigold dust.

His eyes darted back and forth from her shocked face to his own disarray as he continued to brush himself off. She noted his feathered hat, plume up, between the marigolds behind them and bent to

26

retrieve it for him.

"Fine way to greet a king's envoy here in France, a place supposedly known for its elegant hospitality," he said at last, his voice gruff. "Or do pretty maids alway dart out of nowhere to bowl over innocent men on duty to the Queen Mother, and so carefully garbed to look their best? Hell's gates, but you've really done it now as I look more like a gardener than a fine, new duke."

"Duke? King's envoy?" she managed, her mind still annoyed by rude Fitzroy, let alone this. "To Queen Henriette Maria from King Charles?"

"That's my mission, mistress, and now you've made me late as well as dirty with no time to go back as I sent the others by another way to meet me on the terrace. Damn, but I hate to get into court finery anyway. She is still receiving on the Grande Terrasse, isn't she? Not a bit of French accent in your English. You are one of her maids, aren't you?"

The green eyes with golden glitters of sun glow fell into instant shadow as he took his hat from her and replaced it on his full head of curly, brown hair. She stared foolishly up at him for a moment without answering as her quick brain tried to assess the various questions he had asked. His face wasn't quite handsome but—strong, maybe arrogant or a little rough. His chin was very square, stonelike; his brows were slightly shaggy, not elegantly arched as King Louis' or even like that rotten little Fitzroy's; his mouth was firm, his lower lip was full; the slight ruffian look about him came, she decided, from the little bump on his nose where he had probably been in a shameful brawl and broken it and from the small, jagged white scar on the smooth, brown skin of his left high cheekbone. Surely, he looked more like some privateer or brigand than a king's envoy.

"If you're finished staring now, mistress, give me a hand here while I try to repair a little more of the damage you've caused."

"I really must be off. I said I'm sorry for the mishap. And I'm not just one of the queen's maids."

"She's the Queen Mother now," he corrected rudely. "And I see you had a bit of an accident before you crashed into me. Do you make a practice of catastrophes? Your bodice is soaked."

To her dismay, he reached out a long arm and leaned on her slender shoulders while he smacked the dirt from the white boothose covering the backs of the strong calves of his legs. His weight on her seemed enormous even though he still stood on one leg and then the other. His arm was very strong and he smelled of some clean musk odor she could not place. No man, no one, had dared to almost embrace her like this. Stiffly, she stood pulled close to him, a strange, brazen man who knew King Charles and who would probably tell him everything about this, or worse, tell the Queen Mother, as he insisted on calling her.

She suddenly pulled away from the warm contact with his arm and strong ribs and was nearly shouting at him before she knew she was even speaking.

"I am not some maid or flower girl to be leaned on and corrected, envoy or duke or whatever you are! You might just watch where you're walking too, I vow. I am Lady Frances Stewart, maid of honor to the Princess Henriette-Anne known as Minette, and I am

28

daughter of the Queen Mother's late physician, Walter Stewart.''

"And like to go far at someone's court if you grow up a bit from the fiesty, slender maid you are now into the tempting and beautiful woman you promise to be, Maid of Honor Frances Stewart,'' he cut short her tirade. "Good day to you. And should you ever be sent for to King Charles's court in London, and can bridle that shrill voice a bit, remember that the Duke of Richmond will be the first to volunteer to have you run him down. Your servant, Lady Frances.''

He took two steps away and glanced back for one instant, grinning wickedly at the furious effect his parting words had created. She stood, slender arms on hips, her pert breasts thrust up as she held her beautiful head high. The defiant tilt of her jaw bespoke elegance and temper, and her face was already a woman's face—strikingly lovely, somewhere between temptress and angel. The full curls of her disheveled coiffure were tawny brown with reddish highlights in the slant of sun. Her face was a perfect oval, cheekbones high, the nose straight, the sensual mouth with bowed upper lip and full lower lip drawn into a pout, and the heavy fringed eyes a heavenly—an icy—blue. She stood tall, probably only six inches shorter than he; very slender, but never quite delicate with that fiery spirit and exciting challenge in her mouth and eyes.

Still in half stride, he shook his head to throw off such foolhardy thoughts. He was full twenty and a recent widower only newly out of mourning, and this tempting little vixen was surely not much younger. On impulse, he drew his decorative sword while she stepped back startled. He strode to a leggy rose tree they had fallen under and cleanly cut a white rosebud on full stem in one quick slice of sword. Suddenly feeling doltish again, he swept off his hat and flourished a low bow, extending the rose to her. Their eyes snagged and held as he looked up.

"I—you said you are already late, Lord Duke," she faltered.

"Then when next we meet, perhaps you'll make it up to me, Lady Frances Stewart. A proud Scottish name and I'm Scottish myself," he said and turned away as soon as she took the rose careful not to touch his fingers or the large thorns it sported. He moved quickly now, without looking back, but his words floated clearly to her: "I've been sent to prepare a visit to London for the Queen Mother and the Princess Minette in November, so perhaps you'll be coming along too."

She stared at the end of the hedges where he had only a second ago taken up so much space. She glanced down at the white, lovely rose, unspeakably sweet. She counted to ten and followed him to peer around the tall yew border.

He was far down the terrace already and two other men had joined him. And there was little Sophia and Walter she'd been sent to fetch ages ago running along in his wake. She had to go back too, but she'd sooner perish than ever face him again after the things he'd said, the way he'd rudely studied her and dared to put his arm on her without begging her leave!

She hurried toward the cluster of silk awnings and people on the Grande Terrasse. Thank heavens, her bodice looked drier now, not so blotchy. Everyone rose as Henrietta Maria stood to greet her guests. In the sudden upward movement of heads and shoulders, Frances lost sight of the duke's tall hat and sweeping plume.

"Frances, Frances, three men from London, from the king!" her eight-year-old brother Walter shouted to her the minute he spotted her in the fringes of the attentive retinue.

"Sh! Just stand here quietly," Frances hissed at him, inadvertently pricking herself with a rose thorn as she moved to put a hand on his shoulder.

The Duke of Richmond's words floated clearly to her, but the Queen Mother's were more muffled.

"Welcome to our English court in France, my lord," the quiet words of greeting came from Henrietta Maria. "And now, I understand something of great joy is all settled. This November, everyone, the Princess Minette and I shall be visiting our beloved King Charles in London, home at last if only for a while. Ladies, and my dear Lord Jermyn, may I present to you the king's fourth cousin, who even bears the same name and proud Scottish heritage, the fourth Duke of Richmond and sixth Duke of Lennox, Lord Chamberlain of King Charles and Lord High Admiral of Scotland, Charles Stuart."

Some people clapped; everyone murmured, and Lord Jermyn's low voice said something. Frances' insides tilted over at the raft of important-sounding titles—and he was related to the king! Worse, he was his Lord Chamberlain, and she and Minette had spent hours since May studying English court etiquette and organization for when Minette would visit or go home to live. Lord Chamberlain—oh, heavens! He resided at court in the king's livery and lodging, served his monarch at coronations, sat at the king's right hand when Parliament opened, and administered the whole Palace of Westminster. But he had seemed so young, somehow unsophisticated, and rough mannered!

"Frances," little Walter whispered up at her, much too loudly, "that one tall man there talking to the queen. Is he all those things? What's Lord High Admiral of Scotland do? If he fights in warships at sea, I've got to go tell Fitzroy!"

"Quiet! I want to hear what they are saying, Walter!"

The public, formal greetings and conversation went smoothly enough in the beginning though Frances could tell the Queen Mother was becoming more and more annoyed that all the detailed plans for her trip to London were already decided by her royal son. Mercifully, Lord Jermyn at last spoke up to change the subject.

"And James, duke of York, the Queen Mother's second son," Jermyn asked smoothly. "Does he fare as well as our sovereign?"

Frances heard no immediate answer from the duke, and she dropped her hand from Walter's shoulder to move closer. She could see the duke clearly now: he was as young as she remembered, probably only in his early twenties, so that whole string of honors must be only because he was lucky enough to be the king's fourth cousin.

"The Duke of York is well and busy, of course, Lord Jermyn," the duke said. "More of him I prefer

32

to speak to the Queen Mother later."

"But he is well?" Henrietta Maria's voice cut in. "They are both well?"

"Indeed, Your Majesty, hearty as ever, the Duke of York is a fine Lord High Admiral of the English fleet from whom I hope to learn much as I govern Scotland's navy."

They strolled off the terrace, coming toward her now, and the little crowd buckled inward to clear a path. Frances stepped back behind a portly lady, so the duke would not see that she stared so avidly, but he was frowning down at the diminutive Henrietta Maria and did not cast the slightest glance her way. After they passed by, Minette appeared, linking her arm in Frances' and pulling her along behind.

"Isn't it terribly exciting about London, Frances? You'll be going too, of course, you and your mother. I cannot wait to see my beloved Charles again. And we'll be able to meet, at last, all the wonderful people of the court, men like the Duke of Richmond."

"Richmond? He's hardly wonderful, Your Grace. He seems rather uncourtly and rude to me."

"You silly goose! Because his stockings are soiled, I suppose you mean. After all, he is Lord High Admiral and we'll be going back on a vessel under his honorary command since my Uncle James is too busy in London, so you'd best keep such thoughts to yourself. I swear, I thought he made a rather dashing seaman, roguish and yet stern. And whatever happened to you, Frances? Your pink skirts are dirty here along the hem and your tresses are all pulled out of the bodkins in back."

Frances felt herself color as she cursed both that

little monster Fitzroy and that big ruffian Richmond, but she kept her face calm and her eyes steadily ahead, on the Queen Mother and the duke, as they all paraded toward the château. The king's tall envoy and the little woman who came not even to his shoulder were off to the side away from their little retinue now, and even Frances' mother had dropped back quite far.

"About my skirts," Frances answered Minette at last. "I hate to admit it, but when I was looking for Walter and Sophia, I fell, and then, wouldn't you know, the two little darlings just appeared on their own."

"You fell," Minette repeated, her voice somehow amused. "And did you fall into a rosebush laden with afternoon dew to besprinkle your bodice like this and then come up holding this lovely, cut white rose, drearest Frances?"

Minette's silvery laughter was pierced by the sudden shrieked words of a woman. "Oh! Oh, it's mother screaming something about my brother James," Minette cried and dashed away even before Frances could clear her own thoughts to decipher the strangled shouts the little woman had hurled at the stiff figure of Richmond up ahead.

Frances ran toward her own mother who pulled her back. "Mother! What is it? Whatever did he tell her about the Duke of York?"

Her mother's voice seemed strangely pleased and triumphant amidst all the turmoil a few yards ahead. "It seems, my Frances, the present heir presumptive to King Charles's hard-won throne has married a commoner—one which he got conveniently with

34

child first. The poor queen will never, never get over this affront after the way she's coddled him, loved him. But I could have told her. And she should see trouble in her son, the king's ordering her about these last years—never trust a man, for they always hurt you. Never trust them and never, never love them.''

This familiar litany about men washed right over Frances. She never questioned or argued that credo of her mother's anymore.

"The commoner he wed with, Mother—who was it? Did the duke say?''

"Chancellor Clarendon's daughter, it seems—Anne Hyde, poor soul. And now so that he might desert the poor lass, the duke's comrades all claim to have known her favors too.''

"Which duke? Not Richmond?''

Her mother's eyes narrowed as she suddenly noted the disarray of her daughter's usually immaculate clothing. "Richmond? We were hardly speaking of Richmond, Frances, though I vow, he's as much a scoundrel as the next one—as them all. I'll get the two others and we'll go in now. The queen won't be desiring our company tonight.''

Her mother turned back toward the terrace to summon little Walter and Sophia as Frances, oblivious to thorns, tightly gripped her pure white rose and gazed wide-eyed across the vibrantly painted vistas of Saint-Germain.

Charles II, king of Great Britain, Scotland, and Ireland, stepped jauntily out of bed and patted

Barbara Villiers' voluptuous, bare buttock before he stretched, quite naked, and strode to the little walnut sideboard to slosh some malmsey wine into a goblet.

"Od's fish, but lying with you makes me thirsty, Barbara," he said and shot a dark, hot look back to where she sat up nude on the rumpled sheets, leaning back on her hands so that her lush, full breasts hung brazenly pink-tipped under his gaze.

"Thirsty just for wine, sire, or for more of the way I slake your eager thirst?" she murmured throatily and deliberately lifted the sole of a bare foot to stroke her other knee.

The king's eyes raked over her soft, ample flesh again, and he wavered in his resolve to be off on the afternoon's business. The courtiers knew his hearty constitution never needed a nap—never had or never would. Now, obviously, Barbara Villiers would be missed and word would spread like straw fire he had been at her and in the middle of the day. Damn, but his lust for her had made him careless lately. Anyhow, he'd sent for his brother James and Lord Chancellor Edward Hyde to settle this dangerous flap about the very pregnant Lady Anne Hyde once and for all so he couldn't afford to be dallying with Barbara anymore—at least, not until after supper tonight.

She rose too when she saw mere provocative posing would not bring him back, and wrapping her discarded, nearly diaphanous chemise about her like some sort of Roman toga, she padded barefoot over to him. Leaning heavily against his side, one arm possessively around his narrow waist, she drank from his goblet, then ran a tip of pink tongue over her

36

coral lips.

"You'd best get dressed, my dear," he said. "Hurry and I'll help lace your bodice because I'm going to have to get Prodgers in here to clothe me so I can face James and Hyde to settle the Anne Hyde marriage mess."

"Oh that," she said only and snuggled against his hard frame as if he had just invited her back to the royal bed for another extended tumble.

Barbara Villiers, Madame Palmer, was twenty and had been Charles's mistress for almost a year now, despite the increasingly obvious grousings of her cuckolded husband, the Catholic Royalist Roger Palmer, who had been with Charles in the last months of exile in the Hague. Barbara came from a fine Royalist family also: she was too young to recall the loyalties and courage and noble causes of the Royalist side in the civil war, but old enough to remember the deprivations and rudeness of exile. As a result, passionate, beautiful Barbara loved plush pleasures, expensive entertainment, and utter luxury, and with her it was so easy for him to forget the harsh past ever existed.

The king was so very tall at six feet two inches that her tossed chestnut curls nestled against his black-haired chest. She murmured something he did not catch and turned her enticing face with full mouth, long nose, and langorous eyes into his shoulder to lick and nibble at his olive-hued skin.

"Now now, I said, Barbara. Best get dressed as I don't intend for Prodgers or the others who will be in here soon, like my pack of spaniels, to see all *this*!" He smacked her rump playfully again and pulled determinedly away from her embrace.

"But *we* didn't finish what *we* were discussing in bed, my love," she said low, and her crooning voice suddenly annoyed him. He loved women, in the pure sensual sense, but he hated feeling manipulated as he had always felt with his mother. Why couldn't women just be themselves and not so clinging, not so damned demanding!

He turned quickly back to study Barbara with his black slate eyes that set over the large nose and the full mouth with the narrow, ebony mustache. His gaze was so threatening that she looked for a moment as if she might consider a retreat from the topic she had dared broach again.

"I think you'd better learn, and quickly, when to leave well enough alone, my pretty," his deep, lazy voice warned. "*We* really weren't discussing one damned thing of import in bed except how much I liked you on your plump little knees and hands for me today."

"Gad, Charles, you'll give me the vapors talking like that and then they'll all see me fainted dead away on the floor like some delicate flower out of water."

He shouted a laugh and shook his luxuriant head of shiny, coal black hair as he stepped hastily into the breeches thrown across a chair back.

"'Sdeath, Barbara—you delicate and with the vapors? Now that's rare."

"Pooh! You know we were discussing your marriage. I still don't see why it needs to be with some foreign Catholic princess you simply cannot abide!

Your adoring subjects would cheer a true English marriage!"

"Which subjects, madame? You and your wildcap cousin Buckingham? You know why a foreign marriage, Barbara, and probably, yes, to the Catholic Portuguese princess at that. Prestige, allies, bloodlines, and more important than that, a fine dowry. Money, Barbara. I know you understand that, so enough said. Anyone can get used to anyone's face in a few days if it's a princess royal."

"Now you're not being fair, sire! You are king now and not sitting around some foreign court without funding waiting for your mother or her dear lord Jermyn to put food on your table or give you a new shirt. There have been fine, pure English marriages for English kings before and I just know—"

"Fine English marriages, she says," he mocked as he jammed his full linen and lace shirt in the top of his velvet breeches. "List me some, pray, Madame Palmer. Anne Boleyn? Catherine Howard? 'Sdeath, I told you to get dressed and get out before the court jackals all descend, lady! The only all-English marriage I have on my mind right now is a catastrophe as far as it has gone, and I have to see to that mess without your creating new ones. Now before Prodgers and the rest get the misconstrued notion I intend to display and hire out your exceptional talents to rebuild my treasuries, get out!"

While she stood furiously sputtering her rage, he shoved his bare feet into his shoes, scooped up his other garments from the chairs, went out into his privy Green Room, and closed the door quietly behind him. As he feared, both his brother James and Chancellor Edward Hyde were there already, pacing and not saying a solitary thing to each other. He hoped his last shouted words had not carried clear out here, but they both looked engrossed enough in their own considerable problems.

"Ah, good," he began, hoping he sounded in control of his voice, "you could both make it. James, open the door to the Vane Room and summon my Page of the Backstairs, Prodgers, will you? I need his help to get back together after my nap."

James's nervous mouth only twitched once as he complied, but Edward Hyde's face was its usual stormcloud when it came to any of his mistresses. The king knew the old man heartily disapproved of Barbara, but at least now, beset by his own daughter's dangerous antics, the clever politician in him made him forgo his standard schoolmaster lecture.

Stony-faced as though nothing was amiss, Edward Prodgers darted in and proceeded to make his disheveled master regal again while Charles ignored his ministrations and turned his attentions entirely to James and his chancellor.

"The scandalous situation of this marriage is totally out of hand," the king began slowly, trying to keep his impatience in check. "Everyone is talking, and of course, some unfortunate things are being bandied about. The Stuarts need solidified prestige at home and abroad, not this. 'Sdeath," his voice dripped sarcasm now, "I can just imagine how our dear, supportive cousin King Louis XIV is embellishing it for his court."

James's elegant eyebrows shot up over his heavy-lidded blue eyes. "You think mother has been told? Gads, I vow, she'll be beside herself with fury at the idea of your heir wedding a commoner in secret."

"Of course, she knows, James," the king said, understanding fully the panicked expression on his brother's handsome face. "She had to be told and, I thought, better by us officially than through gossip from someone like that foppish Philippe, who rides over to court Minette when he's not busy with his intimate male friends, damn him. I told Richmond to inform the Queen Mother when he went over to arrange for their visit this November. Let her rant and throw things at Richmond now and she'll be all calmed down before her arrival here."

"I doubt it," James said only, and shook his head so that his curled brown locks swayed.

"Now, my Lord Chancellor," the king said, shifting his attentions totally to Clarendon while unceremoniously stepping into his stockings and the shoes Prodgers held. "Let's face up to it—between my royal brother and your daughter, the deed is done. They were legally, if secretly wed. And she's far into a pregnancy."

"I loved her, of course, before, sire, but now—she ought to be sent to the Tower and beheaded!" Clarendon blustered, looking close to tears.

To both royal brothers' mutual surprise the jowly, wooden face of the usually imperious old man actually wobbled: his wispy, gray mustache and little, pointed beard shook even as his voice did. The king chided himself for enjoying the moment of revenge for all the pious, interminable lectures on

41

morality his stern, if trusted, advisor had subjected him to over the spare, lean years of exile.

"Chancellor, I hardly think that is called for," the king went on. "The Duke of York is twenty-six and is hardly some innocent, seduced stripling. I have spoken with the Lady Anne and believe her to be honest, virtuous—as these things go, that is—and very much in love with my brother. If you would await us in the Vane Room, the duke and I need a little conversation on how to best present this . . . this uncomfortable dilemma to the court and the realm. Meanwhile, I expect you and I charge you to treat the lady kindly. She'll no doubt be moving here to court or at least to the duke's suite in St. James's Palace soon enough so you won't be tempted to imprison and decapitate her in the Tower."

The Chancellor looked disconcerted that his king might be jesting at such a time. "I see, Your Majesty, that you have decided," he intoned gravely. "Then I can only say I regret the circumstances and would have you know that I in no way promoted or condone my daughter's rash deeds, but then, I know better than to think my political enemies would ever believe such honesty of me." He bowed stiffly to both of them, his gray eyes suddenly very sad and tired. "Your Majesty. Your Grace. I shall be in the Vane Room with the others as you bid then."

When the heavy oak door snapped shut, the king turned away from his furious brother to dismiss Prodgers. From James's livid face he could tell he was ready to explode, and Charles hated conflict. Why, when he'd been through so much tension abroad in exile did he have to face it continually here in the intimate circle of his confidants and family, he fumed silently.

"I believe the lady in the next chamber has had time to get herself together, Prodgers," he said low, still ignoring James. "Knock before you go in, though, and when the duke and I leave here, see she gets down the privy staircase and out with some semblance of propriety."

He turned back to face his brother, his heir, for whom he truly felt loyalty and affection despite their numerous differences and opposite humors and personalities. Ever since their father's head had been struck off on a scaffold outside this very palace, he had tried desperately to be both elder brother and father to all of them, especially to James, Mary, and dear, beloved Minette.

"Why did you not address me, ask me? What about my part in this?" James shouted the moment King Charles's slaty eyes looked his way.

"Keep your voice down, brother, or your words will be all over London town from the Inns of Court to the whorehouses of Saffron Hill. I assure you, I am painfully aware of your part in this, as you put it. 'Sdeath, brother, your penchant for seducing plain women never ceases to amaze me!"

"I know she's plain! I only wanted to bed her, not marry her!"

"So she held a knife to your throat and forced your chaplain to marry you to her, is that it? Grow up, James. She's not some strumpet you picked up off the street for a quick tumble, nor does she have a husband whose name could cover up such little indiscretions as the big belly she's sporting."

"Nor did Lucy Walter have those attributes when she birthed your Fitzroy!" he dared, his blue eyes blazing.

"*I* am king here, brother, and we are not discussing me."

"But I am your heir."

"Granted, for now at least."

"You surely don't intend to send for Fitzroy to legitimatize!"

"I may send for him but hardly to make him my legitimate heir. I can't stand the idea of mother rearing him there among all those women, though—and with that wily companion of hers, Henry Jermyn. Od's fish, but I suppose I'll have to create that slippery bastard an earl of something or other. No, James, I spoke of sending for a royal bride to get legal heirs of my body. Until then, you are my trusted heir and my obedient brother, I am certain."

All the fight, the hostility seemed to flow out of the younger man. He sighed, and his shoulders slumped. "But so many others have come forward to say they have had Anne Hyde too, Charles, so how am I really to know the babe she carries is mine?"

"Do you believe them? Do you really? Most of the claimants are the chancellor's political enemies or so unscrupulous they can't be trusted to care for chamber pots, let alone a young and very plain girl's reputation."

James heaved another sigh and leaned his shoulders back against the carved wall. "I know, damn me, I know."

"All right then, it's settled. The Hydes are a fine family after all—stout gentry with healthy Wiltshire

44

blood. Make love to her with the lights out, and see someone more fetching on the side."

"Gads, brother, I already have." James managed a wan smile as Charles clapped him on both shoulders.

"That's that, then," the king added awkwardly. "A stiff lip and calm eye to the world. I tell you, James, your present estate is far better than to have gotten tangled with a woman you really care for."

"You mean you and Madame Palmer—" James floundered.

"No. No! I just meant that's my philosophy in general. Let them have all of your body, a little of your brain, but none of your heart, James, and if you ever see me deviate from that creed, you have my permission to have *me* sent to the Tower and beheaded."

They both laughed in unison, but at the jesting reference to beheading, neither looked each other in the eyes. Then King Charles opened the door to the Vane Room packed with courtiers, and they both went out smiling.

Chapter Two

Frances Stewart stood in the window of her bedchamber at the Palais de Louvre and watched the River Seine sparkle in the last sun rays of the warm August evening. The river traffic was quieting now, but most of the day she had watched barges and ferries with goods and people ply the mighty, flowing highway of Paris. Most of the day she stood here and remembered while waiting for the Princess Minette.

So much had happened in the eleven months since last September when they had all been together at Saint-Germain—it had begun with that very day she had crashed into the Duke of Richmond in the gardens. He had given her a single, cut rose that day, but before he had returned to England, he had brought a whole armful of the vibrant, seductively scented blooms to her. Afraid of her rush of feelings for a man she had literally bumped into as if she had been some clumsy, stammering ninny, she had intentionally avoided him during the two brief days he'd met with the Queen Mother and Princess Minette at the château. The River Seine blurred all silvery before Frances' eyes as she remembered: like a petulant child, she had tried to avoid him because he moved her, as no one ever had before, to feel herself a willful woman.

He had actually dared to visit her room the day she had heard he was leaving. How he had known which of the small cubicles in the mazelike halls of the château had been hers—how he had known she would be there alone—she had been too astounded to ask. Suddenly, he had stood in the dim hall, his brown velvet arms full of red and yellow and salmon-hued roses when she answered the knock on her door.

"Oh—you!" she could hear herself flounder foolishly, even as the too-familiar memory assaulted her again.

"Lady Frances," his velvety, resonant voice had replied, "may I be so bold as to reintroduce you to an admirer, if an unfortunately distant one, the Duke of Richmond. It seems he has not been able to get you out of his mind and comes a poor, fond penitent to apologize for being so brusque in the gardens the other day—and to offer the most exquisite woman he has even beheld these exquisite roses."

She had blushed hot; her blood had pounded. "Not been able to get you out of his mind," his words had reverberated in her brain as she had stared, unbelieving, one moment. Heavens, it had been the same for her, thinking of him, but she'd die before she'd ever admit it to the rogue.

"You mock me, my Lord Duke," she said instead, "but I would be remiss if I did not thank you for the

48

roses which I am certain you asked permission of King Louis' gardeners to cut." She held out her arms stiffly as if to take the flowers.

"*Touché*, sweet lady," he laughed. Then to her alarm, he not only settled the fragrant flowers in her arms, but most brazenly stepped forward himself to move by her into her room.

"My Lord Duke, you can hardly—"

"—stand in the hall where someone might see me and tell the Queen Mother or your own watchful mother, so I hear. I swear, lass, but your whereabouts are better kept than a state secret and I'm only fortunate the naïve Princess Minette was finally the informer I needed."

He looked so large standing in her familiar, little chamber that the entire room suddenly shrank. How sure he looked, how very—dangerous. Her blue gaze locked with his green-gold eyes with jarring impact, and she felt for the first time in her sheltered life a distinct, terrifying stirring low in her stomach and at the very tips of her breasts, as if invisible, rough velvet caressed her there.

He took one long stride toward her and, reaching behind, shoved the heavy door closed.

"I mean not to alarm you nor to have you fear I'm some sort of raiding brigand," he told her low. "It is only that I'm leaving within the hour and I foolishly, desperately needed to see you again—to say goodbye properly."

Properly, he had said, but nothing was ever to be proper again, she feared. She tried to think of something to say. He must believe her a rural dolt, a green girl reared so far from civilized courts like that

49

of the French Louis or the English Charles that there would never be hope for her. "Goodbye then," she had said in such a breathy sigh she inwardly cursed herself for not finding her Stewart backbone to order him out before what she very badly wanted to happen did happen.

He leaned over her—that was the only word for it, he was so tall—and carefully rested a long forearm on each side of her head against the door. "When you come to King Charles's court be it with Minette or on your own, I shall see you there," he rasped, and his warm breath stirred the ringlets along her left temple. The scent of roses assailed her flared nostrils, unutterably sweet, and their leaves rustled slightly in her arms as she trembled at this rapid turn of events. She prayed he could not hear her heart pounding, pounding beneath her taut satin bodice.

He bent his elbows more so that he touched her from shoulder to elbow in a firm caress; his mouth slowly descended while she stood suspended, adrift in a sea of sensuous roses.

The kiss she dared to long for despite her fears was warm and tender, then firm and fluid as he slanted his mouth across hers. Awed, she tasted him back, savoring the smooth feel of his shaved face, shamelessly anxious he would stop. He pulled slightly away, then to her surprise, kissed her again, his lips more deliciously demanding, his warm tongue skimming her lips and invading her mouth.

Startled, she went momentarily stiff and moaned deep in her throat before his velvet arms tightened around her, roses and all, in a crushing embrace. His possession of her mouth deepened while she returned his kiss tentatively at first and then with head-spinning ardor.

"Damn, my sweet, damn but I knew it," he whispered, his lips lowering to nuzzle her throat. "I just had to see you for one moment to know if I would feel it again for you, and here under the demure demeanor of a fiery desire to match my own—"

"No. No, I can't—"

"Can't what, my sweet lass, hm? Hell, but I curse the fact we'll soon be the whole wide Channel apart!"

She tried to clear her brain, to think how to argue. Mother and the queen would have her head for allowing this—for liking it. Heavens, she had to get his hands off her waist, his treacherous lips away from her nearly bare shoulder.

"Satin—such satin skin like these rose petals," he breathed as he traced his open lips hotly down the curve of her shoulder to the top of her gown sleeve and then back up to the trembling hollow of her throat.

"You must go," she managed, but her voice was low and strangely, melodically, not her own.

"If it didn't mean my career, I'd take you with me," he said, so earnestly she stared agape before he kissed her again briefly, as if he were fighting to lighten his own mood. "On my ship—would you like that? I swear to you, Frances Stewart, someday I'll arrange it and we will do in truth what I will do only in my fondest dreams until then . . ."

The next kiss, it had been her last from him, she mused dreamily, even as she felt that same treacherous caress now as if rough velvet moved enticingly along the insides of her thighs—that last kiss had been dizzying as he embraced her, his arms like iron bands around her slender waist and too-pliant back. She had felt that last assault of lips and tongue, of his hard body pressed to her soft arms and hips and thighs as if she had fallen from a great distance—spinning, whirling downward into some wonderful abyss. . . .

Fallen into a deep pit of shame and degradation, she scolded herself, as she tried to seize control of her traitorous body even here, now, in Paris, waiting for Minette. She had let a man she hardly knew step into her room alone and kiss and fondle her—and worse, she had reveled in the rush of rapture he'd awakened in her virgin body and he knew it. He knew it when he took his leave to return to England that day eleven months ago, and he probably knew it now while he chased some other lady—if he ever thought on her one bit while she still reminisced entirely too much about him, the pompous, pushy—pirate!

After he had left there had been the exciting plans to visit the newly restored King Charles in London. But Frances had fallen ill of a lingering fever and she and her mother had never made that triumphal journey with the royal party. In January, Minette and the Queen Mother returned, but from then on, it seemed Minette was lost to her: she spoke incessantly of her beloved brother Charles to whom she owed her eternal loyalty. She made frequent journeys to Paris to visit her dear friend King Louis whom Frances was now certain poor Minette loved secretly. Then, in March, Minette had wed Philippe, duke of Orléans, King Louis' elegant but somehow disarming younger brother.

The wedding had been splendid: Minette and Philippe had ridden gaily away to their new lives in a string of gilt carriages bedecked with garlands of the orange blossoms King Louis favored all year round. And then, without Minette's close, sustaining friendship and lighthearted love, Frances had settled back into life at Saint-Germain waiting for she knew not what.

A flutter of light knocks on the door broke into her reverie and before she could even turn or respond, the door flew open and Minette entered with a cavorting, yapping pack of spaniels and her high-heeled silk slippers. She waved and pushed the dogs back out into the hall before she floated toward Frances across the spacious room.

"My darling goose, little Frances, how you have changed!"

Frances' eyes filled with tears despite the fact that, for good things or ill, she never cried. "Princess—I mean, I am so glad to see you at last, *ma grand Duchesse d'Orléans*!"

"No, when we are alone like this, I shall always be only the English Princess Minette to my family and to you, Frances. But how you've grown and filled out since I saw you at the wedding. Your waist is still petite but the bosom is more a woman's, I see."

"But I am not a bit taller, Your Grace, though I know I have gotten rounder here and there and now I am a woman in all ways too."

"Perhaps not all ways, Frances, but enough for now. But still you are so slender, even as I. King Louis teases me and says I look like the bones of the holy innocents, and he tries to fatten me with court

53

banquets and spoils me with marchpane and macaroons.''

"You see him a great deal then—the king?'' Frances ventured.

"Of course, Philippe and I are both with him and the queen often,'' Minette said in a rush and her delicately beautiful face under the blond, flowing ringlets grew ominously wistful.

Frances' eyes took in the sumptuous richness of the princess' garments. She herself had worn her best pale green, watered silk skirts drawn back to reveal layers of cream-hued, lace-edged petticoats and topped with a tightly laced, low-cut, jade green bodice. There was an elegant ribbon in her hair, but Minette's garments dazzled even in this small, dimly lighted bedchamber.

The princess was garbed entirely in rose and pink satins, in skirts edged in Chantilly lace arched back with ruby clips to reveal underskirts woven of lace and ribbons. The bustline of her plunging bodice, drawn taut to elevate the rounded tops of her small breasts, was scalloped with layer upon layer of ribbons, and little tufts of ribbons dripped from the tresses so gracefully wired out at the sides of her lovely face.

"You like the dress, I can tell, Frances. Ribbons are all the rage at Louis' court, you know, and when you go home to London, you must take the style with you.''

They sat in two upholstered chairs, facing each other across a tiny, inlaid and lacquered table. "But, Your Grace, I vow, I have no plans to go to London. You aren't going back soon are you?'' Frances asked.

"Soon? No, I fear not. Philippe probably wouldn't allow it. He's anxious for an heir of course—I suppose all men are. . . ."

Her voice trailed off and she looked down, frowning at her satin-covered knees before her pale blue eyes darted up again. "But as for England, dearest Frances, I do want you to go. I plan for you to go. You see, King Charles will undoubtedly marry the infanta of Portugal next spring and she will need maids of honor about her from good English families as well as her own Portuguese women."

"I—my family is Scottish."

"Of course, dear, but Royalists in long service to the English crown all these past dreadful years. Now the times are happy again and rewards like titles and positions are given gratefully and freely to those who have loved the king."

"I see." Frances wanted to protest, but against what, she was not certain. Her mind skipped back to the young Duke of Richmond at Saint-Germain last year as it did all too frequently: had his endless string of titles and duties come to him only because he was the king's cousin and bore the same name?

"You have heard, Your Grace, that the Queen Mother's advisor Henry Jermyn has become Earl of Saint Albans?" Frances put in to break the awkward calm while Princess Minette studied her face.

"Yes, I heard. Dear, lovely rose—do you remember the Queen Mother and I used to call you that when you were a mere child? No, I suppose not. Please listen carefully, so I might explain because Philippe may be along to fetch me soon when he sees I'm gone. You see, it was for—some unannounced duties with my husband that I could not come to you as early as I had planned today and I am regretful you had to wait."

Minette's mind flashed horrid pictures at her of Philippe's continued, degrading demands on her body—whenever the whim took him and almost any place despite the realms of propriety. That would not have been nearly so unbearable if it weren't for his simpering, clinging male friends who would wait for him continually outside their door no matter what was going on within.

"I didn't mind waiting," Frances was saying. "I would wait longer, and happily, too, to see you again now that you can so seldom come to visit, Your Grace."

"Then let me explain some things that shall be a secret between us. If you stay in France much longer, I have no doubt Philippe or King Louis will notice you and marry you to some rich Frenchman to get you to stay. That is somewhat a—a trend here, you see, to get pretty ladies about the court married but available to—to flattery."

"But I could be with you then, and we could be fast friends again. I vow, it is terribly dull and lonely without you at Saint-Germain, Your Grace, even though little Sophia grows to be less of a heathen every year."

The princess smiled fleetingly, then reached over to pull one of Frances' hands into hers on the cold, inlaid tabletop. "No. Saint-Germain, even the French court is not what I think best for you, Frances, if only you will be ruled by me in this. Believe me, I know!"

"But you wanted to come here—to live in Paris near the king and marry the Duke of Orléans."

"Yes, I swear, I did, didn't I? Then, I believe I must tell you everything so you truly understand. I wed with Philippe for many reasons, my dear friend— partly love of France, the only real home I have ever known despite the fact my heart is yet pure English. Then too, I knew I could serve as a link between Louis and my dear Charles. They are so alike in many ways and yet do not get on well at all, you know. But the two nations must. The two men as kings must!"

She loosed Frances' hand and stood to pace, her heels making little forlorn tappings on the fashionable parquet floor newly laid to help modernize the huge, stony Louvre. "Also, I married because I had lived long enough under my mother's rule and not always happily so. Also—Frances, please try to understand," she said and lowered her voice to a mere velvet rasp, "I married Philippe so that I could be near King Louis whom I believe—believed—I desperately loved and could not live without!"

Frances' sharp little intake of breath was lost as Minette's heels tapped an even quicker pattern on the floor. "I know that sounds foolish to you, Frances, but your heart is a virgin heart yet, untouched by a man you desire even as your body is. I beg you to understand a little."

Frances rose to her feet, and Minette stopped so close to her their skirts swished together. "I do value your kindness and love to me so, Your Grace, and I shall try to understand. Then, tell me, why are you so unhappy now if you are near the man—you favor."

"Oh, Frances, I swear, but it's a long, complicated

story not fit for your ears. Another time, perhaps, when I am not so afraid Philippe and his friends will descend to summon me back. He's very watchful of where I go, you see."

"Because he knows you love King Louis?" Frances gasped before she could grab the impetuous words back.

"No, not really that, for he knows full well now, I think, the king's affections are rooted firmly elsewhere. Please listen now, Frances. It is of utmost importance to me because you—you can take your mother too, of course, the whole little family can live somewhere on royal property in London—but you must go home to England to serve in my dear brother's court. This French court is no place for you and since I shall never be going again, you must go for me—be my gift, as it were—to grace my family's restoration court!"

"But, of course, you shall be going to England again, Your Grace, for private or state visits with your mother or even with your husband."

"Never mind all of that now. I may not see you again until the great celebration in a few days and even then I may not be allowed to see you alone at all. Frances, please promise me you will go home to the Stuart court, and happily so, when I can arrange to send you as the Portuguese Princess' maid of honor."

Their eyes held, and Frances read in Minette's fierce gaze a smothered grief she could not name or fashion. It frightened her, and she knew once again that mother's words of warning about men were true. "Of course, I shall go proudly and joyously, Your Grace. Of course, I shall."

Minette sighed, and as she looked away, Frances realized for the first time how very tired, almost beaten she looked. "Thank you, Frances. I shall send a note in my weekly letters to my brother suggesting the appointment then. At least my letters pass untouched."

They both started at the metallic pounding which seemed about to shatter the door. "It is Philippe," the princess said quietly, "so I shall be going back now. I hope to see you over the next few days before the great fête at the Vaux-le-Vicomte, Frances, but unless Philippe and his friends go off hunting, I fear I cannot promise. I shall remember your vow to go to England for me though."

Frances stared astounded. It was suddenly as though her dear friend had walled off her liveliness, and some sort of passionless, waxen image spoke and moved to open the door. Over Minette's petite height, Frances could see the hall outside full of handsomely attired, elegantly coiffed men, and she could hear the ever-present spaniels again.

"*Ma chère, ma chère,*" the clear, high voice of Philippe, duke of Orléans rang in Frances' ears and seemed to echo in the room, "how I have fretted some harm had befallen you, dashing off this way without any maids or ladies-in-waiting."

"I told you, my lord, my childhood companion is visiting from Saint-Germain and you know I have been detained all day and unable to see her. We were only just now finishing chatting of old times, and I am ready to go back with you," Minette said calmly as if she were reciting a memorized litany.

"Ah, *oui*, I do recall you mentioned a dear

companion, *ma chère*," the duke's voice shrilled as he shouldered past Minette into the room while other staring men moved in so quickly behind him that the princess was lost in the press.

The Duke of Orléans, King Louis XIV's brother, was small and dark featured with raven locks, but the man himself was nearly overwhelmed by his elaborate costume and coiffure. His face was powdered and rouged, and it was obvious he blackened his eyelashes as a courtesan might. Puffs and ridges of lace dripped everywhere, from cuff to cravat to silk stocking tops; and clusters of silk ribbons ran riot, pinned by winking jewels to breeches, shoes, and satin waistcoat. A rainbow of colors seized the eye from iridiscent peacock blue to coral to palest yellow. Frances had seen Philippe on his wedding day in full ornate military dress and on one earlier occasion when he visited Saint-Germain, but there was such a change! Her eyes widened as she noted the two young men closest to the duke were dressed in identical foppish profusion, but she remembered to curtsy.

"Lovely, isn't she, Lorraine?" Philippe rapped out to the man on his left. "So very slender yet not with the duchess' transparent boniness."

Frances frowned at him that he dared say aught to affront her dear Minette, but the princess was hemmed in so far back in the cluster of men, she surely had not heard.

"A stunning young woman," someone remarked. "We ought to fetch her to court, bait a hook or two with her, and see how long it takes the king to forget his whims for Louise de La Vallière, *mon Duc*!"

Several snickered and the duke smiled coldly as his

dark eyes glittered over Frances. For the first time in her young life, she felt the instinctive desire to cover her breasts and cross her legs, though she was fully clothed. There was something awful about this powerful man who had married her dear Minette, something metallic like the carved, beribboned walking stick in his ringed fist—yet also a slithering serpentine quality. And then, when he smiled indulgently and winked at her again and turned away, she knew with stunning impact what it was. As the Duke of Orléans' high voice shooed everyone out ahead of him, as he walked mincingly away, he openly fondled the tightly silk-clad buttocks of the slender young man who walked closely at his side.

The door remained open into the hall as the group's chatter and the sounds of shoes and walking sticks striking the floor grew fainter. Frances' heart thudded against her taut, jade silk bodice as she stood frozen, staring at the open, empty doorway.

Poor Minette—all the half-whispers Frances had heard about stylish, elegant Philippe rushed back. And Frances' mother had said King Charles did not favor the marriage until Minette herself assured him it was what she wanted. Philippe's fantastic garb, his men, Minette's nervousness, his gaze, that touch of the boy—her beautiful, beloved friend Minette had married a man who could not love a woman at all!

Surely, she thought, they weren't all like that here. That could not be the reason the princess insisted she not come to the French court. But now she was here for the remainder of the week and would mingle with them all at the fabulous fête at Vaux-le-Vicmote to which Minette had invited her. Philippe and his dandies would be there, King Louis himself and the Queen Marie Thérèse. And if Minette had married Philippe because she loved and wanted to be near Louis, then who was this mysterious Louise de La Vallière to whom they referred?

At last when the hall went silent, before her maid would come back to prepare her for supper, Frances moved to close the door and then went to stand again at the window where she had spent most of the day staring out. The Seine glittered now, almost blood red in the sunset, under a line of frowning gray clouds, and the sight strangely suited her more than she had known it could.

Charles Stuart, duke of Richmond and Lennox, hereditary duke of Aubigny with estates near Berri in France, Lord Chamberlain of Charles II of England, and Hereditary Lord High Admiral of Scotland admitted finally to himself that he was not happy. He sat, apparently at ease, under a big chestnut tree, his long legs sprawled out amidst piles of financial records, his arms clasped behind his head. But he frowned and stared out moodily over the sedgy, reed-studded bank of the Thames a little distance from his apartments at Whitehall Palace in the section of that vast labyrinth of courtyards and suites called the Bowling Green. Its northwestern side sported a grassy alley where the earlier kings had liked to play peacefully at bowls—but this present king was made of continual crashing bolts of energy, and his casual attitude often belied the sly and explosive strength beneath. This king for mere play preferred rising at five for a pounding game of tennis, walking miles at a clip no one but six-footers like himself could hope to match, swimming in the cold Thames, and reveling in women like that spoiled, haughty, insatiable Barbara Villiers at all hours.

Barbara Villiers, the duke mused, had enjoyed a string of lovers before she married Roger Palmer, but it had appeared she'd settled down to just the king until a few weeks ago when she had made it abundantly if privily clear she'd enjoy an afternoon visit from the Duke of Richmond when the king was in council. She fancied another tall, handsome Charles Stuart she'd said, to entertain royally. And, despite all this, the king had decided to try to rescue her from exile in the country to which her unhappily cuckolded husband had recently dragged her.

"Damn, but I'll have no part of that slick snare!" Richmond said so loudly that the lone bagpiper playing a mournful, moodily dissonant tune at the river's edge stopped to look up. "What say, Yer Grace? A march or jig to cheer you a wee more?" Cradling the sprawling set of pipes between tunes, the piper strode over to the duke.

"What? No. No, Roger. Sit down her awhile and rest. I was only making a disparaging comment about a woman."

"Only that, Yer Grace, nothing more important? Then I shall sit me down for a spell before we get back to the finances at hand."

Roger Payne, a big, burly, red-haired Scotsman whose rich lowland burr, love of piping, and kilts all blatantly bespoke his proud Scottish heritage, sat down beside the duke whose vast estate at Cobham in

Kent he now managed as steward. He shook his big head as the pipes he laid down sighed out their final droning notes. He had only come to London for a few days to report on the fruit, rye, and hop harvests, and to clear the audit accounts for Cobham, and here he'd ended up playing every tune he knew for his young master who loved piping but had never had time to perfect the art as a Scots lad actually reared in Scotland might have.

"Any particular woman, Yer Grace, or all women in general?" Roger Payne picked up the thread of conversation. "Cobham needs a lady, that she does, though not so much as she needs her lordship back."

"*She* needs," Richmond mused. "That's strange, my man. I always think of Cobham as a woman too—and a beautiful but damned expensive one, I'm afraid. I wasn't cursing women in general, for I've seen a few fine ones, though that breed seems to be nearly extinct here at court. There's really been no one of import for me—not more than a passing glance or passing night—since Elizabeth died."

His voice trailed off and he frowned. That wasn't really true, of course, as there had been the foolish, utter and total impact of that infatuation he'd felt for the beautiful, little goddess Frances Stewart in France almost a year ago, but he hadn't been sent back since and was not likely to be. Never in his life had he been so instantly smitten with a woman, but he was over that fever of the blood now, and he should have taken into account that she'd probably be sent to French Louis' court and he'd never see her again. He needed to take into account how starved he'd been for a woman then and—

His head snapped up and he saw Roger Payne staring at him. "What is it, man?" he said almost too brusquely. "Let's see what we can make of these accounts, I said. Damn, but I hate to be so saddled here with all these duties when I should be home at Cobham overseeing all this first hand. It's going to take us years to dig the estate out from the debt-ridden mess it was in when I inherited last year, and my Lennox lands in Scotland are not much better off. Our loyalty to the Stuart kings cost us a great deal more than years of exile under Cromwell's bastard government so prettily dubbed 'The Commonwealth!'"

"Aye. Granted. But you love the land, love husbandry and farming, Yer Grace. It's only been a year you've had lordship of the estate. Ye'll pull Cobham out from under and Lennox too, I warrant. I'd wager my best set of pipes on it, Yer Grace!"

The man's plain, honest face reassured Richmond and gave him the nudge he needed to tackle the tedious paperwork again. The man read him well: he would rather be out from under the mountainous burden of these complicated court duties where he could oversee his estates or sail his new-bought yacht, that was flat! He had to continually push himself to bear up under this service to the crown, the ceremony, the need for political wiles to stay afloat, the long hours of duties hovering over papers or giving orders to underlings he hardly knew and didn't trust. He bent a piece of parchment so hard in his grasp, it crinkled. At least the honorary fleet command would give him an excuse to escape this city upon occasion. But, damn it, he could see no other way at present to solidify his lands and position but to serve King Charles in any capacity he placed him.

As if his rampant thoughts had been prophetic, he heard his name called from near the stretch of buildings called the Bowling Green. He recognized the man instantly—a king's messenger, and one who all too frequently came to summon him when there were questions or commands.

"Roger, my man, I'm caught off duty attempting to escape via riverbank with my favorite Scotsman, it seems. Gather all these accounts up and come to supper later in my suite. I'll get us some good beef and country ale, eh?"

He rose and was off in his long-legged stride toward the distant messenger before Roger Payne could answer. How good it felt, Richmond thought, to be able to trust someone like that. If he ever found such a woman here at court—and one the king had not bedded at all hours—he would marry her in a trice and whisk her off to Cobham forever before this place sullied her.

"His Majesty wants me?" he asked the messenger curtly and strode on past while the man hurried at his heels. These summons always came decorated with the term "immediately," so he'd have to rush to get suitably dressed in his chambers.

"Yes, yes, indeed, my Lord Duke," the man gasped out, hurrying to keep up with him. "His Majesty requests you attend him immediately in the Green Room. Several pressing matters, he said, Your Grace, and I said to him—"

"Fine. I'll be there immediately," Richmond

rapped out and closed his chamber door behind him.

He knew he shouldn't take this hemmed-in feeling that oppressed him out on others, but sometimes he couldn't control his desire to lash back. Now he'd square his shoulders, bear up under the pressure, discipline himself to his tasks again. It was what he expected of his yacht crew; it was what all his sailors at sea needed; and, damn it, it was what he needed too. In five minutes his wardrobe keeper had him dressed and in ten minutes more he stood in the immediate presence of the king.

"Richmond, glad you could make it so quickly. Sit down," his sovereign began with the usual, deceptive casualness. His full mouth curved into an easy smile, but the slate eyes were ever sharp despite Charles's easy posture across the small table. "You seem always adept at handling a mishmash of things and that is what I have for you now."

"A variety of things, sire," Richmond challenged subtly, "and not things you believe I'll make a mishmash of."

"Quite right. I stand corrected then. You canny Scots always were a picky, persnickety lot."

"I am English born and bred even as you, sire, though I would never deny my proud Scottish heritage." Richmond paused when he saw the king's lip go taut under the narrow mustache. He'd better get hold of himself here; it was one thing to fume internally, but even this indirect censoring of the king's commands could be dangerous. When goaded, even slightly like this, King Charles looked almost exotically moorish and resembled the portrait of his powerful ancestor through his Italian bloodlines—

the Renaissance Medici, Duke Lorenzo the Magnificent, Richmond thought.

"Od's fish," the king was saying, "this mention of proud Scottish heritage does bring me to my first point—a niggling one, I admit. Some courtiers have complained again about those blasted bagpipes being played in your chambers at all hours."

"I see. Neither I nor my steward who visits from Cobham on occasion ever play before nine of the morning, sire, and rarely in the evening."

"Nine of the morning sounds eminently practical to me, Richmond, but to the others who need more rest—'Sblood, let's not haggle over it then. I don't know how you can abide those wailing things at all. When I was in Scotland during the exile, I had to put up with those screaming war songs every night, so I must say I sympathize with the complainants here. Couldn't stand the pipes any more than I could stomach their haggis, the Presbyterian piety, or their desire to use me to gain their own ends. You can bet I know you're true-bred English and a capable, clever fellow at that because I don't put up with Scots for a moment. I don't care if my grandfather was once king of their moors and mountains before he came to London to reign. I am king of Scotland today with much restraint and not much love, Richmond—I cannot help it."

"I'll see to the bagpipes."

"Excellent. I don't know where you get the time for the things anyway. No interesting ladies in your life? No tempting, come-hither-to-bed invitations of late, my lord?"

Richmond smiled broadly, both with admiration

at the king's clever smoothing over of his anger and with amusement at the fact the king would explode anew if he but realized his little wanton, Barbara Villiers, had profered the only invitation to bed he'd had in the last month. His mind skipped back to the slender, alluring Frances Stewart as he'd seen her last, her lips tinged pink from his kisses, her arms full of roses. How he would have loved more time there to woo her—and to bed her. He pulled himself back from the foolish fantasy, and awkwardly cleared his throat.

"Not really, sire. There's been no one in the year and a half my wife has been gone. I was hoping the arrival of your princess this spring might bring an infusion of new and pretty females in as maids of honor. Perhaps there are even a few English maids still in exile to bring home—someone with your sister, the new Duchess of Orléans, for example."

The king's heavy black eyebrows lifted, and he grinned like a schoolboy. "Spoken as a true Stuart, Richmond. As a matter of fact—Od's fish, now where it that letter? Oh, here. It's almost as if you've been reading my mail. My sister writes from Paris that she had one such candidate in mind for the Portuguese princess' maids of honor—a loyalist girl who's been reared at the Queen Mother's court, and who wouldn't want out of there for greener pastures? But you were there as an envoy a year ago to Saint-Germain, Richmond. You know what I mean about how stodgy it can be there."

"I found it not so stuffy as I had expected, sire. The grounds and gardens there are beautiful, and the vast, deep hunt forest is full of rich game."

"Gad, I do remember that too, but Her Majesty Henrietta Maria at times can scotch any dreams of freedom. At any rate, Minette—the duchess—writes here that 'I can assure you I should feel very sorry to let her go from here'—the maid of honor, she means—'for she is the prettiest girl in the world and the most fit to adorn a court.' Sounds promising, eh? I hear the maids the Portuguese Catherine will bring are all older, you know, protective dowagers, guardians from Hades or some such. 'Sdeath, I'll worry about that next May when my bride gets off the ship."

"The girl the letter recommends, sire," Richmond asked, seeing his king about to plunge into another topic, "does the duchess not give the name?"

"Oh, yes, here—further up in the letter. The daughter of the Queen Mother's doctor, a man who died in exile some eight years or so ago. You ought to favor this one, Richmond, Scottish and all, even has the Scottish spelling of our royal name. Stewart. Frances Theresa Stewart."

His insides cartwheeled over. "Really? Mistress Stewart?"

One coal black eyebrow quirked up. "You were only there once, Richmond. She wasn't in the Queen Mother's party that visited here last year. You know this girl?"

"Truth is, sire, I ran into her in the gardens the day I arrived. That is all," he said, hoping he sounded calm.

"And is she pretty and—ah, fit to adorn a court, as my sister puts it?"

"I suppose so. A lovely face, but really, a mere,

slender maid."

"Od's fish, Richmond, young? Is that a drawback these days? Besides, it seems King Louis XIV himself has become fond of this maid—during a visit she made to Paris, I take it and even Minette's effeminate husband has too. It will be a year almost for her at Louis' worldy court before she comes home to England, so how 'young' she'll seem after living in that sophisticated viper's nest remains to be seen. Besides, all maids grow up, thank heaven for us wretches who appreciate them so, but now to business."

A year at the court of the infamous "Sun King" of France, Richmond thought while the king's voice droned on. A year to be pursued, enticed, misled— damn it all, fondled or worse by French fops or the king himself whose reputation surely rivaled that of King Charles himself as a *roué*.

"Richmond, are you listening?"

"Yes, sire, sorry, only I was thinking at least the Duchess of Orléans will have a dear friend with her until you wed and send for her."

"Still on the subject of Frances Stewart, Richmond? Indeed, Minette needs friends with that husband of hers. Then too, there've been those terrible rumors she foolishly fell in love with the king himself and that's why she consented to marry Philippe in the first place."

"Rumors, sire? But I know she writes to you constantly and has told you her heart's thoughts over the years."

"Her heart's thoughts—a strange way to put it, Richmond. Yes," his deep voice went on low, almost as if he were speaking only to himself, "but because our relationship is so special, she would hardly dare to tell me of that. Truth is, as I read between the lines of her missives, I have the greatest fear she did wed with Philippe to be near Louis and now he has turned away from her to someone else. Curse the rumors, but my informants tell me he has actually deserted her for one of Minette's companions, a Louise de La Vallière, damn him if he has dared!"

Richmond listened intently to the whispered, vehement words. But did not this king, too, think naught of turning from one mistress to the other as he had once from Lucy Walter and might even turn again from the volatile Barbara Palmer who so obsessed him now? And would he care enough for his own queen someday to grieve for her feelings as he did now for those of his dear sister Minette? He forced Frances Stewart from his mind with a final, impassioned prayer that the French court would not do to her what it evidently had already done to the once innocent Minette. The king, of course, was speaking of his own hardly innocent, Madame Palmer.

"So you see, I need someone I can trust, Richmond, to perform a rather delicate duty for me as I cannot send my Lord Chancellor Hyde. He detests the lady in question here and seems to have conveniently forgotten that he owes me a favor for naming him Earl of Clarendon at the Coronation last April and for pulling him out of that mess with his daughter last year. He thinks just because the child Anne Hyde bore to my brother died it clears the slate, but it doesn't. I'm certain he'd handle it badly anyway; but Barbara Villiers, Madame Palmer, likes you,

I believe."

"I shall help if I can, sire."

"Oh, you can. You can. As you know, her husband, Roger Palmer has gotten some ideas into his head about his honor being besmirched and all that since I show Madame Palmer my favors and want her to live permanently at Whitehall. You do know that?"

"Indeed, sire. I would venture to say most everyone at court knows that."

"Damn you, Scottish Richmond, but aren't you the one with the honest answers to your king today? But, that's fine, just fine. I need honest men, so I'll be blunt with you. I want you to drop things here to ride into Kent, visit the Palmers and offer the bastard an earldom to bring her back. He brings Barbara back and stays out of her way and he's Earl of Castlemaine. And one more thing—you'll have to make it eminently clear to him that any real financial rewards will go to Barbara's heirs."

"I understand, sire."

"Od's fish, I don't doubt you do, Richmond. The lady amuses me, and I want her back. She's nasty tongued, vile tempered, and greedy but I want her back. I don't doubt that's why the wily Roger Palmer gambled that I'd miss her and so has hauled her off to Kent, hoping to catch some reward or honor. Let him know, if you must, he's won that much, but the earldom is my top price I'll offer for her. He's to keep out of the way hereafter."

Richmond shifted his big frame in the hard, carved chair across the cluttered table from the king. The lady was in Kent, the words pounded repeatedly in his brain—Kent, near his own beloved and much neglected Cobham. As distasteful as it was to be sent as king's panderer, he could stomach it for one reason. It was just the excuse, the break he had been looking for.

"Your Majesty," he began, "I know—I am certain—I can handle this suitably for you. Might I ask a small favor from you then?"

"Everyone does, Richmond. Ask. Somehow, with you I trust the request to be appropriate and not some sky-high sinecure for life. Well?"

"After I visit the Palmers and obtain the lord's vow to bring Madame Palmer back, I would like to stop a few days at my Cobham estate near Gravesend. It's harvest time and I have not been able to spare time from my duties here for over three months." Their eyes met and sudden guilt for what he was undertaking washed through Richmond. Hell, he told himself, if Roger Palmer was unprincipled enough to let the king buy his wife like a common whore, they all deserved what they could get out of this.

"Is that all?"

"Yes, sir."

"Granted, but remember I need you here too, and Westminster's like to go to Hades without your careful hand, so don't stay away long."

"Something else, sire."

"Od's fish, I thought that was all."

"It's only a moot point, really. You said I should ride to Kent. I have my new yacht moored in the Upper Pool of the Thames near the Tower. I'd like to sail at least part of the way."

Richmond relaxed as he saw the nearly rapturous

look which lit the king's features. "A damned fine idea! A man after my own heart. A new yacht, you say? Listen, when you get back, I'll take the *Royal Charles*, we'll get the Duke of York in another and let the court see a good race from Greenwich and back."

"I'd be entirely delighted, sire. Sailing always clears my mind and heals my heart."

The king's black eyes narrowed despite the fact his mouth under the mustache still lifted in a smile. "Now, whyever would your heart need healing, Richmond? Just see to business and keep clear of women's clutches—if not of their all too obvious charms—and you'll live to be a hundred."

Richmond saw he was dismissed and rose to his full height across the table as the king stood too. King Charles Stuart was the only man the duke knew who was taller than he—a full two inches.

"I'll be off to Kent by sail then on the morrow, sire, and hope the news of your lady will be all that you would wish."

"I won't forget this, Richmond. Perhaps someday I shall help you win your lady."

"I shall remember *that*, sire."

The duke went out through the ever-crowded Vane Room, carefully fielding the subtle and blatant attempts of courtiers to find out why their king had met with his Lord Chamberlain in total privacy. He strode quickly through dim corridors, through numerous chambers, and emerged in the late afternoon sun along the riverbank.

The Thames looked almost golden in the low western sun—his golden path to temporary freedom, he thought. There was that nasty duty with the

Palmers, but then all those involved would do nothing they did not wish to do.

He hurried toward his suite, planning his next few days. He'd take Roger Payne on the yacht with him, of course, and then get the accounts and much else settled during his stay at Cobham. He really did have a woman's wiles to thank for this trip, highborn slattern that Barbara Villiers was.

And best of all, today had brought him a fondest wish he had dared not even hope for. Soon, but not soon enough, the entrancing Frances Stewart would be here at the Stuart court. But, after months in Louis' dangerous royal world, perhaps she would not be the same naïve, natural charmer at all. Then too, when this king saw her—the other court gallants, also—there would be such an upheaval that England would not ever need another civil war. He smiled grimly. No matter what, he would stake his claims to her heart and body first. He would, he must, he chanted to himself as his feet hurried along the path by the shifting Thames. He began to whistle a wild Scottish dance tune as his long strides ate up the stretch of riverbank to his little chambers in the Bowling Green of Whitehall.

Chapter Three

Frances gave another quick shake to her graceful blue satin skirts and hoped fervently the wrinkles from the long journey would not be noticed. Chambermaids were definitely in short supply here at this old medieval fortress of a place in Portsmouth, England, overlooking the Solent and the English Channel. She had only arrived this morning by ship from Le Havre in France. Already they expected her to be presented to both King Charles and his newly wedded queen of one day, the former Portuguese Princess Catherine of Braganza, despite the fact she was travel weary, still felt salt spray clinging to her hair, and had only unpacked these few garments. At least a careless, nearly disheveled look of *la négligence* held full sway in fashion at the great Louis' court, she thought wryly.

Here in this little chamber she was to share with Amanda Wells, another newly appointed maid of honor whom she had not even met, her boxes and coffers were stacked in terrible disarray, and with no ladies' maids, she'd only pressed these skirts out with her hands on the bed. At Louis' court, even on progress, there were numerous chambermaids to handle such tasks. What sort of barbaric court had Minette exiled her to, she mused grimly as she surveyed her eyelid color in the small mirror her chamber partner evidently owned.

Knowing no one, she felt a terrible jab of longing for France. She had served Minette for the last year, thanks to King Louis' benevolent influence, and she missed her in a huge rush of emotion. Heavens, she was certain she even missed her mother and brother and sister who would be leaving Saint-Germain in four months for good, to join her in London when the Stuart court resettled at Whitehall Palace for the autumn and winter. She missed her cats, Perth and Aberdeen, she'd kept with her at the Louvre and at Fontainebleau when everyone else kept spaniels— one of the things she had done at Louis' court to feel different from the others. But her mother would bring her pets in August when she came. At least she had insisted on carrying her green and red talking parrot, Joli, in his gilt cage on the ship with her, and she hoped Amanda Wells could abide a clever rascal who preened all day and scolded worse than a fishwife.

"Joli. Joli. What do you think of England so far, Joli?"

The bird's pinkish eye closest to her swiveled almost coyly away and the hooked yellow beak picked at a lime green feather. "Keep a smile! Keep a smile! Keep your distance! Auwak!" the bird screeched, and Frances laughed at the appropriate-

78

ness of the message. Joli was a young bird who so far spoke only five phrases, and Frances never knew which ones he would spout when. It was terribly in style to keep cages of parrots or canaries at King Louis' court and that, along with her love for and flair for French fashion, horseback riding, and dancing were the main ways she believed she had finally become somewhat "Frenchified."

There was no knock on her door, but she clearly heard her name repeated—no, rather bellowed—on the other side. She stepped carefully over her piles of coffers and boxes and opened the door. A black-garbed gentleman—quite an old man compared to those she was used to—with white hair, a wispy mustache, and a goatee, faced her in the hall. His small eyes widened and his plump cheeks lifted in a smile evidently in approval of her appearance.

"Mrs. Frances Stewart?" he asked.

The term "Mrs." jolted her, but she remembered Minette had told her, among a thousand other things to remember, that Mrs. was the proper English address for any respectable lady since "Miss" denoted very young girls, harlots, or a woman maintained by a man strictly for his sexual pleasures.

"I am Frances Stewart. Am I sent for as promised, sir?"

The man swept her a little bow although he had no hat to flourish and was really dressed quite somberly compared to other English cavaliers Frances had glimpsed so far.

"Edward Hyde, the King's Lord Chancellor Clarendon at your service, Mrs. Stewart. I shall escort you to the king's presence as I'm going there myself."

"It is your daughter, of course, who married the Duke of York," Frances observed conversationally as he led her down numerous hallways. "I met the duke once at Saint-Germain when I was very young but, I vow, I can hardly recall him."

"Then you have also met the king before? I tell you frankly, Mrs. Stewart, I am delighted at your appointment, a maid from a fine Loyalist family like yourself, and reared in the strict, moral atmosphere of our beloved former queen, Henrietta Maria's court. The king—this court—is in need of pretty ladies with strict upbringings like yourself. Even my own daughter—well, enough of that."

"You do know, my lord, I have spent this last year at the French court?"

"Yes, yes, but you've Scottish blood, and have not, I dearly hope, swayed much from your strong beginnings, eh? I would be a friend to you if ever you need advice, Mrs. Stewart. Let me just say then, before we go in here, I ask you to serve the new queen well as she will need loyal friends. It is a most fortuitous marriage for our beloved sovereign, of course, despite the fact the new queen is solidly Catholic."

"I do know King Louis greatly favored the match for his cousin, my lord, as it is said he even offered King Charles three hundred thousand pistoles as a betrothal gift."

"Ah, well, that. I should realize, of course, you have been privy to French reasoning for a good while now. You see, King Louis prefers England to have an alliance with the smaller nation of Portugal rather than forging ties to some Spanish princess as he was.

You must see, Mrs. Stewart, King Louis has only his own motives at heart."

"I have found that to be true of men in general, my lord," she replied before she could check her vehemence.

"I see you have learned a great deal that will serve you in good stead while at the French court, then, eh? But perhaps love will come to our king here through his marriage union as it never has to poor Louis with his stodgy Spanish Queen María Teresa. But, unfortunately, our monarch tends to favor many women. Despite my warnings to him over the years, my admonitions, that is one way, I fear, the two kings are alike. But King Charles is wise and clever, never doubt it, Mrs. Stewart. He does not marry the Portuguese infanta only because his brother king bribes him a bit. She brings a rich dowry of power—two million crowns for his weakened coffers, control of Bombay in India, and Tangier to oversee the entry to the Mediterranean, a bride well worth her price for England whether he loves her in the end or not."

"And so, Mrs. Stewart," Chancellor Clarendon intoned after the little silence of his schoolmaster's speech when she did not answer immediately, "I repeat, the new queen will need loyal friends. Choose your companions cleverly, and try to steer clear of entanglement with Barbara Villiers' camp, especially her rogue of a cousin, Buckingham."

Before she could even react to that last hurried advice, he nodded to two men with tall, ceremonial pikes evidently guarding a door which they swept open. Chancellor Clarendon and Frances went into what appeared to be a small antechamber: forest green velvet draped most of the stone walls; a dark oak table and four red brocaded chairs were the only furnishings.

"Surely these are not the queen's chambers." Frances voiced her surprise aloud as Chancellor Clarendon bustled over to another door to rap on it sharply with the silver head of his walking stick.

"The queen's, no. She and her large party of Portuguese ladies have the royal suite along the sea on the ground floor where I'm sure you will be going shortly." He lowered his voice. "There's been no consummation of the royal marriage yet as the contracting was done by proxy and the lady felt ill her first night here, so Her Majesty is keeping to her suite and His Majesty is here for now. The king wanted to greet you before you settled into duties. Sire, Mrs. Stewart is come from France!"

The door opened and a very tall, dark-haired, olive-skinned man dressed casually in breeches, shirt, and vest filled the doorway, his eyes like polished pieces of obsidian. The room behind him was bathed in light and the tang of sea air, and there was no evidence of the noisy courtiers Frances had come to expect around King Louis at all hours. Surely, she thought, the king of England does not answer his own doors, but his identity was unmistakable. She dropped him a hurried but graceful curtsy as Clarendon stepped aside.

"As always, my Minette told me true, Frances Stewart," the low, slow voice said, and a huge hand with long, elegant fingers extended to her. She put her small hand in his as she rose. "Indeed, you are a beauty and a sight for sore eyes beset as we are by all these Portuguese dowagers looking like floating men-of-war in those massive farthingales, eh, Chancellor?"

"Sire, I believe the Portuguese princess—I mean, our English queen's virtues and modesty quite surpass any temporary deficiency in style or custom."

"Ever the politician, aren't you, my lord? But here is something entirely charming thrown into this whole marriage deal—an entrancing lady from France to grace our court."

Frances pulled her eyes away at last from King Charles's fixed gaze to note the sudden uncertainty on Chancellor Clarendon's jowly face. "Mrs. Stewart, of course, is full able to serve the queen, sire," the old man clipped out even as the king drew Frances past him into his privy room. "After all, she has been a favorite of the Queen Mother who will visit this autumn and dear companion to your sister, the Duchess of—"

"I am very aware of Mrs. Stewart's qualifications, Chancellor," the king interrupted. His voice seemed mocking, but not angry at the none-too-subtle lecture, and his black eyes glinted in a sort of perverse merriment. "Wait for us in the anteroom and we'll all go visit the queen directly."

To her dismay, King Charles dared to swing the door shut in Clarendon's face, but she soon saw her increasing unease with the tall, magnetic man was mere foolishness. The room was not a bedchamber as she had feared, but a sort of makeshift laboratory, and there were two gentlemen fussing over flasks, bottles, and long bars of glass. He ignored the men and the

83

clutter and indicated she should sit in one of the two tall-backed, upholstered chairs under the large window overlooking the green-gray Solent. Sun poured pleasantly in wrapping them in a warm golden pool and turning his full black head of shiny hair almost bluish in places. He sat facing her; with his casual posture and long legs and arms, he seemed nearly to lounge in his chair.

"I trust Minette is well. We shall call her Minette when we speak of her together, you and I, because she is so dear to us both." His voice was low and easy, a charming voice.

Instantly she began to relax. All this had been so sudden, so rushed, but here in sun and sea breeze while his apparently oblivious men clanked bottles together across the room—even with his dark eyes completely upon her—she began to feel a deep calm.

"Yes, sire, the Princess Minette is quite well, and I have letters and gifts in my things for you and the new queen."

"Splendid. And, may I say quite frankly, *la petite belle* Stewart, you are the fairest gift she could have sent to grace our court."

He noticed how prettily she colored at the compliment and his thorough perusal of her. Od's fish, but she was a vision from heaven after the shock of meeting his bride and all her dark-hued Portuguese guardians two days ago. This young women—let's see, she must be just a bit younger than Minette—dazzled the eye and raped the senses with her tawny hair touched with reddish highlights in the sun and her luxuriously fringed, eggshell blue eyes. The face was perfect; the body, pert breasted and slender; the legs, unfortunately hidden by the satin skirts and ribboned petticoats, evidently as elegant as the trim ankle and slim feet he could see. She seemed untouched somehow, balanced on that tenuous edge between virgin and temptress, yet terribly self-contained and calm.

He heard himself heave a heartfelt sigh before he could stop himself. They had sent him a Portuguese bat of a woman to wed and at Hampton Court where he would soon take his new bride for a two-month honeymoon, a demanding, bad-tempered and pregnant Barbara Villiers awaited them. Now why, damn it, hadn't fate or the Lord God or whatever controlled such affairs handed him something like Frances Stewart to wed?

She stared at him, puzzled, as she caught his sudden, almost guilty smile. But here, indeed, was Frances Stewart, he mused, in his court to live, and there was plenty of time and there were plenty of places to win her heart even if he had no intention of risking his. Suddenly, that single thought pleased him more than anything had since his coronation over a year ago.

"Forgive my rudeness of staring and smiling—a prerogative of kings," he offered.

"I have found—of men, in general, Your Majesty."

He shouted a laugh of pure joy. Gads, she was clever and spirited too. "I do not doubt you find it so, beautiful Frances, but Minette vows you have had no real—attachments, as they say, not in your year at my cousin Louis' frivolous court."

"No attachments, sire, and not likely to, I vow. I prefer to be—well, free."

85

His eyebrows shot up and she noted at last she had unsettled him a bit. He had a strange effect on her, this apparently relaxed but intense man, this king who seemed right now not like a king at all. He exerted a sort of disconcerting pull over her as only one man ever had before, but that had been so long ago when she was a mere unsophisticated maid, and she had tried to forget that. She was grateful that she had become so very adept at hiding whatever feelings she did have under a veneer of controlled calm.

"Not likely to be attached?" he was saying. "But, Frances, you are so young and now that you're home, everything is possible. I do hope your stay in France has not made you—shall we say, soured on men. You have, of course, observed Minette's husband, the Duke of Orléans, at too-close range, damn him, or is it something my pious chancellor has said perhaps?"

"No, sire, not really. Chancellor Clarendon was most instructive and as for Philippe—"

"Philippe! That bastard, forgive me, Frances, but he riles my blood! I am haunted by what Minette doesn't tell me, but what I just feel in her letters. Dare I offend you by asking, my dear, in your opinion, is my beloved sister just some sort of pretty smokescreen for Philippe, Duke of Orléans—Od's fish—for his male friends? I believe she thought, the way he is, he would give her some freedom at court, but does he still expect a willing wife?"

Frances felt herself go hot under the king's steady perusal. His dark eyes were wide; his large lower lip trembled. How much he obviously loved Minette, she marveled, even as Minette loved him. Frances pictured the tearful woman's impassioned last words

86

to her, words she had spoken more than once over these last months they had been together in France: "Love my brother for me, Frances—love him!"

"I believe, sire," she began, selecting her words carefully, "that despite the fact that duke is the way he is and continually has about his presence such . . . favorites as the Duke of Lorraine—"

"Damned catamites! Say on, my dear."

"That—heavens, he expects an heir of the duchess as all powerful men do of their wives."

He nodded and his coal black brows crashed down over his obsidian gaze. "As all powerful men do, kings especially," he said low. "You know, my dear, I could strangle that French bastard Philippe with my own hands, and smile despite my most heartfelt vows to never take to violence again for any cause."

"I am so sorry, sire. It is the Princess Minette's continued love and good wishes for you which light her days, so I am certain she would not want you to be so bitterly unhappy, and not for her especially."

King Charles's saturnine face lifted; one corner of his full mouth turned up in surprise and then all-too-obvious appreciation. "Od's fish, my dear Frances, you do know how to comfort as well as dazzle. And Richmond only spoke of you as young, the rogue."

Her calm demeanor shattered as she fought to keep her face composed. "Richmond?" she asked, her voice a bit too strident. However, at his mere name, a flood of emotion-drowning memories washed over her. "The ambassador who visited Saint-Germain once?" she faltered, relieved her voice sounded better now. "I can barely remember him," she lied. "Young, did he say? And—nothing else?"

King Charles laughed lightly, feeling his poise restored. "No, sweet Frances. Perhaps he did note you were lovely, but he'd have been a blind man not to note that."

His deep baritone voice trailed off but his eyes ran quickly, if not quite covertly, over her. "More, much more on how lovely you are later. Come, I am expected in the queen's suite and you and Clarendon might as well come too. You mustn't let his pontificating bother you, my dear, as I never do. If you'll just be so kind as to trade places with him in the antechamber while I get a little more formally attired and have but a quick word with him, we'll be off."

She stood with him, threading her way carefully past the tables of delicate glassware to the door before she asked in the awkward lull, "Then you will still be living up here and Queen Catherine downstairs, sire?"

Despite her tallness for a woman, he towered a full, eight inches over her as he stepped closer and took her hand. "To tell true, Frances, beginning this evening, I believe I shall spend my nights down with Her Majesty. Last night after the Anglican and Catholic wedding ceremonies and the feasting, my bride was a bit indisposed for a bridegroom's first visit. As for this chamber, I carry a few of my various scientific experimentations with me wherever I go. I always have to have someplace to which I retreat so I might be unattached—to be free, as you put it."

She looked back at the two men hovering intently over their liquids and bottles and curiously colored glass bars held up as if to catch sun rays. "We're working with diffusion of light through prisms and various diffractions of light," he said low. "I have an extensive laboratory in St. James's park in London as well as a telescope to view the stars and moon. I can show you if you'd like." He seemed suddenly more like her younger brother Walter, all self-important and eager to please.

"Yes, I'd like that, and I am sure the queen will too."

"Yes, the queen. You know, *la belle* Frances, here at court, wherever our court may be, gentlemen have a custom of greeting ladies with a kiss on each cheek."

Her high-boned cheeks colored entrancingly again, but she stood calmly, apparently unmoved. It intrigued him greatly she did not flit or simper or flirt like so many women he knew; yet his vague memory of her widowed mother was that she was a perfect match for his own high-strung shrew of a woman.

"It is in fashion at the French court too, sire."

"Od's fish, you're at the English court now, so for you, I shall change the custom," he said and, before she could react, his warm, hard mouth pressed a kiss on her lips. Startled, she felt her lips go soft, half open under his before she seized control at the sudden onslaught and drew back. He gave her no chance to scold or smile but opened the door quickly and summoned his hovering Lord Chancellor in with a flick of a lace-cuffed wrist.

Frances stood slightly dazed outside the door as they went in and closed it. She decided not to sit, for that would make more of a ruin of her wrinkled skirts. Minette would be scandalized that she had met both her beloved brother, the royal Charles, and the new queen in a wrinkled skirt, Frances mused. And would she be scandalized that Charles Stuart had kissed her full on the mouth?

Frances touched fingertips to her tingling lips. The kiss had been quick and alarmingly pleasant. Again, she pictured Minette's teary-eyed face three weeks ago just before she had turned back to join her waiting husband in the Louvre when Frances had left Paris for Saint-Germain and from there the trip to England. "Love him for me," Minette had whispered fervently. "Love him and watch over him for me, Frances, please!"

This king obviously did not need watching over, Frances realized, and as for the idea of loving him— heavens, let his new queen and mistress Barbara Villiers worry about that! She wanted no involvement with him, whatever he hinted, anymore than she did with any man—the vile Duke of Richmond included. After what she'd learned of men this last year and what her mother had told her before— heavens, despite that strange blood-coursing rush of fever back there when the king had merely spoken Richmond's name, she wanted none of him!

Her reverie was shattered by a suddenly raised voice penetrating the door she stood beside. Surely, that was not old Chancellor Clarendon daring to yell back at his sovereign like that!

"I tell you, sire, that is impossible—abominable, and I shall not, *shall not* be a party to it! I believe I have oft heard you say you did not believe in mistresses flaunted by married kings and certainly the new queen will not agree to appoint that Palmer woman as her lady of the bedchamber or to allow her to lie in to deliver your second illegitimate child while you and the queen honeymoon there!"

"Look, Clarendon, I will spell it out once again clearly. I want Madame Palmer there. She's been abandoned by her husband, she's carrying my child, and she is dear to me so just get the queen to sign the appointment. I do not intend to flaunt the situation but neither do I want a scene from either woman."

Frances' pulse pounded in her ears. So this king was only a man and just like the others mother had warned of or she had encountered herself at closer range: conceited, cruel, crass—and of course, the woman who most desired his love and goodwill would suffer at his hands. She trusted no man— none, including this powerful king on whom her livelihood now depended.

"I, sire, am not the chancellor of a bedroom crisis!" Clarendon's high-pitched voice was croaking.

"Evidently, you do not wish to be chancellor in any crisis! I must say, you were not much help last time I really needed your services, Clarendon. I had to send the Duke of Richmond who is equally as busy, if not as self-righteous and self-serving as you, to fetch Barbara back to court last year."

Both of Frances' hands flew to her mouth. The Duke of Richmond! Fetching the king's mistress Barbara Villiers back for him! That meant Richmond might be somewhere about here. Wasn't that just like the man she remembered, running errands for the king to justify all his important titles—and to fetch back a poor woman who probably just wanted

91

to escape the king's grasp?

"Sire, I feel you are just pent-up over all this new business of having a queen and marriage to care for now," Clarendon's strident voice plunged on. "After all, you have been a rather carefree bachelor your thirty years and—"

"Pent-up? 'Sdeath, of course, I'm pent-up! Catherine is nothing like that pretty little miniature picture of her some cock-eyed moron painted! If I'd have gone to Portugal to sign the contract instead of Ambassador Fanshawe, I tell you, I'd have forgone my rights to lie with her that night! Actually, I'd never have signed at all, foreign policy be damned! Granted, her eyes are lovely and her voice is pleasant, but she's skinny, heavy-faced, buck-toothed, and swarthy and you know I favor fair brunettes—like that stunning little Frances Stewart!"

"Really, Your Majesty, I hardly think—"

"No, you don't think much of late, do you, Clarendon? Oh, don't worry, I'll make Catherine of Braganza happy and as soon as she's over that squeamish fit of vapors or unexpected blood flow or whatever, I'll do my damnedest to get her with royal child. Od's fish, even dear cousin Louis across the Channel, they say, lies with his plump, black-toothed queen every other week."

Frances' heart pounded against her dark blue satin bodice at the heated, intimate exchange. If the king hadn't told her to await them here, she'd flee. Minette must have written him that about the king and queen of France, for it was true!

"I only say these things, my Lord Chancellor Clarendon," the king's voice came lower now, "so that you understand why you will ask, at the earliest opportunity, the queen to appoint Barbara Villiers to the honor of serving as one of her ladies of the bedchamber. It will ease my situation greatly, and that is one of your functions as Chancellor. Just slide the appointment in with the list of others. The queen's English leaves much to be desired as well, and she may not even know what she is signing. There, my wardrobe man's done fussing with my waistcoat now, are you not, man? Let's collect the little Stewart and be on our way.''

Frances stepped back away from the door so quickly she nearly tripped over one of the chairs as they came out. Clarendon looked livid-faced and grim, but King Charles appeared relaxed as he smiled at her and offered her his flame-hued satin arm.

Since she had observed King Louis' skill at masking his true feelings under pleasant smiles and placid brows, King Charles' similar ability did not surprise her one whit. As a matter of fact, Frances thought smugly, she, too, fancied herself rather adept at the practice, and among other things, it protected her from the so-called attachments the king had mentioned quite well.

The new queen of England, Frances realized a few minutes later when she was formally presented to her, had no such courtly skill among her practices. Perhaps, she mused, it was because the queen had been convent-reared in Portugal for her twenty-four years, and knew nothing of deceit. The heavy-lidded, liquid eyes of Catherine of Braganza followed her new husband everywhere, and she obviously adored him.

All warmth and kindness now, King Charles bowed over his bride's hand, and he kissed her plump, sallow cheeks too, avoiding her slightly protruding lips pushed forward by slanted front teeth. As Frances watched, her mouth tingled again most annoyingly at the thought he had only a little before kissed her full on the lips.

The queen's English was indeed stilted and accented, but her voice was low and musical. And the gowns of the queen's formidable, Portuguese ladies were at least forty years out of date even as those of Louis' Queen María Teresa had been at first, though since she had learned to dress quite stylishly. Perhaps this foreign queen would learn too and no longer look like a stumpy mushroom in a room full of graceful flowers.

"Zounds, it's really something, isn't it?" a roguish, blond man who suddenly materialized from behind Frances, said. "The Portuguese Armada invades England. We've nicknamed those horrible, fat-skirted farthingales *guardas infantas*, as no man can get within five feet of an *infanta* or any woman in them. You, beautiful damsel, I see, wear no such battle garb."

"I do not believe I know your name, my lord," Frances replied as coldly as possible to buffer his intimate words and piercing stare. He was quite handsome really, in an almost effeminate sort of way as were many of the French cavaliers.

"A temporary, minute obstacle to be soon swept away, pretty lady. I am George Villiers, Lord Buckingham, at your service."

Her brain raced. Buckingham, the very man

94

Chancellor Clarendon had warned her of a little while ago. She wasn't certain if he knew who she was or had singled her out merely as a new face among so many.

"George Villiers," she drawled thoughtfully, and arched one brow the way she had seen the French ladies at court do to precede a snub. "You know, that last name rings familiar somehow, but I simply cannot place it."

She watched his astounded, then amused, expression and judged he would try another tack to ingratiate himself if she didn't dispense with him entirely. "Excuse me, Lord Buckingham, but as maid of honor, I need to see to the queen now. I vow, I have the surest feeling she will need all the trustworthy friends she can get here."

She ignored his grin and the way his eyes swept over her as she moved away. She scanned the crowded, shifting room of rainbow satins, velvets, lace and jewels. No familiar faces but Clarendon's and the king's. At least that insulting Duke of Richmond wasn't in evidence here to make matters worse than having someone like Buckingham hanging about. He was, no doubt, here to keep an eye on his cousin Barbara Villiers' interest in the king even while His Majesty entertained his new royal bride.

This was just like King Louis' vast court, she thought grimly, complicated and potentially treacherous, despite the sophisticated polish and veneer of gentility. But she knew how to care for herself now, especially with men: no more Buckinghams or Richmonds would ever rattle her again!

Bravely, she went over to a little whispering cluster

of obviously English maids to introduce herself and see if her chamber mate Amanda Wells was here in the press of people surrounding the new bride and groom.

Frances' first month in England blurred by on gossamer wings. The court traveled northward to spend a summer idyll with the king and queen at red bricked, turreted Hampton Court on the broad River Thames. Charles and Catherine had ridden the last twenty miles in a gilded chariot drawn by six white horses, followed by a two-mile train of ladies, cavaliers, and guards on horseback; then came the baggage wagons, one of which, the king had jested, was needed to carry the huge farthingales Queen Catherine and her Portuguese women still favored.

Frances had fallen in love with Hampton Court at first sight: a fairy city of gilded weather vanes and twisted chimneys and turrets with cupolas silhouetted against the stunning azure sky of May 29, 1660, the king's birthday and second anniversary of his triumphal return to England. The Thames was so green here as it arched around the richly planted grounds of lime trees in the park, the patterned rose gardens called the Parades, the massive stretch of tall, shady wych-elms, and the intricate hedge maze. A perfectly lovely place, she thought frequently—a perfectly lovely place for a honeymoon.

And, thank heavens, there was never a dull moment, for she had come to expect lively times at Louis' court, and that kept her from missing Minette and her family more than she already did. The king had confided to Frances that he had been wretchedly bored in exile and had vowed never to be so again: there were concerts and masqued balls, gambling and sporting events such as hunting and strolling, and hundreds of new people to meet including five other newly appointed English maids of honor whom she soon came to call friends.

But there were two sad things Frances felt deeply and which somewhat marred the eternal round of festivities for her: the poor queen obviously felt more uncomfortable in the boisterous gaiety of the court, and as August approached, the king and queen were hardly speaking to each other over what everyone now called quite blatantly, "the bedroom crisis."

Tonight amidst the crowded gambling tables in the grand salon, everyone was whispering of it, and some even wagered on who would win and how. The "bedroom crisis" had begun when someone had informed the shy queen before she signed the appointments for lady of the bedchamber who the lady named Madame Palmer really was, and she had stricken that one name from the list. An obviously pregnant Barbara Villiers had ranted and raved at the king who took out his fury first on his chancellor and then on his queen. All of her Portuguese ladies but two had been sent home, and he amused himself elsewhere than the queen's chambers at night. But this evening, the ubiquitous Duke of Buckingham had been slyly spreading the word among the gambling revelers that the king had a new surprise tactic in the feud—and Barbara Villiers had insisted on coming downstairs to get into the fray.

Everyone bided the time chatting, laughing, and

lounging easily among the green-felt-covered gambling tables after they heard that last bit of news. The king himself detested heavy wagers, seldom betting more than five pounds in a game of dice or round of cards, so no one was particularly waiting to gamble with him. But Barbara Villiers was known to risk hundreds of pounds on a wager—and to lose.

Frances sat in a window alcove overlooking the terraces reaching toward the dark gardens. She had ridden all afternoon in the Park with the queen's retinue and the wine at dinner had made her unusually drowsy. Then too, she didn't really care for gambling any mor than did the king, nor did she have money to wager; although both the king and that sticky Buckingham regularly offered her use of their privy purses, she always refused. Besides, an apparently innocent game like whist or bassette or ombre too often turned to wagers for kisses or other favors if there were ladies at the table, and she wanted none of that. The clicking of dice in the little wooden casting boxes, the fluttering shuffle of cards lulled Frances nearly to sleep.

The deep, velvety voice jolted her: "I was certain I would find you out darting through the hedges, crashing into innocent men, Frances Stewart."

"Oh! You!" She stood quickly only inches from the rakish figure of the Duke of Richmond who had leaned rudely over her with one booted foot on the window ledge. Damn the lout, but he'd startled her. She hadn't seen him anywhere, hadn't seen him at all. Worse, she blushed fiery hot and her knees went all watery.

"I am elated you remember me from that day so

long ago at Saint-Germain," he went on smoothly, one elbow carelessly draped across his raised knee as he studied her.

She was grateful the light of the crystal chandeliers and flaming wall sconces did not illumine her flushed face in this alcove. The duke looked windblown somehow, not combed or carefully attired as the others, nor was he dressed half elegantly enough to attend court. When she spoke, the calm coldness of her voice pleased her.

"I do recall your face, my lord. You were sent to the Queen Mother for some reason, I believe. But," she lied, her face impassive, "I am sorry to say I do not know your name."

His eyes darkened, and his mouth hardened into a finely chiseled line. She wasn't certain for an instant whether he felt insulted or only hurt.

"I can understand that," he said low, "for you were a mere slip of haughty girl then, and, of course, since that time no doubt dozens of men have kissed those sweet lips and drowned you in roses. Charles Stuart, duke of Richmond, at your service, Frances Stewart. The king has, of course, welcomed you to your new position here warmly."

Damn this wily man she had thought entirely too much about over the months since they had met, she fumed. Now whatever did he imply by that last comment? If he thought he could rile her, he had better think again. She decided to try another subject which might make him ill at ease.

"My Lord Duke, you evidently are still off playing king's envoy or messenger these days as I don't believe I have seen you about the court."

"My duties, Lady Frances, are in London, so when the court is at Whitehall I can easily attend, though all of a sudden I can think of some new reasons to come to Hampton Court besides that the king sends for me."

Her heart beat faster, and she strolled away from the intimate, dim window alcove with a practiced backward glance that indicated he might accompany her if he wished. She had forgotten he was so tall, nearly as tall as the king, and she wished that, attired as he was, she had not come out among the tables to show herself with him.

"I was told on the way in from the barge landing that Madame Palmer, the newly declared Countess of Castlemaine, is rumored to be making an appearance this evening," he said low to her as she hesitated near a group of courtiers hovered over a dice board playing hazard. "Has she been down yet?"

"Not yet, nor the king or queen. His Majesty went up to speak with his wife, I believe, so perhaps they shall patch up their argument before anything more happens."

"You like the king, of course. You're very admiring of him and impressed by him as indeed he is of you."

She looked astounded at the way he'd put that comment when she turned to him; he was all too sorry to see what he'd said was evidently a statement of fact. Her sea blue eyes glittered in the light, and her lovely mouth pursed in a pout. Damn, but she was lovely, a full-grown woman now, so elegant and desirable, he thought, but with some sort of icy veneer that almost set his teeth on edge. Surely, this practiced coldness could not just be the result of an embarrassed memory of their first meetings, nor of the fact he'd risen to her subtle insults to tease her back. A frown grooved his brow under a stray curl as his gaze went carefully over her to drink in her beauty, yet not to offend. Still, he felt a distinctive stirring in his loins, and for the first time in weeks, since he had been working nearly day and night lately, he begrudgingly admitted how good a woman would feel in his bed.

"Everyone at court, of course, admires Charles Stuart, my lord," she was replying cleverly although he could hardly remember what he had said.

"I meant nothing sinister by the statement, Lady Frances—that is, not unless it should be taken as a sort of warning. His Majesty, you have surely noted, does favor pretty ladies like yourself."

"Your rude implications astound me, my lord, even though I am taking the source into consideration."

"Your sharp tongue and lack of any sort of smile on that stunning face astound me, my lady, so we're even. Look, there's a seat at a bassette table. Let's gamble for a while until His Majesty appears. I was supposed to report to him directly on my arrival," he rushed on, afraid she would dart off because of their harsh exchange and afraid someone else would snap her up. "I've no intention of getting in His Majesty's way now if he's with either the queen or Barbara Villiers," he concluded.

"I don't really care to gamble, my Lord Duke," she protested as he moved her adroitly toward the bassette table with a firm hand in the small of her back and seated her with a warm press on her bare shoulders.

"No? I do. It's sometimes the exciting chances in life that make it all worth while, you know. Just sit and watch me if you don't want to play. And why not call me Charles or at least Richmond? Everyone does. Arlington, Clifford, Lauderdale, good evening to you," he greeted the other players at the table.

"Richmond, didn't know you'd been summoned. 'Sblood, I know damned well you don't hang about here of your own accord like the rest of us," Henry Bennet, Lord Arlington, Keeper of the Privy Purse, replied jovially despite the awful black plaster patch on his nose, which Frances thought abominable even though it did mark his glorious injury from the civil war. "Come to see a new marriage gone sour?" Arlington continued. "It can hardly be you're sent for to fetch *la mistresse en titre* back again as she's not only here but expected down soon, we hear."

Everyone at the table but Frances laughed. She knew, of course, they referred to the duke's errand to bring Barbara Villiers back from her legal husband to her royal lover. Typical actions from both Charles Stuarts, she thought.

The Duke of Richmond leaned casually over her shoulder to take the cards the dealer drew from the box in the center of the table for him. His velvet hip brushed against her bare shoulder, deliberately she supposed, as she sat stock still; she could feel his deep voice reverberate through her chair back to her spine when he spoke or laughed; his breath—wine or sweet ale and some sort of intoxicating tobacco fragrance— drifted down to envelope her.

He thumped his little suede purse of coins on the table and changed some for the metal bassette chips. When he leaned over her, he was certain she did not know he could see the delicious swell of her milk white breasts over the low lace rim of her chemise pulled fashionably up over the top of her taut satin bodice. He felt the foolish stirrings in his loins again. He tried to reason how old she was. With that haughty elegance, she must be sixteen, maybe seventeen, and very marriageable if not pliable; eminently desirable if not wholly lovable. He longed to bend and untie those silk ribbons wound delicately through her tawny, burnished curls to loose the shiny hair over those nearly naked shoulders she had a nasty habit of shrugging when she acquiesced even a little. Damn, but she was enticing and the scent of frangipani that rose from her body was drugging his senses.

It shocked him that he held the cards to win the hand. "Luck of a new player," Lord Lauderdale groused. "Or maybe, Mrs. Stewart brings you luck, Richmond. If so, I'd like to borrow her. I need a run of some hot cards before I get in much deeper. Gads, but what's keeping the triumvirate we've been promised from appearing?"

Across the crowded room there was a murmuring ripple of whispers and movement. It must be the king or queen because chairs scraped back as people stood. The duke's fingers were warm on the smooth skin of her arm slightly up under her flounced sleeve as he steadied her while she rose.

Willingly, she let him escort her closer to the king and queen. Frances breathed a sigh of relief. The royal couple were together, looking as if they had struck a truce, and the king was politely presenting the queen to individuals in the crowd as he frequently had before their disagreement so she could learn the many names and court positions so new to her.

Before Frances could believe what she saw, Barbara Villiers, dressed in sumptuous crimson skirts and a gold bodice which her breasts nearly overflowed, appeared across the room behind the queen. A wave of expectanty hushed the crowd. The woman radiated exotic sensuality; even in midpregnancy she emanated force and passion. An emerald and diamond necklace blazed on her full bosom and matching earbobs caught the light against her dark brown hair.

"I really am sorry I'm here to see this," Richmond hissed in her ear. "Let's go outside and not get caught in it."

She shook his insistent hand off her arm. "And this time," Frances said, her voice mocking, "you didn't even get sent to fetch her nor, I vow, did Chancellor Clarendon."

"I should have known His Majesty would have made you privy to his past doings by now," he shot back. "And you surely can't have been here more than a month. Then you may take my earlier teasings about him as a full warning so you don't find yourself in over your very pretty head."

"Your implications are as crude as you, my lord," she said, evidently too loudly as both Lady Arlington and her friend Amanda Wells turned to stare.

Fuming, Frances stood next to a now-silent

Richmond as the king's introductions to the queen went on. Frances saw Barbara Villiers had edged closer, so near she pushed between Lauderdale and Arlington directly ahead of them in the crowd. The king's mistress swished her hips to settle the crimson skirts she wore drawn back by gold and ruby clasps over petticoats. She wet her lush lips with a tip of pink tongue, smoothed an arched eyebrow, and turned back to see who stood nearby.

"Richmond, you rogue! Gads, something must be up if he's summoned you. Or," she said and winked at Frances, "did some sort of other compelling cause drag you here? Zounds, but I wish I had your figure for this bloody fracas, mistress," Barbara addressed Frances. "This belly the king's ah—ardor—has given me is like to ruin all my bodices and my waistlines. Oh hell, just so I can begin this appointment before my official lying-in to birth the child." Her curls and dangling earbobs bounced as she turned away.

Those close enough to hear her outrageous words stared agog at each other, and behind her, Lord Arlington mouthed something to Richmond Frances did not catch. She held her breath as the king actually began to present his wide-eyed queen to Barbara Villiers not five feet away. It was painfully obvious to everyone in the room the poor queen had no idea whom she was greeting.

"And, Your Grace, a lady I believe you have not met, one I am certain you would like if you could but come to know her," the king was saying with a grandiose gesture.

Catherine of Braganza's lips set in the continual nervous smile Frances had come to expect from her whenever she faced anyone outside her immediate circle of ladies. The queen nodded and extended her hand to be kissed. Barbara Villiers dipped and bent to comply.

"You have new coming to this court?" the queen inquired in the halting, stilted tones to which Frances was nearly oblivious now as she accompanied the queen wherever she went almost daily.

"No, Your Majesty, not newly come to court, but I am well pleased enough to greet you for the first time since I shall be one of your ladies of the bedchamber," Barbara's clear voice rang out.

The queen's limpid eyes darted to her husband's seemingly impassive face, and she whispered something to him. "A lady I want you to come to know," his words carried in the room's deathly silence. "Her name, my dear, is Madame Barbara Palmer, the newly declared Countess of Castlemaine."

The queen's eyes darted, jumped. A low, guttural sound strangled her reply. She raised both hands to smack herself on the forehead and screamed. Frances glimpsed blood under her nose, a common complaint the queen suffered from lately. She heaved another scream and collapsed heavily to the floor.

Frances tried to dart forward into the press of people around the queen, but Richmond's firm grip pulled her back.

"Stand away! Just give her air," the king's voice reverberated through the murmurs and whisperings.

"Damn him and his fancy whore for this wretched trick!" Frances heard Richmond say so quietly she thought for a moment her own words had echoed in her head.

106

"I must go to her," she said. "I've helped her with her nosebleeds."

But Richmond tugged her away, back into the crowd and to add to Frances' outrage, his other hand dragged a sputtering Barbara Villiers behind.

"Loose me, Richmond, leave off," Barbara hissed. "I'm not some sack of barley from your damned Kent farmlands, you know."

"I do indeed know that, Madame Palmer. I'm only trying, though for the life of me I don't know why, to rescue you from your own rash stupidity. They're going to carry the queen out now and I suggest you make your own exist, albeit not so dramatic as you prefer for once," he challenged her.

Barbara Villiers drew herself up to her full height and defiantly stuck out her chin. She shook the duke's arm off, and he released her so quickly, she almost fell.

"You arrogant bastard!" she hissed. "If you ever lay a hand on me it will be only because I send for you to amuse me!" Her furious brown eyes darted to Frances' startled face, and she looked as if she would hurl another insult, but instead she smacked her hands down hard on her thighs through her skirts. "I shall be off now, of my own accord, but I'm sick— sick to death of being ordered around here by you, Charles Stuart—and the other royal one. Good night!"

Barbara Villiers had flounced off around the edge of the large raucous crowd with her cousin, the Duke of Buckingham, in quick pursuit, before Frances even realized Richmond still held her firmly by her upper arm. Their eyes caught and held. It seemed she had been holding her breath for the longest time as she breathed out slowly.

"That sort of despicable scene is the fate of most mistresses, however once favored, Frances."

"Another lecture, my lord?" she managed. "And loose my arm, please."

He did at once, but he stepped treacherously closer to take her by her elbows. "It is only that I want you to be aware of the dangers, Frances, as you are very young and new here."

"Thank you, but I can take care of myself. Please don't bother yourself with me."

"But that's just it," he murmured low, and his eyes searched her face for something. "I am already bothered with you—by you."

She almost swayed against his hard chest, but she pulled free. "I really must go up now. Good luck with your gambling."

"I wish you were more of a gambler, Frances. It would make everything much more exciting."

She meant to turn on her heel but the intimate rasp of his voice held her captive on a silken thread of magnetism one moment longer.

"But—I prefer to be certain of things."

"Of a man."

"A man. No, I—"

"If you're so very certain you will never be the slightest involved with the king, make me a little wager, Frances."

The man was a sorcerer with that rugged look that had no place at any fine, elegant court. She stared at the little scar on his high left cheekbone afraid she would be lost in the depths of his green-gold eyes if she looked into them again.

"Since you're so very certain of things, just wager me that I can have the identical—ah, favors you allow the king," he urged almost soothingly.

Her head snapped up, her jaw went taut. "What? You are insane!"

"Of course, if you're uncertain, you wouldn't dare agree to such a wager," he plunged on. "If you weren't certain of yourself, you'd never dare wager anything to an—what did Barbara Villiers, the decorous Madame Palmer, call me?—an arrogant bastard."

"You are, you know."

"You are unspeakably arrogant yourself, ice goddess."

To her horror her palm reached out to slap his smug face as the terrible memory of the teasing, insulting comments of other men—French fops, even King Louis and the Duke of Orléans stabbed at her.

"Oh!" she said as he gingerly fingered his cheek where her hand had struck him. "Oh, I am certain of myself with the king as I am certain you shall never touch me again for any reason!"

"Then, of course, I have my wager?"

"Yes! Just leave me alone!"

"Good night then, Frances Stewart. You do realize, you're the only woman I've ever let accost me twice without retribution—yet." He bowed mockingly to her and was off into the crowd now resettled at the gaming tables.

Her palm tingled and her eyes stung with unshed tears. Damn him! Barbara Villiers was right to call him an arrogant bastard. She'd be very certain to steer clear of him in the future. Chancellor Clarendon had warned her against the wrong man. After tonight it was Charles Stuart—both of them—she'd have to work to avoid.

Chapter Four

It was several weeks before Frances saw London for the first time. With their courtiers, the king and queen made a triumphal river journey from Hampton Court to Westminster while all England, it seemed, lined the green river banks in joyous abandon. Frances with other selected ladies and cavaliers rode the ornately bedecked royal barge seated directly behind their majesties who were ensconced on a dias under a canopy of gold cloth supported by Corinthian pillars festooned with garlands from Hampton Court's bounteous gardens. Like a parade of grand ducklings behind their decorated mother, a string of other less festive barges followed.

Somehow, the king had managed to smooth things over after that terrible night two months ago when Queen Catherine had been carried swooning from the grand salon amid the gambling tables. Evidently he had gambled on shocking his bride into realizing he would have his way, whatever the cost to others, for she seemed stoically resigned to the presence and reality of Barbara Villiers at last. Barbara had been duly appointed Queen's Lady of the Bedchamber, but Catherine of Braganza had her rewards also. The king visited her chamber almost every afternoon while her ladies were dismissed to amuse themselves, and Barbara Villiers had been left behind at Hampton Court to complete her lying-in for this second half-royal babe.

As the line of barges were rowed even closer to the city, Frances could sense the burgeoning excitement. The green-gray river banks birthed droves of boats from which people rang bells, threw flowers, and shouted blessings and good will. Cheering citizens crowded the shoreline footpaths: wild, little boys ran screeching along and women waved and danced along meadows and the rural villages of Chelsea.

The king's twenty-four bargemen decked in scarlet royal liveries not only bent to their oars now, but also sang some sort of rowing song which evidently pleased His Majesty mightily as he occasionally turned and added his fine deep bass to their chorus— and each time he did so, gave Frances a look and flashing smile.

The warm, clear day was so unutterably beautiful that Frances felt deeply the thrill of finally arriving in Minette's beloved London. She could settle down in her own small, private four-room suite at Whitehall Palace now, a suite the king had told her would be in easy reach of the queen's rooms. Also, her family would be here from France to settle in Somerset House a little way down the river and deliver her two cats she missed so much; her dear, stubborn little parrot Joli was being cared for by a baggage boy on the barge directly behind. Everything today was going so well—of course, with the one exception that after several trips to Hampton Court this summer where she had managed to avoid to avoid or snub him, the Duke of Richmond was here on the royal barge and, unless she chose to dive into the crowded river, there was obviously no escape from him this time if he chose to approach her. Yet he had done naught amiss so far and surely they were nearly there.

Under their own flapping red silk canopy to shield the queen's ladies from the sun, Frances' friend Amanda Wells, a pretty if freckle-faced maid with red hair, leaned over to tap Frances' wrist with her fan. "He's staring again, Frances," Amanda whispered.

Guiltily, Frances' eyes darted to see if the king had turned about in his seat again to sing with the bargemen and eye her.

"No, silly—Richmond. Despite the fact you treat him abominably, I swear, he's going to saunter over here for more," she chortled.

Frances felt herself blush. Her lack of internal composure where the man was concerned annoyed her, though she fancied she kept a fairly calm outward demeanor over the trying situation. "I doubt it, Amanda. He's not so dense that I haven't made my feelings perfectly clear on it."

"Your feelings—I wonder. Gads, any woman in her right mind would at least get the vapors over that tall one. He's a little rough looking, I admit, compared to someone like young Jermyn or Buckingham, but that always gives an added little fillip, I dare say. Besides, he's cousin to the king and has extensive lands in Kent and Scotland. I swear, if you don't fancy Richmond, I think you need your head knocked—or, is it just you don't wish to rile the king?"

"Dear Amanda, your teasing chatter is about to absolutely ruin this lovely day and our friendship, so cease, if you please!" Frances stood and shook her pale yellow silk skirts out. They were caught back gracefully with fashionable rosettes of woven yellow ribbons to match the fluttering ones in her blowing tresses. Ribbons were coming to be the rage among the English courtiers, and even the queen had added festoons of them to her new bridal bed of crimson velvet, embroidered with silver, an expensive gift from the States of Holland that Chancellor Clarendon vowed was worth at least eight hundred pounds. The silk ribbon mania was a style Frances knew her recent return from the French court had helped to establish and she was proud of that.

It felt good to stretch her legs at last even though the river breeze tugged at her pale cream, embroidered underskirt and rustled her lace petticoats into her legs. Several other ladies seemed to take her cue, even as they had in copying her French-made garments these last three months: they stood and began to stroll about despite the narrow, restricted open areas on the barge. Frances moved over to lean lightly on the carved rail from which smartly snapped vibrant banners sporting the Stuart coat of arms. Along the bank, the green meadows had turned to trim gardens and ever-larger villages.

"My kingdom, *la belle* Frances. You do approve?"

She turned, smiled, and squinted directly into the afternoon sun as she faced the king. "Yes, sire, it's beautiful. And the people love you so!"

They both turned to the rail, and his hands nearly swallowed by long lace cuffs under his deep red silk waistcoat dwarfed her hands by comparison. "I want to be loved, Frances, very much," his words floated low to her amidst the shouts and shrieks of people in boats and along the shore. "By certain individuals more than others," he said emphasizing each word. "Is it not so with you?"

She did not dare to look at him so she stared at the passing lapping water line where river met land. "Of course, sire."

"Then assure me it is just my fancy you avoid me."

She gasped at the direct assault of the words before she could make her face impassive again. "Of course, that is not so, Your Majesty. I see you daily as I serve the queen so closely. I—for Minette—I care greatly for you."

"For Minette! Od's fish, that's a charming put-off if I've ever heard one. Frances, I must return to sit now. Richmond told me he saw six orchestras and veritable flotillas of fancy city barges on his way out this morning, so it won't do for the king to be chatting with some beautiful wood nymph while his new queen drifts in alone in all this planned chaos. However, since you have assured me my feelings are mere imaginings of a too fond king, I shall expect to have many chances to converse more privily with you soon."

He was gone from the rail as quickly and silently as he had appeared; she heard him chatting to many on his way back to his seat on the dais, his laugh easily discerned above the swell of noises.

As the barges with their little armada of smaller boats swept around a northward bend of the river, towers, steeples, and a distant huddle of gabled, steep-roofed houses swept into her view. The stiff breeze batted harder; suddenly her skirts billowed and lifted, nearly into her face. She squealed and turned, fighting to control them. Other hands besides hers pushed them down and wrapped them to her sides where she could hold them. The Duke of Richmond towered over her and quickly snatched his hands back from her hips.

"I would have warned you that shift of breeze always occurs at Nine Elms Reach, Frances, but you were talking with another gentleman and I knew better than to interrupt."

She shot him a quick perusal, then looked away. Unlike the other bareheaded men on board whose blown hair seemed somehow bizarre and freakish, except for the king whom protocol dictated was the only one with a hat, the Duke of Richmond's mussed hair looked natural and only carefree. He seemed to relish the sun and breeze, drinking them in and letting his rakish brows and brown hair be whipped about as they would.

"Thank you for helping me out of that situation," she said low, feeling she was being extremely kind in return for his favor. "I really had best sit down now so I can see London."

His voice stopped her as surely as if he had held out his arms to block her way. "You won't really see London this way, Frances, and there will be a large, rowdy crowd at Westminster when we arrive. I have a carriage waiting. Let me show you the heart of London and then drive you back to Whitehall today."

"The offer is kind of you, my Lord Duke—"

"Richmond."

"—Richmond, but I could not possibly leave the queen's party."

"There will be rows of carriages for that last little jaunt between palaces. No one will think a thing of it if you're not in one particular vehicle."

"I thank you, Richmond, but I do not wish to go. Excuse me."

"Not yet. There is one other thing. You do remember our little wager where you allot me whatever privileges you do the king? You stood and listened to him, and I want you to hear something from me."

She shrugged her shoulders and continued to gaze out at the numerous, large approaching barges sent by the city guilds to come out and meet them near Westminster. "I understand you've been given your own suite of rooms at Whitehall," he went on when she was silent.

"What of it?" her voice came shrilly to her ears. "They are in close proximity to Her Majesty's."

"And to King Charles. As a matter of fact, they are almost directly above his as, I understand, Barbara Villiers' suite will be directly below, and there is a privy staircase connecting all three stories. Actually, your suite is far better than Barbara's, for the river-level rooms flood at times."

He watched her beautiful profile intently as she

took in his words. The woman really did astound him with her apparent ability to appear unruffled or to dissemble, but he was pleased to catch the slight tremor of the full lower lip, the furious frown that wrinkled the clear forehead under the wind-tossed curls. Hallelujah, he exulted silently—she hadn't been a party to whatever nefarious seduction plans the king evidently harbored for her, not yet, at least.

"The court can be a dangerous place for a young, beautiful woman, Frances," his voice went on when she still said nothing. "I understand your mother will be here in London, but Somerset house on the Strand is not Whitehall if you're hoping for her protection."

"You think you understand a great deal, do you not, Richmond?" Her voice dripped sarcasm now.

"I wish I understood you," he began as, still holding her wayward skirts down, she hurried back to her seat. She knew he still stood at the rail watching the guild's massive barges that were cleverly disguised as floating islands complete with river deities spouting verse which the various orchestras on shore drowned out even as they did each other. Cheers and the pealing of city bells added to the jumbled cacophony as they passed Lambeth on the right and swung in toward Westminster stairs under the gothic abbey, medieval palace, and Hall of Westminster.

Despite her anger at Richmond's words and what they imported—damn, but she had to put up with his lectures the same way the king did with Clarendon's —her heart swelled at the joyous welcome London lay before the feet of its monarch and his new queen.

Those shouting boatmen, those pompous, grinning guild members, and that little boy there on the wharf with his squirming puppy—what did they know of their new queen's loneliness in England and of her sad parting from the Portuguese ladies the king had sent home to show her who would rule the marriage? What thought of sympathy did any of them give to a marriage already gone rancid because the nature of a man was always to be hard on a woman foolish enough to adore him?

Yes, she'd let the king talk to her privily as he wished and soon! She intended to have his word her chambers were hers alone to use, privy staircase, favored upper story, or not. And if he wanted to punish her by sending her to some scullion's room far off in the reaches of Whitehall, let him! Minette would just have to understand that her plea to love the king went only so far.

The barge nudged, then bumped the stone steps crowded with Londoners. Frances craned her head to see the first baggage barge had pulled in farther down the river landing since additional of the king's guards were on it. She had made certain her parrot was on that one as the others in the water parade from Hampton Court would go directly to Whitehall: she had no intention of letting someone deliver her pet parrot to the wrong chamber there or filch the valuable bird. That barge looked stacked and cluttered, and she wished for one moment she would have asked the king to let her bring Joli with her, but she did not need to start owing him favors. Of that, she would be very careful.

Everyone streamed up the steps through the press

of shouting, waving people behind the king and queen. The scarlet-liveried Yeomen of the Guard from the royal baggage barges held off the crowd from their majesties well enough, but everyone else, it seemed, had to fend for himself. Above, at the top of the stairs, Frances glimpsed the Duke and Duchess of York, Chancellor Clarendon's daughter, greeting the king and queen. The odor of unwashed, unperfumed bodies assailed Frances as shouting citizens hemmed her in. Some strange, cavorting woman jumped out ahead, cutting Frances off from sight of Amanda Wells. She nearly tripped over her skirts. Instantly, hands were on her narrow waist from behind to steady her. She darted a frantic look back fully intending to have to shove some overzealous bargeman or stinking dockboy away.

She smiled to see him despite herself. "You again, Richmond. Do you make a practice of rescuing ladies?"

"Only stubborn ones who never admit they need—a hand now and then. Since you have so pointedly refused my offer in a carriage today, I will see you safely into the nearest one in all this mess, sweet lass."

Sweet. Sweet lass, the nonchalantly offered term of endearment echoed in her mind. Her Scottish father had called her that; she had not heard it or felt that poignant pull of emotion it evoked for so very long. It was as if he knew all about her past, this tall Duke of Richmond, as if he termed her "sweet lass" to apologize for dubbing her "ice goddess" the evening she had slapped him. He had turned her toward the line of waiting carriages before she remembered Joli.

"Wait. Wait! I have to go over to that other barge to get my parrot."

He stared at her a minute, pressed close by the jostling crowd from which he shielded her. "A parrot? But surely it will be delivered with the other things."

"No, my lord. No. I want to take him back myself."

He did not argue as she had thought he might, but led her the other way, pulling her against the flow of revelers. They went down a narrow flight of stairs to a shady stretch of dock where the second barge was moored. A strip of grass with tall trees ran along the river here by Westminster Palace.

"These planks to the barge aren't very steady, Frances. Just wait here and I'll fetch the bird," he said as he started across the two-foot-wide gangplank.

"No, I'll come too. I vow, I know exactly where they put him," she declared and traipsed across the pliant boards right behind him. "There—that little towheaded baggage boy was watching him. Hello, lad! I've come for my parrot!"

The boy nodded and jumped off his lofty vantage point on a tall crate. He scrambled up and over a pile of slatted boxes which Frances recognized as those in which the king's traveling scientific laboratory was transported from place to place. The lad disappeared, then returned with Joli's gilt cage swinging from his scrawny arm. Leaning precariously forward from the top of a crate, he proffered the cage even as a sudden loud boom rattled the barge.

"Yipes!" the boy squealed and dropped the cage. Another echoing, deafening boom exploded from somewhere as Joli's cage crashed down onto the deck.

Frances screamed, the duke cursed as the cage door broke open and the frightened bird shot skyward in a burst of powerful, green flapping wings.

Frances turned, bounced off Richmond's rock-hard body and was instantly down the swaying planks to the dock. "Joli! Joli! Oh, no, my Lord Duke, wherever could he have gone that fast? Joli!"

"He must have gone up into that first tree, the tall chestnut," he called to her. "Stop shrieking like a Billingsgate fishwife. Speak calmly to him and maybe he'll come down. We'll look in the tree."

She peered up carefully, through the leafy branches. Perched a good twelve feet off the ground, the lime-hued bird calmly picked at his ruffled breast feathers. "Yes, yes, he's here. Oh, thank heavens, he's not hurt!"

The duke came up behind her, the dented cage in his hand. "He's very dear to you, isn't he, lass? I swear, I envy the little green bastard even though you keep him in a cage. If we hold it up to him, any chance he'll fly down into it?"

"I doubt it. He loves to perch on high things, and I always have to bring him back." She noted how warmly the duke's free hand rode on her shoulder, and for the first time, she did not shake him off or scold.

"Maybe he's hungry enough to come for some fruit if we only had some," Richmond offered.

"But we don't, my lord."

"Then, my lady, we can't stand about here all day gawking when there is all London for the three of us to see. Here, hold my coat and vest. I'll go up after him."

122

"Heavens, you'll fall!"

White teeth flashed in a broad grin as his eyes went over her. "I'd like to think my demise would sadden you, Frances, but I'm afraid I know better." He divested himself of a magnificently tailored, dark blue satin filigreed waistcoat and a gold brocaded vest which she held for him. He loosed the drawstrings of his long, lace shirt cuffs with quick pulls and shoved his elegant white shirtsleeves up over brown, heavily muscled forearms. "Don't fret, sweet lass. I'm an old country tree climber from way back."

He started up the tree directly above, affording her a view of brawny calves and hard-muscled thighs despite the narrow hips. About five feet off the ground, he bent to look down at her. "I suppose," he gasped, "I should take the cage up but I don't know how I'd manage it. Should I just grab him or what?"

"I'll call gently to him. He should perch on your hand or shoulder if he's not frightened. Oh, there are those awful booms again that scared him and made that little wretch drop the cage."

"Gun salutes from the Tower," he grunted. "More damn royal celebrations." He went farther up, praying each limb would take his weight. At least the stupid bird had not flown clear to the top of Westminster's towers, he fumed. He had scraped his knuckles, and his big onyx ducal ring bit into his finger at each grasp. He knew his shirt and chin were filthy. In that instant, he almost laughed aloud at himself. Hell's gates, but he wanted to please Frances Stewart, wanted to possess her too. But he figured he'd gotten himself into a terrible spot and not just out on a tree limb he wasn't certain would hold him.

The woman, as unconsciously sensuous as she was, had erected some invisible, icy barrier around herself and he wanted it down, melted or broken. And, whatever it took he meant to have it down!

When the bird started shrieking, it startled him so much he almost fell. "Keep a smile. Keep a smile. Keep your distance!" the high-pitched voice scolded. Damn, he could tell for certain Frances Stewart had taught the parrot to talk now!

"Good Joli. Good boy," he said as he reached out a tentative hand toward the eight-inch-tall bird. It shifted two quick sidesteps out on the limb away from him. Far below, Frances' nervous crooning to the bird drifted to him. Hell, he cursed low again. This had better be worth it! The spoiled little chit owed him some pliant sweetness after this fiasco.

"Come on, Joli boy, for Frances. Come on," he murmured. He shuddered with excitement as the bird stepped calmly onto his arm. The black pupil of the closest eye rolled as if to examine him. The bird began to preen his wing feathers as Richmond glanced down.

He could not see anything below but leaves and branches, and it occurred to him he'd never be able to back down with only one free hand. He lifted and bent his arm with the bird as he felt talons walk to his shoulder and settle there. Afraid his voice would startle the bird if he answered Frances' questions below, he started carefully down. He bruised his chin and bumped his thigh hard, but still the bird sat stolidly preening. Richmond's arms were trembling from the strain by the time he was low enough for her to see he had the parrot.

"Richmond! Oh, thank you, thank you! Joli, you bad boy, here, come to me!" The parrot stepped easily from his shoulder and into the broken cage she held up while Richmond sat down, his back against the tree. His shirt was ruined now anyhow, so what did it matter?

He felt a flash of irrational jealousy which heartily shamed him as she petted and fussed over the green culprit sitting innocently enough back in his cage. Richmond watched her tie the broken cage door closed with one of her yellow hair ribbons, and a heavy, loose curl tumbled down her slender arch of throat to bounce once in the cleft between her breasts before she straightened. He gave an inward groan at the lewd thought of reaching out to tug those pert breasts free to cover the satin skin and pink nipples with kisses whatever sort of struggle she offered. But he steeled his temper and his passions. Damn, he did want that, but he wanted much more and not just once. He was amazed to see tears gather in her lovely, sky-blue eyes.

"I can't thank you enough, my Lord Richmond. You took a great risk. Thank you."

He stood slowly at last and brushed off his soiled midnight blue velvet breeches. He knew his white boot hose were devastated and he hardly gave them a glance although he saw she did. "I told you, Frances, I like risks and gambles, if the prize is good enough." His eyes caught hers and he almost kissed her, but there were still others on the steps above and someone might tell the king. When she spoke next, her voice was so soft and sweet—he had never heard it so—that the desire to touch her staggered him.

"It does seem, my lord, I am always causing you to ruin your best garments. As I said, Joli and I thank you."

"I would have waited to ask you for a carriage ride to Whitehall if I had only foreseen this turn of events," he said as she helped him don the vest and waistcoat she still held. He fancied he could smell her intoxicating scent of frangipani on them where they had lain over her arm.

She stared one moment at his shoulders stretching the dirtied shirt and the waistcoat taut. His brown neck was strong, his chin square with a tiny cleft, his green eyes lit by moving shards of gold when he faced her in full sunlight as now. Something ticklish like Joli's feathers fluttered low in her stomach. Then she said the words that pounded in her brain: "I will go in your carriage, if you still wish, my Lord Duke."

She thought he would look more delighted, but his mouth went slightly taut as he nodded and lifted the damaged birdcage to lead her back up to the landing. How long had all that taken? she wondered. The crowd had thinned and the carriages for the royal retinue had departed. They walked across a courtyard and then a grassy square to a fine-looking carriage with massive backwheels and a huge embossed *R* on the door. Four black horses stood patiently stomping the cobbled street.

"M' lord, what happened? Did you have a fall, m' lord?" his brawny, black-haired coachman asked in some sort of rural drawl as he hurried up to them.

"A fall of sorts, Jenkin. This is Mrs. Frances Stewart and her thankfully caged parrot. Take us to Whitehall via St. Paul's and Cheapside."

"St. Paul's and Cheapside, m'lord," Jenkin repeated, knowing full well that was as about a circuitous route as anyone could take. Gads, they would be a good two hours in this traffic with the royal entry today and all. "Aye, m'lord, Whitehall via St. Paul's and Cheapside, it is!" he said, and caught a good glimpse of slender female ankle as his lordship handed the pretty lady up into his private carriage.

Frances settled Joli's cage across on the other seat as Richmond climbed in beside her. The carriage was a fine one with leather-tooled interior walls, seats and footstools and cushions to brace one's back as they jolted and swayed along. From a brass box on the floor, Richmond immediately drew out a metal flask. Then he surprised her by dashing the amber liquid on his linen and lace handkerchief rather than drinking it.

"I'm sure my face is filthy from that climb, so I'll just clean up a bit if you'll tell me where the smudges are," he said. "I don't usually use this stuff to wash in, but it's too strong for a lady to drink anyway."

"Yes. All right. Your chin is scraped—and farther up too. Here, I can do it, my lord."

She took the damp square of cloth from his proffered fingers before she wondered if he had meant for her to wash him all along. She dabbed at his reddish scrapes and smudge marks, her heart thudding as he studied her face at such close range and as her shoulder lurched against his when they turned a corner in the swaying vehicle. There, that would have to do for now. She could feel her cheeks and bosom getting prickly hot, and he looked as if he would like to seize her.

She moved swiftly away to sit by her partly rolled-up window and offered him his handkerchief with outstretched arm. "There. I vow, you look much more presentable now. Where are we anyway? If this is a city tour, should you not point out all the important sites?"

He slid across the seat almost touching her again and leaned over her to roll the leather flap up even higher. "We're riding through St. James's Park, north toward Pall Mall," he said, his mouth so close that his warm breath ruffled the loosed ringlets along her left temple. "We just passed Birdcage Walk where His Majesty keeps cages of singing birds. Now, Joli would really appreciate that."

His shoulder leaned ever so lightly against hers which was barely covered with satin, lawn, and lace. A little tremor shot clear down her spine to the very pit of her stomach, and his low, raspy voice seemed to ruffle something deep inside her again.

"It's a lovely park," she said. Afraid to turn to look at him at such close range, she leaned farther toward the breezy window to let the air cool her face. "Look. Cattle and deer grazing right there and so many people walking."

"The king keeps ducks down on that lake. He feeds them daily on his long walks when he's in residence. Our new sovereign, as you will see, has many pursuits, some admirable, some not."

She tensed waiting for another scolding warning from him, but he said no more of that as the carriage passed a huge, sprawling complex of brick buildings and rolled on.

"What was that big place?" she asked. "It went

128

on forever."

"That, lass, was Whitehall, your future home for who knows how long."

"But you said you would deliver me there! Surely, I will be missed."

"I told you I would deliver you there after you'd seen London. You can show them Joli's cage and explain it took you several hours to get some poor, trembling bloke to climb a giant tree for you. You see this row of grand houses along the Strand here?" he changed the subject adeptly. "Homes of rich courtiers when they're not at Whitehall or in their country houses."

"Do you have one along here then?"

"I? No. I live at the Bowling Green in Whitehall in a suite traditionally given to the King's Lord Chamberlain and when I get any sort of chance to be free, I go off to my lands at Cobham near Gravesend in Kent. I'm a Scottish crofter or poor sailor at heart, Frances, and London would hardly see me if I had my way. Look, that large place there is Somerset House where your family will live."

"I vow, but it's grand too. They should be here soon. It's not far from Whitehall, at least."

"Far enough as your busy duties and general court frivolities will probably claim most of your time, but you won't be so busy," he said and one hand warmly covered her hand on her knee, "that you won't agree to see me once in a while."

Coward that she was with this man, she stiffened and didn't dare turn to face him. "Of course, I'll see you, Richmond. As you have said, we both live at court."

His voice was treacherously low in the jolting, swaying carriage as his rock-hard thigh gently pressed against hers. "Don't fence with me, Frances. I'm afraid I don't appreciate catty cleverness the way some cavaliers do. I only learned last week you spent almost a year in Louis XIV's court with the Princess Henrietta-Anne before you came here. I had always pictured you still there at lovely, rural Saint-Germain and here you've had to fend for yourself in Louis' fashionable, dangerous court."

"I got on quite well. I vow, I have become very adept at taking care of myself."

He heard the iciness begin to creep back into her voice. "I can see that, and I am not criticizing. I hope you will continue to get on and take care of yourself in Charles's court, and I want to offer myself as a friend."

When she turned to look at him briefly, their noses almost touched. She leaned her head back against the jolting carriage near the open window. For the life of her, she could not seem to compose a properly assured retort.

"Of course, I don't mean to imply I wouldn't like for us to be much more than friends," he murmured, his green eyes lit by gold flecks burning into her half-lidded gaze. "Damn it, sweet lass, shall I take that smoldering silence for acquiescence then?" he groaned, and his big hands reached for her.

He pulled her so swiftly into his warm, hard embrace that she did not even protest or turn her head away. Long arms enveloped her shoulders, back, and waist as his mouth took hers determinedly, posessively. Startled at the sensual pressure of his lips, she opened hers against him only to have her mouth invaded by his darting tongue. It caressed her moist inner lip and moved deeper as if to challenge her. She stiffened against his chest as she felt her breasts crushed to him, but he only slanted his mouth sideways and moved his head in enticing little circles as the kiss deepened.

Her eyes flew open only to stare at closed eyelids and his dark, thick lashes spread along his high-boned, brown cheeks. He was moving against her everywhere, his chest, his thigh, his mouth, his hands on her back and waist. Her pulse pounded in her ears and all reasoning crashed into some deep pool of unfathomable feeling as something in her very core poured out to drown her.

His senses reeled so dizzily, he thought he might lose his hard-won control. She was very inept at kissing; didn't even really purse her lips for him, but the reality she was still inexperienced with men thrilled him as much as her sweet fragrance, her hair, her skin, and the apparent submission of her response. If only the king didn't seem so obviously set to woo her, for that might take her out of his reach. If only he could drop these window flaps and tell Jenkin to drive off to Cobham while he pressed her down against the cushions here and—

"Mm. Noo—no," she managed shakily as she pulled her mouth away. "No more. Loose me."

He feathered little kisses down her slant of cheekbone to her jaw line. "All right, all right, I will." He nuzzled the smooth, scented skin along her neck glancing down to the alluring line of bodice that displayed the pushed-up twin mounds of her creamy breasts. His hands tingled at the nearly overwhelming desire to tug her bodice down and press his hands to her there. He hoped she didn't glance down because he knew his rampant desire was all too obvious in the bulge of his breeches, and he drew his legs closer together.

Her voice sounded very small and frightened. "When will you let me go? Now, please."

Reluctantly, he released her and watched her stare immediately out the window almost as if he had never touched her. But her breasts rose and fell noticeably and her lower lip trembled discernibly.

"You're a stunningly beautiful woman, Frances Stewart, so don't expect an apology for that."

"If not an apology, then some restraint please," she managed. Her heart thudded; her stomach fluttered; her breasts tingled. Never, never, she thought, had she been so—so out of control as that, and she was as determined he would never know it as she was it must never happen again. Heavens, if it hadn't been for his rescuing of Joli, none of this insanity would be happening now either!

"I can't promise, but I am pleased you evidently haven't liked such attention from men before."

The controlled profile whirled to reveal an angry face. "You have no right to claim such a thing! You don't know anything about it!"

"Then Frenchmen, fortunately, kiss very badly. Pray, Frances, do not slap me because it is just the excuse I need to put my hands on you again."

"You are insufferable. I should have known you couldn't be civil! You belong on your barbaric Scottish lands or Kentish farm!"

"I shall take that for the truth it is, and not an insult, sweet."

"Ask your coachman to put me down, please. Joli and I are getting out."

"Not in Cheapside uncovered by a shawl or mask, you're not. Stop pouting and look out and you'll see what I mean. You'd never even make it across the intersection in one unmuddied, untrampled piece."

Her eyes took in the scene around them. Large carriages and numerous smaller black hackneys were jammed to a stop as two carriages had collided farther up ahead. Drivers in the affected vehicles screamed obscenities at each other as street boys and vendors converged on the area evidently hoping for a scuffle. Housewives with stringy hair hung from second- and third-story windows to shout insults or heave out jars of slop with the warning cry of "Garde loo!" Along the edge of narrow, mud-rutted curbs, posts at regular intervals kept pedestrians from being hit by horse or carriage traffic. Frances was in awe of the raucous, congested chaos.

"Whyever did we come down here?" she asked him, pretending to ignore the fact his body pressed hers intimately as he leaned over to look out with her.

"I told you, I wanted you to see London. The sacred precincts of Whitehall or St. James's Palace are not London although you'll note a veritable parade of Londoners traipsing through since the king allows it. But it is important to remember how the others live when you're tucked away at court."

She arched one eyebrow at him, weighing his final choice of words, then turned back to the potpourri of street life outside their window. Ballad singers, their tin dishes out for coins, had begun to stroll among the halted vehicles and beggars wailed from the curbs. Vendors' cries assailed their ears in dissonant counterpoint, both ragged and tidy men and women offering pies, Venus oysters, gilt ginger-bread, China oranges, pig trotters, or lemons. Richmond leaned past her and held two coins out the window for gingerbread.

"Here, Frances. It's hot," he said, evidently not thinking he might have asked her what she wanted first. "We hardly need the oysters, you and I. They're aphrodisiacs, you know."

He grinned at her and in a moment she managed a careful smile at the tease. She broke off a small piece of the pugnent gingerbread and fed Joli.

"I just knew under that stiff Scottish-born, French-reared exterior," he dared, "there lurked a sweet smile and at least a little sense of humor."

"You are despicable."

"At least, lass," he replied, his mouth full of gingerbread, "having me around lets you keep those barbs you like to launch well sharpened and oiled."

He bought them oranges too, big juicy ones he showed her how to cut a small hole into and suck all the sweet juice from. He talked on and on about London as the traffic snarl eventually unwound and as they rattled back down Fleet Street. He showed her where the Drury Lane Theatre was being built and promised to bring her fashionably masked to a play there some afternoon. He told her each major type of food had its own market area in teeming London: Billingsgate for fish, Leadenhall for poultry, Smithfield for meats, and Spitalfields for fruits and vegetables. He talked on and she listened, her quick mind taking the information in, her mouth reluctantly lifting in a smile at his occasional outrageous comments.

"Street names, sweet Frances, are either for great people or whatever is sold on them. There is Candlewick Street, Bread Street, Hosier Lane—which I had better visit as I've ruined these boot hose tree climbing this afternoon—and even a Pie Corner. Also," he said and leaned toward her to encircle a slender wrist with his warm fingers, "a Love Lane."

Despite herself, she felt relaxed and content again now, bold enough to get caught up in the spirit of his apparent lightheartedness.

"And do they sell love there, my Lord Duke of Richmond?"

"Alas, it's inhabited by wantons. Barbara Villiers might be at home there, but never someone like you, Frances."

He had cleverly shifted the mood on her again, she realized entirely too late, as his hand on her wrist gave a little tug that brought her mouth within inches of his. She did not flinch away as she had meant to but stared as if suspended, mesmerized, in the swaying carriage. Her free hand dropped lightly to his upper chest to brace herself. When he took her lips, she yielded them coolly, feeling as much an experimenter in a laboratory as the king amidst his bubbling liquids and fragile bottles. Determinedly, she willed herself to feel nothing at the kiss.

But tiny, treacherous tremors tickled along her skin only to run rampant in the stretch of muscle and coursing flow of blood. He slanted his mouth crazily along hers, and she leaned into him to return the kiss. She moaned low in her throat as his arms lifted to pull her upper body half across his lap, her head resting on his shoulder, her back in the crook of his arm for support.

The kiss went breathlessly on, making her press up against him while his free hand brushed down her arch of throat with the backs of bent fingers. He loosed her slightly, dropping his lips to the little pulse at the base of her throat and lower. His caressing fingers hooked into the very edge of her bodice and ran gently along its width scraping sensuously over one breast, then into the little valley between and up over the other.

"Let me. Let me, sweetheart," he breathed. He reached behind her and loosed the window flap which smacked down to dim the carriage.

"No, I cannot," she thought she said clearly through the golden haze of his touch, but he must not have heard her.

She moaned as his mouth and fingers stroked her throat, her shoulders, shoving the thin material on both sides slightly down to kiss the hollows under her collarbones. He bent into her clasped in his arms now, his full head of hair tickling her chin and throat as he trailed kisses lower. Then, before she realized he had done it or that she wanted him to do it, he stroked her bodice and chemise away from both shoulders to partly bare her damp bosom.

She drew in a sharp breath as his tongue tickled little paths of molten fire in the warm valley between her breasts. His fingers dipped into her still taut corset to tease a hard peak of nipple.

"Damn corset," he murmured almost inaudibly. "Lean forward to me, love. I'm going to unlace it just a little."

Her brain screamed no, but her voice would not speak and her body did as he asked, only he must have unlaced the taut whaleboned corset completely as he merely lifted it away to bare her pointed, heaving breasts to his avid eyes and skillful hands.

Her own deep moan of pleasure whirled in her ears with the exhilarating buzz of coursing blood. Every nerve felt alive, every stretch of skin longed for his touch as his firm lips closed enticingly around her right nipple. He kissed, he pulled, he suckled the pink bud sending such a shower of rapture through her she could not bear it when he pulled away only one instant to nuzzle the valley between her firm breasts, then to move to the other pulsating bud. Each caress of lips and tantalizing tongue she felt clear down between her thighs, and she fidgeted wildly on his lap as his hard thighs pressed up against her soft hips.

After an eternity of ecstasy, when he lifted his rugged, passion-glazed face to kiss her lips again, she kissed him back with an intensity she could not explain, a wantonness she had never fathomed in herself. Her slender fingers entwined in his mussed, thick hair to hold his lips to hers. When one huge hand slid heavily up a silk-stockinged leg even above her garters where bare flesh began, she welcomed his touch as one possessed.

Somehow she was down on the soft leather seat, amazed she could feel its cool, soft suppleness on her bare back and even her buttocks. Her gown, the gown he had helped to keep from blowing up earlier in the river breeze, had been pressed up to become a mere, wispy ruffle around her waist. His face over her, close to her spun dizzily to match the sweeping sway of the carriage. Perhaps they were flying now, high above London, sailing in the cloudless heavens like his ship adrift in rapturous seas.

His mouth and hands were everywhere now, and she reveled in it, cherishing each fiery touch. How—how could it be this way for her, for them, this overwhelming rightness, this natural desire to be as one? When he moved heavily over her on the swaying carriage and she felt hard, hair-flecked thighs against her own which she displayed for him so mindlessly, she jolted as if awakening from a lovely dream.

"No, no, my lord, we can't—" she said, but her voice was a mere breathy moan and not the harsh command she had intended.

"I love you, Frances, love you—I have from afar and now so close. I have since I first saw you there so disheveled among the roses. I'll care for you, protect you. . . ."

Impossible! her mind screeched, but all protest crumbled beneath his next searing kiss. She couldn't breathe, couldn't think, could only feel the unquenchable desire she had had for this one man ever since he'd given her that rose—all those beautiful, seductive roses.

Like a vibrant bloom of silken petals, she opened herself to him at a mere nudge of knee between her soft thighs. In that careening instant of time, nothing but him mattered, pleasing him, desiring him, yes,

138

even deep within her like the sweetest thorny stem could pierce the rose.

She gasped, startled at the pressure, the push of sharp possessiveness. One little thrust of thorn, a blindingly beautiful blending and they were one.

He looked as startled as she for one moment while he paused to kiss her, then lifted to gaze deep into her wide stare with his green-gold eyes. "I didn't mean at first for this to happen—not today," he rasped out, "but we'll always be together now. Always, my little love . . ."

His words trailed off as the swirling plunge swept them higher, higher. The deep ache subsided, at first soothed, then fired by his insistent thrust and pull inside her quaking body. Never, never had she imagined anything could be like this, so sweet and so utterly poignant.

The sight of her legs still ludicrously stockinged, the pert satin shoes quite unperturbed, amused her. Men, all those deceitful men—no wonder women loved and desired and clung to them, all dizzy-headed like this.

"Yes, yes, love, lift your sweet knees—oh, Frances, Frances, damn but you make me mad for you!"

Something foreign yet completely fantastic feathered out from their fierce union to make her go all weak and wild at once. Her arms around his big neck, she pulled him down for a brazen, open-mouthed kiss even as he pulsated into her, each reverberation as distinct as her own rampant, rhythmic rapture.

He held her tightly to him as their breathing quieted. Everything slowed—thoughts, pulses, feelings, the riotous rattle of the carriage.

"Oh, damn, I think we're stopping," he ground out and pulled her quickly upright on the seat. Dazed, dizzy, she watched his big bronzed hands as he pushed her skirts down across her blatantly bare thighs and laced her corset at her back.

"I'm going to put my head out and tell them to drive on," he told her. "Here, straighten your bodice and I'll have them take us to the ship."

"The ship?" she echoed. "No, you can't. We can't—we can't do this!"

Pressing her back firmly against the seat, he opened the flap a crack and thrust his head out even while he recomposed his own garments.

"Hell!" he ground out so fiercely it jolted her at last to her senses. "We're at Whitehall trapped in a line of carriages!"

"Whitehall, m' lord. West Gate!" the driver's voice seemed to jar the whole world.

"Stupid fool," Richmond's voice shot out. "Too late now. Here sweet, straighten your bodice a little more as coachmen often greet carriages here and just open doors."

Flustered, stunned, she pulled away to straighten her hair. Her lips trembled visibly, and she looked dazed, he thought. He steadied her with one hand while he rolled the streetside window flap up and secured it. They both blinked at the sudden rush of late daylight.

"I—I just wasn't thinking," she breathed.

"I also, most willingly, and now that you know how I really feel for you, let me take you in and we'll talk. I may have lost my head, but I meant all the things I said, Frances."

"Take me in? No, you can't. No, this wasn't good. I cannot—"

Angered, he gave her a little shake. "It was good and what we both obviously wanted desperately—maybe had since France when I came to your room."

The carriage door snapped open and a liveried footman looked in as Richmond reluctantly released her.

"My Lord Duke of Richmond," the apparently passive-faced man intoned. "As you always come by foot or water, I didn't recognize the carriage at first."

"This is Mrs. Stewart, man, whose parrot escaped from one of the king's barges earlier and she had to chase it. Please see her to her suite in the royal wing."

"Of course, my lord."

Richmond regretted instantly how stony her face looked as he handed the footman the parrot's cage and she gathered her mussed skirts to get out.

"Frances," he whispered, "I will see you tomorrow morn then. Do not be upset. We need to talk about the things I said earlier."

"No, I don't want to talk to you," she whispered back. "Please just stay away." She pulled her arm firmly away from his steadying touch on her elbow and the stiff-backed footman handed her down. Richmond hit his knee hard with his fist as the carriage door slammed shut on her slender form and the footman with the swinging parrot cage.

He felt suddenly bereft. He wanted to run after her, to kneel before her feet there on the very steps of the king's palace to declare his love for her, but she obviously needed time to learn that what she had yielded him today was not all he wanted from her, nor was his strong and skillful body all he meant to give her.

He peered out again as his carriage pulled away from Whitehall. He stretched his feet out on the opposite seat and smiled grimly. A parrot—he had a damned, silly parrot to thank for today, for arranging the carriage ride and for not screeching "keep your distance" when he had touched her.

At least today the woman who had haunted his thoughts for so long had been his at last: virgin, untouched, his. He'd been longing for someone like Frances Stewart all his life, someone not only to marry, for he'd done that once before, but someone to love. He heaved a deep sigh and let his mind drift back over how beautifully she had responded when he'd loved her.

Chapter Five

Frances' world was never the same after that first day in London—that day in Richmond's carriage. He haunted her nightly dreams and her daily thoughts despite how busy she was at court. But almost as if she had asked the king for help in this obsession which she, of course, never would share with a living soul, the king had sent Richmond on various duties to Scotland for several months and, despite the letters he sent her, she began to relax at last. The court was as big as it was busy—filled with so many people to hide behind if need be when the duke would return and try to speak to her alone. She threw herself headlong into everything and vowed that one foolish and passionate mistake would not ruin her life here.

She settled easily at least into not only the luxury and excitement of living at the English royal court but the delight of being home in England. The Duke of Richmond had warned her once that Whitehall was not London and it was certainly not England, but for now, it was enough as she lost herself in the social and cultural whirl. She smiled and laughed and listened; she taught the courtiers the newest French dances, including the stately minuet; she loved theatricals and riding her own horse from the royal stables through St. James's Park. She worked very hard at her duties, accompanying and pleasing the queen who finally seemed to be adapting somewhat to English court life. And Frances worked harder yet at trying to push away the all too vivid memories of Richmond's hands and mouth on her body and of the rapturous, crowning union with him that had changed her world. Now he was back at court and she had quite simply refused to see him or to open his letters. Today, today perhaps, was the first day in weeks that she would really have to face him and she had no idea how he might react—or, oh heavens, what she herself would do if he turned that devouring, gold-green gaze her way. This new year of 1663 that was almost here, she vowed, simply must be a more sane and reasonable year than the turbulent last one had been.

She stood studying herself in the tall mirror Minette had sent her from France for Christmas while her wardrobe maid Gillian fastened the braided frogs on the front of her warm, soft velvet cloak. A pert blue hat with a red plume set off her outfit beautifully, and for one instant, she wished she had accepted the stunning filigreed brooch Richmond had sent her at Christmas and which she had returned. It would have looked perfect on the shoulder of this deep blue velvet.

"Frances, I swear!" Amanda Wells's voice rang out

from the drawing room outside her partially open door. "Hurry up. The sleighs are all waiting in the courtyard." Amanda's red head, topped by a becoming, green feathered hat, popped in. "You can make the king wait, I don't doubt, but not when he's entertaining the ambassador from the Tsar of Muscovy."

"Don't scold. I'm ready. Thank you, Gillie, and for heaven's sake, don't let the cats out in the halls as we don't need another scrap with the royal spaniels."

Frances and Amanda quickened their steps down the corridor and staircase when they saw the area was nearly deserted.

"His Majesty was in a royal pique all day when your felines scratched those dogs," Amanda said. "If Perth and Aberdeen had not been yours, I swear, he would have had them tossed in the Thames. Gads, everyone smirks and whispers about it every time he sits on a chair in your drawing room and finds white cat hair on his velvet breeches."

"Really, Amanda, if that's the best everyone can do for amusement, they must live wretchedly boring lives."

"I suppose they just want to see how much he'll take from you. You and Joli amuse him but the cats—gads!"

"His Majesty realizes he does not need to visit my suite if it bothers him. Indeed, if he visits I make certain it is with a crowd of others who can suffer the cat hair too. They all know my rules so let people whisper," she finished grandly, but Amanda only sniffed at what she considered pure foolishness.

It was obvious enough to Amanda that Frances

Stewart was a cold fish—and moonstruck, too, to try to keep off both the exciting Duke of Richmond, who was an entirely eligible widower, and an obviously enamored King Charles, who spent more time gazing at Frances these days than he did his own mistress, Barbara Villiers, the snobbish Countess of Castlemaine.

Fortunately, everyone was waiting inside in the black-and-white tiled grand foyer and had not ventured out into the crisp air to fill the waiting sleighs for the ride through the foot-deep snow, rare in London. Frances noted instantly that the Duke of Richmond was here today, garbed all in finest dark brown boots and cloak to match his hair, but when Amanda remarked how handsome he looked, she chose not to answer. He had accused her in a letter from Scotland of being a coward and cold-hearted and of teasing both himself and the king, and she had no intention of discussing that with him now. Her heart beat faster, but she pointedly ignored him as she and Amanda descended the sweep of stairs to join the waiting courtiers.

"Zounds, it's going to be cold out there on this jaunt," Cynthia Boyton, another maid of honor, was saying as they joined the group. "I took a good jog of buttered ale to get me through it. At least, His Majesty's guest is the ambassador from Muscovy who is used to such torture. I heard he is bringing some unique gifts downstairs to present to the king and queen before we set out, and, my chambermaid told me he will be wearing a coat made of over a hundred red fox pelts. How utterly barbaric!"

Everyone murmured and chattered wondering

what sort of gifts could possibly come from some-place as uncivilized as Muscovy and however did Cynthia Boynton's chambermaid know about the ambassador's wardrobe? Frances was starting to feel warm standing here all bundled up, but when she turned to speak to Amanda and saw her across the foyer laughing up at the Duke of Richmond, she began to feel hot all over.

Then, amidst brightly garbed ceremonial guards on the staircase, the king and queen descended, and moments later, the four bewhiskered and fur-bundled ambassadors from the tsar followed them down.

Frances concentrated her attention on greeting the foreigners, a repeat of what surely must have gone on a few days earlier when the Muscovites had first presented their official papers. It annoyed her that Amanda and Richmond were almost directly in her view across the room, and from somewhere a green-velvet-swathed Barbara Villiers and a smirking Duke of Buckingham had joined the group. Why couldn't they just get all this over with and go out in the fresh air? she fumed, as a parade of the ambassadors' servants entered to present brassbound boxes of gifts.

Two of the Muscovites spoke passable English with distinctive French accents, but Frances noted, under no circumstance was the king going to converse with them in common French however fluent they all might be. Although the Stuart sovereign like his Francophilic courtiers eagerly emulated French fashions, this was, after all, not Louis' court, but that of English Charles. She herself had learned quickly enough never to refer to "great

Louis" in the king's presence, however much he loved and missed Minette.

Lush, shiny furs in every hue of brown, red, and black spilled from the ambassador's first several boxes. The king nodded at each presentation, a few brief words, a set smile ever on his lips under the small mustache. Queen Catherine stroked some of the furs and handed them to those closest to her for petting.

"See, Countess Castlemaine," the queen said, "this one dark brown, so pretty—matching your hair for winter muff, no?"

Many exchanged glances and nudged each other at the queen's continual, almost fawning kindness to her royal husband's mistress who only three months ago had borne a second Stuart bastard son. The queen assiduously used the new title the king had bestowed on the Palmers to get the cuckolded husband to bring his wife back to court from rural exile.

"Yes, Your Majesty, it is wonderfully soft," the beautiful Barbara crooned and rubbed it up and down her rough cheek, her painted eyelids closed and her coral mouth puckered enticingly.

The queen's near servility to her husband and his mistress, and Barbara's continued pluck and daring astounded Frances anew. She could barely stand it when the king took her to dinner in Barbara's posh suite of rooms, but she tried to be polite to the woman. Frances was even starting to feel Barbara might look on her as a rival, but that, of course, was ludicrous. At least Barbara and her clever cousin Buckingham seemed to like her well enough and she did not intend doing anything to change that. She had made one enemy in the Duke of Richmond because—because it just had to be done, and she needed no others.

Additional brass boxes revealed bolts of delicate, diaphanous cloth as fine as tissue and jars full of something called sea-horse teeth. Everyone strained close for a look, pressing in. The room was getting stifling. Several Muscovy-bred, ornately hooded hunt falcons were brought in; four massive Persian carpets unrolled to display the rich generosity Muscovy offered England. More stilted pleasantries and gratitude were extended on both sides and then, gratefully, everyone trooped outside.

"Twice around the Park before we stop at the Ice House and the pond," an apparently buoyant King Charles was calling out to many of them. "One ambassador per sleigh," she heard him tell someone close behind her. She turned halfway around even as the king's hand touched her elbow. "You'll ride with the queen, Ambassador Slanovitch, and me, won't you, Frances? Barbara and Buckingham can ride with the Duke of York."

She nodded and smiled up at him as they crunched through deep snow to the first in a line of ten sleighs. They were really just converted carriages on rails, she thought, for they had told her London seldom had snow on the ground. This seating arrangement would make Barbara fume—and it would give the others better gossip fodder than cat fur on the royal britches!

"Something amuses you, my dear Frances?" the king inquired.

"No, sire, not really amuses, only—well, I vow,

whatever will you do with sea-horse teeth?"

"Make you a bracelet or an anklet of them if you'd let me, love. I've a mind to give you one of those bluish Persian carpets they brought too. The color matches those tantalizing eyes," he said low as they approached the sleigh. "Would you accept even that from me, dear?"

Before she could answer to tell him no, he handed her in to sit by the furry bulk of the bearded ambassador. Queen Catherine's face lit all too obviously to see her because she would not have to bear the insult of staring at Barbara's smug face. King Charles jumped in next to the queen, across from Frances, and they were off.

"I vow it's much smoother than those swaying carriages," Frances said. "Oh, it's fun!"

The ambassador was eying her intently. "Come to Muscovy. We have this now many times."

As they pulled farther away from the cold shadows tall Whitehall cast, the sun on snow glared brightly in their eyes. As Frances and the ambassador rode with their backs to the following parade, she twisted once to dart a quick look back. A string of sleighs strung behind them around the curve of the lane, the bouncing bells and brasses on forty horses' harnesses jangling musically in the crisp air.

"I was told, Your Majesty, bells keep off evil eyes," the ambassador shouted over the jangle and turned to wink boldly at Frances.

"Just an old English superstition," the king bellowed back over the rhythmic racket, "but I'm afraid Mrs. Stewart here still believes in it."

"I, sire?" Frances said and then, while the

150

ambassador stared blatantly at her again, the king quickly imitated the man's ogling, fish-eyed stare. Despite herself, she broke into laughter as the king's face became instantly passive again. Thankfully, she was rescued by King Charles's detailed explanation of the Ice House he was now pointing out to the ambassador.

"We import huge blocks of ice from Norway, Your Excellency and store them in that cottage there," the king went on. "The floor is underground and the walls are thick dirt stuffed with layers of straw. Then, in summer, we can have cold drinks to please lovely ladies like the queen and Mrs. Stewart."

"Good. Good. I will send you plenty cold ice. Lovely ladies in Muscovy wanting hot drinks, *da*."

They clambered out around the pond south of St. James's Palace as the other sleighs halted in an arc behind them. On the distant duck pond, people were sliding across the frozen surface on their feet.

"We have heard St. Petersburg is known for beautiful women," the king asked the ambassador. "Is it true?"

"*Da*. Many. Many. Muscovite beautiful women has best legs in world!"

The king's sable eyebrows arched. "Really, Your Excellency?" The courtiers were catching up with their lead party now. Frances noted with chagrin that Richmond, with Amanda Wells draped all over his arm, was only a few strides back. Something sharp twisted deep inside her at that, but it only told her what sort of despicable man he really was. What was it to her if he dared to make wild love to that damned Amanda right before everyone's eyes here today?

"But you do think, for example, Mrs. Stewart here is a beautiful woman, do you not, Excellency?" the king pursued.

The man's narrow eyes popped wide under bushy brows and moved to survey Frances as they had in the carriage. "*Da*! Yes! The legs she has is beautiful too?"

"Indeed, they are!" King Charles's voice boomed out. The queen gasped, and those courtiers close enough to hear twittered, but the king seemed unperturbed. "Richmond here can vouch for it, can't you man?"

Frances' head swiveled and her gaze collided with Richmond's devouring green stare. She felt herself go hot even out here, and her knees shook before she seized control again.

"Your Majesty," she heard her own loud voice rise above the murmurs, "whatever are you trying to do to my reputation for strict upbringing in your own mother's court?"

"When you dancing, ankles and legs showing," Queen Catherine put in helpfully. Frances tore her eyes away from Richmond to smile her thanks.

"And riding—and that day we came back to London on the Thames and the wind caught your skirts about the same time Richmond did," the king said, his black eyes on Richmond now.

Behind the king, Frances could see Barbara Villiers' face was an absolute thundercloud; her frown became even worse when Buckingham, standing next to her, urged, "Let's have the lady in question lift her skirts a bit then, so the ambassador can judge."

Everyone but Barbara and Richmond laughed

and cheered until Frances had to grin herself. She liked all the attention, she realized, without having to do anything really outrageous. "I vow," her voice rang out, "anything to uphold the honor of English ladies." She laughed as, on the snowy, windy path, stared at by a hundred eyes, she lifted her skirts just above the knee.

The Muscovy ambassador bent and stared, fingering his shaggy chin whiskers. Barbara glowered; the queen smiled faintly; the king's gaze went slaty black. Richmond she was afraid to look at at all.

"Muscovy ladies bigger legs than that," the ambassador intoned gravely as if the whole game were deadly serious.

Frances could feel the cold creeping up her unstockinged upper thighs now, clear to the warm skin of her belly and hips under the double chemise she had worn.

"Od's fish, ambassador, you're beaten," King Charles said and jovially slapped him on the back although his eyes still stared at Frances' legs. "Admit it, Your Excellency, and someday I'll return the favor by sending some of my cavaliers as ambassadors to St. Petersburg to judge your ladies' legs, eh?"

"*Da*. Beautiful legs and lady," the ambassador said over and over again as the comedy was ended and everyone trooped toward the pond.

"You didn't mind that, I pray, Frances," the king said low to her as people gathered at the edge of the pond to cheer and applaud the clever Londoners sliding across the ice on little rails strapped to the bottoms of their shoes.

"No, sire," she smiled radiantly up at him, totally

unaware the look almost staggered his poise.

"Then if you'll do it for the whole damn court on a whim, why not for me in private?" he hissed.

The smile froze on her lips as he stepped quickly away from her and turned back to the queen and his guests of honor. She felt suddenly alone in the crowd, and almost frightened by the intensity of the king's look and tone. She had felt so certain she had been both holding him at a good distance and pleasing him, but inside he must be very angry at her and she could not have that. Perhaps this lighthearted approach where she let him treat her like an indulged child while she flirted gaily with him was not a good idea. Perhaps the king wouldn't turn out to be as easily handled as the whole Duke of Richmond problem had evidently been, at least these last few weeks when she had merely not read his letters.

"Those skaters look pretty clever and fleet-footed, but then they manage to end up on their backsides quickly and painfully when they least expect it," the low, disturbing voice slightly above and behind her murmured.

"Good afternoon, my Lord Richmond," she said. She did not even turn to look at him as he moved to stand closer, staring out over the pond, but she knew they were momentarily alone and she felt the sudden intimacy intently. "I take it this is some sort of veiled warning for me," she went on. "Did you call them skaters? And, I vow, whatever have you done with our friend Amanda?"

"Allow me to answer that flurry of questions in order of increasing importance, Frances. One, the English call the new phenomenon sliding, but it was imported by some of the king's people who were with him in exile in the Dutch Estates. Those are iron skates on their feet so the correct word is skating. Two, I fobbed Amanda off on one of the ambassador's furry arms and she could hardly protest that. Three, yes I have been north to my Scottish lands and very busy here so I have missed you too."

"I did not ask that!"

"Sh. I missed you and want to see you alone soon. If not, I shall be forced to call on Joli as I understand he has rooms with you."

"I don't believe the king would bring you to sup with the others and I do not wish to see you alone," she said archly and turned to regard the skaters again.

"From what I hear, I take it you do not wish to see His Majesty alone either, so for now, I content myself with that and the fact this icy demeanor could hardly be melted by anyone else. Quite in your element here in the frozen snow, aren't you, Frances? You slapped me once for dubbing you ice goddess, but if that is not true, prove it to me."

"I detest you. Leave me alone. Barbara Villiers and Buckingham are staring."

"The king probably is too. He certainly remembered the day I helped you with your skirts on the barge last summer, didn't he? Seeing us together will probably enrage him, so I suggest we meet secretly where we won't get his royal blood up."

"He will banish you."

"I think not. For now, he needs me to administer Westminster and act as liaison to his Scottish navy. If you banish me as you have tried this autumn, Frances, I'll be forced to take you off in my carriage for another exciting ride through lively, passionate London.''

She felt her cheeks go hot pink at the memory. That day she had been grateful to him for rescuing Joli and she had let her guard down. That woman in the carriage so willingly seduced by his touch—that had not really been her, but however could she convince him of that and certainly not out here. She managed to beat down the panic and anger this man aroused; she felt the welcome chill breeze across the icy pond nip at her face again.

"Come over by the Ice House, Frances," Richmond's voice came quietly, and they moved toward the crowd clustered around the king and the ambassadors.

Good, she thought, the king probably hadn't noted their heated exchange even if Barbara Villiers had, though she might be one to tell him. Richmond was not touching her so she moved willingly enough behind him through the press of people as his big body made a little path for her. They stood behind the queen and two of the ambassadors when Richmond turned back to press a warm brass mug into her hands.

"It's called Lamb's Wool," he said. "The country folk around Cobham love it dearly."

She noticed others were being served cups, hot enough to fog the crisp air, from a big kettle over a fire. The hot liquid smelled of cloves and cinnamon as she inhaled its fragrant steam. She stared at Richmond over the lifted rim of her mug as he raised his Lamb's Wool to her and drank. When his face caught the sun reflected by the white surrounding stretch of ice and snow, glittery shards of gold glistened in the green irises of his eyes. Despite her careful aplomb, the look warmed her insides as much as the sweet, pungent drink.

"It's marvelous, my lord. Whatever is in Lamb's Wool?"

"Pulp of roasted apples, white wine, spices and sugar. Someday," his voice came so low to her it was almost a raspy whisper, "we'll take some bagpipers out to the village at Cobham with us and mix a kettle of it when there are not so many others."

The audacity of the man, she mused, but it would do no good to put him off with some cutting comment here in this crowd where the king had just motioned to her and smiled. Standing close to Richmond, she took another slow sip of the hot drink before she threaded her way to the king's side for the sleigh ride back through the snow.

After a huge feast and a performance of Shakespeare's tragedy *Macbeth* in the cleared Banqueting Hall that evening, the king, the Duke of York, and several of the king's advisors disappeared with the Muscovy ambassadors. Frances made a hasty retreat herself as she saw Richmond had been left behind and she had no desire to be alone with his sharp words and accusing stares. In the dimly lit hall by her chambers, she heard hurrying footsteps behind her and moved even faster. Surely he would not dare to chase her up here and if he had, she would not even open the door to her suites but go back down. It was early yet and her maids Gillian and Jane would not even be about and she would be forced to face him alone.

She whirled, casting a quick glance over her shoulder, and was surprised to see a woman's form revealed by the sconces lit down the length of the hall. She realized who it was only when the blaze of diamonds at the woman's throat caught the flare of the flambeau by her door.

"Barbara Villiers!"

"Disappointed, little Stewart? Expecting the king in hot pursuit perhaps? 'Sblood, but you're in a damned hurry to get up here. I know you hardly have some randy beau stashed away, though I swear Richmond would be first in line to volunteer."

Barbara's shapely arms went to voluptuous hips as her coral lips pursed in a practiced pout. "Well, let's in, Frances. I need a private word with you and I don't have all day to stand about drafty halls in December!"

"Nor all night, I warrant," Frances threw at her, pleased with the jab. But Barbara only laughed in that annoyingly metallic way of hers.

She ushered Barbara in through the small black-and-white tiled entry hall lit by two big candles in glass chimneys that reflected in two gold-speckled mirrors. In the carpeted drawing room, Barbara perched immediately on a brocade settee and smoothed her skirts while Frances lit other candles. She wondered what was forthcoming since this woman had never sought a private audience before: this narrow, tastefully decorated room with its moss greens and creamy satins and brocade upholstery, its polished wooden buffet tables, and woven, flowered carpet touched by the rich glow of expensive wax candles seemed invaded and cold now for the first time.

"Of course, I do admire your cleverness for one just starting out," Barbara drawled as if voicing a challenge to battle.

Uncertain where this was going, Frances sat stiffly on a small armless French chair across the room from her uninvited guest. "I'm afraid I do not quite catch your drift, Countess."

"My drift. Pooh! You are a damned clever one, Frances Stewart, and don't bother to mince words with me about it. You have those baby blue, seemingly naïve eyes on the king and hope to have him hooked soon with this innocent routine you're so adept at. I'm here to tell you flatly to keep back or, I swear, you'll wish you'd never come to England!"

Frances' mouth fell open at the sudden, acrid assault. This woman had been openly kind, even if she had given her hard glances and cold shoulders. She was proud her own voice sounded so calmly controlled when she answered.

"I believe the stupidity of your deductions astounds me even more than the rudeness of your words, Madame Palmer."

Barbara snorted inelegantly at Frances' instinctive reversion to her previous, married name. "Don't try to spar with me, Stewart. You're out of your league. And, no one dares call me Palmer anymore now that the king created my husband Earl of Castlemaine to get me back from prison in the damned boring countryside. Countess of Castlemaine, if you please."

"Are you saying your presence here has been

merely purchased then?"

Barbara jumped to her feet and began to pace, her bright yellow satin skirts and ribbons swishing and swaying with each step. "I said, don't be clever, girl! Of course, I've been bought, time and again with power, money, and now the two lovely titles of Castlemaine and Queen's Lady of the Bedchamber. Bedchamber—now that is rare. We've all been bought and delivered, so don't simper like some damned country-bred green girl about nobility and honor to me!"

She whirled to a sudden stop several feet from Frances, her eye wild, her face and hands totally animated as she punctuated her words with fingers jabbing the air. "Listen to me, Frances Stewart, and listen well. I am the king's *mistresse en titre*, I have borne him two sons, and there will be others. He may bed with the queen out of duty on occasion, but I have his damned, fickle heart!"

"Indeed? I vow, I heard His Majesty tell Clarendon once he would never give his heart. Are you quite certain you aren't mistaken?"

"*You* are the only sadly mistaken one here if you are angling for his fidelity, little Stewart. Give in to him and let him get between those chaste, cold virginal thighs if you must, but cease these sluttish games you play!"

Frances' nails bit deeply into the palms of her hands as she fought to keep from slapping the contorted face so close to her own. "You certainly know whereof you speak about sluttish games, king's mistress, but you have no right to council or accuse me of them. Take your vile thoughts to His Majesty if

160

you wish, but leave my rooms!"

"Pooh!" Barbara sniffed again. "Since they're your rooms—and a lovely suite they are—you'd better hike your skirts up for Charles, king of England, and start paying your rent for them. He doesn't give something like this for mere sweet smiles—not for long."

She backed off a few steps amazed at her failure to reduce Frances to a cowering wretch no matter what she said. Perhaps she had misjudged her power to control the girl. After all she didn't want enemies who had the king's ear since she didn't need anyone to tell him that young stud Jermyn was with her whenever His Majesty was not in her bed.

"'Sdeath, I am going though," Barbara said. "I know His Majesty will be heading for my suite soon after he dispenses with those furry, whiskered freaks from Muscovy. I only mean, Frances, I came to warn you that you cannot hope to get away with leading the king around by a ring through his nose as you have been doing. If your intentions are honorable, you'd best leave the court because he can be a rutting, rampaging bull when he's crossed whatever gentlemanly exterior he puts on. He is king of England, a wencher at heart, and if you're not careful, you'll find yourself raped and enjoying it, Frances."

"No! Never!"

"Really?" Barbara drawled as if amused at her vehemence. "Or," she went on with her ringed hands up as Frances started to protest and rose to show her out, "the other possibility is, as I said, you mean to become his whore and in that case—"

"Get out of here! Now! And do not be so one-minded that you confuse your own character with mine!''

"Zounds, but aren't we haughty? He'll tire of these delicate virgin theatrics one way or the other, Stewart, I'm warning you. Protected honor, hot blushes, no touching—it's new to him, that's all, but your little game with all its pretty rules will go down just like that card house he built for you the other day. Either decide to be his willing whore—when he's not with me—or back off, little Stewart, I'm warning you!''

Frances yanked open the door to the hall and glared defiantly at Barbara Villiers' flushed face. "Now I'll warn you, Madame Palmer. Do not confuse the motives of honorable people you cannot hope to understand with those of your own. Discuss all this with the king or Buckingham or even your friend Jermyn if you will, but never speak to me of it again!''

In the corridor, Barbara spun back, her usually beautiful face a mask of fury and frustration. "You sly little slut! I swear, I'll ruin you and have your sweet, little ass clear out of London when I'm done with you!''

Her heart pounding against her satin bodice, Frances merely stared as impassively and condescendingly as she could manage; then she swung the door shut in Barbara Villiers' livid face. Through the door she heard a shouted string of oaths and then the click of heels fading away. Her hands trembled and she felt hurt and dirtied. It frightened her that Barbara Villiers had come so close to shattering her poise: she had wanted to scream, scratch, and tear the chestnut curls from that witch's head! Those vile demonic creatures in that play *Macbeth* tonight— even the treacherous, murderous Lady Macbeth— were more honorable characters than Lady MacVilliers!

Despite her fury, she started to giggle soundlessly as she pictured Barbara with indelible blood on her hands for every knife she had ever plunged into someone's back here at court. But now that the woman had really shown herself, she must be very careful. She would not actually tell the king of his royal mistress' visit, but she could always make Barbara think she had if she overstepped so badly again.

Startled, she jumped away from the door as she felt and heard a series of low knocks. Surely that termagant would not dare to come back for more, nor would Richmond be so foolish, and her maids merely called out and did not knock.

The door she tried to pierce with her eyes resounded again, and the king's deep voice halted her frenzied thoughts.

"Frances, are you there?"

She pulled the door open fully expecting to see King Charles with a raft of other courtiers, but he was utterly alone, his plumed, broad-brimmed hat in one hand, a flat black velvet box in the other.

"Now, don't glare at me that way, Frances. Let's just say a friend missed you downstairs and came calling. May I not come in out of the hall before someone comes along?"

"My maids are not here."

His dark eyes glittered in the reflection of the low-

163

burning wall sconce. "Marvelous, as I hardly came to call on them. Come on, dear, you look like you've seen a ghost. It's only that here it is four days after Christmas, and I still haven't found the opportunity to give you this gift alone so I gave everyone the slip. Move back, dearest. Let me in."

He stepped past her into the tiled entry hall and went on through to the drawing room and sat on the settee Barbara Villiers had only recently vacated while Frances unwillingly closed the door behind him and followed.

"Sire, you know we agreed you would not come here alone."

One black eyebrow went up as his gaze swept her carefully. "The agreement, I believe, was I would not use the privy staircase entry over there unless you gave me permission, and I haven't."

"Your Majesty, I believe you are splitting hairs and I'm afraid—"

"No arguing, Frances. Please. It's been a long day with those beady-eyed ambassadors. I can't tell what they're thinking half the time. Od's fish, I only came to give you this little gift, I said, so come over here and don't quibble."

His mouth set in a grim line as he waited for her to comply. Her gaze fixed on the little black velvet box on his knee, she sat next to him on the settee where he indicated.

"That's better, love," his voice came treacherously low. "I don't want us to argue ever. 'Sblood, I get enough of that from Clarendon and Barbara. Here, open this."

She took the flat box, and his fingers intentionally

brushed hers. "But you and the queen gave all her ladies and maids lovely gifts only last week at Christmas, sire."

He leaned closer, one long arm snaking along on the settee in back of her, the other hand reaching out as fingers tapped the box. "This is different. Only from me to only you."

She could smell spiced wine on his breath, hear his quickened intake of air, feel his thigh against her skirts. She opened the lid and blinked down at a necklace of flawless pearls. The lustrous, creamy hue of each pearl, big as a chickpea against the bed of black velvet utterly entranced her.

"So perfect with your fair skin, Frances. Here, lift your back curls and ringlets and let me put it on."

"Sire, it is so lovely, but I cannot accept it." Barbara's vile accusations echoed in her brain as though the woman sat here between them on the settee shrieking them anew: he doesn't give anything like this for mere sweet smiles . . . not for long . . . you'd better hike your skirts up for Charles, king of England. Her mother's numerous warnings over the years, her own observations of men in France all collided and crashed in raucous cacophony as he lifted the pearls up over her head and lowered them past her face.

"Your Majesty, I cannot accept them."

"No arguing, I said. Turn you back and lift your hair while I work this damned clasp."

Feeling as if she were floating closer and closer to a whirlpool she could not escape, she stilled her inner voices and complied.

He smiled behind her back, pleased he had found

the way at last to get even a smidgin of compliance from this stubborn yet delicate girl. A blend of kindness with brusque firmness, a little frown and touch of authority and she obeyed at last.

He pretended to have trouble with the clasp. Meanwhile his pulse pounded as his practiced eye skimmed the nape of her neck and the sweep of elegant bare shoulders to the ruffled edge of her bodice. She was the only woman who had ever made him almost lose control enough, to force her, but then, all the others had come easily, offering themselves to him at a mere nod or snap of fingers like fawning spaniels. This girl, aloof, untouchable he wanted more than he had any other. The pearls rested perfectly across her neck now. His arms shot out to encircle her, his lips to touch that bare nape before he knew he was moving.

"Sire!" she protested although his arms only linked in front of her in a sort of loose hug. She stared at the way one of his big hands grasped his other wrist as if to lock her in. His lips were warm and gentle as he kissed and nuzzled her satin nape, and then as she quickly loosed her lifted curls to try to pull away, his mouth moved to caress where her left shoulder curved to the side of her neck.

"Sire, please!"

"Frances, Frances," he murmured low along her skin where his hot breath and lips burned her. "Cease the fluttering. I have to touch you, just a little. For six months I have held back. Od's fish, Frances, hold still."

His powerful arms tightened to pull her protesting hands into her lap and, as he leaned forward into her, he gazed directly down her bodice between the firm, high swell of her breasts under the pearls.

As if he were some country bumpkin who had never had a maid yet under him, he gasped, a sharp intake of breath, and felt his loins go tight. 'Sdeath, he cursed to himself, this was ridiculous. He ought to just seduce her and have done with it!

Icy chills raced along Frances' spine as the king enveloped her from behind: his strong chest and flat stomach, hardened by his athletic endeavors, pressed into her back while one elbow lay heavily along a soft thigh and the other moved against the side of her right breast as he held her quiet by gently manacling her wrists with his big hands. His mouth, his moustache and nose tickled along the skin of her neck and throat. But what frightened and infuriated her more than anything else, was the fact her mind dared to torment her with pictures of Richmond warm against her like this in his carriage. No, she told herself, as though the king of England were not even nearby, I cannot still be cherishing those thoughts.

"Be calm, love," he whispered. "Let me show you how wonderful it can be for us. Here, darling, lean back against me, just be calm."

He settled her closer still, holding her arms gently down. His kisses dropped lower over her shoulder to her fluted collarbones and to the arched hollow at the base of her throat. She feared for a moment she would spill back across his lap, but she hung there frozen and suspended as he trailed flickering kisses and a tip of tongue across her skin.

Love him for me, Minette had begged, but she

surely could not have forseen this. Or had she? Frances' eyes flew open and she stared down at the ebony head of thick hair so close as he turned her slightly in his arms to bend even lower toward her breasts. Her head cleared instantly.

"Wait. Please, Your Majesty. I—I love the pearls and will be proud to wear them, but you must not rush me so fast. Please, sire, you're frightening me!"

The slitted eyes lifted and stared into her wide blue ones. "Frances, damn it, just trust me a little. I won't do anything to hurt you. The moment you don't really like what I'm doing and ask me to stop for that reason, I will."

She returned his intense gaze at that challenge, her mind racing for a safe escape from the looming precipice. "But, heavens, I can't just rush like that," she floundered, groping for reasons, for words. "I am not ready yet."

"I can get you ready, Frances, so ready you'll welcome my attentions, want them as desperately as I desire you."

"No, I don't mean that sort of ready, sire. I mean, I am sure you know a million ways to make a woman care for you . . ."

"Do you care, Frances? Even a little? Od's fish, do you?" His arms tightened perceptibly, and he considered using his strength and the persuasion of lips and hands to take her so far down the path she'd never pull back when he moved finally to fully possess her, but something in her look held him back. He fought the building sexual tension in his body and brain, pressing it back, struggling to control his frustration. Hell, when he came in here,

168

his goal was only to get one sweet kiss and here he was considering seduction or rape!

"I'm sorry for the unwanted affection, Frances, but you drive your king distracted half the time, you know." He loosed her carefully, expecting her to scamper away, but she sat, apparently composed, next to him on the little settee, her hands clasped in her mussed lap. She did not look at him as she answered.

"I would not call the affection you show me unwanted, sire, only unprepared for."

"I see. Now, since I've been forced to listen to that Muscovite gibberish all day without understanding a damn word of it, translate that for me and maybe we can negotiate a trade agreement or some sort of truce." She turned to look at him and his pulse quickened again.

"I cannot promise you anything, but I do know I like to please you, sire."

He smiled inwardly as he took a challenge she no doubt did not even realize she'd offered. Od's fish, if he just held himself in check a bit longer, he'd bargain his way into her bed if he couldn't seduce her outright.

"Then, Frances, please me and I'll be very patient and not push. Only, 'sdeath, pretty dancing partner and sweet listener that you are, I want much, much more."

"I cannot freely give much, much more, sire. Heavens, I realize you are used to women who—"

"—we are not speaking of other women here, so do not cloud the subject. If you cannot freely give me what I want now, give me a little."

"A little?"

"Don't freeze when I put my hands on you in the affection I feel and cannot stem. Little kisses—returned kisses—a fond caress now and then, a little lap sitting or petting, a private glance at those fabulous legs upon the proper occasion. Say yes, Frances, and I won't allow Ambasssador Slanovitch to take you back to Muscovy however many sea-horse teeth and furs he offers for you."

She laughed despite herself, and he grinned like a schoolboy. Here they were enjoying each other's company and he wasn't angry at the fact she had talked her way out of his volatile predicament. After all, these new rules of his did not supersede the others that he would not use the privy staircase, and in six months, this was the first time he had managed to corner her really alone. Tomorrow, with Barbara Villiers' rude visit a fading memory and things back on even keel, this determined assault would all be in the harmless past. Surely, she could handle this every bit as adroitly as she did Richmond's latest advances, and certainly, neither of these men would ever get her alone again.

He studied her beautiful face as thoughts evidently dashed behind that pure white forehead, and he wished he could read them. He had her now, whether she realized it or not. She didn't want to displease him or lose his affections even if she wasn't just his for the taking quite yet. He'd woo her, seduce her bit by bit until she was, as she said, ready—or at least too committed, too dependent on him to pull back or defy him. Yes, he could steel himself to work for that and for the delicious, pleasant torment of teaching her day by day the arts of love.

Love—the word startled him and, suddenly, he wanted to be out of here. He would go to Barbara's room where everything was simple and so easy. Lust. 'Sdeath, with Barbara and all the others besides his poor, adoring queen where duty called, it was simply lust. Here, with Frances, he was not so sure.

"We have a bargain then, Frances—some new rules, as you like to put it," he said matter-of-factly as he stood and pulled the satin sleeves to his waistcoat down and then tugged his lace shirt cuffs over his wrists. She stood too, her hands clasped over her flat stomach. "If you won't agree," he went on, regretting the brusque tone he could not control, "let's sit back down now and pick up where we just left off."

"But I do agree," she said, her mouth lifted in a taut smile.

"Then, good night, Frances." He leaned down swiftly touching her only briefly, his hands on her shoulders and his mouth on hers in a warm kiss he hardly gave her time to return. But starting tomorrow, he thought, tomorrow, after he'd relieved himself of this pressure in his loins by lying with Barbara and cleared his head with a good night's rest and some morning exercise, she'd be no match for him.

Silent at first, she accompanied him to the door. But then she surprised him with a quick move to stand against it. "Sire, even though we do have new rules, I think our reputations are still of value. I thank you for not coming by the privy stairs, but could you not please leave by them so no one in the hall sees?"

He shouted a laugh at the wench's daring to demand so much while fighting to give so little. But, starting tomorrow— He had her now. "Of course, my Frances. Excellent suggestion."

Then, at the little door which Frances had stubbornly put a chair across to block, he decided to show her he would not always be so amenable. A sardonic grin on his face, he lifted the chair away and opened the door into the dark staircase. But instead of stepping immediately through as she expected, he reached for her and adeptly tipped her back over one arm to arch her throat and bosom to his view. Swiftly, he pulled the taut satin off one shoulder, them moved his fingers to deftly slip one breast free from the press of bodice and corset. He heard her gasp and felt her try to struggle as his mouth descended lightning quick to cover the rosy-hued nipple.

The move had been so sudden and so swift when she thought she had mastered the situation that she was stunned. He supported her with one iron arm under her shoulder blades; the other held a wrist and steadied a hip as he teased her bared nipple back and forth with his insistent, slick tongue.

There was nothing but his big shoulder to push out against and that wouldn't budge as the terrifying, delicious torment continued. He suckled on the taut tip until it was as firm as a big, shiny pearl between his lips. He licked in wet, hot circles around the pink aureole and then tugged sensuously at the perky peak until she moaned and bit her lip to keep from crying out.

Then, as quickly as it had begun, he loosed her and leaned her back against the wall. She heard him, out

172

of breath, panting, and she feared for one minute he would lift her or maybe even push her to the floor. She opened her eyes and stared into glittering slits of pure black power.

"Think tonight in bed about how sweet things between us can feel, Frances," he rasped. He grabbed the single candle from the little inlaid table and disappeared down the wooden steps.

She leaned where he had left her, listening to his fading footsteps echoing up the stairwell to her. He had traversed two landings already, and yet she heard his quick feet sound on another, lower flight of stairs. He was nearly running, she thought, running clear down to Barbara Villiers' suite of rooms on the ground floor under his own.

A door banged in the hollow darkness of the shaft. At last she moved to straighten her gown, tugging it shakily up to cover the pointed nipple he had so expertly ravished. That was what Richmond had done to her that thrilling day in his carriage, she told herself—kissed and licked and suckled her ready, willing breasts and then he had possessed her so completely he had taken her to heights she had never imagined could exist.

"Oh!" She twisted and pressed herself face inward to the wall. Just the thought of Richmond doing that to her brought back the memory of kissing him, of letting him—wanting him to unlace her, to do that and more. But, with the king, it was different: she wanted only escape without his anger.

She turned back, closed the door to the privy stairs, and placed the little chair to block it. Then she changed her mind and shoved the large, drop-leaf

173

buffet table across the door, huffing and groaning as she did so.

She detested both men, she told herself with crystal clarity—detested what they did to her, their assurance, how they made her feel. But she could reason her way out of this mess, out of anything. All these emotions were deadly dangerous. They were what had doomed Minette and, no doubt, her own, unhappy mother although she would never understand how her father, as she remembered him, could possibly have hurt anyone's feelings.

Let the king revel in Barbara Villiers' ready bed and Richmond fawn all over Amanda Wells who had been her friend first. She was going to bed, alone, to think, and tomorrow everything would be under control again.

She straightened her mussed skirts and went toward her bedroom as she heard her maid Gillian call to her and come in from the corridor. Then she saw the king's hat where he had left it on a drawing-room chair, and she swept it up to hide under her bed before anyone could see it.

Part II

That Very Face

The Constant Lover

Out upon it! I have loved
Three whole days together;
And am like to love three more,
If it prove fair weather.

Time shall molt away his wings,
Ere he shall discover
In the whole wide world again
Such a constant lover.

But the spite on 't is, no praise
Is due at all to me;
Love with me had made no stays
Had it any been but she.

Had it any been but she,
And that very face,
There had been at least ere this
A dozen dozen in her place.

—Sir John Suckling

Chapter Six

It seemed to Frances that half of London had turned out to see the king play Pall Mall in St. James's Park. The rickety galleries were packed with all sorts of city folk, from rich merchants to impoverished carters, while most of the courtiers stood along the perimeter of the playing alley, a narrow rectangle of grassless soil into which ground cockle shells had been trampled. Frances guided her mother, sister, and brother into the only open spot along the side of the crowded alley she could find.

She regretted instantly that they stood directly across the narrow gaming area from the Duke of Buckingham and Barbara Villiers. At least Barbara had enough sense of propriety not to flaunt her lover, young Henry Jermyn, before the king, she thought. Frances acknowledged Buckingham's jaunty salute of a flourished handkerchief and looked pointedly away as Barbara made some obvious snide remark to her cousin who stood behind her chair. The imperturbable Countess of Castlemaine was *enceinte* with her third royal child, but it had hardly improved her temper nor the rude way she treated "the little Stewart" when the king wasn't looking. Heavens, at least there had been no repeat of the screaming fit Barbara had had during that surprise visit to Frances' chambers.

Frances breathed deeply of sun-swept spring air to clear her head. It was a rare and beautiful mid-March afternoon, and since her family was visiting for the day, she had no intention of letting the Villiers-Buckingham cousins spoil her enjoyment. She hoped the king would notice her where she was standing, for she had arrived later than she had promised him she would and the game was already well underway. At least she didn't see Richmond lurking anywhere about to throw a pall on this lovely spring day.

"Frances, who is that lady sitting in her own chair across there? Is it the queen?" her sister Sophia asked. The fourteen-year-old girl was blond with hazel eyes and would soon be appointed to the Duchess of York's household as maid of honor. The king these last few months had subtly but persistently bestowed kindnesses on her family. These she could hardly refuse as she did his other, more tangible presents. That after-Christmas pearl necklace had taught her a good lesson.

"That lady is not the queen and she has a chair because she is with child, Sophia. The queen isn't here today," Frances replied.

Her mother clucked her tongue in disdain and took up the answer to Sophia when she saw Frances intended to say no more. "That, my dears, is Lady

Castlemaine, His Majesty's mistress. She gets chairs fetched and many other gifts, yet the king, no doubt, plays her for a fool."

"Mother, for heaven's sake," Frances protested quietly as both younger children turned their attentions back to the game.

"For heaven's sake nothing, Frances. He'll eventually toss her out as he did poor Lucy Walter who died in some wretched Paris garret. Men!" she snorted. "And king's men and kings—the worst!"

"Actually, mother," Frances retorted, although she could clearly see her mother thought the subject was closed, "I believe the Countess of Castlemaine can take care of herself. She gives as good as she gets, it seems to me."

Her mother's white face, taut under the ruffled bonnet, turned to her, sharp eyes narrowed. "I certainly hope and pray you do not defend her as a friend of yours, Frances, nor the king, though in his case, of course, it is important you get on well with him."

Frances breathed a sigh of relief for at least the hundredth time that day, glad that her mother lived her own life at Somerset House down the Thames where she was not about to see how fondly the king carried on with her daughter. Frances realized she was nervously fingering the braided front lacings of her new buff-colored brocade bodice and she let the ties drop to clasp her hands against the elaborately embroidered material. Then, in the awkward pause, she silently blessed her twelve-year-old brother Walter for interrupting with a spate of shouts and questions.

"Gad, Frances! Look at the king hit that ball to score right through that high-up hoop there. Zounds, can't wait 'til I'm old enough to play with him!"

"Yes, His Majesty is a marvel at Pall Mall, Walter, but it will be a few years before you're big enough to play with the king's men," Frances observed.

They all watched the next charge of mallets into boxwood balls: wood smacked wood and balls thudded balls as the players ran up and down the field trying to align their shots so they would fly through a suspended oval ring dangling nearly fifteen feet above the ground.

"Why?" Walter challenged when Frances had almost forgotten what they were talking about. "If I am old enough to go back to France to be trained in Lord Douglas' Scottish regiment, I am sure as Hades old enough to play Pall Mall. I wish they'd play it on horses, because I can ride almost as well as you, Frances. Can't I, mother?"

"Almost, my dear. Few, including most men I've seen, can sit a horse as well as Frances. And I told you I do not want to hear those vile oaths like gads, zounds, or worse coming from your mouth. You are not some foppish courtier, my lad."

"Aw, everybody uses them! Even Frances says 'heavens!' all the time!"

The king had noticed them now and was waving during a moment's respite before he dashed back after his six-inch boxwood ball with mallet flying. The nine other heated, panting, but elegantly dressed men on the field converged to discuss a point until someone finally thwacked a ball and it spurted away.

"Frances," little Sophia said quietly and looked up into her older sister's face in awe, "the king waved and winked just at you and now everybody else is looking."

It was true. Even the dolts jammed in the shaky galleries shaded their eyes against the slant of afternoon sun to see whom the king had waved to when his mistress Castlemaine was so obviously seated on the other side of the field. Frances kept her face impassive, but under the partial protection of her ruffled, beribboned bonnet, she blushed. It had been like this at court for her ever since His Majesty had cleverly coerced her into giving "a little." To her dismay she even heard the sibilant sound of the *ss* in her name whispered behind them as someone evidently pointed her out.

For over three months now the courtiers had amused themselves with rumors and wagers over the new turn of events: King Charles was obviously smitten with Frances Stewart, and she with him, for he kissed and caressed her openly and she allowed it. He got her into corners and nuzzled her; his hand gracefully rode her hip or waist or shoulder on strolls or at the gaming tables—yet, as far as anyone could tell, the little Stewart still held the king at bay and did not see him alone. In satisfying his most intimate of needs, everyone was smugly certain, the Countess of Castlemaine reigned yet supreme.

Frances tried to concentrate on the increasingly boisterous game. How relieved and grateful she had been today to discover no one had told all this to her mother. The court and city might buzz with it, but no one had dared whisper it to her own mother.

However, if the king walked over here between games to take his usual good luck kiss, she would be lost . . . or if Barbara or Buckingham knew what grief they could cause by merely stepping over to give her protective, obsessed mother one mere hint of this.

Suddenly, the Duke of Richmond was sweeping her a low bow. He was elegantly attired in deep hunter green hues that highlighted his eyes which always disturbed her so. "Frances, I see you have your family here today. I am certain the Queen Mother, Henrietta Maria greatly misses the companionship of your mother at Saint-Germain."

The elder Sophia Stewart eyed Richmond warily, with a taut smile. Before he could say anything else, Frances took over. "Mother, may I present the King's Great Chamberlain and Lord High Admiral of Scotland, Charles Stuart, duke of Richmond. He was king's messenger to Saint-Germain once as you may recall. My lord, this is my sister Sophia and brother Walter."

"Lord High Admiral of Scotland," Frances' mother repeated, and her pinched lips curved to more of a smile than Frances could remember her bestowing in the presence of any man. "My homeland is Scotland, you know. Aberdeen."

"Aberdeen—a beautiful sea town and one the navy frequently puts into. My Scottish lands are more western, my lady, the Lennox estates near Lethington."

"Oh, Scottish lands too. How I still long for Scotland after all these years, though most of my people are gone now."

"Anyone who loves Scotland as I do is welcome

always at Lennox, or indeed, at my lands here in Kent, Lady Stewart."

His eyes lifted at last to Frances' annoyed face, and she shot him a withering glance of warning which she immediately regretted as he evidently took it as a challenge. "I am so busy serving the king as so many of us are here that I don't often see your lovely daughter, but please consider my invitation, Lady Stewart."

"Unfortunately, my Lord Duke," Frances put in, "I really doubt if my mother or any of us will be visiting either Scotland or Kent in the near future."

"Pity," he replied, a hint of laughter in his voice which increased Frances' frustration so that she clenched her mauve satin skirts, burying her fists in the soft folds of material before she realized what she was doing and let go. "I'm afraid we all must comply when royal duty calls, right, Frances? You are, no doubt, proud to hear how well Frances is getting on here after such a short time, Lady Stewart."

Frances' heart began to pound. The wretch! He wouldn't tell her what he'd seen or heard, but it would be just like him to shame her. She detested herself for stepping so willingly, so open-eyed, into his trap, but right now she would do almost anything to avoid the days of berating lectures her mother would subject her to if she knew what favors her daughter allowed a man . . . and a king.

"My Lord Richmond was kind enough to climb a tree for me one day when Joli got loose, mother," Frances said and shot Richmond her sweetest smile. She plainly saw him waver at the tactic and hesitate to voice the tormenting comment with which he had

183

intended to annoy her.

"How very kind of you, my lord," her mother said, "though, I dare say, a mere pet is hardly worth putting yourself in danger. You know, I had a spaniel once in Aberdeen which would have drowned had not a young man I knew waded into a wild spring burn to save him for me."

Frances listened to her mother ramble on to the attentive Richmond who still held his plumed hat in his big hands. The woman hadn't chatted so in years and certainly not to a man. Heavens, it was her fault for mentioning he was Lord High Admiral of Scotland. Scotland—and to her mother! She should have known better, and now her mother was rattling away to him about having to rear the three of them after father had died. The rogue would have their whole life story to taunt her with if it suited him.

"Mother, excuse me, but you said you wanted to head back before five, and I'm sure it's nearly that. If the duke will excuse us, we had best go over to the royal mews now."

"The *royal* mews?" Richmond echoed and Frances cursed herself upon realizing she had given her mother another opening to cause more trouble.

"Oh, yes, Your Grace," Sophia Stewart said, gazing up at the tall duke as he easily fell into step beside her. "You see, King Charles has offered us the use of his carriage to visit and return home today."

"How kind! I know he and the queen appreciate Frances' efforts as maid of honor despite the fact she is the youngest of the queen's ladies and still, no doubt, has much to learn. Frances, I hope you and your mother won't mind if I accompany you. I am

184

going on a carriage ride myself, you see."

She read the tone of voice, the subtle challenge in the green, green eyes. "Of course not. Please come along," Frances managed. She turned away to control the urge to slap that smug, square-jawed face for the little triumph he had won, and she only hoped he would not stoop to such blackmail in the future to assure her compliance.

"Walter and Sophia—come on now," she called. "Walter, if you have any more questions about Pall Mall, I am sure the duke will be glad to answer them as he has played against the king—"

"Played against the king for interesting stakes— and won, Walter," Richmond cut in. Despite the fact he used the boy's name, he smiled directly at Frances. She noted the devilish glint in his eyes was for her, but he offered his arm to her mother as they strolled through the trees of the Park toward the mews.

Ten minutes later both Richmond and Frances waved her family off as the coach, decorated with the gilded royal crest, rolled away up the Strand. Walter still had his head and one arm out the window as he shouted something, but Frances didn't even wait for that to end.

"I hope you are pleased with yourself today, my lord!"

They walked across the central courtyard of the big square of royal stableblocks which, with the king's falconry and dog kennels, comprised the mews.

"Very pleased. I believe I understand you a little better now, though it hardly excuses the stupid way you've been conducting yourself at court since New Year."

"Let go of my arm. I'm going back to the Park."

"Frances, where's all the sweet compliance—the smiles—I got just a bit ago for not spilling the news to your naïve mother hen that her Frances allows the king outrageous liberties in public?"

"I vow, I knew you'd get to that. They are not outrageous and they are only in public, though it is none of your damned business!"

"You're shouting, Frances. Granted, stablehands and grooms seem to be in short supply right now, but do you really want them to know all your business— more than they undoubtedly already do?"

"I'd rather have them know than you."

His eyes narrowed and dipped once to her heaving buff satin bodice so prettily laced up the front with braided silver cord; then they dropped to her mauve skirts before they returned to her flushed face again. "If that foolish statement is true, Frances, it's only because, like most Londoners, the stablemen would snicker and not give a damn. I don't laugh at you, sweet lass, and I care very, very much."

Her eyes locked with his as firmly as his hand was locked on her wrist. "I don't believe you."

"Frances, I can see your mother usually doesn't trust—people either, but I assure you, my feelings for you are sincere. I told you plainly I loved you from the first and I meant it. Am I to be punished because you wanted to kiss and touch me in return? I will not just nod and smile like the rest and let you plod your pretty path to destruction with the king."

"I am not. I have it under control. I owe him nothing this way."

His mouth set in a hard line, but he said only, "But

now you do owe me something."

"Because you didn't tattle on me to my mother, I presume you mean," she shot back. "I don't want to go on a carriage ride with you as you so cleverly hinted before."

"No, you owe me because gamblers sooner or later must pay debts."

He moved them steadily toward a tall, open stable door as he spoke, his lock on her wrist unbroken. "Let me go, Richmond. I said I do not wish to go for another ride."

"Look for yourself, Frances. There are no carriages in here. It's one of several parts of the mews that have not held horses since the Restoration as His Majesty has never quite yet managed to recoup the extensive array of horseflesh his royal sire lost in the civil war."

"I don't want to see a stable or anything with you. I want to go back."

"Back to be publicly fondled, caressed, kissed—pawed by the king?" His voice was louder now; his face looked carved from granite in the shade of the courtyard.

"Believe me, Frances, it will be nicer in private and between us. You promised—you wagered—you would give me whatever you allowed him, remember? I saw you last week when I came to court to look for myself. I couldn't believe what I'd heard, and I didn't want to. You looked calm, even happy when he touched you and got you off in the window seat to kiss and pet you, Frances, but I believe you were almost as unhappy inside at all that as I was."

"I didn't see you."

"I left to avoid challenging His Majesty to some

sort of duel. I don't need to have my lands or the yacht he fancies confiscated on charges of treason or worse."

They stood in the open door of the deserted mews, and she darted a quick look in behind him. It smelled of fodder, leather and wood here. Within was naught but shadow behind deep piles of loose, stored straw. Despite his hold on her wrist, she took a step to run even as his arms moved to lift her. She kicked and squirmed but he took her in and the door banged hollowly behind them. He stood her on her feet and shook her hard once, his hands on her upper arms.

"Stop fighting unless you want to wrestle in the straw with me, lass; then we'd both ruin our clothes for certain. If what you're letting the king enjoy daily, publicly, is causing you no concern and is fully under your control, surely you can pay me off without batting an eyelash and be back at Whitehall before supper. Or could you not let me touch you, little ice goddess, and remain so outwardly calm and in control, as you say?"

She glared up at him, her ruffled lace bonnet awry and two long curls tumbling loose from their dangling silk ribbons. "Of course, I could," she heard herself say, but it infuriated her that her voice shook. "If I wanted to."

"Then you'd better want to, or I swear, you'll be very, very late to supper. You see, I don't give a rap if I'm dismissed in disgrace for disappearing for hours and holding up the royal meal, but I think you do."

He stepped close to her and lifted her chin for a kiss. He seemed to be only sampling her lips, tasting them, and she relaxed a little. If she just made her

188

mind a blank as she sometimes had to do when the king became especially persistent, she could give Richmond a kiss or two and insist she had to go back. Despite trembling legs, she gazed defiantly at him as his fingers awkwardly untied her bonnet string and he dropped her hat onto a pile of straw behind them, tossing his own after it.

He pulled her gently to him; she moved as if she were dazed. He kissed her nose, her eyelids, her cheeks, then nibbled at the corners of her mouth pursed for a kiss. "Is that what he expects?" he said low. "I prefer things more spontaneous, more exciting."

A warm tip of wet tongue traced the outline of her lips once, twice. He felt her shudder beneath his hands. He moved to hold her tighter without alarming her, one hand across her shoulder blades, one pressing her to him at the small of her back. His lips opened perfectly under his as his mouth took hers repeatedly until he could bear no more restraint and thrust his tongue into the warm honey of her mouth to taste her intoxicating sweetness.

She fought to keep calm, to keep control, but he was not just kissing her the way the king did, or else, it was just he was so—different. She had meant to let him kiss her once, she told herself desperately, maybe twice, then to step away to show him he moved her not at all. But he did. He did!

"No. My lord, stop. Stop!"

"I can't and you don't want to anyway," he groaned and slanted his hard mouth across hers as his hand dropped to knead her hip, then gently but firmly clasp her derrière through the sliding satin.

This time her tongue met his in a little duel, first in her mouth and then in his. She leaned against him, trembling, moaning deep in her throat as her hands lifted to caress the thick brown hair at his temples. It was so dim in here she couldn't see anything. No, she had her eyes closed, she was drifting off somewhere, she was dizzy.

The crushing embrace ceased. He leaned her back against a wooden post and she almost cried out at his desertion. Then she opened her heavy eyelids and saw he had stripped off his blue waistcoat and vest and laid them in the straw, patterned silk lining side down. She fought to clear her head as he reached for her.

"Richmond, no."

"We can't be comfortable standing like that, not with how dizzy I get when I touch you."

"You do?" she said wordlessly, awed by the knowledge she did the same thing to him. He lay on his side and she leaned easily into his arms on the soft bed of straw and brocaded satin. His kisses demanded, deepened, and she was lost. Her hands lifted to stroke the back of his head, his curly hair, to grasp the muscles of his shoulders as he pressed her down. Her thoughts became liquid flow, then mingled with an engulfing torrent of emotion she could not control.

His mouth was everywhere and she reveled in it. Why, why was it like this? The king did not sweep her away like this.

One big thigh moved to trap her shifting legs; a hand was untying the front laces of her elaborately embroidered bodice. She could feel the lean strength of him; big powerful muscles where she had smaller ones; hard, taut sinew where she had soft flesh.

His fingers caressed the valley between her damp breasts open to him now as he tugged the embroidered bodice apart. Her corset, a new French one, laced up the front, and hurriedly, he pulled at its laces while his mouth rained kisses on her earlobes and jangled her metal earbobs. Like him, she breathed heavily, evenly, as she fluttered tiny kisses along his hard jaw line where he smelled wonderfully of musk and some unnameable, intoxicating male scent.

He pulled her up against him. He returned to claim her mouth again and again until she clung to him. Then, his warm fingers briefly moving along each rounded shoulder, he slid the buff-hued bodice and ruffled sleeves down her arms nearly to her elbows and opened the stiff corset with its steel supports to bare her to him in a huge V to her waist.

"Sweetheart," he breathed as she looked dizzily at his rapt face. Her arms were nearly immobilized because of the way he had peeled the layers of garments down, but she didn't care. A little warning voice chattered in her dulled brain, but she shoved it back.

Each inch of naked skin came alive under his gaze, and she knew her nipples, taut with desire, were giving her emotions away. He moved one hand to support her back and she arched it, presenting more fully to his ravenous view two proud, perfect breasts. He stroked, he touched, he gently squeezed each ivory mound until a tear forced itself from beneath her thick eyelashes at the pure rapture of his caresses.

"This is the real Frances," he murmured, his mouth so close to her right breast that his breath scalded her skin. "Passionate, honest, loving, knowing whom to trust. I'm wild for you, my sweet, sweet lass."

Her head began to clear as a protest tried to surface through her swirling desires, but his mouth dipped to cover one pointed peak which trembled under the teasing touch of tongue. He traced icy, liquid fire across to the other rosy nipple, then back again pulling, kissing, until neither of them could breathe again. They clung, mutually, magnetized, her arms low around his waist and back, pressed him so hard to her that her soft breasts felt intimately, distinctly the imprint of heavy lace and ribbing on his shirt.

One hand was on her knee now, where her skirts had fluttered up. The long fingers caressed, gripped her leg through the silk stocking as he slid his hand heavily up her thigh. When his thumb stroked bare flesh above the ribboned garter holding her stocking, she made a desperate grab at sanity.

"No."

"I won't. Not here, not now, damn it, but somewhere more private and protected—soon." He felt her smooth thigh quiver when he brushed it, and reluctantly, he drew his hand back down and out from the ruffled warmth.

"Sweetheart, there's so much I want to tell you, to show you. I knew it could be like this for us."

He looked so smug and self-satisfied, she thought, and panic crashed in. "No more, my lord. I must go back."

His face became wary at the new edge to her voice.

"You're not going to tell me, Frances, that all this was only to pay the debt. You loved it as much as I."

"Did I?"

"Very, very obviously."

She pushed his hands away and started to lace her corset while he watched seemingly impassive. "It was your idea, my lord. You dared me. And you trapped me and dragged me in here. It won't happen again."

"Won't it?" he asked, his gentle voice sharply edged now. "I suppose you intend to keep me at bay for weeks, maybe months until we just happen to be alone again and the explosive alchemy we feel for each other ignites—like this."

He seized her to him, crushing her hands against her still disheveled bodice. His mouth took her fiercely, tasting her, probing, while his hands ran riot up and down her slender back. Her own sweeping response astounded her and overwhelmed them both. Explosive alchemy, he had called it, this ignition of her passions when they looked or touched. They moved down together onto the bed of prickly straw, entwined and melding everywhere.

He rolled her up over him, then down his other side into the depths of straw and skirts and abandonment. Her breathing seemed to stop, then crash alive like waves in the Channel. His warm hand was on her thighs again, across her flat belly, then gently if insistently at that fiery juncture where her legs joined.

"I didn't mean for us to do this now—here," he rasped out, his breathing as ragged as hers. "I wanted to ask you to come away from Whitehall with me, maybe to the ship, but Frances, with you I can never think, never stop—"

"No, no," she heard a woman's breathy voice say, "please, please do not stop."

He moved over her and nudged her knees apart even while they were lost in the throes of a blazing kiss. The stables, the lofty roof overhead, all this straw seemed to be whirling them down into some magic vortex she could not control. "I need you, want you—" she whispered hotly against his ear as the sweet piercing thrust she recalled so clearly from their union that other time turned her wild wanton in his fierce embrace.

She tasted his tongue as well as his earlobe and his mussed, rampant hair as he moved over her, in her. He murmured love words, distracted words she tried to treasure as they blurred by. "I can't believe how you do this to me, lass—make me lose my head like this—like no one else ever has," he gasped. His tongue now traced the delicate shape of her ear, then darted madly inside. His plunging increased in pace until rainbows of vivid color exploded before her eyes. Again, effortlessly as in his carriage, with him she climbed and flew and then soared sweetly back to earth.

For long floating minutes, she clung warmly to him, wishing everything outside their mutual embrace could go away. She felt drowsy, relaxed, and utterly fulfilled. His breathing quieted; at last a big hand covered her bare hips with her rumpled skirts.

"I just meant to kiss you once more to demonstrate the futility of your telling me you can just dismiss how we feel about each other," he said low as she sat to lace her bodice under his steady gaze. With his

194

help, she stood unsteadily and flipped her skirts a bit while he quickly brushed straw from the inside of his vest and waistcoat.

"But it's crazy—it's all wrong," she ventured at last, as much to convince herself as him. "I really can't see you like this—not at all."

"I told you I want to court you properly. It doesn't have to be in places where we just find ourselves when neither of us can hold back."

"Neither of us? I believe you pulled me in here!"

He sighed as he retrieved her bonnet from the straw and held it out to her. "I forget how young you are—young and inexperienced, Frances, but I do intend to help you grow up."

"How kind of you," she said as icily as she could manage. She grabbed her bonnet. How dare he imply that any of this was really her fault—her desire. "Heavens, I'm afraid in the future you'll just be spending your precious time on a lost cause, my lord. Obviously there are many less young and more experienced ladies about for you to choose from. Maybe Castlemaine will tire of hiding Jermyn and has as spot for you or there's always Amanda Wells!"

She could tell he was getting furious at her sudden shift of mood; a little muscle twitched tautly along the slant of lean cheek under his little scar. But he only opened the stable door, checked the area, and they went out.

"I do appreciate your advice if not your protestations of naïve innocence, Frances," he said at last, "and seeing how much advice I give you, perhaps it is warranted. Perhaps I'll just follow your suggestions and probably be far better off for it. So—as soon as you willingly take all my advice, I'll follow yours to the letter and will chase Castlemaine and your willing little friend Amanda.''

With a stony stare he swept her an apparently mocking bow and watched as she headed, without glancing back, into Whitehall Palace through the Holbein Gate.

Barbara Villiers, Madame Palmer, countess of Castlemaine, blew warmly in her lover's ear, then darted a pink tip of tongue in to arouse him further. Henry Jermyn was just twenty, three years younger than Barbara, but he had been a skilled and practiced pleaser of women in France, in exile, and now, like many other Stuart cavaliers, he had come home to reap the full benefits of the royal return. Only he had never in his wildest dreams imagined one of these benefits would include the lush plunder of the king's voluptuous and insatiable mistress, Castlemaine.

Her skillful hands were again on him so enticingly he could hardly hold back although he'd already had her once in the half hour since she had returned from the Pall Mall game at St. James's. While her hands worked wonders at the juncture of his thighs, her tongue scorched slick little paths down his chest and belly as her thick chestnut hair trailed tantalizingly over that same stretch of sensitive skin.

"Damn me, Barbara, are you trying to kill me?"

"Mm. You know you love it." She smiled up at him, her heavy-lidded brown eyes languorous. "My dearest, randy Jermyn, you have never yet failed to rise to the occasion, and I can see plainly you do not intend to fail me now. Oh, you're lovely. Here, I'm going to climb on."

He sucked his breath in as she did just that, hoisting one leg and moving instantly astride his hips to take the hot length of him. His eyes raked her, but he put his hands under his head and let her do the work. Her bobbing breasts were huge, their nipples large and tawny, but then she had borne two children and her belly was slightly rounded now from a third royal pregnancy. He winced. He knew this babe could just as well be his, but then again, she did lie with the king four or five times a week.

"What's the matter?" she asked as one brown eyebrow arched and she halted her quick up-down gyrations for a moment. "You're jumpy today."

"You're several months pregnant. Don't you think you should be more careful?" he said thickly.

"Pooh! I carry bastard babes more easily than most men fall off horses, but the king will provide for them—for me too. He loves his children."

"I know. Loves his eldest son by poor Lucy Walter enough to have brought him back from the Queen Mother's court at Saint-Germain to rear and marry off well here."

"Gads, Jermyn. Whose side are you on? I swear, Queen Catherine's barren as the moors and I have sons that someday—well, who knows! Now hush up and let me finish so we can go down to supper."

Her commanding rhythm increased and he lost himself as usual in the sensual sweep that came over him in her bed or anywhere he took her. Her appetites were obviously too much for even the bawdy king to fulfill now, or else she craved a variety

His Majesty was unwilling to give her—a change of positions, of places, of men.

He throbbed into her evidently before she had even began the multiple waves of pleasure of which she was usually capable.

"A pox on it, Jermyn," she hissed and collapsed against him, "I'm not even spent yet and you're no good now."

"'Sblood, Barbara, we've been at it hot and heavy twice. I swear, but the king ought to bring his entire Yeomen Guard regiment up here for you!"

"You bastard. You never used to speak to me thus or act so lazy—no, not at first," she taunted.

A flutter of knocks sounded on the door, and panicked, he lifted Barbara off his hips. "Sarah," she screeched as she watched him jump up and yank his breeches on, "I told you, I'm seeing no one until supper. I'm not to be disturbed!"

"The king, madam, the king is in the hall!"

"Zounds!" Barbara cursed. "At this time of day and after Pall Mall all afternoon—I can't believe it."

"What the hell's wrong with you, Barbara," Jermyn hissed. "Get up!"

She lay back among the rumpled silk sheets and bolsters and stretched luxuriously as his handsome, muscular body was hastily covered by unfastened and untied garments. He jammed his feet into his shoes and grabbed his stockings and hat, while his mussed blond hair nearly obscured his furious face.

"No, my lord, I'll greet the king as I am, I believe. He'll love it. Perhaps *he* can be attentive enough until I'm quite finished," she drawled.

He felt like screaming names at her, but he didn't

intend to be banished or imprisoned at some fancy whore's whims, whoever's child she carried. "Hide me, damn it, Barbara!"

"I think you'd best be out the window, my lord. It's a mere six foot drop to the muddy river bank since His Majesty has given the little Stewart slut the better chambers upstairs. Perhaps I will see you tomorrow then?"

He stared, aghast at her outrageous audacity, for a minute and then disappeared, hat and stockings in hand, over the sill. She heard him drop and scramble away.

She plumped the pillows up and smoothed the sheets a bit, then stretched again. Could that damn maid have been mistaken about Charles in the hall? She'd box her ears roundly if Henry Jermyn had been hurried away for no reason, for she'd known him often to be coaxed to take her a third or even fourth time in one bedding. It wasn't like the king not to use the privy staircase, but his coming to her openly through the halls could at least enhance her reputation with the fickle courtiers a bit more.

Another flutter of knocks made her smile. "Madame—Countess of Castlemaine—His Majesty is here."

"He may enter, Sarah."

King Charles closed the door behind him and stopped in his tracks half way across the poshly decorated room. The massive bed was so hung with velvet swags, clusters of ribbons, and gold braid and tassels he could barely make her out and the open window glared in his face. Then his eyes took her in—stretched utterly naked, one leg provocatively

199

bent—on the bed. He moved to stand over her.

"What the hell are you doing in bed just before supper, Barbara?"

"Such a scolding tone, my King. Here. Sit here," she murmured and patted the bed by her hip. "I am with child, remember, though I swear, I don't show it too much yet so I need a bit of extra rest now and then."

"Indeed? You've seemed as active and lively as ever to me lately."

"Are you sure you don't have a few minutes before supper, sire?" Her hand caressed his velvet thigh, creeping higher. "You wouldn't even have to get completely undressed, you know—"

"I believe I am aware of the varied possibilities, madame. Have you seen Frances?"

Her face went instantly flushed. She snatched her hand back. "What? Frances? Here? You must be jesting!"

"She put her family in a carriage, I suppose, but she hadn't come back yet."

"Frances! Oh, I dare say, you are aware of the varied possibilities, Your Majesty!"

"Just hush, Barbara. I'm not in the mood to argue."

She scrambled up to sit on her flanks, her bare feet tucked in under rounded buttocks. "Zounds, I guess not, but you are in the mood to fawn and paw that little virgin so everyone can laugh behind your back! If you had any sense at all, you'd rape her and have done with it."

"No, madame, if I had any sense at all, I'd send Jermyn to the Tower or Tyburn and toss you out, though I'd see our children were well enough reared and loved."

Jermyn! He knew about Jermyn! She made a quick grab for his arm across the bed as he stood. "Our children. Please, sire—it's just that carrying this royal babe I get all emotional sometimes and don't know what I'm saying. About our children—now that you've brought Fitzroy back and created him Duke of Monmouth—"

"—and plan to make a fine marriage for him next month to the Earl of Buccleuch's little heiress—yes, Barbara?"

"Gads, what about our children? There will be three soon."

"I can count, madame. As for the children, I shall provide well for them, however rashly their mother chooses to behave."

Stark naked, she ran after him and wound her arms around him from behind, pressing her soft body to his back. "If I would ever leave for any reason, sire, they would, of course, go with me. I'm no Lucy Walter to be fobbed off somewhere."

He gently but firmly disengaged her clinging arms and turned to face her. "No, but you're not Frances Stewart either. You know, a little more sense and restraint wouldn't hurt you."

She yanked away violently and, before he could stop her, picked up a Chinese porcelain plate loaded with oranges and heaved it against the wall. It shattered into a thousand shards as the king grabbed her and half lifted, half carried her back to the bed. She was so beside herself with fury he wasn't sure she was even aware he had pushed her down and covered her. He leaned stolidly against a ribbon-festooned bedpost and glared down at her, brocaded arms crossed on his chest.

"How dare you lecture me of her!" Barbara screeched when she righted herself. "How dare you! I give you everything—everything I have and yet you fall all over her for a few icy kisses and a little squeeze of tit! I will never, never have that strumpet here in my rooms again, so you needn't ever look for her here again!"

"Rest assured I won't, madame, but then, I'll not be here either."

He heard her gasp as he turned away, heard her scramble off the bed again. He turned back once more at the door as she stood five feet from him on the thick Persian carpet next to her gilt dressing table cluttered with crystal bottles and various tortoise-shell mirrors and brushes. This time tears coursed down her cheeks.

"Please, sire, don't be angry. I didn't mean all that, of course. I know—I know these past few months since you have shown Frances your affection more openly you've thought of her even when you've lain with me. I was hurt at first—gads, any woman in love with you as I am would be, but I'm used to it now and I still desire you terribly. Please don't go off in a huff. She—Frances—probably just took a lot of time to say goodbye to her mother and those two children today."

"Perhaps."

She reached for his hand and tugged him back a step into the room. She smiled provocatively at him now, but her tears had smeared her eye colors creating dark streaks under her bleary eyes.

"We could do whatever you'd like in bed now, my love. Anything. If you want me to lie very still under you, I can, or moan or kick or whatever you want, sire."

"I grasp the message, Barbara, but I hardly think you need to pretend you're Frances Stewart for me. That fantasy just isn't possible."

"But I know you have wished, pretended it was so. Why isn't it possible? I want to make you happy."

"You wouldn't really understand, Barbara," he said patiently. "You have so much of the aggressor, the wanton in you and she doesn't. She makes a man feel totally a man. Wash your face now and I'll find Buckingham to fetch you down to supper after you get dressed. Tonight—late—I'll be back and there will be no arguing. Then we'll see."

"Oh, yes, yes. How wonderful. I'll be waiting, sire."

He did not kiss her as she was certain he would. He patted her naked shoulder as though they stood fully dressed in chapel service and went out.

When she was sure he was gone, she smashed a crystal bottle full of expensive Genoa water and collapsed in sobs on the carpet. Damn him! Damn him and that Stewart slut! There had to be some way to rid Whitehall of her simpering, pretended virginal presence!

She lifted her head at last and wiped black running eye color from her wet cheeks. Where was that stupid maid Sarah? Buckingham would be here soon and she must be ready and beautiful.

Buckingham—he could help. He had a hundred

spies, a hundred clever tricks. He could seduce Frances himself perhaps, or get someone else to do it. Maybe that rural rake, the sly fox Richmond, would want her. After all, Richmond had sought out Frances' family today at the Pall Mall alley and then had walked off with them. Yes, Richmond. The haughty bastard had turned down the chance to lie with her, the king's mistress, three times these last two years. Maybe, Frances was even now with Richmond, and she could bring them both down together!

Barbara Villiers, Countess of Castlemaine, smiled as she got slowly to her feet and sat, her interest revived, at her cosmetic table. "Sarah! Sarah, get the maids in here to prepare me!"

The silly wench must have been nearly at the keyhole because she tumbled in instantly. "Yes, madame. At once, madame."

"And fix my face. I'm in a hurry now. My cousin, the Duke of Buckingham will be here soon."

Already, Barbara could feel her mind plotting, clicking away to shape the inevitable. She smiled beneath the cool linen cloth with which Sarah sponged her lovely face.

Chapter Seven

Whitehall Palace was ablaze with lights for the wedding of the king's son by Lucy Walter, Fitzroy, recently dubbed the Duke of Monmouth. Glass-covered lanterns hung from fruit trees to illumine gravel paths in the Privy Garden and were suspended along the Thames clear to the watergate; sconces lit the labyrinthine halls and the intricate maze of chambers from the Bowling Green to the Cockpit to the royal rooms; thousands of thick wax candles set aglow the ornate Banqueting Hall where the dancing would soon commence now that the long formal wedding feast had ended. And scented tapers lighted the queen's quarters, newly decorated in her favorite cool greens, where Catherine of Barganza, her maids, and ladies had gone so that Her Majesty might change her gown before the dancing.

"Gads, at least she has grown to see the error of her ways and put off those mushroom farthingales," Amanda Wells whispered to Cynthia Boyton directly behind Frances.

"Of course," Cynthia's hushed voice replied. "Her Majesty would do anything to please her unfaithful lord husband—even be slavishly polite to that witch Castlemaine. Look, she's letting that woman help her change her gown right now."

Frances swiveled to face Amanda and Cynthia. "After all, that is part of a lady of the bedchamber's duties," she said low, eager to speak for the queen if not for Castlemaine. "I only wish Her Majesty would get with royal child and that would be the end of Barbara, Countess of Castlemaine."

"That or something else perhaps," Cynthia whispered pointedly, as she and Amanda exchanged knowing looks. "I swear, Frances, if I had the king in hot pursuit of me, I'd not be returning his gorgeous gifts or denying him private entrance to my rooms. King or no king, the man is handsome, sensual, and, I warrant, a marvelous teacher of the arts of Venus."

"Just hush, you two. I vow, I'm sick of your silly teasing."

Frances edged toward the queen to stand behind Barbara. Despite the fact that the king's mistress' belly had greatly grown in this most recent month of her pregnancy, the flagrantly hued red gown she wore over a gold bodice and lacy underskirts hid it fairly well. Rubies dripped from her ears, wrists, and nearly naked throat and breasts.

Queen Catherine caught Frances' warm gaze and nodded to the girl with a smile. Now *there*, the queen mused, was someone on her side in all this host of laughing, pretty English ladies. Although her dear husband, King Charles, had been careful never to let her see it—*Santa María*, bless him for at least not flaunting his attentions to the pretty Frances before her—she, the queen, had heard the gossip. But the rumors said, and the queen believed them true, that the girl was entirely chaste and would not see the king alone. Let this serpent's Eve, Castlemaine, here in the royal garden of her life whisper to her that the king was smitten—besotted—with the little Stewart. She, Catherine the queen, judged the girl loyal still and prayed mightily to the Virgin she would remain so.

The queen sucked in her breath as they laced her blue satin bodice tightly up the back. Her large, dark eyes darted to the face of that serpent's Eve they all called *mistresse en titre*. Ah, *Santa María*, if only she, Catherine, could bear His Majesty a child, a son to set all these Castlemaine's sons and Monmouth forever aside! She could see Castlemaine was preparing to say something clever and she, Catherine, proud daughter of the king of all Portugal, would have to be kind to her again.

"Your Majesty, I really must praise your patience in standing there so still like that when they fuss over you. I swear, I'd fidget and jump all around myself," Barbara's speech ended and all whispering ceased.

The queen bit her lower lip to keep from grinning as the thought came to her: "Ah, but I have so much practice bearing much worse things, it is nothing to me, my dear Countess of Castlemaine."

Someone far back in the group dared to titter. Barbara frowned and held her tongue for once. The queen looked preoccupied, as if totally innocent of the jab. Frances' heart flowed out to the queen; she wanted to laugh and applaud, but instead, to break the uncomfortable hush, she said, "Your Majesty, will you change your jewels as well as your gown? I can fetch them for you."

"Yes. Excellent idea, dear Frances. Here—take back these emeralds; bring the sapphire pendant like to this blue satin. My Lord King does so love blues," she said with a lightning-quick glance at Castlemaine's stark red skirts.

The ladies gasped again at the queen's clever ribbing of Castlemaine tonight, but Frances stepped behind the queen to unclasp the heavy emerald necklace as though she noted nothing. Perhaps, she thought, the queen had heard what everyone whispered of late and the knowledge made her bold: that now since Castlemaine was pregnant again, His Majesty might look elsewhere, or, perhaps, though no word had come of it yet, Her Majesty might, indeed, be with child. Everyone knew the king was ever attentive to a husband's rights and lay with Her Majesty two or three times a week.

Lady Anne Scroope, whose proper duty Frances realized too late she was usurping by handling the queen's jewels, offered Frances the carved jewel box, glaring down her long nose as she did so. The box was not large, but amazingly heavy, and when Frances opened it before the queen, she saw why. Not only the sapphire pendant must be here but at least four or five other large, gem-studded neck chains all entwined.

"Oh," Frances said low as she stared at the bounty. "So many."

"No—not one hundred of the number I have," the queen said and winked almost conspiratorially.

"Lady Scroope, please to come hold this box for us." Anne Scroope was forced to step in front of Castlemaine to display the jewels for the queen's perusal.

"Here, this one for me," the queen said as she drew out a chain from which dangled a huge tear drop pendant, "and this for you tonight, Frances."

Frances stared down at the tumble of blazing diamonds which lay across the queen's plumpish fingers. Castlemaine gasped; several others stepped forward to look.

"I, Your Majesty? But I am wearing these pearls." Frances' heart began to thud so loudly she was certain everyone would hear. Surely, the queen could not know about these pearls, the only gift of jewelry she had ever accepted from the king. Amanda had assured her she had heard His Majesty had not taken the pearls from the Stuart cache but had paid eleven hundred ten pounds at a Strand jeweler for them.

"But with such a pretty black and white gown, these are best. For me, Frances," the queen coaxed, ignoring the taut, jealous stares surrounding them both. "Tomorrow, you give them back, I give you back pretty pearls, yes? After all," she said so low only Frances could catch the words, "diamonds looking better than Castlemaine's rubies once were in this box, I think."

Startled anew, Frances caught the queen's barely imperceptible nod. "How very kind of you, Your Majesty," she said loudly enough for everyone to hear. "I would be thrilled to borrow them for the evening."

As they all swept down the curving marble

staircase to the Banqueting Hall, Frances could fairly feel the thrust of Barbara's narrowed eyes stab her back. Glittering blue fire in candleglow, the diamonds hung from her hair, her earlobes, and wrist to the awe of all the others and the smothered rage of Castlemaine. Frances shrugged her bare shoulders slightly. Let the woman fume and the queen have this small victory. She only hoped the king would understand, and Richmond too, who was certain after all that staring down the table at her tonight to notice the queen was not the only one who had changed her jewels.

This black and white striped skirt and ebony satin bodice with tiers of lace around the neckline was perfect with diamonds, Frances assured herself, as the beginning strains of the orchestra floated up to greet them. Now that the court had adopted and mastered the rage of French ribbons it was fully time to stun them with something else, and inset stripes it was. She was certain that, like the other French innovations Minette wrote of to the king and to her, inset stripes in gowns would sweep the court in the next months even if the ladies had trouble copying this veritable flood of diamonds.

The king and the Duke of York stood across the room amidst a group of men which included the Duke of Buckingham and Chancellor Clarendon who were seldom ever civil to each other. Then the group parted and Frances saw they surrounded the sixteen-year-old bridegroom and twelve-year-old bride. Lady Anne Scott, heiress daughter of the rich and powerfully landed Earl of Buccleuch, looked every bit the child she was, but of course, the young couple would only be put to bed in a brief ceremony tonight and their marriage not really consummated to solidify the family alliance for several years. Then too, the earlier contracting of the couple had hardly included the privilege of young Monmouth to lie with his betrothed when their fathers had helped them sign the promise to wed.

Monmouth, who had grown into a handsome if pompous and petulant young man, saw Frances with the queen before anyone else turned; he nodded coldly despite the way his eyes widened as he took her in. In a great rush of annoyance, she recalled how the little wretch had doused her gown with a hatful of fountain water over three years ago at Saint-Germain.

Buckingham's startled gaze, then the king's lazy eyes swung to follow Monmouth's stare. Frances nearly panicked at how shocked the king looked at first, or was that, indeed, raw and blatant hunger in his eyes? She distinctively heard Barbara's too familiar, derisive snort behind her as the queen swept her along toward the king.

"My dearest Catherine," His Majesty drawled low. "You have changed your gown and how lovely you look. And Frances—in satin stripes and glittering diamonds. Stunning."

The queen's face lit like a torch as she turned to Frances. "My dear husband and King, I hope you not minding. I ask my friend Frances wear these jewels of mine with her new dress tonight, so pretty, no? I think our Frances not getting many jewels to wear as some others of my ladies."

The king looked as if he would choke or explode in

laughter, but he did neither. "How kind of you, Catherine. At least, beauty like our dear Frances possesses needs little adornment." He shot Frances an unreadable look and swiveled his head of rich, coal black hair to Buckingham. "Od's fish, better choose a partner, my lord. The queen and I start out this pavane with Monmouth and our little bride here, but don't leave us out there floundering alone all night. And," he said low so no one but Buckingham could hear, "I suggest you start with little Stewart because Barbara is too heavy to dance long and looks furious enough to fully devour the first man she gets hold of."

Buckingham bellowed a roar of laughter that made little Anne Scott jump and everyone else in earshot stare. The king without another word swept the smiling queen onto the floor to the stately accompaniment of viola, harpsichord, flute, cithern, and lute.

"Frances, will you join me?" Buckingham said. "I dare say, the king can hardly dance with you yet, and if I don't have my chance now the other wolves like Richmond will be slavering at your diamond-decked feet in a trice," he added, his eyes going thoroughly over her.

"Heavens, my Lord Buckingham, how you ramble. I do not have diamonds on my feet, and you're hardly one to save me from the wolves. Besides, I don't intend to dance at all with Richmond."

"Really? Yet I hear the king brought him to a supper party in your rooms once or twice recently and a good time was had by all."

"By all except your cousin Barbara, my lord, and

since she is, no doubt, the fount of all this arcane knowledge of Richmond you seem to have, I suggest you consider the source.''

"Zounds, Frances, what sharp little fangs you have when aroused. I swear, sometimes I think you almost could be a match for Barbara, but not for me, so let's be friends, hm?''

"Friends, I can't say, but I will dance if you'd like,'' she said hurriedly as she caught sight of the tall Duke of Richmond across the room evidently preparing to take the floor with Amanda Wells.

"I'm afraid that will have to satisfy a poor humble soul like me for the moment,'' he said and ludicrously placed his hand over his heart as if smitten to his very core. He grinned like a charming schoolboy when she laughed at him and then guided her smoothly out onto the vast parquet floor.

They fell into the pavane's slow steps easily. It was unfortunately, she thought, a dance which allowed for easy conversation unlike some of the others that would surely follow.

"The king is terribly taken with you, Frances, has been for the entire year you've been in England. What is it you really want from him?''

"Want? Why, to be his friend and ever loyal subject, Buckingham, even as you.''

"*Touché*. But I have been with him from his boyhood years through the best and worst, you know. Our fathers and his grandfather were fast friends. I know His Majesty far better than you do, far better than most, pretty lady.''

"Does anyone really know him, my lord?'' She pivoted, arching under his raised arm as the pattern of slow, sliding steps began again.

"He is terribly private despite his apparent openness and keeps his own stubborn counsel at times, I admit that, Frances. That's part of knowing him. He learned that through the awful days of the war, a fifteen-year-old boy trying valiantly to lead his father's conquered armies, the close escape from capture in that debacle at Worcester, then to keep his safety and his spirits up in the years of exile."

"I know all that."

"Then you realize too, he is determined, tenacious. Life has taught him not only to survive in difficult circumstances—when deprived of things he wants, for example, things rightfully his—not only to survive, I say, Frances, but to win, to possess, and to conquer any obstacle, so to speak."

"I believe I have had this identical discussion several months ago with your cousin Barbara, my lord, though of course in somewhat less clever, more—earthy terms. Please leave off. I warrant the only virgin who will be brought to bed around here for a long, long time is Monmouth's pale, little bride, so cease your sage advice, if you please."

He sucked in sharp air between pursed lips. "Ah—more than *touché*, Frances. A hit! And *that* little virgin won't really be bedded, will she? You're proud of flaunting, of teasing with your virginity, aren't you, beautiful Frances? So aloof and yet so utterly tempting. Zounds, I can't say I blame His Majesty for his tormented twistings and turnings over you, as I'd gladly dance to your tunes too, but only so far. Then, I'd lose that hard won, disciplined patience the king has steeled himself to, tempered by his disappointments; and your precious virginity would be no more. You'd be happier, Frances, believe me. Yes, I really feel I have something in common with His Majesty."

Thankfully, she heard the interminable, slow music end as the orchestra began a faster courante, which had been the King of France's favorite dance the year she had lived at his court.

"I will say thank you for the dance if not the erudite lectures, Buckingham," she said low as she saw the king had passed the queen to his brother, the Duke of York, and was making directly for her like a determined ship through a gale. "And I must say I do agree, you and His Majesty indeed have something in common. You both have wives who adore you as faithfully as you are unfaithful to them."

"I swear, you little vixen, you try a man's patience, and I'd just love to teach you—"

"Teach her what, Buckingham?" the king's voice cut in as he joined them.

For once Buckingham looked at a loss for words, like a little boy caught with his hand in the sugar box.

"Actually, sire," Frances put in, "we were speaking of the duke's wife."

"If so, it's for the first time in years for him. Here, Frances," His Majesty said and offered her his arm effectively dismissing Buckingham. "I hate courantes, but let's dance."

She knew the courante's quick running and gliding steps in triple time were too much for the king's long legs and big feet however naturally athletic he was, so she suggested, "Let's just watch this one and maybe the next will be a minuet or sarabande."

"Or a pendant gavotte?" he teased. "We've surely got to have at least one kissing dance at a wedding." They stood under the sweep of windows, near the huge ornately framed Italian and Dutch masterpieces the king had begun to reassemble from his father's once fabulous art collection. For a moment they did not speak as the others passed quickly by, but she knew he stared broodingly at her. To her annoyance, across the room, the Duke of Richmond, almost as tall as the king, managed the fast dance steps perfectly with the simpering Amanda on his blue brocade arm.

"Od's fish, Frances, he didn't say anything out of line, did he?"

She tore her eyes away to look up into the familiar, slaty royal stare. "What?"

"Buckingham. He's really not to be trusted, I suppose, anymore than his female counterpart, Barbara, these days, but under my protection surely you're safe enough no matter what."

"Of course, I am, sire, but he does run on in the longest, most complicated thoughts I've ever heard. Anyway, the Villiers clan should realize I'm not out to usurp Madame Castlemaine's position."

"Damn it, Frances, you know how to puncture a man's pride faster than anyone I've ever seen. And I don't like the word *usurp* anymore than I like words like *overthrow, conquer,* or *war.* I only want you to love me. It's been a whole year, my dear, and you've never looked more beautiful than you do tonight— stunning, absolutely ravishing. When I first saw you

216

there across the floor by Catherine, I thought I'd love to make an utter fool of myself putting my mouth and hands everywhere those blazing diamonds are."

"Sire, please, I—"

"There, the dance is changing. I'm going to put you back in the circle with the Duke of York and go play fond uncle to Monmouth's little bride again as they're both jumpy and nervous. Od's fish, you'd think they were bedding in a contracting or marriage ceremony when it's to be entirely Platonic for several years yet. But I will see you by privy staircase tonight later. No arguing—and no damn buffet table or chair blocking the doorway. I promise, I won't stay long, Frances. I swear, I will only kiss the satin skin where my diamonds are now and then be banished like a little lamb as usual. Come on. The Duke of York prefers plain women like his wife, but he'll just have to bear up with you so all the other greedy jack-a-dandies keep their hands off."

She danced the sarabandes and pavanes that followed with various partners after the sloe-eyed, handsome Duke of York let her go at last, reluctantly. She loved to dance almost as much as she loved to ride and few were the partners who could match her style and grace. The newly popular minuet she had brought back from King Louis' court began again, and as all the men rotated one lady to their left, the Duke of Richmond took her hand.

"You know, my lord, it seems I never see you coming until too late. You were several partners down."

"Then you've been watching me the way I have been you, Frances."

"It is only I do appreciate a good dancer and that is all. I noticed you in the first courante with Amanda."

"Ah, yes, Amanda. Please do not think I'm taking your advice to really court her, Frances. I must say, she's as good a clinger as Madame Castlemaine."

"'Clinger'?"

"Someone who doesn't know when to let go. May I come up to see you tonight after the dancing?" he asked suddenly as they turned, lifted joined arms, and paraded in the opposite direction in the line of dancers.

"Of course not. Just because you talked the king into bringing you along to supper a few times—"

"I enjoyed myself tremendously, Frances. You and I get on well together when you give us a chance."

"I? Besides, we weren't together. There were at least fifteen others there."

"I'm fully aware of that, but it is one step up from being deprived of the sight of you which is what you did last time I made love to you."

"Would you lower your voice, please?"

"Of course, it wasn't really making love at leisure the way I want to do to you, if you'd ever give me the chance."

The dance ended as she whirled back to face him. "I think you had better see Barbara Castlemaine or someone of that ilk, my Lord Richmond. I believe your idea of 'making love' is what they give out for a fee."

"You wouldn't recognize love if you fell over it on a dance floor, Frances. You've proved that. And I believe, I've about had my fill of chasing a stone-hearted little lass who lies constantly to me—and worse, to herself. Hell's gates, I believe I do prefer a clinger to a block of ice, however beautiful in ropes of glittering diamonds another poor hopeful dolt has given her."

He spun and was half a room away before she could even reply. A pox on that vile wretch and good riddance, she told herself. Of course, he'd accuse her of taking these diamonds from the king. At least now she was certain Richmond would not come upstairs to her rooms where he might run into His Majesty. Damn men, all of them, Buckingham, Richmond, royal Charles—all, all!

She went over to stand by the Duke of York and his Duchess Anne, Chancellor Clarendon's daughter. Suddenly, she was hot and tired. She let the duke fetch her goblet after goblet of champagne and let it tickle her nose and cool her blood. She steadfastly ignored Richmond across the way with Amanda, and she disregarded the scathing looks of Barbara Villiers who sat, noticeably not dancing, in a chair in the corner by the door, with Buckingham and his poor wife who had materialized from somewhere.

At last the music ceased and selected courtiers trooped up the stairs for the bedding ceremony of Monmouth and his bride. The stairs seemed a long way up to Frances now—the laughing voices a steady buzz in her ears. She smiled gratefully at the Duke of York when he offered her the arm opposite that on which he escorted his duchess.

Herbs and perfumes hung heavy in the bridal chamber. Anne Scott's ladies had already prepared her for the formal bedding: her long brown hair was loose to symbolize virginity and caught back in a garland of tradition myrtle leaves. The conventional stocking was not flung, nor were there bawdy jests or obscene encouragements as there might have been if the marriage were truly to be consummated that night. While the large copper bowl of the good-luck posset went around among the bystanders, James Crofts, Fitzroy, duke of Monmouth, eldest illegitimate son of the king of England merely touched his wide-eyed bride's bare leg with his under the coverlet and that was that.

Standing in the crowded room in the press of people, Frances began to feel very sleepy. Just as the Duke of York handed her the posset bowl, she saw Richmond and Amanda leave the room, her red head on his dark blue chest. Frances shrugged her shoulders to beat down the little twist of anger she experienced, and she took a long draught of the hot spiced milk drink deliciously curled with wine.

"Enough, Mrs. Stewart, on top of all that champagne," the fine-featured Duke of York was laughing at her. "Here—best pass it on and the duchess and I shall see you to your chambers."

"Thank you, Your Grace. My suite is upstairs."

"Right above the king's, I believe," the duchess put in and smiled so stiltedly Frances wondered if she could be in Castlemaine's camp of followers. But that could not be because the duchess' father, Chancellor Clarendon, hated the Villiers and they hated him in return and—

"Here you are, my dear, safe and sound. You dance like an angel," the duke was saying.

"Thank you," she managed. "Thank you both very much."

Her maids Gillian and Jane were about her instantly when she entered the drawing room. "Oh, we heard, we heard you were in the queen's diamonds downstairs tonight and Castlemaine is fit to tear her hair out," Gillian gushed.

"Don't shout, Gillie. These diamonds are very heavy and this necklace bounces in courantes and sarabandes, that's all I can say. Just take them off and loose this corset, please."

She closed her eyes to stop her head from spinning as they fussed over her. Should she send the jewels back tonight? No. No, the queen had said tomorrow and was probably still with the king. Her eyes shot open.

The king! He was coming here—late, he'd said—and wanted no furniture to block the door. And here she was already stripped down to her chemise and petticoats while Gillie helped her on with her yellow silk wrapper.

"I have to get dressed again."

"What?" Jane squeaked. "Now?"

"Yes. Oh, heavens, the king is coming for a little visit, and I can hardly look like this. Damn that wedding champagne and rich posset. I feel wretchedly dizzy."

She sat on the settee in the drawing room since that was where they had partially undressed her. Jane lifted her legs up and plumped a bolster behind her head and shoulders. "The king, oh, Lady Frances, the king coming here tonight!" Jane whispered, and Frances forced her eyes open again.

"Only for a few minutes and just to say good night. And I want both of you to wait in the bedchamber and tear out here if I call. Is that understood?"

They exchanged half-bemused, half-tolerant glances. "Of course, m'lady."

"Good. Then hide these jewels under the pillow in my bed. He said he'd be late so I will just doze a minute and then put on another gown, the high bodiced one, the green watered wilk."

"Yes, m'lady."

"You'd best shove the buffet away from the privy door—and don't let me sleep long."

"Yes, m'lady."

She heard them scrape the heavy buffet along bit by bit and scamper away whispering. She heard Joli squawk, "Keep your distance!" and "Joli likes fruit." Evidently they had fed him. Why didn't they cover his cage and leave him alone? It was so late. The cats were probably wide-eyed, perched on the slightly recessed bedroom window sills over the Thames to watch for flies or millers in the glow of shore lanterns. The cats stayed up all night sometimes, and she was so tired.

Yet her feet still moved to the music and swept her along in Richmond's arms. His hands were strong, his feet were sure. But that half-dream disturbed her, and she shifted nervously on the settee, unaware her silk wrapper fell open. Richmond was off dancing with Amanda now, touching her, loving her. Since she hated him, why did that hurt so much?

Richmond smiled and stopped whirling around her in the elegant way he danced despite his size. He was a fine dancer, like herself, but they had danced together such a little while. His hands were on her waist and hip as he moved closer. She was glad her

222

wrapper had fallen open, glad he would touch her naked skin and undress her to press his hot mouth to her breasts and lower. His hands were on her waist and hip as he moved closer. She knew he would—she wanted him to press her down and make love to her—

"Frances. Frances, love, I'm here. You look even more beautiful lying here for me like this than you did in diamonds earlier."

She felt her mouth curve into a deliberately seductive smile as she pulled her heavy eyelids open. But instead of Richmond, the king's intent, dark face was only inches from her own.

"Sire!"

"Were you expecting someone else?"

"I—no, of course not. I fell asleep. I have to call my maids and get dressed."

"Nonsense. You look absolutely perfect for what I have in mind and if you call your maids I'll throw them out the window into the dark Thames."

Despite her panic, she managed to return his little smile. He, too, was dressed very informally, his white lace shirt aglow in the dimness but wearing no vest or waistcoat, and no hat. "You are a tease, Your Majesty."

"Well, my sweet love, it takes one to know one." He bent to take her lips warmly; his hands dropped to her wrists as they often did by habit to still any half-hearted protests. His brother James had told him Frances was obviously dizzy from too much champagne, but Od's fish, the very look of her made *his* head spin crazily and champagne was hardly to blame for that.

When she did not try to push him away, he loosed

one wrist to free a hand to caress her. She moaned low as he deeped the kiss and stroked gently along her slender waist to untie the robe's ribbons. He lifted his head. A mere brush and the silk parted completely under his hand, sliding away to reveal her lace petticoats and the thin linen chemise over her high, firm breasts. His own voice sounded strangled as he gazed down at her so still and unprotesting.

"Frances, love—I want you so!"

His eager, shadowy face nearly blurred before her when she gazed up at him—so close. His features melded to Richmond's, but then that wretch was somewhere loving Amanda, maybe even like this. How she'd like to hurt him—let the king do something Richmond had never done, would never know of, never be able to claim from her as one of his vile gambling bargains!

But now the powerful man had to be held off, had to be controlled—or she was lost and no better than that witch Castlemaine. She had to stop being so dizzy, so sleepy. He had to stop looking at her with such burning eyes.

"I have to sit up. Please help me sit up, sire."

He obeyed instantly, gently pulling her up, but then his big warm hands moved to steady her by cupping her breasts.

"No."

"Frances, look at me. We care too much about each other for any more of these games. I know you've never lain with a man. I will be very gentle, very tender. That thrills me, pleases me, and I have been patient."

Her wrists grasped his to try to pull his hands

away, but he didn't budge. Instead, he flicked his thumbs back and forth through the chemise over her nipples which, unfortunately, sprang instantly erect for him.

"Your beautiful body will love what I can do for it, Frances, I swear it."

"Perhaps, so, sire, I don't know, only my body is not all of me. You want my heart too, do you not, my Lord King?"

"Yes, yes, of course, but—Od's fish, Frances, why do our intimate moments have to turn to clever lawyers' debates? I just want to love you and, damn it, that's precisely what I am going to do!"

He shoved the silk wrapper back as she tried to grab at it; then he pushed her chemise down so quickly she could not even find a big hand to seize. His mouth covered hers to still her cries for her maids. Her eyes flew open in real fear as she felt his fingers at the waist ties of her petticoats.

She squirmed under him, her soft, naked breasts pressed to his chest hard, through his shirt, but her movement just seemed to excite him more. When she began to kick under the layers of petticoats, he tried to move atop her to still her, but his body was entirely too long for the settee.

"All right, all right," he ground out and, to her amazement, stood abruptly; then he pulled her gently to stand against him, supporting her with one hand flat against the small of her back and one pressing her clasped hands to his chest.

"I know you're tired, sweet, and I don't want to ruin our growing love and trust. I want your trust, your reliance, and I won't destroy that however desperately I want to bury myself in you. Besides, you're going to come to me and want me too, you'll see."

He towered over her as she was barefooted and he wore shoes to increase his six-foot-two-inch height another two inches. "Thank you, Your Majesty. I want—to trust you."

"Then, will you not call me Charles when we are alone? It would please me."

"If you wish."

"Why can I not have that sweet submission from those tempting lips when I ask for other things? Say it then."

"I am going to summon my maids—Charles."

"No. I am going to put you to bed—Frances," he mocked gently.

"The maids are discreet but sometimes I think the walls have ears. You cannot."

"I can. It's the only way you'll get me to leave. Frances, don't look at me as if I were some sort of ogre! I have done without things dear to me for years and learned to bear it."

"The throne, you mean."

"Yes, the throne, and it was rightfully mine during all those years of exile after my father was murdered—rightfully mine as you are. And, as with my exile, Frances, there comes an end somewhere. At some point, the master claims what is his."

"But not tonight. Promise me, Charles."

He smiled—a flash of white teeth—at her use of his intimate name. "I promise. Now call the maids out here," he said.

Once again, she thought, in partial compliance lay

escape and at least a temporary victory. She stood somewhat dizzily while he helped her don her robe after she tugged up the chemise to cover her naked breasts. Leaning on his arm, she walked to the bedchamber door and opened it. Both maids darted up from where they sat on the upholstered chaise longue when they saw the king standing so tall behind their mistress.

"The king is going to see me to bed, girls. You are to wait in the drawing room the few minutes it will take and if anyone outside this chamber ever learns of it later, I swear, I shall dismiss you both."

A jumbled chorus of "Yes, m'lady, no m'lady" came from the pair as they hurried out.

"Please leave the door a bit ajar, sire."

"Od's fish, woman, but you try to run me as completely as Barbara does, so why do I enjoy it so much more?"

"You didn't need to mention her. I intend for you not to confuse the two of us." She fought to control her wavering strength, the whirling dizziness, but the minute he took his arm from hers to remove the silk wrapper she tottered into him.

"Here, love," he said low as he steadied her with one hand and lifted the wrapper away. "Just stand against me a minute. Would you believe I used to be very adept at loosing these damned, fussy petticoat strings?"

"Yes, I believe it. In exile, no doubt, when there weren't hovering ladies' maids everywhere."

She felt their layered warmth drop away, and she quickly turned to get under the coverlet the maids had turned down before he could touch her further through the thin chemise. She tugged the coverlet to her chin and gazed up at him.

"You're a coward at heart, my Frances."

"But I always wear a chemise at night."

"You won't when you bed with me—and soon."

He looked so big and dark—almost demonic with those black eyes and that raven hair—standing over her. She almost panicked. Her voice sounded very small. "Good night, dear Charles."

He smiled. "You'd better mean that, Frances—dear Charles. I have never put up with more sweet torment than I take from you. Never. King of England playing lady's maid and going away disappointed and—unfulfilled."

"I'm sorry."

"Are you, Frances?" He bent quickly, awkwardly to kiss her lips, a mere brush of his hard mouth on her soft one.

"The real reason," he said most unexpectedly as he turned to go, "that I don't dive in there with you, whatever rash promises I might have made, is because I'd get that damned white cat fur over myself everywhere—absolutely everywhere. Good night."

She smiled despite her exhaustion as she heard him go out. How often his clever if sardonic wit had smoothed something over or restored her shattered poise. She did appreciate and admire that about him. Maybe she loved him a little for it, but not in the way Minette had meant. Why did dealing with men have to be so tangled and confusing? And, worst of all, why did every warm feeling she felt for any man always conjure up before her mind's eye the roguish face of Richmond?

She heard Gillie's light footsteps come into the room. "Snuff the candles, Gillie. You can pick up in the morning. I'm exhausted."

"Yes, Lady Frances. Only Amanda Wells is here to see you."

"What? Was she here when the king walked out?"

"Well, no, m'lady. I had her waiting in the hall a few minutes as I told her you were sick and she said she'd wait."

"Thank heavens. Fetch her in then. Thank heavens," she murmured again. That was all she needed—the whole court would know, Richmond would know. Oh, damn it, if that woman had come to gloat over being with Richmond until this late, she would just perish!

Amanda came in and walked halfway across the room. Her face looked pinched as if she had been crying; her hair was mussed and her lip color smudged. Frances swallowed hard.

"I'm sorry you had to stand in the hall, Amanda. I had entirely too much to drink tonight, I'm afraid. It's late. What is it?"

"I came to tell you that you've ruined my evening—all my plans—and we cannot ever be friends again, that's all."

"I don't understand."

"You may have had too much to drink, but I have had entirely too much of Charles Stuart, alias Duke of Richmond."

"Really, I can't help—"

"Frances, you're the most beautiful woman at court now that Castlemaine's got the big belly again—everybody says it!" she shouted. "So why

229

cannot you just enjoy the king and leave Richmond alone! It's not fair! You say you don't love him, but I swear, you must lead him on in private!"

"I do not! I don't know what vile lies he's told you, but—"

"Oh, he told me nothing except he called me Frances when he didn't even realize it the other day. And then tonight—tonight in his rooms he just stopped right before and said he didn't want to go further and it wasn't fair to me, some such slop. I'd have had him caught then! There I was—damn you both—lying there all ready for him and clinging . . ."

Her words dissolved into a sob and her shaking hands shot up to cover her face. Frances tried to get up to go to her, but the room moved and shifted, and she sat back down dizzily on the side of the bed.

"I am sorry, Amanda, but it is not my fault. You must learn to do as I do and not trust—not love—a one of them. Richmond is naught to me."

"Gads, you stupid blind fool—you liar! I never ever want to lay eyes on you again, Frances Stewart. The thought of you or that selfish, pious bastard Richmond gives me the absolute vapors!" A swish of satin skirts, another stifled sob, then she turned, ran, and slammed the door behind her.

Frances pulled her feet up and fell back against the pillow. Her head ached wretchedly from all that screaming. Maybe she would actually be sick. What a horrible night this had turned out to be—but then something had stopped Richmond from making love, as he called it, to Amanda Wells, maybe at the same moment she was dreaming he touched her. . . .

As she moaned and shifted sideways, her hand struck the diamonds under the pillow where she'd told the maids to put them. They felt cold, hard, scratchy. Their bright pinpoints of shattering blue fire spun at her from behind her closed eyes as the room slowly revolved around her head. Diamonds, queen, king—some sort of clever card game. Games, king, queen, diamonds, hearts, knave, Richmond. Heart—love.

Love me, love me, Richmond. Exhaustedly, she let herself be swept over the edge of dream-haunted sleep.

Chapter Eight

In July, Queen Catherine and her entourage vacated London to take the healthful waters at Tunbridge Wells. The accommodations for nearly forty ladies, their maids, guards, drivers, and occasional visitors were hardly royal, but the little spa was exactly what the queen wanted: everyone knew that King Charles II's own mother, Henriette Maria, had become pregnant with her heir after a visit there to drink and bathe in the curative waters. The iron-rich chalybeate spring discovered fifty-seven years before in 1606 was commonly called "the cure" because it was supposed to remedy barrenness, as well as numbers of more plebein ailments, none of which mattered to a childless queen.

For Frances, the rural sojourn was a blessed escape from court restrictions, from Amanda's frowns and glares, from rumors which did her reputation no good, and from the king who had, of necessity, stayed behind in London to tend to business. The English were fighting the Hollanders in America, where the king's forces were trying to seize the city of New Netherlands with the intent of victoriously renaming the little town New York after the king's brother. Relations with the French were uneasy and Parliament, growing ever more stubborn about larger grants to the king's privy purse, was especially furious that the king had sold Dunkirk to France for four hundred thousand pounds last year. In short, His Majesty had his hands full of problems other than his queen's barrenness, Castlemaine's antics, and Frances Stewart's stubbornness.

Frances smiled at that thought as she sat under a leafy apple tree on a wooden settle and gazed far down the lane to the grassy square of the small Kentish hamlet for once deserted of court folk at play. Time lay heavy on all their hands when the queen retired to her rooms in the inn, where she had a little Catholic altar before which she kept a prayer vigil every third day. If she could not imbibe away her barrenness with that foul-tasting water, Frances mused, she would definitely pray herself to pregnancy. So on days like today her ladies created their own amusements by picnicking or rollicking with beaux or husbands who had traveled the thirty miles from London to visit.

Buckingham had come and gone after conferring with his very pregnant cousin Barbara, who would soon be temporarily retiring from court for her third lying-in to birth the king's child. French ambassadors had visited briefly, dubbed the whole once-quiet village a scandal, and gone back to London. Several visiting young men, including the lighthearted

George Hamilton, had worked very hard to have Frances return their admiration with amorous favors, but they were easy to discourage and soon left her alone.

Today she had turned down a day-long jaunt into the forest with most of the others to just stay here at the three-room cottage where she resided with the Greenwood family who owned several surrounding fruit orchards. Her roommate and new friend, Susan Warmestry, had gone off with a beau, the Greenwoods were all out with their apple trees somewhere, and here she sat, feeling unexplainably restless.

Surely, she didn't really miss the king, though perhaps his fervent attentions at court did make her feel important, and his cynical wit and teasing flirtations certainly amused her. She looked down at the folded paper in her lap and opened it again. Yesterday she had received this note from him—a *billet deux*, Minette would call it. Almost everytime a messenger came to the queen from London, Frances, too, received a letter, only a secret one she hoped only Susan knew about. But this one had been different; it revealed a new depth of desperation in the king's affections.

It was only a poem—but from a scientific, practical-minded man who never wrote poetry. The word *love* was used repeatedly by a man who never employed that term save in mock derision or as a flippant sobriquet. It referred to her by a pseudonym, Phyllis, which he had promised her he would use in case his correspondence was ever seen by someone else, but the impact of this was undeniably clear: the king of England presented himself before her as the most impassioned and humble of lovers.

I pass all my hours in a shady old grove,
But I live not the day when I see not my love;
I survey every walk now my Phyllis is gone,
And sigh when I think we were there all alone:
    O then, 'tis O then, that I think there's no hell
    Like loving, like loving too well.

While alone to myself I repeat all her charms,
She I love may be locked in another man's arms,
She may laugh at my cares and so false she may
    be
To say all the kind things she before said to me:
    O then, 'tis O then, that I think there's no hell
    Like loving too well.

But when I consider the truth of her heart,
Such an innocent passion, so kind without art;
I fear I have wronged her, and hope she may be
So full of true love to be jealous of me:
    And then 'tis I think that no joys be above
    The pleasures of love.

"The pleasures of love," she repeated aloud. Could it ever be so for her, these pleasures of love? There had been Richmond's fierce declarations of love, of course, but he had been away for weeks from court on royal duties, and she could not possibly love Richmond despite the fact she thought about him and his love-making, as he termed it, entirely too much. Closer to the truth about love was this second verse about the hells of loving too well. At least she

236

had a respite from worrying about love, or Richmond, or the king now as she was to remain here for another week. She folded the paper and put it down her bodice until she would go back inside to hide it with her other letters.

The morning was warm but with enough of a breeze to rustle the heavy-laden apple boughs over her head and to push little puffs of clouds across the azure sky. A whole day to herself and what to do with it. Truly, she thought, what she would like most of all was a fine horse to streak across the meadows on, perhaps to stop and dine with the others in some glade, and then to be off again, alone with the wind free in her hair. She stood and sighed. The courtiers had taken all the mounts with them except the drayers' stolid horses which pulled the heaviest baggage carts.

She stood and shook out her pale green linen skirt. They all dressed less formally here except for supper at night, but they were usually playing carefree shepherds and shepherdesses, the queen said. Frances' bodice was pale pink with embroidered dark green summer roses along the front lacings, her shoes mere green slippers to match. And she wore but one linen and lace petticoat as she knew the day would be warm and she would see no one important unless she went in to await the queen's brief emergence from her chapel vigil for a light meal. But no, she wanted to be outside today and her body ached for some sort of freeing, physical action.

Her longing for something outside of herself was so intense that at first she thought she imagined the quick, distant, rhythmic beat of horses' hoofs. She turned eastward shading her eyes to gaze down the lane she had just walked. One white-shirted rider on a large horse, apparently pulling another mount riderless.

Her heart began to pound in answer to the horses' hoofs long before she recognized the man. It couldn't be, not here, not when she hadn't seen him for almost three months! It frightened her how, with the cadence of hoofs, her heart lightened to see him.

The Duke of Richmond pulled up so close to her she stepped back, looking up. He was dressed very informally, with shirt sleeves rolled carelessly up to his elbows and a leather vest. The open neck of his shirt revealed brown skin and dark, curly chest hair in a V almost to his belt. His hat and some sort of waistcoat half protruded from his saddle sack, and his soft leather riding boots came clear up to his breeches to hide his stockings. His face was bronzer than she remembered it being, and he shot her a broad grin that even reached up to lift his rakish dark brown eyebrows.

"Mistress Stewart out for a solitary stroll. This place looks hardly as exciting as rumors in London would have it. Fancy running into you here, lass."

"My Lord Duke, I vow I share your surprise. Has the king sent you to fetch the Countess of Castlemaine back to court or on some such errand?"

He dismounted in one smooth motion and moved toward her, holding both horses' reins.

"Ever the sharp tongue for protection, eh, Frances? Have you been drinking or soaking in that foul Tunbridge iron water? I think we'd best find you some sugar water hereabouts as you're the last one to need more iron in that steely little backbone of yours. No, I am not here as king's lackey or to join the general frivolities we hear so much of in London."

His eyes surveyed every inch of her in the most disconcerting way as he spoke, and his deep voice seemed to caress her very backbone which he had mentioned so jestingly. "Everyone went off picnicking today, Richmond, and for once, I chose not to join them," she said to break the awkward moment in which she was suddenly certain he wanted to kiss her.

"What good fortune," he said, "but then, I would have found you there too. I came across a rowdy game of hide-and-seek down the road and Susan Warmestry told me you'd stayed here."

"Heavens, I'm glad it was Susan and not Amanda."

He slowly raised one big hand to touch her shoulder. "Listen to me, Frances. Let's not talk about any of the others today. I haven't seen you for endless weeks as I've traveled to Scotland and been kept busy at Westminster in His Majesty's service. Your staying behind today is a gift from heaven. I've just been a few days at Cobham and you know how much getting away there means to me."

She nodded, her blue gaze linked to his green eyes lit with golden shards like a sunny meadow pond. "But I've left Cobham to have a day with you if you'll let me," he went on. "I've brought my yacht up the Medway River, Frances, seven miles from here and I'd like you to see her. It's too far to get you to Cobham for the day, but I love the yacht too and—I'd like you to come with me if it would only please you to."

The honest intensity, yet the humility, of his tone nearly swamped her aloof stance. "Oh. So you brought these horses—one for me to ride."

"I borrowed them from a friend." He grinned again at some thought. "No room for horses on a yacht, but my crew will lay out a lovely little dinner for you, if you'll come."

"And would we sail her?"

"If you'd like. The Medway's not the Thames or the Channel, but we can sail her up and down a bit. Will you come with me, Frances?"

Her words, her ready acquiescence surprised her. "To tell the truth, my lord, I've been wishing for a fine horse to ride today and that one, I believe, will do."

Laughter shivered through his voice as he moved to help her mount. "Ah, Frances, you don't know how long I've hoped I'd sooner or later be the answer to your maiden's prayers. Let's ride like the wind, my sweet."

She laughed in return and settled carefully, sidesaddle, on the horse's broad back. Even her flimsy little slippers would not keep her from reveling in this ride today, she vowed silently. "Which way to the Medway, my lord?"

"Follow me, lass," he threw buoyantly over his shoulder as he mounted and kicked his horse to a gallop. "Follow me!"

She followed him only until she caught up with him. This was wonderful. She was crazy to go off alone with him like this, but the day was so fair and it all felt so good. Only seven miles to the yacht he had said and, after all, his crew was there. She'd be back by supper and no one the wiser. She laughed aloud and shook her ribboned, tawny curls loose in the wind as she passed him on a stretch of wooded road and thundered on to stop at last on the rise of hill that overlooked the broad river valley.

"It's a lovely view, Richmond."

"All of Kent is beautiful, Frances. You would love Cobham. And will you not call me Charles?"

The king's nearly identical words to her last April thudded in her ears and she frowned. She should never have come away with him like this. Her two Charles Stuarts, alike in some ways but so different, yet both so—alarming.

"Frances, come on. This way. The yacht's beyond that curve of river there. Don't look so grim, sweet lass. I don't mean to push you. Call me Richmond, Charles, or 'that vile wretch' as you usually do, but come along."

She smiled at him for that and relaxed again. Through the trees, the midmorning sun glinted on the broad green river and birds twittered overhead. Two boys in a skiff in midriver shouted with joy as they yanked up a squirming, silver fish, but no one else was in view. Then the path curved to the right, slanted down, and there she lay nestled in a broad stretch of tree-lined water.

"My yacht, the *Francis*, lass, but speaking of names, don't let that turn your pretty head. It is spelled *i - s* like a man's name as it was called so for its previous owner, though, of course, I might be sweetly persuaded to respell it someday."

"My lord," she smiled at him, "you are indeed a wretch, but not a vile one right now. Let's ride down and see her."

They tethered the horses to crop grass in the shade and took a little flat-bellied rowboat out from the bank. The ship soon loomed tall over them, very ornate and with a carved and gilded stern where a huge, colorful flag with the Richmond coat of arms shifted slightly in the river breeze. The ship sported one big mast and a cobweb of rope rigging, but the sails were all furled. A red-haired man on board waved and threw a woven rope ladder over the side.

"It's a big yacht," she said as their rowboat hollowly bumped the hull.

"Forty-five feet, larger than most, a good racing size and enough at sea. She's ninety-four tons and has a three-man crew plus Windy, who's my cook and cabin boy. Shall I help you up then?"

"No need. If I can beat you riding, my lord, I can make that little ladder," she laughed and had started up before she realized what a view of her petticoat and legs she must be affording him below. It was more difficult than she had thought as the ropes gave way and bumped and shifted, but he came up close beside her with his head at her waist level and one arm practically behind her legs for security.

The red-haired crewman helped her up, grinned at her, then disappeared toward the bow of the boat. "That was First Mate Jonathan," Richmond said and clapped his hands to clean them before he took her elbow. "Here, let's look around and then later, we'll take her a little ways."

He pointed out the gaff sail, square topsail, the foresail and a new innovation called a jib, though she heard too many unfamiliar terms to remember them

242

all. He showed her the small ceremonial guns, on a private ship like this used only for salutes, and she noted how clean the decks looked and how imperceptibly the ship tilted even at anchor in a river. Below decks, the *Francis* was like a little suite of tiny rooms with crew's quarters, a narrow galley, two small storage rooms, then the large, luxurious stateroom in the stern.

"It's lovely," she admitted as she surveyed the stateroom's wood-paneled walls and the sweeping curve of six windows set ajar to catch sunlight and breezes. The room had tall, recessed cabinets for storage, and a long oak table with six carved chairs; but the table was set for two. Four oil paintings of other ships graced the walls, and a long, narrow bed stretched under the set of windows to their left.

"I'm pleased you like it, Frances. I do too—freedom, quiet, fresh air, privacy. I'll leave you for a minute to tell the men we'll take a sail after a little food. There is some wash water over there, and chamber facilities. I'll knock before I come back in."

He smiled as his eyes went over her before he closed the door quietly behind him. She heard his footsteps echo down the hall as he began whistling. Nervously, she did as he suggested, then walked around a bit. The room was quietly elegant, she decided—lovely but spare and masculine. There were rolled maps in one corner protruding from a brass urn and several swords mounted on one wall. The bed was very long and not so narrow as it had first looked. It and its big bolsters were covered with a rich green, figured brocade which looked every bit as fine as something one would find at Whitehall. She jumped away from

243

the bed when he knocked.

"Come in."

She realized she was famished the minute she smelled the food the man named Windy carried on a big tray behind Richmond. The cook was gray haired with freckles and one tooth missing in front, and his voice was distinctively Scottish. Sitting across the narrow, polished width of table from each other, she and Richmond devoured a shrimp and vegetable pie, spinach and carrot salad, rye bread, gooseberry pudding, peaches, and golden cheese all washed down with delicious Galloway wine.

"No champagne and no Lamb's Wool today," he teased as Windy cleared their large plates away and the door banged shut behind him.

"Mm. I like this better, at least it fits better out here, my lord. You know what else I like—that new, rich drink chocolate, only it's fearfully expensive. Mother buys the solid chunks of it from a shop in Queen's Alley near Bishopsgate and melts it in warm milk."

He had set a little smile on his lips, but she saw he wasn't really listening. She felt nervous again as if she had been chattering just like Joli did, and she fell silent. He leaned casually forward on the table, one big bronze hand curled around the delicate stem of his wine goblet. When he spoke, she was surprised he had heard her. "I will send you some of that chocolate, lass, when we're back in London. I know the shop."

"Oh. But I didn't mean you should buy it for me."

"I know. But is that one gift you might accept from me?"

Their eyes locked. "The Christmas brooch was

elegant, my lord, but I just could not accept it then."

"And could you now, lass? I still have it though it's at Cobham. And I did purchase a little gift I want to give you later."

She felt the mounting tension between them—the tension that used to anger her so. But now she wasn't angry, only . . . intrigued perhaps by the magnetism of the man as the river current shifted them in harmony ever so gently.

"Do you have family at Cobham, my Lord Richmond?"

He began to tell her how he had inherited his vast estates at the death of Esme, the previous duke in 1660. He wanted to tell her other things he was not saying about how he planned someday to divide his time between Cobham, the Scottish lands, and sailing, how he would go to London only on visits or shopping jaunts someday when he had a wife and heirs of his own.

"Then your wife never lived at Cobham with you?" she was asking almost as if she'd read his mind about a wife.

"No. Elizabeth died of smallpox in 1660, the year I inherited. We had some other lands at Lichfield where we lived. She would have been a great heiress someday. We were married very young."

"Something like Monmouth and his little Anne?"

"Not that young, and my marriage was consummated for over two years. Elizabeth was older than I, and we were happy enough as such marriages go. When I marry next time, it may be for other reasons. I will choose the lady myself and to hell with big dowries and settlements."

245

"Are you so wealthy then?"

"I wish I could say yes, especially if it would make a difference to you. Rich in lands, Frances, rich in hope and stubbornness. Actually, my vast inheritance came to me greatly in debt, but I shall work it out over the years."

"I vow, I seldom think about money. Living at Stuart courts as I've been all my life, enough of everything has just been there."

"And bounty lately compared to the Spartan years in exile, eh? Now, don't start, lass, as we're not arguing over anything today for a change. We'll tell Jonathan you're to be my first mate for the little jaunt upriver. He won't mind a bit when he gets a better look at that stunning face. Come on then."

She went gladly and even laughed at herself when she wore his big plumed hat to keep the sun from her face. The men unfurled only the loose-footed gaff sail and the smaller, triangular foresail so they could control the yacht on the river without tacking, and off they went. They talked and Richmond pointed out nameless little villages to her as they went by. They waved at herders, fishermen, and at housewives spreading laundered linens on the riverbank. She took the wheel for a while but he stood close behind and placed his big hands over hers—and she let him. Near Maidstone where the river became busier, they turned back.

"What o'clock is it, my lord?" she asked him as she leaned over the bow rail letting her skirts and hair blow free.

"About two, lass. If you're going to be a sailor, you'll have to learn to read the sun and stars."

"I swear, it's been a wonderful day," she said and smiled radiantly at him from under his broad-brimmed hat. "It will be hard to ever have another quite like this."

He joined her at the rail. "I hope you mean that, sweet, but about other days for us like this, you never can tell how many we could manage if it's what we both want. I do and if you'd just cooperate, we could find much more time alone, you know."

"Cooperate? I don't want to talk about that now, and I do have to head back."

"Of course. I'll get you there in plenty of time. Come back down to the stateroom and we'll have a little more wine while Jonathan puts us in by the horses. The way you and I ride, it's a mere half hour back to Tunbridge."

Below, she drank most of her wine in the goblet immediately. "Mm. I was thirsty."

He finished his wine and set the goblet down carefully on the table. "I too. Sometimes there are just some things I cannot get enough of."

He stepped closer to where she leaned her hips along the edge of the table and lifted a wind-blown curl from her bare throat. She stood quietly, her pulse accelerating as though they already rode pounding horseback. She did not protest when he took her goblet and set it back beside his own.

"You must realize, Frances, I adore you, but I wanted to say it. You boil my blood, I worry and think about you much too much—constantly, even when I'm not within miles of you."

She stared up not moving, hardly breathing, watching his lips as he said those words. His nearness, the broad shoulders, his deep voice—everything set her to trembling but she was not afraid.

"I know you're very fond of claiming you can take care of yourself, sweet lass, but I want you to know that anytime you need help, I will do my utmost in your service and you have only to ask."

One big thigh almost imperceptibly rustled her mussed linen skirts; one hand lifted to touch her waist as gently as his other held her long, tawny brown curl entwined between his fingers.

"Thank you. I vow, I won't forget, Charles."

He bathed her steady upward gaze in the most radiant smile he had ever bestowed on her. The impact of it warmed her, thrilled her, then devastated her as she returned it in a moment of aching, shattering silence.

She stepped against him as readily as he tugged her forward. Their lips met gently, then with a sudden, mutual intensity that made her sway into him. Her palms and fingers splayed across his hard chest and she felt the resilient curl of chest hair beneath his white shirt; her green skirt and single petticoat were crushed to nothingness by the powerful press of his thighs on hers.

He tipped her slightly sideways holding her securely and took her eager mouth repeatedly until her mind spun and rocked like a ship plunging wildly into a beckoning gale. Her hands lifted to link around his strong, warm neck as she returned kiss for searing kiss. The fears and angers, the warnings and restrictions she had clung to were swept into the stunning vortex of his touch.

He was murmuring her name in her hair, along her temple, in her ear, a delicious, raspy whisper. An icy chill raced along her spine and fingered the nape of her neck, even as he had.

She fought to open her eyes, to still the tilt and sway of the room. The air about them was sprinkled with golden sunbeams washed by the river breeze. "Oh, Richmond—Charles. I can't breathe."

"I know. I love you, my sweet Frances—need you, need you so much. Here."

He lifted her high up into his arms and strode around the table to place her on the soft stretch of bed and lay immediately beside her. When he moved to kiss her again, her hand was on his bare slash of chest, and that undefinable male fragrance he always had about him emanated from his skin and hair to pull her deeper, deeper into the sensual swirl enveloping them.

"Charles—we have to go back."

"Sh. We will. Just let me love you a few minutes and we'll go back."

Yes, a few minutes. She, too, wanted that much at least, and then she'd stop him and step away intact the way she had with the king. All day since Richmond had ridden up to her at Tunbridge with the horses like some medieval rescuing knight, she had wanted to touch him, feel him like this. His hair had glinted in the sun, a wayward curl had danced on his bronzed forehead in the river breeze. His casual garments were stretched taut over his muscular back and shoulders, soft Spanish leather boots covered the hard calves and feet which had once climbed that tree for her, for her.

249

Another woman, a warm, wanton creature possessed her body now. The woman kissed him back, her tongue eager in his mouth as his plundered hers. The woman did not protest, but cooperated as he untied the front lacings of her bodice and corset and peeled them and her thin chemise gently but firmly down to bare her to his skilled hands and burning gaze.

She reveled in the hot, wet touch of his mouth on her breasts—pulling, licking, nipping her taut, pink nipples. His lips moved over them leisurely, tormentingly until she thought she would scream with pleasure. But instead, she lifted her palms to his bare chest again to caress his shirt lacing back and away.

"Frances—sweet. You'll push me over the edge and we'll both be lost again," he groaned.

He frightened her then at the swiftness with which he stripped off the shirt and threw it somewhere behind him. Boots thudded beside the bed; stockings and breeches went while she stared mesmerized at the vast length of his lean brown body. She tore her eyes away, but not until she had beheld the blatant proof of a man's desire—this man's desire for her.

"Please, I don't think—" she managed before his mouth descended again to still her half-hearted, yet unvoiced protest.

His hands and mouth were everywhere. Then one hand pressed beneath her to stroke her back and lift her slightly as he tugged her rumpled garments down off her hips in steady, rhythmic pulls that matched the cadence of his kisses.

Yes, they were riding along again or sailing in great, rolling billows and it was wonderful. But she jolted instantly sober as his naked body pressed full length along her soft, nude flesh.

"Oh, it feels so wonderful," she managed, but her voice trembled, much as she did, with feverish anticipation.

"It's always like this for us, my love, always will be—always," his voice came to her like rough velvet from where his lips were pressed to the tiny swell of her satin belly.

His skilled hands stroked, caressed, lightly squeezed her everywhere, leaving streaks of incandescent fire which flared somehow in the very core of her stomach. The heat spread, feathering out to her thighs until she writhed under him, shifting her hips.

"Oh, damn, my sweet," he ground out drawing in an almost painful breath. "You're driving me crazy enough already. Love, I'm trying so hard to go slowly—"

She meant to stop at that half-gasped warning, but she knew she could not. She couldn't stop touching his back and kneading his shoulders as her hands ran over them; then his face went even more darkly intense as his tactics suddenly changed again. He was no longer beside her on the bed with only his upper torso twisted over her: he lifted himself and moved completely above her to press her into the sleek brocade now warm against their damp bodies. She meant to draw her legs tightly together, but too late. As he hovered above touching her everywhere, one big knee and thigh held hers apart. She moaned and shook her head, tossing the wild bounty of her tresses across the bed to tangle with his own tousled hair.

"Too late, sweet lass. Much, much too late for us to stop ever again. I love you, Frances. Trust me. I'll take you away to Cobham and we'll ask for permission to wed from there."

She tried half-heartedly to shove him off, but the man's weight was tremendous. With one hand he moved to hold her wrists gently above her head while he supported himself with only one elbow and arm. He began to kiss her again, and she let him, encouraged him, opening her mouth to the sweet assault until she felt his other leg also move between her spread thighs. She tried to kick, but he only settled closer in when she lifted her knees, and her feet thudded against nothing but brocade-covered bed. A shaft of sun slanting through the windows above them gilded his hair and lit the crags of his face to highlight the rugged bend of his nose and the tiny, white scar on his left cheek as he gazed raptly down at her. The green eyes were slitted, his mouth slightly open. Her skin tingled everywhere he looked as he rasped out hot words to calm her futile movements. Her eyes suddenly met his, both awed and eager.

"I love you, Frances, I always will whatever befalls," he said, so low she almost didn't hear the words above the rush of her own blood in her singing veins.

As he loosed her wrists, she felt him touch her between the thighs with his free hand—a stroke, a caress, a tiny exploratory penetration. Then his mouth dropped to cover hers again. He positioned himself and pressed into her slightly, a pleasant intrusion. Then, as her freed hands moved to bury themselves in his thick mane of hair, his hips surged toward her soft, open thighs.

He rocked against her, deep, deeper into her readily accommodating warmth. She began to shift and twist in her own counter movement—with him, then against him—relaxing, reveling in the vibrant, building tension they created together.

"Oh, oh, Charles. Oh!"

"I knew I hadn't misjudged you, Frances. That façade—it's not for me, is it? Never has been?"

It went on, the whirling, spiraling heat where they were joined, the trembling desire to be just as she was under him, part of him like this. The pleasures, the pleasures of love, the king had writteen, for she might be locked in another man's arms. Heavens—this, this was whom and what she wanted.

The crescendo of rapture moved upward—outward—until deep within her something turned, uncoiled, exploded in wildly rolling waves as he collapsed along her, his hard body slickly damp against her moist skin everywhere. She drifted back down from wherever he had taken her as she clung to his neck, her deep breathing through parted lips almost synchronized with his.

After long, silent minutes, he lifted himself and pulled slightly away from her. She felt strangely at ease, even as he gathered her against him and lazily, possessively, stroked her bare flank and hip. They did not speak as the breeze and pool of sunlight in which they lay licked the veneer of warmth from their entwined bodies and as his green-gold eyes studied her face.

Soon, too soon, he noted the blush that spread along her cheeks and her graceful throat, the tiny frown that barely creased the smooth brow over her sky blue eyes. He admired her for not acting defensive or outraged as she had so soon after they had lain together the other two times.

"Want to talk, sweetheart?" he said low.

She looked away, up at the wood paneled ceiling now so far overhead. "What is there to say? It wasn't exactly rape, but, I vow, the result is the same."

"Is it, Frances? Which result is that?"

"You probably believe you can have me anytime it hits your fancy when we are alone—and what if I get with child?"

Her voice sounded more her own now, he thought. Gone were the soft murmurings, the low endearments. Her mother's wary tones had already crept back in, damn it.

"Should I pout and fret that you think you can have me anytime it hits your fancy when we are alone?" he teased gently. "And, about a child, haven't you been listening? I will ask the king to let me wed with you as soon as possible, although that will probably mean the ruination of my career and who knows what else."

"And mine," she said before she realized how calloused that sounded when he'd just proposed marriage again and not even in the throes of passion. She raised herself on one elbow carefully covering herself with brocade from the armpits down while he lay there like some centaur or satyr in a mythological painting sprawled nakedly at ease. "You can't mean that about marriage, Richmond. He'd take all your precious lands you so worry about and this lovely yacht and you'd have nothing but a little prison cell in the Tower."

"Would I? Perhaps. We'll see, because since it was so unbelievable marvelous for both of us even from your first time—well."

"You are the height of presumptuous conceit, my lord."

"Spare me the well-timed barbs, Frances. I am not some fop you brush off at court, and I think you're woman enough to know that now. Today, as you said earlier, was absolutely wonderful—all of it— and I believe we can have more days of loving if we are merely honest with each other and careful where others are concerned. And I was in deadly earnest about marrying you if you would wish it—"

"But I won't. Ever. I won't ever marry, especially not you. This—today—doesn't mean you own me."

He sighed and frowned. "Frances, because the hour is growing late and I do not wish to have your associates at Tunbridge beating the bushes for you, I am going to take you back now. Otherwise, we would discuss this and I would either seduce or rape you, whichever came first, to teach you several lessons which, I fear, will have to wait a bit. Here, wrap my shirt around yourself and go sponge off. Or, I shall do it myself as I have no objection whatsoever."

Recognizing that challenge and noticing his single arched eyebrow, she donned the proffered shirt he'd grabbed from the floor and scrambled off the opposite side of the bed.

He watched her covertly as he bent to retrieve their scattered garments. On the far side of the bed, he reluctantly turned his back and pulled on and laced his breeches, then bent to touch the folded paper that

255

must have fallen from somewhere. His hands opened the note; his eyes skimmed it. He cursed low, then read it once again before he refolded it and put it between the rumpled chemise and pink bodice it must have fallen from.

He dressed, combed his hair, took the little gift book he intended to give her when he left her today, and went quietly up on deck to allow her some privacy until she joined him. The seductive lines of the poem in the king's flowing, ornate script, which he recognized only too well, taunted him.

At least, he told himself, the note undeniably proved the king had not had her. Hell's gates, the royal bull wouldn't have her at all if he could help it, but until she got herself in so deep she had nowhere else to turn, there was probably no way to really secure her. He would never regret what had happened today whatever the results, only he had meant to woo her more carefully than this! Damn, she had that nervous, frightened streak in her about men, but that might save her from the king's clever clutches whatever a shambles she made of her reputation in the meantime.

Then too, she was warmly passionate underneath that carefully tended, icy veneer; he'd die if the king or anyone else ever discovered her deep sensuality as he had. But she evidently wasn't ready to be honest with him or with herself, and he didn't intend to push so hard she'd do something utterly foolish.

He heard her step up on deck, felt her eyes on his back, but he did not move until she spoke. "I am ready to ride back now, my lord."

He turned and forced a little smile. "I want you to

know, my lady," he said as gently as he could manage, "you have greatly enhanced the chances of my renaming this yacht today, though, I fear, I may have completely ruined my own hopes of ever being called Charles again."

She looked surprised at his teasing jest, but she only gazed down the length of ship. She was nervous, awkward under his stare, and he saw her blush again. He shifted the thin, wrapped book he'd bought her from hand to hand. He fought the urge to hold her, even to carry her down below again to properly say goodbye. Instead, he steadied her over the side of the ship and hurried to keep her from falling as she quickly climbed down the swaying ladder to their rocky, little rowboat.

Chapter Nine

Frances felt utterly staggered by the six hours she had spent yesterday with the Duke of Richmond. Despite her desperate desire to get them out of her mind, to put them behind her, recalling his words, his face, his body, and the undeniable way he had excited her kept her awake half the night and intruded on her troubled thoughts by day.

She had not exactly dreamed of being with him at night; her sleep had taunted her with nightmares of the king pursuing her, his wine-laden, hot breath enveloping her—and his fury smothering her when he found she was no longer virgin. But when she jolted wide awake in the double bed next to a sleeping Susan Warmestry, her mind kept restaging what had happened in the yacht's stateroom: then her heart beat faster, her body warmed, and her loins ached again at the mere memories.

The next morning, with the others, playing a raucous game of blindman's bluff about the village, too often she found herself stopped in stride, just thinking, or not listening to what someone said. Both Susan and the queen had commented on the bluish circles under her eyes from lack of sleep.

If, she assured herself, just if she ever did conceive a child from lying with Richmond—a slip which would never, never be allowed to happen again, she would beg to go to France to visit Minette, then ask Minette to hide her in some country house or convent somewhere until she bore the child. After that, Richmond could rear it at his precious Cobham or something. She knew some court ladies drank all sorts of vile brews and went horseback riding to rid themselves of unwanted pregnancies, but she was too faithfully Catholic and too tender-hearted to ever do such a terrible thing. A child would be her only and final gift to Charles Stuart, duke of Richmond, she mused, since she certainly knew now that she could never see him again in private or intimate circumstances as on the yacht, however lovely his spider's web appeared.

Richmond's gift to her as they had parted yesterday at the edge of the village had been most surprising—a small, embossed book entitled *The Sad and Most Tragic Life of the Lady Queen Anne Boleyn*, a long and pompous title for such a little volume. Frances had pored over it by candlelight last night, intrigued by his choice of gift for her until she had come to the last chapter where the author had waxed eloquent as he moralized about the final demise of the poor lady who had lost her head.

Since those lines had leapt off the thick parchment pages at her, she had been haunted by countless renditions of imagined argumentative debates with

Richmond over his daring to give her such a pointed message. "You're a lunatic!" she had shouted at him in her brain's tormented imaginings.

"I'm a lunatic!" he had yelled back despite her efforts to still her inner voices. "Then you're a spoiled, cold, little ice goddess. Read the book again and learn from it, Frances. Anne Boleyn came to grief and lost her head because she led her king on without honesty. She remained supposedly chaste for years to entice him from his lawful wife and then, when she did submit her body to him at last, she learned she did not love the king. She learned too late she loved another man she had been torn from years before!"

"You wretch!" her fantasy voice screamed at him as she brazenly slapped his smug face always just beneath the thin veneer of her daydreams. "Leave me alone! Get away from me! You vile, wretched— seducer!"

In this haunting, recurrent vision, he always laughed grimly then and waved the little book in her face. "It says here on the last page, Frances," he shouted, "that the sad lady played for high stakes to become a queen and paid the ultimate forfeit of her love—and her life."

"Richmond, I hate you!" she said aloud as she tumbled back into reality to find herself sitting on a wooden bench in the shade of the Two Partridge Inn watching the others dash about like moonstruck dolts at a new game of hide-and-seek. Except for the fact she never intended to see Richmond alone again, how she'd love to throw the book at him and tell him her mind. If he thought for one minute he could compare her humble life to Anne Boleyn's flagrant one, he was more insane than she had thought. She hardly enticed the king and certainly never in her wildest dreams contemplated trying to displace a lawful queen!

Susan Warmestry darted up, her ebony curls bouncing loosely from her exertions, her cheeks pink. "Frances, are you just sitting and talking to yourself again? Get up, silly! Can't you hear them coming?"

She did hear horses—a great many and riding at a good clip. "Who's coming? Who is it?"

"A messenger just came to the queen, I heard, and all in royal livery. It's the king! Her Majesty is beside herself with joy. I warrant this will even haul that lazy, bored Castlemaine out of bed before noon. Come on!"

Already they could see the first riders and guards crowding the narrow main street of Tunbridge Wells, the same road on which Richmond had ridden in to find her only yesterday. Susan pulled at her hand and together they ran toward the grassy square where the other courtiers were gathering.

The king was easy to pick out—the tallest rider of the entire lot of them, the only one, of course, hatted in the group as no one covered his head in the presence of his sovereign. "Now accommodations in this little one-inn village will really be horrible," Susan was saying, "though there are a few of the king's men I wouldn't mind putting up at the Greenwood's."

"Such as?" Frances said, hoping her voice sounded amused. "I vow, it seems you've been doing well enough with the ones already here."

"And now that His Majesty has arrived, what of you?" Susan said low, her dark brown eyes serious.

"Heavens—nothing of me, Susan. Everyone must know he is here to get his queen with child. Look, she's come out to greet him."

Despite the way Susan pressed forward with the others, Frances deliberately stood back. The king's party was welcomed with cheers and hugs and flurries of kisses as the two groups merged. Frances' pulse fluttered a bit as she saw the king's dark face scan the crowd even after he had greeted the queen. Yet she held her ground; she was no Anne Boleyn and this Charles Stuart was no King Henry VIII, and she'd tell that rogue Richmond so directly next time she saw him.

"Hiding back here like some shy country primrose, little Stewart?" a man's voice said.

"My Lord Buckingham, I should have known you'd be along. I'm not hiding, but, I vow, you'd best go fetch your cousin. She tends to sleep late and not appear 'til mid afternoon."

"She won't be out here at all at eight months gone with child. She'll hope he comes to see her later where she can play on his sympathies for her—ah, temporarily incapacitated state. Besides, she's going to be lying-in for this child at Oxford soon and the whole court's stopping there before we go back to London this autumn," he told her.

"I didn't know that. It seems strange not to know what's going on in London."

"Zounds, Frances, you're back with the king now, so I'm sure you'll be instantly on top of it all—unless he gets his way at last and you end up on the bottom.

263

And speaking of that, His Majesty sent me to fetch you. I would have to say he's a little piqued you weren't in the front ranks to greet him."

"I did not think it wise or seemly."

"Wise or— Gads, Frances, you still astound me. That such an angel face can have such an angel brain after living so close to our amorous sovereign for over a year and him in hot pursuit. Damn me, if that isn't the best!"

"I don't appreciate being the cause of your amusements, Buckingham. I am hardly an angel and you may tell His Majesty I will certainly see him at dinner later as I know he wants to attend the queen now."

"Whoa, Frances. Not so fast."

"Let go of my arm, my lord."

"Icicles in August, how enticing. Now listen to me and carefully, mistress. Yes, the king is here to attend his queen and get her with royal child if he can. It's how he was conceived after his own mother took the cure here and he still has hopes. Frankly, I think our little Portuguese queen is as barren as the cliffs of Dover."

"You are cruel, Buckingham."

"No, Frances. I'm realistic, and that's something you'd better learn to be and quickly. Now, I was sent by His Majesty to fetch you immediately to the inn and if you don't wish to walk, I'd just as soon carry you."

She glared up into his narrowed eyes. His face could look so hard and calculating at times—demonic.

"Don't bother, my lord," she said as coldly as she

could manage and shrugged her shoulders. "I'll go along with you. And I can understand why you're miffed to be sent to secure me when it's your cousin Barbara's position you're forced to be concerned with."

"I'm not forced to be anything, little Stewart. Though Barbara's and my names are linked by blood, our positions are not. I have known and served King Charles a good deal longer than he's had any dealings with her. So, am I to conclude then," he changed the subject hoping the little beauty would never find out any of the plots he and Barbara had begun to concoct for her downfall, "that you have not missed the king?"

"I didn't say that. Of course, I have," she told him a little too loudly as they went past the king's guards into the inn where the queen had been staying.

"No *beaux* here either?" he gibed. "I heard George Hamilton made an utter ass of himself over you for a few days but you dispensed with him with one withering glance."

Her head snapped up. "Are you merely a gossip monger, my lord, or have you actually planted spies in this little place?"

"You're such an innocent, pretty lady. They're the king's spies, of course. Hadn't thought of that, eh? Zounds, I certainly hope you've not been off in the bushes somewhere allowing some jack-a-dandy all sorts of privileges."

Her heart thudded despite his teasing grin. King's spies. What if she and Richmond were followed or watched, but no, no. They were out on the yacht and it was very private there, she assured herself as

Buckingham turned her into a tiny eating room with one small window, a table, and four chairs.

"Aha, but I recognize a guilty conscience when I see it on a face," he said smugly. "Good for you, Frances!"

"It is only that I become very annoyed with your company very easily, my Lord Buckingham," she threw over her shoulder as she moved away from him around the table.

"And rightly so. For the moment I do too," a new, yet familiar male voice said, and Frances whirled in a soft rustle of yellow skirts to see the king had come in immediately after them. "Get you gone, my lord."

Buckingham swept them both a low bow as he exited hastily backward, a set smile on his face. He closed the door quietly while Frances stood staring at the king across the table. His size dwarfed the dimensions of the tiny room.

"Here I am so thrilled to see you and you made me send for you, Frances. No welcoming hug, no little kiss, not even as much as you'd give your damned cats or that silly, prating parrot."

She forced a shaky smile. "I am glad to see you, sire, only it is a surprise."

"I thought you liked little surprises, and I think you'd better come here to me before I lose my temper."

She moved slowly around the table toward him, one hand trailing on it as if for support. "But that wouldn't be the Charles I know—to lose his temper," she said low.

"Od's fish, you little tease, it's not the Charles you know to write poetry either, but I've missed you so."

Both of his big hands moved to cradle her face and tip it up toward him. She knew her use of his intimate first name had softened the edge of his anger, and she pursed her lips instinctively to accept the kiss. Still, she was not prepared for the way his arms dropped and pulled her to him, how he bent her back to sample not only her lips but to kiss her cheeks, eyelids, and throat.

"Sire! Sire, please, I—I want to thank you for something."

"Thank me for touching you then, kissing you, desiring you so desperately! That's what I want to hear."

When he took her lips again, she pressed hard against his chest. One big hand held her head in back now so she would not turn her mouth away; one long arm held her to him along her back. He loosed her suddenly as she went completely still in his arms.

"Damn it, Frances, I'm not apologizing. What did you expect—a little wave and more schoolboy poetry?"

"I loved the poetry. That's what I wanted to thank you for."

His slaty black eyes narrowed to study her upturned face. "Do you mean it?"

"Yes. I think I understood it."

"I'm glad, my love. I hope so." He seized her hands in his big warm ones. "Are you angry—that I have come to try to get the queen with child?"

"Angry for that? Heavens, it is grand, and I hope you do."

He frowned. "It's business, you know, Frances, royal prerogatives and all. I need a legal heir."

"Of course you do. It is much better to have one's son than one's brother but a few years younger be the heir."

"I agree. Even the Duke of York says he agrees. But, Frances, neither Catherine nor Castlemaine have my heart, and now that we're to be together again, you'll see how easy, how natural it will be for us to love. You'll see."

No, no, tell him never, tell him now, a little voice inside her prattled on, but he was so calm and amenable now, and she feared another show of his anger or passion.

"I'd best let you go to her now, sire, and I will see you at dinner. It will be harder for us to be together here as it's such a small, open village and you did promise me you would have a care for my reputation."

"Od's fish, Frances, your memory is too damn good for my spur of the moment promises. Yes, love, we'll be careful, but we will be together!" He bent to kiss her once more, still holding her hands to his brocaded and white ruffled chest. He loosed her then, evidently satisfied her silence had been acquiescence. He smiled, turned, and went out.

As she moved to follow him, Buckingham appeared to block her way with an outstretched arm across the narrow doorway. "Frances, I'll see you back wherever you're going."

"No need, thank you."

"Best straighten your coif a bit then. Zounds, but what should we expect when he's been without you, Barbara, or the queen for over three weeks, eh? All he's really had to slake that astounding thirst for ladies were a few prettied-up tavern wench types for an hour or so at night. Now, Frances, don't gape. Whatever did you expect, I said, since he's been deprived of all three of his ladies? I'd venture to say if the queen is ever to conceive a child, it will be now."

"I swear, you're despicable. Let me pass, please."

"In a minute. Frances, let's not play games. I'd like for us to be friends. You'll need friends, you know, clever friends in case anything goes awry."

Richmond's similar words to her yesterday taunted her. They were all alike, these court men—men in general—vowing vows while laying traps.

"I shall remember the offer, my lord, but I doubt it. I believe it might put you at cross purposes with Barbara, and we simply couldn't have that. Now let me pass."

He moved the arm barring her way and let her brush by him. She smelled of forest wildflowers. Her skin was absolutely flawless and especially enticing where it rose rounded above her taut yellow bodice. He watched her got out the back door of the inn so she didn't have to walk through the crowd in the front drawing and eating rooms. Her hips gracefully swayed against her daffodil-hued gown.

He grinned and nodded in anticipation. As soon as Barbara birthed this child and they all settled back in at Whitehall, he had a sure-fire plan or two to get the haughty, little Stewart to lie with the king, and if he was lucky, maybe he himself could sample her virginal wares during the whole little intrigue. Then later when the king tired of her enough to look elsewhere, there'd surely be room for the powerful Duke of Buckingham in her bed at least some of the time. He favored squirmers and fighters to tame women.

He laughed and went out across the grassy village square to visit Barbara.

The talk of all Whitehall and all London that autumn when the court finally settled back into its routines was that the Stuart queen was with child. The foul, iron water of Tunbridge Wells was imported for toasts; huge bets over the sex of the future royal child were wagered. Some even dared to gamble in secret the babe would not be born live at all and that the king's brother James, an alleged Catholic, would remain his heir. Others thought King Charles's eldest bastard son, the Duke of Monmouth, would be legitimized. The Countess of Castlemaine, whose third son, Henry, had been born during the court's brief stay at Oxford two months ago, was grateful, it was whispered, that her new child so closely resembled the king, but she was furious to hear the queen had now joined the ranks of ladies made pregnant by the king. The king himself was jubilant; Frances was relieved; and the solidity of England's Stuart throne greatly enhanced by the good news.

But soon, the joy and high-blown expectations were utterly shattered: the queen had either miscarried early or had never been with child at all. Worse, she had been struck down by a terrible disease. Everyone hovered, whispering, in corridors near the queen's suite, speaking of the vile fever's progress and of who would be the next queen.

Frances trembled inwardly and spent a good deal of her time on her knees in her room praying for the queen's deliverance from death. She also tore out the pages and burned the book on Queen Anne Boleyn which Richmond had given her at the close of their forbidden little idyll in August. Her joy at the fact she had had two months of definite proof she herself was not with child worked on her conscience in that the poor queen was griefstricken over the same result that so pleased her.

Frances rose from her prayers and shook her skirts out. Heavens, no one would believe it of her—that she prayed fervently for Queen Catherine's life, she thought, not with some of the vile rumors she'd heard from her own maids. She absently stroked her cat Perth's flawless white fur as the animal lay stretched on the brocade bed. Frances had kept to her rooms for the first days of the queen's worsening illness save for the evenings when the most intimate courtiers gathered for subdued suppers and to hear the sad recital of the latest sickchamber events. Frances' heart went out to the king: he was worried for his wife, grieved and disturbed, and Frances found it in her heart to love him a little for that.

"M'lady. M'lady Frances!"

"Come in, Gillie. What is it?"

"Susan Warmestry stopped by, m'lady, and says you're to go down to the poor queen's suite and right now."

"Is she worse then? Are her other ladies sent for?"

"Don't know, m'lady. You are sent for, that's all Lady Warmestry told to me."

Frances tucked a lace-edged shawl into the bodice

of her dark blue brocade gown to cover her shoulders. In November when the Thames wind was cruel, icy drafts knifed through cracks and chilled the hallways so that even the smelly sea-coal fires in the grates were not enough for warmth. She hurried out into the hall ignoring both Joli's squawks and the waiting pot of hot chocolate milk Gillie had ready for her.

Richmond had sent the chocolate in a veritable rain of other little gifts, all of which but the chocolate—a moment's weakness—she had returned. He had been gone again in Scotland much of the autumn to visit the eastern ports in case there was a trade war with the Hollanders, but he had been back a fortnight. She had seen him at dinner—blessedly, never alone, however he tried to maneuver her.

She stopped dead in the hall expecting to see Susan waiting. As if her thinking of Richmond had conjured him up, there he was coming at her at a good clip down the corridor. Elegantly dressed all in deepest brown, he was bareheaded and typically windblown.

"Frances, I must speak with you for a moment."

"I can't, my lord. I've been sent for to the queen's rooms."

"I know that. Everyone's heard. I'll go down with you."

It was too late for her to turn around now and take the broad north stairs where the crowd would be. She was nearly to the backstairs and he would know she was afraid of him if she went the other way.

"All right," she murmured and moved past him. "Have you heard anything new from down there?"

"Only that she hovers near death every few hours—

and that the king has sent for Mrs. Stewart. I just arrived from Westminster."

He opened the carved oak door for her and followed her down the twisting backstairs, but she went so quickly that on the first landing, he reached for her arm and spun her gently around to face him.

"Wait, lass. It seems there's been no time for us, and you haven't cooperated as I'd hoped you might. I want to touch you, to hold you, but as you've said, there is no time now."

"Then let me go."

"In a minute, you little coward. Afraid of your feelings, Frances—a woman's feelings for a man who adores her? Afraid some beautiful memories you're trying to bury could happen again if you let them? No—never mind the protests. That's not what I really have to say now. I came over from Westminster to tell you—to insist you be careful."

"Careful? I am. I try to be."

"Do not commit yourself to the king or say anything someone might use to feed these wild rumors you could be his next queen."

"I've heard them, Richmond. They're wrong, just insane stories."

"I'm not sure. The man's so besotted with you anything is possible. I'm certain your sweet Scottish heart flows out to him now, but don't let him get too close however stricken with grief he is, whatever he promises for later. Even if Her Majesty does die, common sense dictates another powerful dynastic French, German, or Spanish marriage."

"I assure you, I am not so foolish or vain to believe he would ever marry me, my lord. Now I must go."

"I should have found you a book on Queen Catherine Howard instead of Anne Boleyn, you know," he said, his grip only tightening at her order that he release her.

"Catherine Howard. Why?"

"She presented herself as a virgin to her bridegroom King Henry VIII and then later His Majesty found out she'd had a lover—still had a lover."

"And then? Finish your history lesson since you favor them so much."

"And then, he beheaded both of them. Just be careful, that's all."

She stepped back from him and he released her. She had never seen him so tense; his shadowed, deep green eyes even looked a little teary.

"Are you afraid for yourself?" she asked low, suddenly entranced by the thought he had come to warn her.

"Only that I'll lose my chance with you, my love." He lifted her right hand and bent forward a moment to turn it and kiss its palm. She had a nearly overwhelming urge to stroke his curly brown hair so close.

"Go on then, Frances. Let's just say your queen needs you."

He did not follow her down the last flight of stairs, and she amazed herself by turning back to call up to him, "My maids have prepared some of the chocolate you sent. Go up to have some if you'd like." Her voice echoed in the stairwell as she heard the door above thud. Not knowing whether he'd heard her or not, she went out onto the second floor.

The hall was crowded with buzzing, shifting

courtiers and servants. Some of the royal retinue had set up little food or drink tables as though they could not bear to break their vigil.

"There she is—she is—is," the hall seemed to echo as Frances wended her way through the press of whispering people. Her ears rang with the hiss of their s sounds even after she acknowledged several people by name. "Stewart, Frances Stewart, she is, there she is . . ." washed over her from behind.

The guards swept open the double doors for her and she went through the candlelit foyer and into the first drawing room. Had Anne Boleyn or Catherine Howard ever been sent for here? she wondered erratically.

One of the queen's ladies of the bedchamber, Lady Scroope, nodded to her and motioned her on. The second drawing room, the lovely redecorated green and gold one, was filled with silent people. She saw the Duke of York and his wife Anne and her father Chancellor Clarendon. Several of the queen's other ladies stood in little clusters but, thank heavens, Castlemaine had had the sense not to appear. However, her Villiers ally, the Duke of Buckingham, was there and he made directly for Frances.

"He'll be out directly, I suppose," Buckingham said as his eyes darted over her. "She was supposedly rallying this morning, but now they've despaired for her life again. They've shaved her head."

"Poor lady."

"Zounds, poor all of us but Frances Stewart, eh?"

"I vow, I should have known you couldn't be kind, Buckingham, even at a time like this."

"Realistic, pretty lady, remember I told you I'm

always realistic."

She was grateful that the old, white-haired Chancellor Clarendon rescued her immediately, and she gladly took his arm to step away from Buckingham. "I can tell he bothers you, Mrs. Stewart. I say, but that villain and his rapacious cousin will yet be the death of us all if we're not careful, especially now. I would really like to warn you about Buckingham. He always wants his way and is capable of the most amoral, if clever, chess moves to attain quite nefarious ends. You will tread carefully?"

"Yes, thank you."

"I appreciate the fact you're honest, Mrs. Stewart, not an intriguer and not at all a greedy harpy like the other lady. Please rely on me if I might be of any service."

They are all offering to help, she thought, all of them beginning with Richmond, and yet that was before he could have known any of this. This is what it is like to be king's favorite, this ability to summon and control people's interest—this is power.

The doors to the royal bedchamber behind Clarendon opened and the king stepped out. His eyes lighted when he saw Frances, but he did not smile.

How lovely she looks, how untouched by all the world's pain and misery, he thought. He held out his hand to her and she took it even as the others were upon him.

"I'm just out for a minute, everyone. It's very grave, and she's delirious. They've used everything they know. The magical cap is in place on her shaved head and the split pigeon carcasses have been placed at her feet. Spotted fever they've decided, though what it is hardly matters now. I'm going right back in after they bleed her again. Frances, come over here with me."

He led her back into the first drawing room and closed them away from the eyes of the others. It was very dim in there but he looked bleary eyed. His face seemed creased with lines though he was but thirty-three, and in the candleglow she noted that his once coal black hair was silvered.

"I am sorry, sire, sorry for the queen and you."

"I know you are, my dear. Probably one of the few. Everyone else would no doubt be happy enough to have a more lighthearted queen, one without a foreign accent and different ways."

She could feel her heart beat and realized she had been holding her breath as he spoke.

"I appreciate your concern, Frances, but I really asked you here just to reassure you," he went on.

"Reassure me? But, sire, I believe you need the comforting."

"Then hold me, love, hold me."

She stepped into the waiting circle of his arms and stroked his back as she would a child's—a tall, powerful child, she told herself. She knew he would say more, that his thoughts were not complete.

"By reassure you, Frances, I mean whatever happens to Catherine in her struggle, we shall still be together."

When she stiffened in his embrace but did not answer, he went on, "By that I'm saying if she lives, nothing is changed, though I shall do my best to give her of my time and care for her recovery. And, if she passes, you may then with an easy heart either be my mistress or maybe more, but I am too distraught to think on that now."

She ignored the last dangerous implications and focused on his other meaning. "An easy heart. How could that be, sire?"

"Because," he said and set her back from him with both hands heavy on her shoulders, "your argument that I am a married man would be of no import. Even though you are a virgin, you would agree to bed with a man you loved had he no wife, I take it."

She wondered fleetingly if he could have heard about her and Richmond; but no, that was her own guilty conscience and not what he meant at all. Her eyes wavered away from his intense gaze.

"As you say, sire, we are too tired to speak of it now."

"You too, Frances? Have the scandal purveyors been at you these three days then?"

She countered with her own question. "Was Her Majesty truly with child, sire, and then perhaps the grief of that loss made her prey to all this?"

He sank onto the edge of the green satin chair behind him, still holding her hand and sighed. "I think there was no child, Frances, but the one her mind desired so desperately, poor dear thing."

"I am sorry."

"I too. I too. And now I've got to go back in as the doctors should be done with their damned leeches. I don't like doctors. Frankly, I don't think they know what the hell they're doing half the time but there's naught else, I suppose, but to trust them. I just pray none of this is retribution on me."

"But you can't mean that. Of course, it isn't!"

His long arms encircled her hips, and he pressed his head to her flat belly. "Damn, Frances, but you're sweet as honey when you want to be and so good for me. If only you'd let me really show you how much I care."

"This—heavens, it's hardly the time, sire. The queen needs you."

He grasped her to him a minute more and then stood abruptly releasing her. She was right. He had to go back in now. He hadn't slept in three days, hadn't been this exhausted since after the Battle of Worcester where he'd even slept in an oak tree for a few hours while fleeing the enemy. Od's fish, but his mind was wandering. He had to go back in.

"Don't bother to wait outside with the vultures, Frances," he heard himself tell her. "I'll send for you again if there's anything to say."

He walked back toward the queen's bedchamber without looking at her again. Damn, but why could he so seldom tell what she was thinking when women were usually so easy to read? He wasn't even certain she really loved him, really would submit to him even if he were unmarried for a while. If Catherine did die . . . he would love to have Frances Stewart permanently, securely, as his wife waiting for him every night in his own bed, but he needed funding so much and she had no dowry. His throne needed another rich dynastic marriage as much as his heart and body needed Frances Stewart.

He ignored the others in the second drawing room and went back into the sickroom. The mingled stench of herbs, potions, sea-coal fire, and pigeon carcasses assailed his flared nostrils. It took a moment for his eyes to adjust to the dimness under the huge bed canopy. He leaned over the queen and stared down.

Catherine looked waxlike, a funeral effigy already, only her poor shaved head was tightly bound with the royal physicians' version of a magic nightcap. A heavily jeweled crucifix had been placed in one limp hand at her request. Her form seemed very slight on the big bed he had often shared with her; she was almost not there at all except for where the coverlet bulged up at her feet because they had bound the pigeons to her.

"You took more blood?" he whispered to the four doctors.

"Yes, sire," one said. "It seemed to arouse her a bit. Now we must wait again."

"Step back then, all of you, and let her be. I shall sit here. Now that you've done your worst, sirs, and she's had extreme unction from her priests, I alone shall see to her for a while. And, Od's fish, air this chamber a bit or the rest of us will be sick of fever soon enough too!"

The purple-garbed doctors moved away with hushed whispers and someone across the room waved a little air in by opening and closing the door to the drawing room several times. He had sent her priests away earlier, afraid their presence would make her believe she was near death if she awoke in one of her more lucid moments free of delirium, afraid the word would spread the Anglican king kept Catholic priests near in time of crisis.

He sat staring at her, even beyond her for a very long time while his mind drifted. He ordered the

280

hovering physicians away again when they approached with their white hellebore root to make her sneeze and their plasters of Burgundy pitch for her feet. He would have pulled that ludicrous tight cap from her shaved head and flung the pigeon carcasses off her feet himself, but he did not wish to disturb her sleep however increasingly restless it appeared to be now.

She moaned almost imperceptibly, and he rose from his chair to lean closer over her. The blotches on her face, from which spotted fever took its name, seemed to blur as he gazed hard at her. Had she said his name?

Her bluish eyelids twitched and slitted open. "Charles?"

"I am here, my Catherine. I am here."

Her eyes flew wide, darted to both sides, then returned, but hardly focused on him.

"The doctors said—everyone says," she whispered, her voice rough, "it is a son, but I am afraid he is ugly."

His pulse pounded. Had he heard aright? "You must rest now, my dearest, rest and get better."

"May I not see him? Your heir—he is not ugly, is he?"

He could barely speak. He could not even swallow. "No, no, of course not," he rasped. "It is a very pretty boy."

The cracked lips they had anointed with marigold balm tried to smile. "Then, if it be like you, it is a fine boy indeed and I would be greatly pleased with it."

Tears blinded him and he heard one plop on the brocade coverlet they had pulled up under her arms.

"Catherine." He knew his voice trembled, his voice that hadn't trembled since his chaplain, Stephen Goffe, had come into his room that cold winter day to tell him his father had been beheaded and he was king. He ignored the doctors who had pressed forward to lean close when she had spoken. "Catherine," he managed, and her fever-bright eyes lifted slightly. "Recover, please, for my sake. Please. Please, live."

She moaned and closed her eyes, but at last her breathing was deep and even. He sat staring again, his mind tormenting him with guilt he fought to exorcise. If he gave up Barbara's body, gave up pursuit of Frances, and only clung to Catherine, maybe there could be a child. But no, no. That was a moment's whim, a twist of conscience he would only renounce later. He was a man of politics and science, more practical than one who believed he could bargain with God. Besides, he knew himself utterly too well to know he would never keep such a bargain. He could give up Barbara's ready favors easily enough, but only if he finally possessed Frances Stewart as his mistress.

And so he sat in a mindless stupor, only aroused when he needed to order the physicians, intent on imposing some new, wretched cure they had concocted, away from his queen. He gave her watered wine himself and guarded her until dawn seeped into the room again. Then, when she still slept heavily and he fancied her fever spots were fading, he went out to breathe fresh air, and eat, and send for Frances Stewart.

Chapter Ten

George Villiers, duke of Buckingham sat with his feet up on the table in his cousin Barbara's elegant dressing room, eating imported quinces and spitting the seeds noisily into a porcelain dish.

"Really, George, you do have some disgusting habits," Barbara chided from across the room where she posed and turned to survey herself in the full-length mirror. She was impeccably attired for the small private supper she was giving for the king in a quarter-hour and everything had to be just perfect. She was certain she looked her most seductive, it being five months since her last child had been born. At least, there had been no sign of another pregnancy yet, even though the king was still at her several times a week.

"*I* have disgusting habits?" Buckingham was saying. "Best not throw stones, as much as I know about your, ah—appetites, my lady."

"Pooh. I still have the king and others I favor too and no one's the wiser."

"We've been over this before, madame. You do not have the king. He has you, and that's not quite good enough. You need his heart back, such as it is, and unless we topple little Stewart off her virginal pedestal and bring her down to your level, you haven't a chance in Hades!"

Barbara flounced over to him, hands on hips, then shoved his legs off her polished tabletop. "Get your feet off my expensive parquet! 'Bring her down to my level?' You vile oaf! You bastard!"

Buckingham grinned maddeningly at her, re-crossed his legs on the floor, and took another quince. "Shut your pretty mouth, Barbara. Save it for dinner chatter for the king tonight. You know I'm right. We've tried every civilized means these past several months to get Frances in his bed and failed. Luckily, the king just hasn't caught on because he can't fathom we'd want Frances to give in to him. Then too, I think Frances almost believes you're her friend now."

"I doubt it. Richmond probably tells her otherwise. He has her ear, you know."

"I know, but I think it's all he has since he acts as beleaguered as the king does near her. Her chasteness and naïveté intact in a court like this for almost two years—zounds!" He laughed half to himself while she continued to glare down at his blond head.

"But not after tonight," she put in grimly.

He stopped chuckling. "No—this should work, but the king harbors some strange streak of protective honor toward her which I've never seen him exhibit but to his queen."

"Gad, at least we made it through that spotted

fever mess unscathed," she said. "Rumors were rampant he would have married Frances if Catherine had died."

"But Catherine didn't die, and I doubt if Charles would have married our little vestal virgin anyway. He needs a continual flow of currency and Frances has nothing to offer there. She might have condescended to bed with him between queens though, and once she's committed, I think we've got her and he'll start to view her more like any pretty lady he desires and can have."

"Let's get the powder out, my lord. I want to look at it again."

"Sit down, Barbara, and just leave things as they are. The powder, the pewter goblet, and the Anguelle wine are all ready, but you're not to be fussing or gloating over it. And it's nothing to brag about afterward or we're doomed."

She stood still across from him, unwilling to sit and wrinkle the jade green-and-white striped skirt her maids had slaved over so long this afternoon. The table for eight in the drawing room was set, the splendid meal was ready, only she was so jumpy over this plan. Damn, but this idea just had to work if only the king would drink enough, if only his frustrated passions for Frances could be inflamed when he saw her offered to him all ready and unprotesting like that. . . .

"What did you say, my lord?"

"I said, if our so-called Committee to Get Mistress Stewart for the King knew of this idea, they'd probably jump ship. Arlington's a coward when it comes to anything that smacks of plot as he's so damned ambitious for himself."

"I know. He even thought we'd gone daft by trying to lure the king away from Frances with that tempting little Jennings wench we brought in and set up under his nose. His Majesty was willing enough to tumble the pretty slut until that selfish, spoiled Stewart gave him the absolute cold shoulder and he sent Jennings away. But this, I'm certain, will work. I'll have Frances drowsy and ready by the time you set him up."

"Royal irony or something like that," Buckingham mused more to himself than her. "Imagine seducing the royal stallion into thinking he's seducing a maiden."

He stood up and threw the last half-eaten quince into the sea-coal fire and watched sparks fly. It was a mild enough February and soon it would be decent riding weather again. He did not move even when he heard Barbara's maids call to her and she hurried out to greet the first guests. It wouldn't be the king and Frances anyway. The king always arrived last. Zounds! If it hadn't been so blasted boring this winter, especially since New Year's when the queen had fully recovered, he would never have hatched this elaborate, delicate scheme. In truth, he'd much rather be bedding the little icicle maiden himself than handing her over to the king, but at least it would be an amusing evening, and if the king would finish with her and give her back while she still was half-unconscious—well, who knew what the hell could happen?

Buckingham stretched, looking in the mirror to smooth the new periwig he'd taken to wearing last month when the king adopted them to hide his increasing gray, and went out to see who had arrived.

"My Lord Lauderdale and lovely wife," Buckingham greeted the powerful John Maitland and his Duchess Bess. Both of them were flaming redheads. Bess's body had gone a little thick of late, but she was still alluring, tremendously endowed with large, sensitive breasts as a great many men at court including Buckingham were fully aware.

"And how is the Lauderdale royal court at Ham House?" Buckingham asked and winked surreptitiously at Bess. "Still entertaining there in a style to rival Whitehall, I don't doubt."

Bess Maitland's laugh was like jangling chimes. "Of course, you truant rascal. You're welcome anytime, you know. Bring your duchess for a visit."

"Mary is much at her family home Nun Appleton with the Fairfaxes lately. London in winter never did please her, but perhaps Barbara and I shall visit soon."

He turned with Barbara to greet Henry Bennet, Lord Arlington, and the rich Dutch wife he'd married in exile. Arlington, who wore a blatant nose patch over his war wound, was a little too stiffly moral for Buckingham's taste, but he was ambitious too—enough to be obsessed with the idea of someday replacing their common enemy Edward Hyde, Lord Clarendon, as Lord Chancellor, and therein lay the ties that bound Arlington in any sort of plan to please the king.

When Buckingham saw His Majesty, Frances on his arm, behind the Bennets at the door, he reached for Barbara's arm to give her a warning shake.

Barbara and Frances were in gowns strikingly similar in color and cut, even to the newly fashionable striped skirts, and he couldn't allow one of Barbara's little snits over imagined insults tonight.

"Sire. Frances," he began, relieved Barbara only swept a curtsy and held her tongue. "You look beautiful."

"Do I Buckingham?" the king goaded, even as eyes went over Barbara. "You dog, I never thought you'd notice."

Everyone laughed at the king's silly gibe. Frances flipped her fan open and eyed Barbara's garb playfully over the top of it. "We do have different jewels and fans, Barbara, and the greens are varied hues. Heavens, let's just say," she whispered to Barbara, her eyes wide, "that we have excellent taste and let it go at that for now."

"Od's fish," the king remarked, "Frances is the best politician I've seen in years. Arlington, Lauderdale, pay attention here—compromise, compliments, and a sweet smile. Let's see if that works for a foreign policy, if you please."

"I believe, sire, the Hollanders and the French would eat us up like little fish if we carried on thus," Arlington said almost condescendingly as he took a glass of Canary wine from the steward's silver tray.

"And the Scots would not be long to rebel," Lauderdale put in.

"The Scots, my lord, are ruffians at heart with small purses and long Presbyterian noses they like to stick in other people's business," the king said vehemently as he lifted his glass to Frances and drank. "The only Scots I can abide at all are you,

Lauderdale, and of course, Richmond."

"But, I vow, I have as good Scottish blood in my veins as they, Your Majesty," Frances told him, surprised at how her long-stifled Scottish pride rose up at their words. "Have I been brought here this evening to be told I'm to be sent packing for the Scottish borders then or some such?"

Buckingham was so amused at the king's sputtered apology that he elbowed Barbara and jolted a drop of Canary on her gown. She glared at him as she brushed at the offending stain and tried to overhear what His Majesty was telling Frances.

"You know I didn't mean you, my sweet. I was speaking of Scottish *men*. And you are the exception of all exceptions when it comes to Scots. Scots are rebels at heart, that's all, and treated me abysmally when I was there during the wars."

"If you knew a few more intimately, sire, perhaps you would not feel that way," Frances soothed.

He took another sip of wine and lowered his voice even more. "If I knew you more intimately, sweet Frances, we could discuss this further, but for now, you, Arlington, and Richmond are as far as I go on trusting Scots, and Richmond even has his dangerous moments, doesn't he, dear?"

She could feel her pulse quicken, and she prayed she would not blush. "Why? What's he done?"

"Only made a bit of a pest of himself as far as I'm concerned, ingratiating himself with you when I let him near you. But he's kept busy enough, he knows his place, and in general seems to be more enamored of yachts and farming than ladies lately, so enough said of him for now."

At supper, she sat smiling on the king's right hand next to the ever-watchful Buckingham. That talk of Richmond—a thin veiled warning it was, really—had taken her entirely unaware. She must be much more careful, even perhaps mention something to Richmond. Of course, she had been spending more and more time with him—little walks, stolen kisses. No doubt, she was beginning to rely on him entirely too much; but he had been such a gentleman lately, although she knew she had begun to lower her guard again. She had danced with him and somewhat encouraged his attentions; she had smiled at and hardly protested his outrageous flattery, and she had even kept a few of his latest little gifts. Now, all that must stop.

Thank heavens, the conversation over the first course of the meal had turned to Parliamentary politics, the looming Dutch War over trade competition, and fashion. Wine flowed more freely than Frances had ever seen Barbara serve it before, even for the king, and the Venus oysters and little buttered scallops slid down smoothly. Fricassees and grilled carbonadoes accompanied a delicately herbed side of lamb, one more main dish than Barbara usually offered at supper parties.

But then other things had changed recently too, Frances mused. Barbara was increasingly kind, even if condescendingly so. A few months ago this similar gown incident would have occasioned a raving fit, but even now she was smiling across the table at her. Frances hoped fervently that Buckingham or the king had talked her into peaceful coexistence, but just in case, she must be very careful.

"The meal is wonderful, Barbara," Frances told her. "I vow, I always learn something by studying your fine table closely. These tarts are a marvel."

Barbara's mouth smiled, but the expression failed to light her dark brown eyes. "Just bananas, dear Frances. Gads, though they're as new as chocolate and as fashionable as our dress stripes and face patches, they are outrageously expensive, that's flat. Do you like them, sire? My cook purchased them from Thomas Johnson's import shop on Snow Hill."

"Delectable, Barbara, everything is," King Charles said and lifted his newly filled goblet of Canary to her with a flourish which evidently pleased her enough to quiet her for several more minutes while the men began to argue foreign policy over their almonds and cheese.

When they were sufficiently sated, the table was cleared and they played one-and-twenty and putt where the Villiers cousins seemed to hold all the honor cards. The wine still flowed with uncharacteristic bounty, but the beautifully painted cards bearing the ornately gilded kings' and queens' heads began to bore Frances. It had been an amazingly enjoyable and calm evening for one spent with Barbara and Buckingham, but she hoped the king would soon decide to leave. That would mean, of course, she'd have to wake up enough to fend off his predictable, erotic assault, but she was very adept at handling that now.

"Trey and deuce is all that I have," Frances moaned dramatically and threw down her cards. "Heavens, you and I would have won sure, my Lord

Arlington, if I'd only had the king in my hand!"

She realized what she'd said only when they all began to laugh—all but Barbara who looked merely thoughtful. The king was grinning ear to ear and she knew his lack of public rejoinder was only to humor her fears for her reputation, which he would be only too happy to destroy when he took her upstairs shortly. At least, Frances thought, after that little amusement, the long evening seemed to be over.

Buckingham was bidding the Maitlands and Bennets farewell at the door. "Are we not leaving, sire?" she asked.

"Yes, love, directly," he whispered low. "His lordship says he has a favor to ask, it seems."

"Oh dear."

"Are you so anxious for what's coming then, Frances?" he teased, and his black moustache and brows lifted when he smiled down at her surprised expression. "I relish delight and wild anticipation unconcealed."

Frances glanced around the elegant foyer and stepped into the drawing room when Buckingham came back in. Strange for Barbara to disappear with the king yet here, she thought. The bedroom door beyond stood ajar. Surely, the favor Buckingham would ask had nothing to do with the king staying to go into Barbara's open bedroom.

Frances turned to go back out with the men, but Barbara appeared, fully garbed, thank heavens, in the doorway. "Gads, Frances, there you are. I think the men have business for a moment. Come here, won't you? I want to show you something."

Frances had only been in the Countess of Castlemaine's highly touted *boudoir* once before when Barbara had been receiving visitors grandly from her bed back when she was merely Madame Palmer. Frances knew many other court ladies spoke of the chamber's flamboyant luxury, but she had never felt the slightest interest in seeing it.

Now she paused in the doorway to take it all in. The bed was monstrously exotic with flying cupids trailing swathes of silk and clusters of ribbons. The other furnishings were carved and gilded or inlaid French pieces, no doubt wildly extravagant in price as well as style. The walls were walnut paneled and inset with painted rectangles framing French wallpaper; a portrait of Barbara reclining nude as the goddess Venus graced the outside wall. The carpet was a deep, bold flowered print.

"I see you have not yet striped the walls or floor, Barbara."

What looked to be rage for a moment fired in Castlemaine's brown eyes and then faded to mere embers. "Gads, Frances, don't goad me. I admit you manage to get the styles from the king's sister Henriette-Anne and pass them on at court. Now if you'd only condescend to wear the face patches like everyone else— Well, never mind. Come over here, will you? Speaking of French influence, I bought some very new, expensive Bordeaux wine I want you to try. If you like it, I'll pour some for the men too."

Frances advanced into the room halfway feeling almost wary. "Thank you, but I had so much already at dinner. Your wine steward really outdid himself."

"One of my two cooks orders the wine. My cooks are a wonder. Here, please, just try some since you've had wines at Louis' court and tell me what you think."

Frances walked over to her and took the pewter goblet. "They say wine is always better in crystal, Barbara," she protested mildly.

"They say—" Barbara began testily, but checked herself. "Not this sort, Frances. It's called Anguelle. Gads, go on and tell me what you think of it."

Frances took a long sip, then another. "It is good, but I remember it being sweeter. This has a bitter tang."

"Oh, I hope not. Are you sure? Maybe it shouldn't be in pewter after all."

"No, it's all right. Let me see the bottle." She took another sip and held it in her mouth while Barbara lifted the bottle. Frances started to read the French words on the label but the lines moved and shifted halfway down. Her head felt light. She sat quickly in the nearest chair along the table.

"Heavens, I've had too much wine tonight. It happened at Monmouth's wedding with champagne," she managed but her own voice sounded very far away. She saw Barbara's blurred face peering at her, very close. She did not resist when someone raised her goblet to her lips and told her to drink the rest. Then a black velvet curtain descended.

Frances tried to pull herself upward from the soft black depths, tried to open her eyes. Her legs and arms felt so heavy—or was she floating? No, everything must be all right. She knew she was being undressed, so she must be in her own rooms and Gillie was seeing to her. It was a woman's hands on her but why was Gillie so rushed and so awkward at this?

She tried to cover herself up at the sound of the man's voice so near. The king—had he come to put her to bed again? Why, why could it not be Richmond . . . Richmond, maybe it was Richmond. They were on the yacht. The river was rocking, rocking and his hands were on her naked breasts.

"George, you greedy bastard," a female voice hissed. "If the king asks if you've touched her or seen her this way, he'll have your head if he thinks you're lying."

"I suppose, but what he doesn't know won't hurt him. Maybe later. She is exquisite. I'll get her upstairs before he barges in here. Go on out and detain him. And reassure him. He looked like a fish wanting the bait, but I'm not sure he's taken the hook yet."

The words flew by and Frances could not grasp their meaning. She wanted to just surrender to sleep. She was being lifted, carried over someone's shoulder. The person's shoulder pressed into her stomach and she thought she might be sick.

"No, sire, put me down," she cried out, but evidently no one heard her.

Steps, steps up. A knock on a door jarred her. Another man's voice. "My Lord Buckingham, what in hell are you doing on His Majesty's privy staircase? Where is he?"

Buckingham, Buckingham was here somewhere, she thought. She tried to clear her brain, tried to kick but she was wrapped in something long and silky.

"Is that who I think it is, my Lord Buckingham?" the new voice went on.

"Never mind, Prodgers. His Majesty will be right down and he'll be expecting the lady waiting in his bed. She's a little dizzy from too much wine. Zounds, don't gawk. Give me a hand here."

She stretched out where they put her on the yacht, and the voices went away. The sheets here were smoothest, cool satin like the wind on the river. She slept.

"Frances. Frances!" Hands were on her bare shoulders. Hands pulled the coverlet gently from her to bare her skin to cool air. She tried to push the hands away. "Frances, it's Charles. I'm here, love."

She sighed and fought to raise her heavy arms to return the embrace of skillful, darting hands. It was Richmond. They were on the yacht and Richmond had come to love her. "Charles. Charles," she repeated.

"Are you all right, Frances? I know you had a good deal of wine, but I can't believe this. I want to but I cannot believe it all."

Richmond's hands had unwrapped the silk robe and she let him. His mouth dipped warm and wet to harden a soft nipple and then a hand reached low to cup and fondle a soft buttock. "You do love your Charles, Frances. I've wanted this so, but I can hardly believe Barbara and Buckingham would help you surprise me like this."

Barbara. Buckingham. Why would they be on the yacht? She made a desperate effort to tear the dark clouds away from her mind even as Richmond's mouth fluttered little bites and kisses across her soft belly then lifted to the other nipple. In the candle-light, Richmond's hair looked so very, very black.

Why ever did he look so much like the king?

"No."

"What, darling? Just relax. We've both had entirely too much wine but, I swear, the sight of you like this in my bed has jolted me stone sober. I should have known you would want it to be here in my bed the first time. We'll threaten Barbara and Buckingham with their lives and keep this our secret, my love, my love."

She grasped his wrist, trying to dig her nails in to stop him, but she had no strength. With one hand he was stripping off his upper garments while the other did strange, drugging things to her where her legs joined. Drugs, drugs, the wine. She made a great effort to pull her legs together where she trapped his hand.

"Let me, Frances, let me. For what else did you undress and hurry down here like this? Buckingham explained, my dear. Just let my fingers in a little and then we'll both be ready."

"No!" She managed to swing her arm in a futile arc to push him away. "Buckingham. He lied."

His frenzied caresses froze. "I don't believe that. I don't want to believe that, but, 'sdeath, my darling, you're more than tipsy, aren't you?"

His fingers still between her thighs, he lifted one of her eyelids with his other hand.

"Don't!"

"Oh, Frances, damn it! Damn it! I will have their heads, I swear it!"

She tried to sit up, and he pulled her, cradled her, against him on his lap. He was swearing a long string of terrible oaths. He wore breeches and boothose still ribboned, but his darkly furred chest and arms were bare. She stared appalled at her own white nakedness across his brown velvet lap. She shuddered. Her legs and arms would not obey; her head ached miserably.

"Please, no."

"I won't, I won't, love. Not now, damn it. 'Sblood, but I've got to get you back upstairs and see to them before everyone knows. You'd hate me then, love, I know, but I can't grasp why they did this. I'm no lecher, Frances, never have forced myself on a sedated or drunk woman, hardly needed seduction let alone rape. You'll want me too. It won't be—can't be—long now after this."

"I'm—not drunk. Just don't—"

He sighed so hard his breath stirred her tousled hair. She tried to speak again. He was stroking her whole side from swell of breast over ribs to hip and thigh as if she were a sleek white cat like Perth or Aberdeen.

"Please, sire."

"I know. I know. You're so beautiful, Frances, so lovely like this. In five fast minutes with very little fuss, I could put you down and change our lives forever, but I can't—can't lose you over some vile Villiers trick. You'll remember much of this in the morning, I'm afraid. Here, my love, I'm going to carry you upstairs and then get your clothes from that bitch Barbara and that damned amoral Buckingham who are about to wish they'd never come back from exile to England at all!"

He stood and leaned over her another endless moment while his black eyes went up and down her limp, helpless length. She tried to watch him don his shirt and waistcoat, but her eyes were so heavy lidded again. She had called him Charles. Had she called him Richmond too?

The tight press of silk felt good around her body, but his arms were trembling as he lifted her.

The spring of 1664 was warm and beautiful, but then this fresh morning might not be so grand, Frances thought. This was the day Buckingham was allowed to come back to court after his three-month exile with his wife at his country estate Nun Appleton, and Barbara, whose banishment had only lasted a too-brief month after the Villiers' aborted plot to have the king bed Frances, was hinting at some sort of fine welcome for her wayward cousin.

Barbara had professed to all the world that she had merely opted for a month's respite from court at the home of her uncle, Sir Edward Villiers, but court gossipmongers knew something was afoot. As for Buckingham, the king gave out he was banished for dueling with the husband of his current mistress, Anna Maria, countess of Shrewsbury, a true enough fact and a timely enough excuse, as the king was adamant about stamping out the dubious practice where men important to his realm maimed or killed each other in politely arranged meetings at rural Knightsbridge or Marylebone Fields.

Barbara, countess of Castlemaine, unfortunately, was hitting her stride again as the imperious termagant of Whitehall Palace. After all, she was once more with child again, and though King

Charles was still foot dragging over proclaiming her third son Henry as his own, he evidently knew the way he had welcomed a momentarily subdued, recalcitrant Castlemaine back to court had produced this pregnancy. Frances gave her yellow plumed hat a toss as she strolled with the king, Barbara, and numerous courtiers, including Richmond whom she had tried desperately to avoid lately because she not only feared she would blurt out to him what had happened the night Buckingham and Castlemaine had drugged her, but she knew only too well that she was weak enough to want him to do what, thank heavens, the king had not. To make matters worse, today Richmond seemed to be dallying with some pretty, new little twit the Duchess of York had hauled in from the country, probably because he knew full well any time he paid the slightest heed to another lady, Frances Stewart was upset. Damn the cad, not this time, she told herself fiercely, not ever again!

"Sire, I just know you and George will make it all up and be fast friends again," Frances heard Barbara drawl to the king in her most annoying, coaxing tones. Lately, Frances and Barbara were icily, assiduously polite to each other within their monarch's earshot as he hated quarreling and had scolded them both for it since Barbara's return.

"That remains to be seen, madame," the king told Barbara low. "I don't approve of dueling—or drugging."

Frances's elegantly coiffed head, its curls tumbled in the best fashion *à la négligence* under her pert, cocked hat, swiveled to the king. "Please, sire. I vow, you said we'd never speak of—dueling."

"We aren't speaking of it, my dear. I just want Barbara to tell that associate of hers to steer clear as I haven't forgiven him. He's always been a clever rogue, but he needs a taut rein. You know," he said and stopped his quick pace as others clustered around him in a growing ring, "the daring bastard had a warrant out on his head almost as big as mine after our defeat at Worcester during the war."

Frances watched the hard, angular lines of the king's face soften as they so often did when he recounted his exploits or sang the old Royalist battle songs. Sometimes, though it really made no sense, she was almost certain his years of exile had been indeed happy for him, at least remembered from this distance. She saw Richmond move into the circle directly in her view, his green eyes on her even as he listened to the king.

"The Roundhead armies were searching every nook and cranny for me and my Royalist leaders and Buckingham—Od's fish—Buckingham was right under their Puritan noses giving public performances on an open-air stage here in London at Charing Cross!"

Everyone roared with laughter, His Majesty the loudest of all. "He wore some ludicrous coat and hat to hide his distinctive blond head and daubed his face with flour or some such and sang ballads right under their damned, out-of-joint noses and spied on them until he could join me in France again," he concluded. Everyone was staring, guffawing; even common folk using the footpath through Whitehall had come over to hear the riotous tale. Oblivious to the hundreds of staring eyes, when the king's laughter subsided, he took both Frances' and Barbara's arms and walked on.

"You see, ladies, I am a man who can forgive, but I won't abide disobedience or treachery. Remember that, Barbara, and remind dear George when you see him."

"I hope, sire, you do not just lecture me. Gads, what about your little Frances here?"

The king turned to Frances. He smiled down at her, his slaty gaze caressing his pearls on her throat, her nearly bare shoulders, and the periwinkle blue satin bodice. "Frances doesn't have treachery in so much as a little finger, do you, love?" he asked low.

She fluttered her fan and thought of Richmond whose stare she could feel on her from somewhere behind. "I am human, sire."

"But when it comes to human passion, Frances— well, enough of that for now. This is not the time or place. Anyway, that's why I am pleased to see you and Barbara getting on. I don't like rebellion and I don't like fuss."

"Pooh! Good hearty arguments, you mean, sire," Barbara put in and smiled up at him. "Now let's see this great surprise the Chevalier de Grammont has given you, which we've all trooped out here to gape at."

The crowd funneled out of the Privy Gardens through the narrow, arched King Street Gate and onto the fringe of St. James's Park. "It's not a coach-and-four, ladies. It's French and we do manage to get some of the loveliest things from Louis' court, though I hate to admit it." One hand briefly caressed Frances' slender waist as he raised his other and, with

302

a carved walking stick, pointed. "Over there beyond the elms—a calash with windows of glass."

Everyone hurried over to surround the tiny, elegant carriage murmuring at its rare features. Two low wheels sported elegantly detailed paint and gilt; swept-up footboards boasted a whole mythological scene of nymphs and satyrs at play. The upholstery was softest black leather wonderfully stitched and ribbed, and the single horse to pull it was a green-plumed ebony beauty. But the crowning touches were the side windows of clearest glass, the first of their kind in England, the king boasted, as if he had made them himself. Even though she could peer into the calash's interior, Frances could see her reflection perfectly in the glass with the dark trees behind at the same time, and she just knew it would go like the wind.

"Zounds, you can hardly take us both for a spin around the park," Barbara was saying. "There's only room for two in it."

"The queen and Duchess of York have had it out this morning," the king said as if he hadn't heard her. "Later perhaps we'll have a ride. I'm due at the Guildhall for that blasted speech at one."

"Then, may I not borrow it for the afternoon?" Barbara pursued.

Suddenly, Frances pictured Barbara greeting the returned Buckingham in the king's fine, new gift just as though they had never lied to her, tricked her, used her, and made a fool of her by delivering her to the king's bed. She worried about facing Buckingham even more than she had the king after she knew they had both surely seen her as naked as she was born.

The thought of that wretch and this simpering woman polluting this lovely little calash made her furious.

"But, Your Majesty," she heard herself interrupt before he could respond to Barbara's request, "I was going to ask you the very same favor. I would just adore having it for the afternoon." She put her hand imploringly on his brocade arm and smiled winsomely up at him.

"The two of you could go together or take turns then," he said, his eyes assessing Frances' eager face and all too obviously surprised she had asked him for a favor.

"No, we couldn't possibly do that, could we, Frances?" Barbara said, warming to the challenge, her dark brown eyes catlike slits.

"No, sire, if you please. I thought I'd take my mother for a turn and I'm certain Madame Palmer has someone special in mind to ride with, don't you, Barbara?"

Despite his annoyance at this tense development, the king grinned at Frances' blatant use of Barbara's old name. Frances always fought much more subtly than Barbara, and she obviously had her hackles up over this. If it hadn't been in public, he'd like to see what letting Frances have the calash would get him, but since he abhorred one of Barbara's public tantrums and was in a hurry now—Od's fish—it was too bad, but then Frances surely had the sweeter temper and would back off here.

"Barbara did ask first, Frances. You may have it all day tomorrow. I'll go out with you if you'd like. Let's head back in. 'Sdeath, but we've got a big crowd here."

Frances had a nearly overwhelming desire to rake Barbara's smug, contemptuous face, but instead she shook off the king's touch.

"No thank you, sire. I'd like it this afternoon, to myself, or not at all!"

"Pooh, you silly little ninny. Can't stand to be beaten at anything but won't return favors either," Barbara taunted much too loudly.

The courtiers clustered around now hushed, to hear the exchange. It was a rare theatrical treat to see the usually aloof Mrs. Stewart take on the king's vitriolic mistress. Frances felt herself blush as she caught Richmond's warning glare over someone's shoulder.

"Now, ladies, let's go back and discuss it further inside," the king said low.

"I won't," Barbara screeched. "Tell her clearly it's mine. You said it's mine. Gads, I'm most like to miscarry this child if I don't get that calash, I am certain of that!"

"And I, Madame Palmer," Frances intoned icily, "will not ever, ever be in the possible circumstance of miscarrying a king's child if I don't get that calash, and I am certain of that!"

There were several gasps, one the king's, Frances thought. He looked absolutely furious, and his hand gripped his walking stick so hard his big knuckles went stark white. All three of them stood there like suspended statues on center stage for one long moment.

"Barbara," His Majesty hissed low at last as everyone pressed in to hear, "since you insist on publicly announcing you are with child, you remind me of my duty. I have heard some ladies sadly do miscarry in riding carriages, not that they don't. For the sake of your unborn child, Frances gets the calash and you will come in with me."

He turned his back on Barbara's sputtering rage and handed Frances up immediately into the calash. His voice was angry, but controlled. "And you, my dear, since you like to advertise you do not sleep with me and may never do so had better realize you're a grown woman now and are likely to be treated as such. Only a little while around the park now. I will see you later."

She didn't dare falter as the king turned away dragging Barbara along. The crowd hurried after him but for a few who stared. Even Richmond was walking quickly now, though he wasn't headed toward the palace. She held her head up, took the reins, and lifted the delicate whip from its holder. With one flap of reins she was off alone, heading for the park.

The whole area, blessedly, was not crowded: too early, she thought, for the fops to be out displaying their current mistresses. Several people she knew called out to her, and a few she did not recognize. She smiled and nodded. By the second time around the whole perimeter, she had calmed herself enough to enjoy the marvelous vehicle and elegant horse. As she turned south under the tall elms just beyond where the crowd had been before, a man stepped out from behind a tree ahead and waved her down. It was Richmond, tall and rugged, looking more a brigand or marauding ruffian than a courtier despite his elegant rust-hued breeches and waistcoat. She reined in as he came closer; with one hand he patted the horse's smooth flank.

"Am I to be robbed by a St. James's Robin Hood who hides behind trees, my lord?" she called out.

"Could be, my beautiful lady, but I must warn you I'm after more than jewels or coins. Besides, after that display of temper I witnessed earlier and with that deadly whip I see poised in your hand right now, I wouldn't dare climb in with you unless asked. And where is your poor, dear mother who needed the carriage ride so desperately this afternoon?"

"You scoundrel. Don't you dare climb up here. We'll be seen and I've got to go back now."

"But you're headed down Birdcage Walk away from the palace, sweet lass, so I think I'll just come along."

Panicked, she tried to bar him with the whip as he clambered up, but he only took it easily from her grasp as if she had offered it.

"We can't," she protested again. "Someone will tell him."

"I see. You really are his property now, a crown possession, just like his pretty calash then."

"You have no right to say that. I am not his property! You're the one always warning me to be careful."

"I know, but you've about driven me to the brink with longing to be alone with you. Besides, if you head that plumed creature out the lane towards Knightsbridge, no one from the palace will see us. You can handle this one horse and tiny carriage outside the narrow lanes here at St. James's, can't

307

you, Frances?''

She moved them out with such a great jerk of the carriage, he was thrown back into the seat and tipped his broad-brimmed, red-plumed hat into his lap.

They didn't speak until they had started up Constitution Hill to cross the Tyburn, but she knew he was studying her. He sat casually at ease in the elegant little calash as only he could: his body was slightly turned to her and one arm stretched behind her on the back of the seat while his other ran the entire length of side window. Even the smallest jolt bounced his hip and thigh into her skirts and he made no effort to move more to his side of the seat. His posture of assumed intimacy made her dart him a narrow-eyed glance.

"I vow, I'm sure you're regretful there isn't room for three here, Richmond. Then I could cart you along *and* that little what's-her-name you've been dragging all over.''

"Jealous?"

"Don't be absurd!''

"Maybe I'm just squiring little what's-her-name around a bit so it doesn't look like I'm mooning over you. You said His Majesty had noted my ardent looks your way.''

"Yes, he has. Buckingham said something more than once about it too.''

"Marvelous. Are you suggesting then, Frances, I may call on you more openly than the secret, brief little trysts you've allowed lately—that is before this new campaign you've had to hold me at a greater distance. I don't have years and years to spend until you not only realize you are attracted to me, but love

308

me too, and want to be mine legally as well as physically. Now, don't protest as this is a very open carriage and someone might notice if we sprawled along this seat. I was hoping at first the king would find someone else or tire of you, but I must have been insane. In his bed or out, it's just not likely to happen that he'll send you away."

"I haven't been in his bed!" she shrilled before she remembered she really had been, but Richmond would never believe that wild story or else he'd talk of gambling debts she owed him to get her to climb undressed into his own bed!

"Frances, what's the matter? You look like you're going to cry, sweet. I believe you."

"I never cry," she croaked out. "Never!"

She would have been all right if he hadn't tugged her to him and spoken low, comforting words when she thought he would tease or scold her. He took the reins and pulled them over under a clump of willows by the babbling Tyburn and held her, rocking her against his hard body gently as if she were a child.

It all poured out in broken sobs—Buckingham and Barbara's plot, the king's restraint and fury, his growing impatience to bed her, her anger at herself today when she'd made such a fool of herself over this damned carriage and lowered herself to Barbara's level before a huge crowd. She cried wretchedly, almost until she couldn't breathe while he held her tightly against him. To her dismay, she saw she'd smeared Belladonna from her eyes on him and smudged his collar pinkish from the Spanish paper she'd used on her lips.

"Oh look," she gasped, "it's all over you. I'm

so sorry."

He pulled her head down again to his shoulder, one big hand carefully cupping the back of her head under her little hat. "It's all right, Frances. Everything will be all right, my sweet lass. You'll just have to stop fighting me and let me take care of you more. Besides, I can only think of one time we've been alone together that you haven't played havoc with something I've had on."

"But I hate to cry," she told him futilely.

"I know. Here. Use this handkerchief and listen to me. It is an absolute wonder to me you've kept the king at bay as you have, but then, he has Castlemaine for his most primitive needs and even the queen upon occasion. Castlemaine's a fool to think she'd even last a minute at Whitehall if you became his mistress except she's mother to his children, though I judge the last boy's probably Jermyn's or someone else's."

She subsided to sniffs as she carefully wiped his lace-edged handkerchief under her eyes. "The only thing that seems to be saving you then is his own pride—that he'll eventually win you over—and the fact his respect for you seems to increase in proportion to how long you deny him."

She blew her nose. "I know. And that I'm so different from Barbara."

"Yes, there is that. But what about us, lass? Now that you've been so honest here today, will you tell me you care nothing for me? Was that day we had on the yacht just some accident? It wasn't so for me, Frances, not at all. It was needed before and has been treasured since."

He looked so in earnest she didn't know what to

say and wanted to protest even less. "But we can't meet like that."

"Why not? If you'll just agree, I can arrange it. We'll have to be careful until we're ready to tell him—ask him, as the case may be. Sooner or later, he'd have to let you go."

She shook her head so hard her metal earbobs jangled. "I couldn't just leave court. I've no money, nowhere else to go. Mother expects it—and he is the king!"

He sighed and released her from his comforting embrace, staring out at the noisy rush of Tyburn over rocks under the droop of slender willow leaves. "Then, for now," he said at last as he lifted the reins and whistled to the horse to wheel it back toward London, "let's talk of something fun and adventuresome. Tomorrow, all day, the king will be in meetings at the Guildhall. So after noon, I shall meet you on the Thames at the Public Stairs south of Whitehall, and I shall take you to the theater."

"Heavens, could we? I know all the ladies wear masks, so no one would know."

He smiled now, and the sad mood he had fallen into seemed to lift. "Exactly, Lady Stewart. And then we'll get a bite to eat at a nice inn I know and you'll be back safe at Whitehall and no one the wiser as long as you manage to hide those tawny brown curls that get all gilded red in the sun—and don't bring Joli for a chaperone. Will you come?"

"I shouldn't."

"But will you?"

"All right. I've never been out to the theater freely like that, without all the others, and never to an inn. I

311

will come just this once."

He kissed the tip of her nose before she could protest and reined in the horse. "Are you getting out here, my lord? But we're not even to Spur Road."

"I know, but I won't have our day tomorrow ruined by someone tattling. I'll just walk up the Mall and find a hackney at an inn somewhere. Go on now and don't fail me tomorrow—the Public Stairs at one. We'll go by barge. And don't forget your mask!"

How excited he looked and sounded, just like her brother Walter had when he was a boy, she mused, as he climbed down. She waved and urged the horse away, still trying to repair her streaked cheeks with his handkerchief.

Tomorrow would be fun, a lark with no worries about being recognized since she would wear her mask and no worries of holding him off since everyone knew barges, inns, and theaters were always crowded. She smiled and moved the horse into a fast canter through the park.

Chapter Eleven

Frances was relieved to see Richmond coming toward her through the noisy crowd as she reached the Public Stairs south of Whitehall, because she had been repeatedly jostled and one burly lout had tried to snatch her mask which kept slipping. Still, whatever happened, she felt vibrantly alive to be out away from court and king like this. Despite the foul-smelling press of loud people shoving into her, this freedom on a clear May day was wonderful.

Richmond's arm went around her shoulders, and he thrust away a man hawking fresh fish in her face. "You're early, lass, and I am delighted. Come on, over here out of this mess. You'll find today that cloak, hood, and vizard won't keep anyone from poking and trying to assess what's underneath."

To her surprise, he hurried her into an empty barge waiting at the side of the broad Public Stairs from which barges plied up and down the Thames to Lambeth or Southwark. He settled her on a wooden bench with a boarded backrest, beside him, while the two dull-faced oarsmen shoved off. The river glinted gray-green in the midday sun as Frances composed her skirts and cloak well aware Richmond's arm had gone protectively around her again.

"You didn't have any trouble getting away, did you, sweet?" he said solicitously.

She could feel the reverberations of his deep voice when he spoke, a sound both compelling and reassuring as the ripple of river under the barge. "No trouble as the queen is in prayer for her ill mother again. But Susan Warmestry said she heard the king's meeting at Guildhall would be over at noon. So," she admitted somewhat sheepishly, "I told Susan I was going to Somerset House in case he returned early and asked."

"And indeed we are off for Somerset, so that was no story. That's where I told them to put in so we can walk up to the Theatre Royal on Drury Lane."

"But that's the king's theater!" she protested.

"Of course it is, but it has the best actors and, even if he sat in the royal box himself, he'd never suspect the slender masked and cloaked lady with Richmond is his little Stewart."

"Don't say that, I'm not his."

"I love to hear that, lass, but you don't need to vehemently protest to me. Save it for the gossip mongers. And I want to assure you I will do nothing to harm your position at court or to cause you dismay—not until you're ready also. We'll be careful today, but as you're *incognito* to everyone but me and no one would ever expect Mrs. Stewart to be loose outside the sacred precincts of His Majesty's protection, just trust me and enjoy the adventure.

314

Will you?"

She nodded and lifted the black velvet vizard for one second to shoot him a swift smile, then quickly replaced it and fussed overlong to resettle its ribbon ties firmly in place. Massive Whitehall swept by and they picked out her own stretch of windows on the third story; both Northumberland House and York House stairs were crowded with hawkers and private barges. The truncated steeple of St. Paul's, which had been damaged by lightning, Somerset House, and the city beyond slid into view.

He held her hand now, and she did not protest. She was glad he could not see her face today for increasingly she admitted it was more difficult to affect the disdain and aloofness she did not feel with him.

"I like the view from here," she said as they put in to Somerset Stairs. "From mother's windows I can see clear to London Bridge. It's too bad the big yachts cannot come up this way beyond it."

"If I could," he said, "I'd sail the *Francis* to fetch my Frances, and we'd be off to visit Cobham and Scotland and the world."

She laughed lightly, but he looked very serious. "Perhaps you'll come on board—in disguise, of course—when I race the king's yacht sometime this summer," he added suddenly as they bumped the wooden barge landing.

"I heard there was to be a race and the women are to watch from Greenwich, but I'm sure I'm expected to be there, so I could never manage going with you. His Majesty would surely glance over with one of his long, thin spyglasses and note a strange deckhand in a cloak and black velvet vizard on your yacht."

"No. We'd garb you as a boy with loose shirt, breeches, and a linen scarf tied slantwise to hold up all those wild curls. It would be great fun but of course you'd probably be afraid and cower below-decks. Then too, you'd never agree to come aboard as on race days all crew members obey any captain's order instantly without protest."

"I wouldn't cower belowdecks, but I might not obey any order, my lord. Aren't we getting out here at Somerset? Next, I fear, you'll concoct some plan where I shall help you and the king open Parliament at Westminster disguised as the Archbishop of Canterbury or some such."

They laughed and strolled up bustling, fashion-able Drury Lane to the new Theatre Royal which had been dedicated a year ago this month with the king presiding. King Charles was patron to the king's Players whose repertoire was now thirty dramas which were enacted on some sort of schedule Frances never did bother to understand. Like the other courtiers, she just went along at least three times a week when the king attended and enjoyed the afternoon performances. Just as His Majesty, she preferred clever comedies to ponderous tragedies, and as was the vogue, she had favorites among the actors and actresses, though today here incognito with Richmond, she hardly gave a thought to who played what for them.

Richmond was paying their entry whereas with the king they'd always just walked in. She spotted the manager of the King's Players, Thomas Killigrew, in the crowded entryway; he stared curiously at her and turned away before she remembered she was masked and he could not recognize her. Painted prostitutes, who always cheered raucously when the king arrived, eyed the theater customers looking for likely prospects amidst the hubbub of gingerbread and oyster hawkers. Several other women went in masked, probably married ladies with illicit liaisons to keep, the king had told her once.

Richmond took her arm as he moved them into an entryway. Frances raised her scented handkerchief to her nose as the mingled smells of the crowd and vendors' foods assailed her. They turned and went immediately up the curtained stairway to their left.

"But, my Lord Richmond, I thought we'd be seated in the pit today," she teased.

"So you can get pinched and pawed? That may happen, lass, but only by me. Come on."

They sat in the balcony box at the back to avoid the royal box and others the court usually used. Frances liked the seats instantly: she could view the whole intimate reach of theater ahead and didn't have to crane her neck to watch the stage.

"What are we to see today, my lord?" she asked as she peered over the rail at the hubbub below.

"Some frippery by a new playwright named George Etheridge, a man said to have been born in Bermuda, lass—another lovely place we can sail to someday. It's a farce called, interestingly enough, *The Comical Revenge* or *Love in a Tub*. I don't care much for revenge but the love sounds good."

"In a tub? But that doesn't make sense."

"Someday we'll see," he said and grinned. "The master bedchamber at Cobham's got a huge, blue-veined marble bathing tub. We'll see, we'll see. Never mind the repartee for that thought, lass. Now listen. Both Charles Hart and that wild, little hoyden, Nell Gwynn are featured today, so that should help. They'll make any play, however stilted, a success."

Frances loosed her cloak slightly and plied her fan. "I vow, at least Nell Gwynn was a success, climbing out of the pit where she only sold oranges to be one of the first actresses, as they call them. The king favors her, I can tell, as he always shifts his legs about a great deal when she's on stage."

To her annoyance, Richmond burst out laughing. "I was wondering what it meant, sweet lass, that I shift my legs about a great deal when I'm around you."

She shrugged her shoulders in great exaggeration, but his outrageous compliment thrilled her. "They all have lovers, you know," he went on. "The gallants are thick as flies in actresses' tiring rooms and several are very handsomely kept by courtiers."

"So I have heard, but you seem to know an especial great deal about it, my lord," she taunted. "Have you ever kept one handsomely yourself, even for a few hours?"

He leaned close, his shoulder heavy against hers for a minute and she could smell sweet wine and a hint of the Virginia pipe tobacco he smoked occasionally on his breath. "I only discuss intimate situations in intimate circumstances, my love. Later, if you wish to know any details, we shall discuss it in great depth."

She fluttered her fan near to his smug face and leaned slightly over the rail pretending to study the theater to avoid having to answer. He was teasing again, she was certain and she'd probably asked for that, but it unsettled her so when he spoke rough and low and got that challenging look in his slightly narrowed eyes.

The stage thrust out into the pit below under a huge painted and gilded royal coat of arms. Men were lighting, then hauling up the chandeliers which burned brightly, forty wax candles in each, over the actors' heads; then they lit big double burners along the foot of the stage. Frances counted ten fiddlers in the orchestra, as Killigrew must have recently hired new ones, and the rabble milling about among the benches on the stone floor clapped and hooted for some particular melodies they evidently wanted played. Girls selling the outrageously priced oranges and lemons circulated among the audience shrilling their wares, tossing back an insult or curse, and generally ignoring the pinches and pokes of fingers or breasts or buttocks.

The curtain was pulled aside, and the movable, painted scenery swayed a bit, then settled as the musicians swept into what sounded to Frances like a plodding coronto. Richmond was still watching her as John Lacy, a fine comic actor, stepped out to speak a prologue.

"This whole play is likely to be as silly as what goes on at court," Richmond whispered nearly in her ear and one hand moved to rest lightly on her knee where she hit it off playfully with her fun. "I said I'd bring you but we can leave anytime you want. Maybe 'love in a tub' means love on a boat and the yacht's just on the other side of London Bridge."

319

"No, absolutely not," she hissed.

Apparently properly chastened, he shifted his long legs and sat back to watch. The wigged and quite fashionably garbed actors and actresses, decked out mostly in costumes the courtiers had donated, began the first scenes with typical caustic wit and clever repartee, but Richmond had rattled her now. She couldn't concentrate, wasn't even certain if dark-haired Nell Gwynn was supposed to be Charles Hart's sister or wife in this comedy.

"Richmond," she whispered, "there's a man down there on the third bench staring up at us. I think he waved too."

Richmond leaned forward, pressing slightly into her again as he did. "The broad-faced man. That's Samuel Pepys, a Secretary of the Royal Navy, a good man. He loves ships—and he's lost his heart, at a distance, to your friend the Countess of Castlemaine for years, until lately, though she doesn't know he exists."

"Then he is as daft as some others I could name."

"Until lately, as I said, Frances. Now he's switched his allegiance to a Mrs. Stewart at court, he told me at the Naval Office last month."

"Then he is daft indeed, because Mrs. Stewart's heart is ever her own."

"Is it, lass?" he asked, his light, informative tone gone darkly rasping all of a sudden. "Permanently under lock and key or frozen in something like the St. James's Ice House with layers of protection to keep it all crystal cold?" His hand was back on her knee as he leaned forward. "Do you really believe that's the way it can ever be for you again now, Frances?"

Her hand grasped his on her knee, but she could not budge its warm weight. The actors were reciting their lines; the pit below hummed with voices as ogling and fondling went on interminably.

"Please, Charles, not here."

"Let's go then. I have a carriage outside."

That surprised her. He'd said nothing of a carriage. A closed carriage with his hand on her knee or his mouth on hers on the short ride to the yacht he'd mentioned. She sucked in a quick breath through the restricting mask at the thought of being alone either place with him.

"No," she managed. "I want to stay here."

"As you wish," he said politely, his face as much a mask as the one she wore. He removed his hand and settled back immediately in his seat as if deeply intent on the play below, which neither of them could even guess the basic story of now.

Suddenly, from the back of the theater in a whispered wave, some subtle commotion ruffled forward. Bodies turned; necks craned. Even two fiddlers in the pit half stood and stared. Then, slowly, the royal box near the front of the theater and the box next to it filled with courtiers while the play halted momentarily and everyone rose noisily to his feet.

"Oh, heavens, it cannot be!" Frances moaned. "Susan was right!"

"Steady. I think headlong flight would tip our hand. We're far enough back they may not even note us. 'Sdeath, if it isn't the king and Duke of York with the duchess and the Countess of Castlemaine and their ladies in the next box. Do you think you were missed?"

"Of course, I was, you rogue. You told me he'd be at Guildhall all day."

"And you told me Susan would tell anyone who asked you'd gone to Somerset House, so stop fussing. You're fully covered—unless, of course, you prefer to be unmasked up there with them and if so I'll deliver you immediately and be on my way."

"Hardly. But I would like to leave now, please."

"No. A moment ago you told me you did not want to leave with me, so we will sit here until the play is over."

She fumed, utterly frustrated, under her mask and warm cloak. She should have known the Duke of Richmond couldn't be pleasant, not for long. Granted, he was a fine actor at times, as fine as Charles Hart down there spouting his lines, but now she was undeceived again. The moment this comedy ended, she'd insist he take her to Whitehall and, if he balked, she'd walk back alone!

She sat rigidly, turned slightly away from him but soon forgot her own pique as it became evident to everyone in the theater that an even more humorous playlet was being enacted in the king's royal boxes. Barbara, Countess of Castlemaine, was apparently most annoyed by the lack of attention the king and duke were showing her in public. His Majesty had his elegant, brocaded back nearly turned to her and was obviously intent on the young actress Nell Gwynne who held center stage and played directly up at the royal box despite where she should have been looking. Behind her mask, Frances barely suppressed a giggle as she darted a look at Richmond's wry grin.

Barbara flounced her skirts, flipped her fan, scraped her chair, and whispered to the Duchess of York and two ladies seated behind her. She produced a small mirror and grandly stuck two additional beauty patches on her painted face. She dropped flowers from her nosegay down on the men seated under her box and Samuel Pepys, below, nearly fell over another chap in his effort to get one. When the king finally swiveled slightly to glare at her before turning back, she leapt from her seat and disappeared.

"She's in one of her vile rages," Frances whispered to Richmond. "She'll probably insist he take her back."

"Sounds entirely familiar," he goaded. "No, there she is. Watch this."

Barbara had appeared suddenly behind the king and duke in their box. Head held high, she stepped in front of the duke and settled herself with great show on the tiny chair the two men had left for comfort between theirs. The Duke of York gaped like a fish, and the king's eyes were black slits of rage at the public tantrum.

"She's almost desperate lately," Frances said half to herself, but she knew Richmond heard. "She's desperate for him to keep up appearances and afraid she's losing her power."

"It's obvious enough the king is tired of her and that he looks elsewhere now. Let's leave. I think you were right to want to go," he said low.

She went with him willingly, glad to be rid of the whole scene and to escape the chance the king might note them and summon Richmond. The carriage was waiting nearby just as he'd said, and she became nervous again and angry with herself because she hadn't insisted he take her home by barge.

"The Bear at the Bridgefoot," he'd shouted to his driver Jenken as he handed her in, and they were rolling away already.

She sat far over on her side of the seat. He said nothing so she began to talk as nonchalantly as she could manage considering the jolting of the coach and her composure. "You heard what Barbara did last week to try to rile him, didn't you, my lord?"

"Enlighten me."

"You know, she thinks His Majesty has Catholic leanings."

"I think she's probably right. And the fact that Minette and you are Catholic may have a lot to do with that as well as the fact that he tends to equate Protestantism more with the fierce Presbyterian Scots and pious Puritans than with the more moderate Anglicans. But say on."

"So Castlemaine supposedly converted to Catholicism, though I vow, I wouldn't give a tinker's damn for her reasons or her piety. Then she announced it grandly and asked him what he thought."

"And he said," he urged her on.

"He said he never interfered with the souls of ladies, only with their bodies when they were civil enough to accept his attentions, so her grandiose power scheme was all for naught."

"And the king's words?" he prompted.

"What of them?"

"Frances, they were obviously aimed at you at least

324

as much as Castlemaine. You were no doubt standing right there to hear them, were you not?''

"Yes."

"He's getting more angry, more impatient with you, lass. Do not make the mistake of the young by believing you always will have the time to have things your way. His Majesty may not wait patiently forever—nor may I for that matter. Your little anecdote of the king reminds me of something else he said once, a deeply held philosophy of his you'd do well to take to heart if you mean to remain living in such close proximity to *that* Charles Stuart.''

"Well, what was it?"

"'Women,' he said, 'are at their prime at twenty, decayed at four and twenty, old and insupportable at thirty.' So, Castlemaine's four and twenty this year, and I am certain she believed it would never come when she was twenty. And where will she be with the king when she's thirty, Frances? And what about you?''

"I haven't thought on it. That's a long ways away,'' she protested, annoyed at the turn the talk had taken.

"Then you'd better. You're the most beautiful woman at the king's court, Frances, and, I believe, a much more beautiful woman within, but courts have a way of changing people the longer they remain. I don't imply that you have it in you to be a greedy, vile, and sexually insatiable Castlemaine, but just think on it, that's all.''

She flushed hot in the restricting cocoon of hood, mask, and cloak. She wanted to hit back with a clever taunt or sharp reply, but no words would come.

Instead, she bit her lower lip and turned to look out the window as the carriage made its way across London Bridge to the other side of the river.

Three- and four-storied houses, built over the passageway, pressed inward, making an actual tunnel for horse and foot traffic with only occasional breaks of sunlight and fresh air along the stretch of old bridge. The span itself was twenty feet wide but the arches and passageways were barely enough for a big carriage like this one, and Jenkin had to shout and curse people out of the way. Beneath the bridge, nineteen arches held its weight and made violently-flowing rapids that the smaller boats and barges shot through while the yachts and fleet vessels rode above the bridge in the great Thames pool to the east. At last in the bustle of hackneys, drays, coaches, and barrows, they rolled under Bridge Gate on the Southwark side, the infamous spot on which many criminals' heads had been displayed on spikes over the years.

"How dreadful," she said as she pulled her head in at the first glimpse of the gruesome sight. "It hardly keeps anyone from breaking the law or there still wouldn't be heads all these years, would there? Is that where they put Cromwell and the other regicides, my lord?"

"What a pleasant turn of conversation just before I offer you a fine meal, lass," he teased. "No, Cromwell's remains they dug up from the poor bastard's grave and publicly hung at Tyburn along with Ireton and Bradshaw's corpses, and a few others at Charing Cross. I have heard your polite acquaintance, Lady Lauderdale, proudly boast more than once that she dangled Cromwell's scalp on her golden belt for several weeks. Here we are, lass. On that happy note, let's go in.''

She let him help her down on the busy thoroughfare in the shadow of St. Mary Overies Church before a quaint little inn and holstery called The Bear at the Bridgefoot. It's timbered roof and the frayed sign boasting a crude-looking black bear made it seem very ancient and droll.

"A strange name," she murmured to him as they went in.

"The best sporting bear gardens were hereabouts in Southwark with the theaters in the great Elizabeth's reign," he told her. As he swung open the heavy oak door, she heard their carriage roll away ito traffic behind them.

The big, central taproom, heavy-beamed and low-ceilinged was crowded with men and a few women of questionable purpose. Smoke from the new rage of Virginia, imported tobacco, hung bluish and sweet in the air. Tables were all jammed together, and Frances could see by looking down under her mask that the floor was littered with oyster shells, nut shells, and even bones. Over by the hearth, a turnspit dog ran around in his cage to rotate a huge side of beef over the fire.

"Milord Duke, you are early, Yer Grace," a man's rough voice said. "But no worry, no worry, Yer Grace. Right this way, an' it please Yer Grace.''

To her surprise, they followed the man up narrow, crooked stairs on which she had to lift her skirts and cloak and peer crazily down through the eyeholes in the mask to keep her footing. Richmond's grasp steadied her, and she held her tongue at the awareness that they were in a little private, low-ceilinged chamber. A table and four chairs, a long sideboard, but unfortunately, also a small bed along one wall crowded the limited floor space.

"Wine now and the food in a quarter hour, Yer Grace," the man said and was gone.

Frances took off her mask and let Richmond divest her of the cloak. The small oak-paneled room had two high, deep-set windows opened to catch the river breeze, and Frances breathed deeply and fanned her face and throat.

"Too warm a day for all that warm disguise, Frances," he said as if to break the silence.

She nodded and moved to rest her elbows on the window ledge and peer out over the busy thoroughfare below. "I've never been in Southwark, only been through it," she said as he came to stand close behind her, not touching her, one hand along the window ledge on either side of her.

He felt her presence, the stunning impact on his heart and body from just looking at her. How beautifully untouchable she seemed in that lavender bodice with rows of French laces, her gown almost the color of Scottish heather, with deeper purple underskirts. Her wooden-heeled chopine-style shoes and piled hair made her tall for a woman, he thought, but he still towered a good six inches over her. Her jewels were minimal today, an Italian cameo on a gold chain at her slender throat, single pearl drops suspended from each earlobe. The scent of frangipani lightly drifting from her hair and skin was alluring, yet delicate. He let his eyes taunt him further by deliberately studying the bare nape of her neck under the tawny brown cascade of curls and tousled ringlets; then he looked lower to take in the straight back, tiny waist, and swell of hip. He ached to touch her; his palms tingled at the mere thought and his knees went weak, but he steeled himself to wait. Wine now and food in a quarter hour, the innkeeper had said.

They toasted their day together almost solemnly over the wine and talked little while two quick-handed lads spread their table under the watchful innkeeper's eye. Richmond almost wished he had made Frances stay cloaked and masked since they stared so at her, but inn workers from Southwark surely never got to Whitehall to recognize who she was. When they were left alone again, they fell to devouring a rich crabmeat bisque, slices of beef, a delicious egg tansy, and strawberries with cream. He was pleased she showed such a hearty appetite despite the awkwardness that suddenly sat between them like a third, unwanted diner.

"The yacht race next week," she said at last, unable to absorb his smoldering, green-eyed gaze another moment without doing something to break the tension. "I suppose you'll wager on it."

"Probably. Many will. The Duke of York will bet heavily, I will try to bet moderately, and His Majesty not at all. Want to get in on the action, lass?"

"Heavens, not I. I was duped into a wager once, and once was enough."

Despite her intended taunt, he grinned. "That wager still runs an open account, you know, Frances—one I'm afraid is seriously in arrears."

"Brave words, my Lord Duke, for someone who admitted once his inherited lands came heavily in debt. If you can remain in debt and live with it, I vow I can too."

"But, sweet lady, I do pay off little bits of the debts whenever I have a good opportunity, even as you do now."

She rose and stood behind her chair as if to place a buffer between them. "Frankly, my lord, I don't like the turn this conversation has taken. I was only asking about the yacht race."

"If I can arrange it, will you come along?"

"I couldn't possibly as I would be missed by the others."

"I said *if* I can arrange it, would you? It would be wonderful, Frances, skimming along with the sails pulling taut, tacking to catch every shift of breeze. You'd have to be careful not to get in the way as all of us are busy the whole time with tiller and riggings during a race. It's all freedom and challenge, pure and lovely."

She stared raptly at his face, almost aglow with his own thoughts as he described the race. She could never go with him, of course. Someone would know, but it did sound exciting.

"Will you come, sweet lass? I won't ask again. It will take some careful arranging, but I can do it."

"All right—if it seems safe."

He smiled, then frowned. "Safe—hell, my sweetheart. Safe is too often sorry. We may have to hazard everything at some point—in racing and in other things, things not quite here yet."

She hardly listened to his last words as her mind

plotted what to tell the others next week and what to wear. Lately there were getting to be too many lies and masks and disguises, but perhaps it just couldn't be helped for now. And for right now, Richmond had stepped closer around the table, much too close.

"Then you will sail with me, and I'll take a little downpayment on that old wager," he was saying, with a new devilish glint in his green eyes.

"I will sail with you, and you'll release me from the earlier wager," she tossed at him, but she took a step back.

"I never cancel old debts except under one rather special circumstance," he said.

"Such as?"

"Such as the debtor becomes part of my family and then we'd strike an entirely new bargain."

She blinked at him. "Rather special, indeed," she challenged and then took another step back before he reached for her. "Richmond, I insist we head back now."

"It will be an hour or so before the carriage returns." He tilted her chin up gently and took her lips. At least, she told herself reassuringly, she was fully aware of what could happen with him if she weren't careful. Just a moment or two before she had demanded he take her back. Now she returned his kiss warmly since he was not pressing her or touching her anywhere but on one shoulder and her throat where his other hand had dropped. But when his tongue darted out to part her soft lips, she drew back.

"Is that my quota, my ration for today, Frances? Surely, you're not afraid you'll lose control."

She turned her back to him but the wall was inches away, and she felt foolishly, awkwardly trapped. "I'm not the one I fear will lose control," she said evenly, but her knees began to tremble as he placed his hands on the wall on either side of her effectively blocking her in as he had earlier.

"Really?" he said low and his voice sounded faintly amused. "Why don't we just put that to the test then?"

"I have no desire to play your little games, and I don't need a test."

"I keep wishing all that were true, Frances my love, but you keep disappointing me by your little girl posturing when I try to deal forthrightly with you. And worst of all, sometimes you aren't even sure what I mean or what I want, are you?"

"It seems eminently clear enough to me," she ground out, her back still to him. "I vow, I am not some rural-bred ninny to not recognize that you want exactly what His Royal Majesty, the other Charles Stuart, wants and—neither of you is going to get it."

His mouth dripped to her bare shoulder and nuzzled her throat as little shivers shot clear down to her toes. "Poor little Frances," he murmured, "beset on every side and can't tell a Charles Stuart who's desperate for a mistress he can possess from a Charles Stuart who's eager for a wife he can love. Poor little Frances."

His voice was condescendingly taunting and insulting, but his lips and hands were warm and she had heard him plainly enough. A wife? He had not proposed it and didn't dare! She was not really free to wed, she had no dowry, and she was assigned to—she was important to—the court, to their majesties. How dare he jest and amuse himself at her expense!

One arm pulled her back against his chest now encircling her with a heated embrace; the other lifted to trace warm fingers along the lacy bodice of her neckline, trailing enticing tingles over the swells of and into the cleft between her breasts. His hard thighs moved closer behind her, pressing into her soft buttocks; she felt his hand at the uppermost ties of her lacings in back.

She stiffened against him, but the top of her bodice relaxed and his fingers caressed her exposed breasts and darted lower to flicker intimately into the top of the corset where her aching nipples were still imprisoned. She was ashamed how taut and swollen they were before he even touched them the first time.

"Oh," she murmured. "Oh!" She twisted to him and wrapped her arms tightly about his waist and hid her face against his chest along the blue brocade waistcoat. He went back to unlacing the bodice ties now offered to him and then the corset while she clung to him unprotesting, trying to assure herself that the undeniable fact she wanted to lie with him, to feel him inside her as that day on the yacht did not mean—could not mean—she loved him. He made her body feel so good, that was all. He was rough yet gentle—reassuring and yet so tantalizingly dangerous.

"Frances, I do love you," he was saying in her ear as his fingers now stroked up and down her bare spine even through the chemise where he had unlaced the corset and gown. "Very, very much and I want you so. Is it not that way even a little for you?

Can you not say it? You've got to stop fighting me—and us—sooner or later. Can you not say it?''

"I don't know."

"I realize you've seen some pretty awful marriages and learned not to trust courtiers and kings, lass. I suppose that's what's saved you from His Majesty so far so I should be grateful, but you can't live your life not trusting and detesting all men."

"I don't."

"No? Name the lucky exception then. King Louis? The Princess Henriette-Anne's homosexual husband Philippe—you have seen him at too close range, haven't you, love? Crafty, little Monmouth? King Charles? Buckingham?''

"Don't taunt me."

"The Duke of Richmond maybe—just a little?"

She sighed against him and slightly loosed her grip around his waist, surprised that she still held him to her so fiercely. "Yes, the Duke of Richmond—a little," she said low against his chest.

"I want you desperately, Frances, always have, and I'm not too proud to say it, no matter how you try to put me off from time to time," he told her, his low voice ruffling her hair. "I want your spoken permission to show you how much I care here, now on that little couch there. And afterward, I want no accusations or hints I forced or coerced you as there have been before." He said no more, but his warm mouth dropped to trace a seductive path down her jawling along the side of her neck and the curve of her throat.

She stood against him as if spellbound. There was no pulling back although she felt that she stood poised on the crowning edge of some rapturous cliff which eternally beckoned.

All these days, these years in which she'd told herself she detested men, she had never really meant Richmond too. He had not deserted her, however aloof and cold she had been to him. And it was true—heavens, it was true as true—that she wanted him too.

"Yes," she murmured, her soft mouth pressed to his sinewy neck.

"What? I said your spoken permission, my love, not muffled or mumbled. Do you mean to say you do want me to make love to you?" His eyes were alight with dancing golden shards of sunglow as he leaned slightly back to look down at her. She swam willingly in the emerald depths of his gaze and took in the slightly arrogant twist of his mouth as well as the paradoxically boyish lift of his brow under the fall of wayward hair across his forehead.

"Yes, yes, my Charles. I—you make me feel so happy and so wonderful."

He shouted a little laugh and picked her up as if to spin her before he realized there was no room for such in the tiny chamber. "And do I not make you feel loved, my sweet lass?" he said, as he sat on the very edge of the narrow couch and stood her beside him so their knees were touching. "I want you to feel loved above all," he rasped slowly, although his hands quickened their movements on her loosened garments.

Gently if hurriedly, he peeled her bodice and unlaced corset down over the curve of her hips and let them rustle to her feet. She watched his eyes light to a more startling green as they went over her bare skin

335

and she stood willingly before him. As he bent slightly forward to untie her garters and peel down her silk hose and remove her shoes, the top of his auburn head brushed her soft belly and she sucked in her breath at the pure, shattering sensation of his touch.

He began to kiss her then even as he removed his own garments. Little fluttering movements of his mouth, tiny nips across her stomach and upward toward her expectant, rose-tipped breasts made her knees go weak and she willingly collapsed across his lap, kissing his bare chest and shoulders wildly.

This was pure madness and she knew it. All the barriers she had ever built up, all the fears she had tended toppled away before the rapturous onslaught of this man's mere gaze and sorcerer's touch. They pressed together on the narrow bed; his hands cupped her bare bottom so perfectly, and she reveled in the feel of her full breasts crushed to his lightly haired chest.

"No rushing, no hurrying today," he told her as his lips and hands began a second roaming tour of each silken curve of her quaking body. He ravished her mouth, her breasts while she mindlessly rained passionate touches along his muscled back and even dared to feather fingertips down his hips and powerful thighs.

She was panting as if she had run miles and miles when he finally could bear their games no more and parted her legs to enter her. "Oh, yes, please . . ." she moaned as he slid heavily in.

"Yes," he echoed, "yes, always, my sweet lass. You are mine. You will be mine!"

Their bodies met in a mutually heightening crescendo that swept them both away, endlessly rising and falling. He marveled that she became more bold to match his frenzied rhythm, but then, had he not taught her boldness? She murmured wild, disjointed love words, but had he not taught her to love?

He turned them, balanced them on their sides, facing each other, but his rapid movements did not slow. She looked dreamy-eyed, and beautiful blushes tinged her ivory skin clear to the tips of her pink nipples.

She darted him a slitted, languorous look, then managed to smile shakily even as he pressed forward to claim her slightly bruised mouth again. At that double joining, she clung so perfectly, so submissively even as her own movements urged him on, that once again their bodies crested and spun and then went limp in utter calm and fulfilled peace.

They curled wordlessly together on the narrow space of mussed bed, and he covered their perspiring bodies with her discarded skirts, lifting them from the floor. She was not certain, but they might even have slept that way for some few minutes until he roused them and they dressed silently.

"You see," she finally broke the quiet, "no protests nor regrets."

He bent to kiss the tip of her nose, then sat on the bed again to pull on his boothose and shoes. "Ah, but my dear Lady Frances," he teased low and winked up at her, "I do have the regret that we must go back. Quite frankly, I am trying to steel myself to behave until we get out of here, because I'm sorely tempted to keep you here, or at the very least spirit you away from London entirely in my chariot."

She dared to smile back at his light, bantering tone. She sat down carefully a little way from him on the bed to replace her own shoes and stockings. "You aren't really serious," she told him low, trying to convince herself as well as him. "You know, you mustn't worry about my living so near the king, Charles."

His mouth smiled, but his eyes did not. "But I do, lass. Come on. The coach is just around the corner in Duke Street Hill. A polite kiss in the carriage, and I'll take you back with plenty to ponder, I warrant."

"Including the yacht race. You won't forget," she asked feeling suddenly every bit the little girl he had tauntingly accused her of being earlier.

"No, my love, I won't forget. And meanwhile, I expect you to be happy to see me at court when I can manage it. About my promise to you, Frances, I won't ever forget."

He had gone somehow pensive and more serious than she had thought he would be after she had given in and admitted how much she loved their loving, she thought. He swept her unwanted, too warm cloak around her shoulders and handed her the velvet vizard to arrange. She hastily lifted the mask and took a long time to fasten it so he would not note the sudden, silly tears which clung to her lashes.

Chapter Twelve

Frances stood as still as a carved statue while the Dutch painter Jacob Huysman completed her portrait on which he had been working for weeks. He hardly needed her here today as the head, face, and hands had long been done and the details and background alone were receiving final, dramatic brushstrokes, but this had come to be a tradition. The king had taken to organizing celebrations for his closest courtiers each time a portrait of Frances was finished, and there had been an absolute rash of them this past year.

The king now owned portraits of his favorite lady by Lely, Wissing, Gascar, and Largillière as well as a set of delicate miniatures. Her profile also had been used as Britannia on the new coins of the realm prepared by Jan Roettiers. It was almost as if, Frances mused, King Charles had decided to possess her image if he could not have her body and heart in truth.

This portrait, though, had been great fun compared to some of the others as it combined the new lady's style at court with the rage of Frances Stewart artwork: Frances posed for Huysman in men's garb, a fashion actually promoted by the queen who had come a long way from clinging stubbornly to her massive farthingales two years before. Then too, both Frances and the queen were slender: the style of men's attire favored them while the voluptuous and ever-pregnant Castlemaine looked merely ludicrous. Off somewhere in another fine snit, Barbara had not even come to this gathering today, though she'd clearly been invited.

"*Finis!*" the mustached, portly artist Huysman shouted grandly. His brush brandished like a sword, he swept a low bow to the king who had been standing just behind him. "I hope you approve, Your Majesty!"

"Od's fish, Huysman, a pretty job, but then how could you fail with *la belle* Stewart as a model? Frances, come look."

The king went halfway to meet her as she stepped from the curtained platform, and everyone clustered about the portrait. The Duke of York, who had become avidly attentive lately, especially when he knew his royal brother was not near, pressed close on her other shoulder and the ever-watchful Buckingham hovered behind. The queen and Duchess of York murmured, nodded, and sipped champagne. If only, Frances thought, Richmond were here to admire it, she might be content with the big portrait.

The lady masquerading like a fancy soldier in the painting looked very serious, she decided, gazing at her own portrait as she drank some of the king's champagne from his proffered goblet. She had chosen to wear a full, curled, blond periwig since they were so fashionable; the huge striped sleeves of the man's doublet which flattened her high breasts did almost make her look like a handsome boy here. The gold sword slung at her hip completed the impact of a pensive, young soldier.

"Zounds, Frances, why so silent on it?" Buckingham asked from behind. "Tell us what you think."

"I vow, it certainly is different from the others you've commissioned, sire," she said.

"It stops a bit too soon across the hips," His Majesty observed. "I'd really fancy a little more of those fabulous legs in the gartered hose showing."

"But she's lovely, sire, lovely in boy's garb or lady's," the Duke of York added, oblivious to the narrow-eyed glare his duchess gave him.

As the rest of them chatted, the king gently pulled Frances away toward the row of windows overlooking the river. Through the panes morning light still bathed the room at Whitehall which an artist was always given for a makeshift studio.

"Do you not like the portrait then, sire?" she asked low.

"I like anything with you, my Frances; but, except for the fact this outfit shows your legs, I prefer you dressed as a woman."

"Heavens, I know that, sire, but fashion is fashion."

"That evidently seems not to matter to you when it comes to ignoring other styles," he accused, his eyes gone to shiny obsidian slits in the slash of sunlight.

"Please, Your Majesty," she said. "We cannot have

a continuation of the discussion on my chastity here and now. It is settled anyway. I thought you understood that last night.''

"We will have the chastity discussion, as you put it, anytime and anyplace I say, Frances. 'Sdeath, I ought to be done with all this foolishness.''

She lifted her chin and her low voice trembled. "And banish me?"

His eyes went over her; his face looked like chiseled fury. "And ravish you," he said bluntly and turned away.

Stunned, she stood alone for a minute gazing out over the busy morning Thames, still holding the king's now empty champagne goblet. All summer he had been more sharp with her, almost insulting at times, like a loaded cannon waiting to explode. More and more she became uncertain and almost afraid she would never be able to both hold him at bay and be allowed to remain at court, although her increasing closeness to Queen Catherine helped to act as a newly erected buffer to the king's almost obsessive desire to possess her. Suddenly, all she wanted to do was go upstairs and get this periwig and tightly laced doublet off.

Across the way with his back to her, the king stood speaking with his queen and the Duchess of York. He did not even turn to see whom the queen was waving farewell to. Frances put the goblet on the recessed window sill, waved back, and went out. Perhaps this was what Barbara felt so much now—this little jab of unease when the king turned away in anger or seemed to lose interest. He was frustrated and irate with her; his back looked very broad and forbidding.

She had nothing to placate him with short of lying with him, and then he would surely know another man had made love to her before.

She hurried down the long corridor to the west stairs. Richmond—she hadn't seen him for over a week although he had sent her chocolate, expensive Genoa perfume, and flowers, all of which she had kept. Now, why did she always think of Richmond's attentions as wanting to make love to her, but the king's as desiring to lie with her? She smiled despite her raging headache. She cared so for Richmond, in a way she never had for anyone else, and had seen him several times briefly when he had not been sent somewhere on wretched royal business and when she could slip away. How thrillingly the thought of him affected her even now, almost as if she were hurrying to meet him. She was lost in musings and halfway up the steep stairs before she heard the running steps behind.

It was the Duke of York, out of breath and scraping his sword hilt along the wall in his haste. Surely, the king would not send his brother like a common lackey to fetch her back for leaving like this.

"Frances!"

"My Lord Duke. Am I sent for in disgrace?"

His handsome features seemed much more refined than those of his elder brother, yet he looked royal Stuart through and through. "Sent for—no, dear Frances. I just thought you might favor an escort back to your rooms as the king's manners seem to be a bit wanting today." He fell easily in step beside her as she went up.

"I truly cannot fault his manners, my Lord Duke,

as he is evidently entertaining both his queen and your duchess."

The man's lower lip actually trembled at what he evidently took to be a snub. She hadn't actually intended that, but then, she was sick of all these cavaliers, the king included, so what did it really matter? But his voice was so earnest, so shaky, that hand on her sword hilt on the top step, she turned back to face him.

"Frances—is—do you mean to warn me off then?" he asked low.

"Warn you off, my Lord Duke? Heavens, from what, pray tell?"

"From paying suit to you if his attentions wane. Oh, don't answer hastily, please. I realize he's still besotted, but by now surely you have made your position clear."

She wondered if her face showed the shock she felt at this unexpected twist of events. For over a year the king's brother had heaved huge sighs in her presence, but she had thought him merely impatient or disconcerted with the king's avid attentions to her. But not this!

"I fear I have not made my position clear at all, Your Grace. My refusal to become the king's mistress is not at all rooted in any desire not to choose him as a person. I respect and admire, even to a degree, favor him, you see."

"But, why then—"

"My Lord Duke, I know it is most unfashionable and it shows that the supposedly most stylish lady at court is hardly in style at all, but I will not bed with a married man, and I wouldn't—I shouldn't—I won't consider it with a man I—a man I was not wed to."

He eyed her strangely at that broken recital. "And if you were to marry like Castlemaine and your husband to retire?" he pursued.

"No. No, never. I do not intend to bear sons as she does to a man not my lord even if it is the king and he is always kind to his children so at least they do not suffer as much as they could." She wasn't certain she was even coherent as the denials poured from her. "I shall never—never wed," she added. "Excuse me, my Lord Duke, but this damned stylish blond periwig is giving me a raging head pain. Good day to you."

He was speechless for a moment and held his ground as she hurried away. But his words floated after her as she went down the hall toward her chambers: "I hope, nevertheless, Frances, you might see fit to cheer on my yacht in the race from Greenwich tomorrow."

The yacht race tomorrow? It had been postponed several times this summer because of royal business. The undeclared war with the Hollanders was wreaking havoc on English shipping and both the Dukes of York and Richmond had been busy with naval preparations. Tomorrow? But the king hadn't said a word and surely Richmond had long forgotten his promise to her she could sail with him. She pretended she had not heard the Duke of York's words at all and went into her drawing room through the little tiled foyer.

"Gillie! Jane!"

"They aren't here. Will I do?"

"Richmond!"

"At your services, Mistress Stewart," he said and

swept her a mockingly grand bow. "Forgive me for startling you but the door was ajar so the maids probably haven't gone far. I thought it best not to stand about outside in the hall nor to invade the little party downstairs as I'm supposed to be hard at work at Westminster. You know, for a minute there when you first came in, I believed I'd have to challenge some other suitor you'd let walk into your rooms to a duel for your fair hand." His rakish gaze swept pointedly over her outfit and periwig.

She laughed despite how he'd surprised her and swept him a low bow to mimic his own. "I fear I'd not have been a match for you at swordplay, my lord. All this wretched weapon does is hit against my hipbone and generally trip me up on stairs."

She faced him squarely, feet planted a bit apart even as he stood now with one hand on hip and one on sword hilt. "And to what do I owe this sudden visit, my Lord Charles?" she asked softly, hoping her pleasure at seeing him and her desire to have him ask her to sail with him tomorrow was not overly obvious.

"You owe this particular visit, sweet lass, to my missing you and to the dire necessity I gather my crew for tomorrow's yacht race with the king."

"You didn't forget your promise!"

"Did you think I would? Has the king announced the race?"

"No, but then, I left the gathering below a bit prematurely. The Duke of York mentioned it."

"Duke Jamie? Did he tell you it's to be from Greenwich at promptly two of the clock tomorrow afternoon? The court is probably going down by barge at midmorn, so you had better let out you've made plans to visit your mother."

"Actually, this periwig has given me a head pain, so that excuse will do as well, I think. Besides, after my exit today, His Majesty may not want me to go at all."

"Another fury over your continued refusal?" he asked tersely.

"More like one of Castlemaine's sulks than an out-and-out fury, I'd say."

"And do you really think you can go on with this balancing act forever without falling off, lass?"

She fumbled to unbuckle her unwieldy sword as she sought to compose an answer. "I suppose not," she began slowly, but stopped to hold her breath as he came to stand beside her to deftly undo her sword belt for her.

"And do not his physical attentions move you?" he pursued. "I worry, you see, as I have found you to be a wonderfully sensual and passionate woman."

At the intimate caress of his words, she almost swayed into him but he only moved a few steps away to place her sword and belt carefully on a tabletop beside Aberdeen, her sleeping, curled white cat. He stroked the animal once, then straightened to regard Frances silently with his arms crossed on his chest.

"The king is very skillful, of course—well, I suppose most men are," she said, touched by his attention to her cats which everyone else politely ignored.

"You know nothing of most men, Frances, but say on."

"I guess I have learned to steel myself against

feelings for him and I do not find it difficult to tell him 'no.'"

"You've always been most adept at saying that, sweet lass, even to me, so then it becomes the puzzle of deciphering when you mean it and when you don't. I just hope he knows you're serious. You have a head pain from that blond, curly thing, you said, so let me play lady's maid again and we'll get it off. Then we'd best lay our plans for tomorrow because I want to get back to Westminster before someone finds out I'm here. That sleeping cat will hardly do for a proper chaperone if some gossipmongers discover us, I'm afraid."

Her acquiescence astounded him, and he was almost tempted to throw caution to the winds and bolt the door to the hall, but he forced himself not to touch her as he ached to. Tomorrow he would have her on the yacht for hours, though the crew would be busy and exhausted and it was actually foolish to let her get underfoot. A year—it had been a whole year since they had lost themselves in rapturous love that day on the *Francis*, but he did not intend to do anything to ruin this placid trust that flourished now between them.

He lifted her heavy periwig off and flopped it onto a tall Chinese vase on the table while she pulled out the bodkins imprisoning her riot of tawny curls and shook them free. "Oh, that feels good," she said, "but, I vow, I must look like a wild woman."

"I like it. Now listen to me, wild Frances all in boy's garb. By nine tomorrow morning, hie yourself out of here and down to the barge steps where we met before."

"In boy's garb?"

"No. We'll see to that on the yacht. Just leave as if you're going out in cloak and mask and be sure you are not followed. I never did trust the Villiers duo not to have spies. Though I wouldn't put it past the king to watch you too, he's basically too forthright to operate so underhandedly."

"And you'll be at the barge landing?"

"No. I can't risk that. Roger Payne, my Scottish steward from Cobham, will fetch you. He's a big, burly redhead who speaks with a real burr and you'll know him by his kilts, but no staring at his legs or flaunting yours."

He grinned at her, then led her by one hand to the hall door with him and leaned his back against it for one minute. "You're the damned best-looking boy I've ever seen," he said low.

"Charles, about what you said regarding my balancing act with the king—I really believe he will finally tire of it."

"Not until he's slaked his thirst with you or you're no longer living under his nose everyday, lass. It's all too utterly tempting for him, and you're just fortunate he's too proud to rape you or too conceited to think you can hold out. I've got to head back now. Don't fail me tomorrow. It will be wonderful. You know, I don't usually kiss boys, but—"

He pulled her against him and took her soft mouth determinedly, his big hand in her tousled hair at the back of her head. Her lips parted under his willingly with a little sigh that shook him to his very core.

He forced himself to set her back as he heard women's voices in the hall. "Look out, Frances, and see if the corridor's clear enough. If not, I can always dare the privy staircase down through dragon Castlemaine's rooms."

She punched him playfully in his hard midsection and peered out. "No one in particular, my lord, though I'm certain Barbara, dragon Castlemaine, would be only too happy to have you stop by. As young Henry Jermyn's been sent to France, she's down to only seven or eight beddings a week, I warrant."

He glanced out, then leaned back in to kiss her cheek and give her buttock a swift pat. "Seven or eight times a week I could like, but not with Castlemaine, sweetheart. Tomorrow then."

She closed the door and went back into the foyer. Such outrageous comments from Richmond tended to amuse or even excite her now, so she must have just gotten used to him, she mused.

Tomorrow would be a fine adventure. Surely, she could manage to see Richmond occasionally when she chose—and when there were sure to be others along. And she could somehow keep the king her friend and not a lover too. She had done it so far and nothing would go wrong in the future.

She jumped when she saw her cat rubbing the blond periwig set on the tall Chinese vase but too late. It toppled off and broke noisily against the carved foot of the table leg. The cat looked up with round, blue eyes and scampered away.

Frances threw the periwig on the settee behind her and knelt to examine the ruins. She picked up the broken pieces gingerly, still thinking of the king.

*   *   *

On the broad stretch of Thames at Greenwich, the three yachts' sails bellied out with breeze to haul the ships eastward on the first leg of the race to Woolwich Ferry. The sky blazed blue, laced with thin ribbons of clouds; the water chopped gray-green against the ornately gilded hulls. Men shouted overhead in the rigging of the *Francis* as they lengthened or shortened sails. The flap of the massive Richmond coat of arms flag on the stern nearly drowned their words.

After they were well underway, a bareheaded Richmond hurried back to see Frances as she stood in breeches, shirt, and headscarf on the portside of the mast.

"The Duke of York's ahead," she shouted.

"We've only just started," he yelled back as the wind grabbed his words away. "He just has a good tackline right now, and he dared to cut off the *Royal Charles*. If we get far enough ahead or fall back, you can help me steer, only keep away from the lee side near their ships. And I'd better fetch you a broad-brimmed hat. Your nose is pink already, sailor."

He was gone, his hair yanked wildly by the wind. He always looked that way somehow—windblown, free, and utterly, casually at ease with himself whatever he wore. With him, of all the men she'd ever known, proper, elegant clothing didn't really matter.

She loved the roll and fall of the deck as they raced northward around the bend of river and then east past Canning Town. More than once smaller craft dashed out of the way of the three plunging barks; people waved and shouted mutely from green riverbanks as they passed little hamlets trailing occasional smoke from chimneys or sprouting steeples in the brisk September air.

Roger Payne, Richmond's Scottish steward from Cobham, came to lean next to her along the rail and play his bagpipes, a sound both resonant and thrilling which brought back memories of her father somehow, though she couldn't remember his ever playing the pipes.

"What was that tune called, Master Payne?" she asked when he took a breath.

The big, burly redhead, who like her had donned breeches to outwit the ripping breeze, grinned at her. "It's a march, my fine lad," he said and laughed. "Montrose's Fifth Regiment March from the civil wars. I hope you like the sound of skirling pipes, for the duke loves them and plays a wee bit himself."

"He never told me."

"He's wanting a lot of practice, but don't tell him I said so. The king hates pipes and the Scots so that's why we're going to play him a few proud, highland and border tunes today!"

He bellowed another laugh, and she grinned at him as the duke ran by again. "Come on, my bonny lass," Richmond called, "no time for Scottish dancing today until after we beat the royal Stuarts. Come on back if you want to help me steer. The *Royal Charles* is tacking crosswise on the port side of the *James* and telescope or not, he'd never see you now."

She ran after him and climbed the little platform where the wheel was mounted. Richmond took it over from his first mate, Jonathan, who disappeared toward the bow without a backward glance. The loose-footed gaffsail shifted just ahead of them, and when they cut back into the wind, it flapped and cracked like cannons firing.

"I'm going to steer until we bring her about at Dartford," Richmond shouted.. "Come stand between me and the wheel and help."

She did and willingly, grateful his hands were beside hers to control the hard pull of the brass-studded, polished wooden wheel. Soon she began to sense the pattern of regulating the roll and direction; a feel of power and freedom assailed her heart and brain as she stood in his half embrace on the rolling deck with flying, flapping sails and rigging above.

"See why I love it, Frances?"

"It's marvelous."

"Wouldn't it surprise them all if, instead of turning back west at Dartford, we just kept going clear to the Channel and sea beyond?"

She laughed aloud at the heady thought. "And, later, they'd find me missing from Whitehall. Would we go to Scotland so you could beguile me with your bagpipe playing Roger told me of?"

"I'll have his head if he told you how I really sound. And would you go with me if I asked?"

"Today, as happy as I am now, anything is possible!"

"Then I regret I'm needed on deck to win this damned race, my lass, for I can think of some other exciting things besides handling this *Francis*. Best go on back by the mast now as the king's yacht is about to come around—and get something from the stateroom to shade your face and nose, I said."

The hours went by as swiftly as the shoreline. She helped Windy distribute cheese and bread to the crew and reveled in the cadence of the great vessel pushed westward now by the wind. She went belowdecks and sat for a few minutes in Richmond's captain's chair at the table in the stateroom. She stared long at the big bed where he had made love to her last summer and noted it had a new brocade coverlet of deepest blue now. She wondered how much time they might have here alone before he had to send her back with Roger Payne or if he would dare to take her to Whitehall himself. She scampered up the swaying stairs when she heard them cheering and shouting on deck.

"His Grace, Duke Jamie'll be in a foul mood for weeks if'n you best him, m'lord," Jonathan, who had the wheel, was shouting to Richmond. "Lord High Admiral of the English Navy beat by Lord High of the Scots! Jamie would rather have war with the Hollanders than lose to his brother and you, I warrant!"

Frances scanned the width and length of the river as they rolled past Woolwich Ferry on the home stretch to Greenwich. The Duke of York's *James* had dropped back considerably but the *Royal Charles* plunged nearly head to head with them.

"Come on! Come on! We can do it!" Frances shrieked, adding her voice to the men's cheers.

Roger Payne in the very bow of the ship played away on his pipes again, and as if that were pulling them on, they began to make even farther headway on the King's yacht. Frances could even pick him out now stripped to vest and blindingly white shirtsleeves at the wheel of his own vessel. She could imagine the intense slits of slate eyes, the flow of blue-black hair as he leaned forward urging his ship on from sheer will power. She didn't want the *Royal Charles* to lose really, she thought, overwhelmed by guilt at the charade she had perpetrated here today— only she wanted her other Charles to win much, much more.

As they approached Greenwich where the king had begun building a palace, she could easily see the groups of standing, cheering courtiers on the bank. She knew several had the long, thin spyglasses Richmond called telescopes, so she stood in the sheltered doorway to view the end of the race. The *Royal Charles* was now almost beside them twenty feet away, but she didn't want to hide belowdecks at the last.

It was like the most thrilling horserace she had ever seen only more exhilarating at that final moment with the stretching sinew of rigging and the white cloudlike muscles of sail overhead. The dust was cool spray and the creak and groan of ships replaced the thud of hoofs. The two ships strained and plunged head to head. Then the crew erupted into wild cheers, the bagpipe shrilling ceased, and they had won.

Richmond hugged her later in the stateroom as she could feel the ship wheel about again. He kissed her heartily and swung her feet off the floor; she laughed crazily and kissed him back, her arms wrapped around his bronze neck.

"We did it, lass, if only barely! I knew you'd be good luck!"

"Did you win much from your bets, Charles?"

"Maybe enough to reroof the stableblock at Cobham," he told her as he sloshed wine into two mugs. "Want a cut of the action, sweet?"

"I vow, if your Cobham horses are getting rained on, I wouldn't dare."

He grinned again as they clanked their pewter mugs and drank. "Look, lass, I've got to go upstairs and be seen for a few minutes as we go past Greenwich again, but I don't intend to put in there. Windy will be in with some real food and we'll celebrate properly here. I'll be right back." His mug thudded down and he was gone.

Now her mind raced even as the ships had. Would the whole crew sit down to a victory feast—and whatever did "celebrate properly" mean? She reckoned she only had an hour at most before she would have to head back to be certain to arrive at Whitehall before the others, and what did he mean he'd be right back?

He returned almost immediately, his previous joyous expression gone stony serious. He took her hands. "Frances, a little change of plans, I'm afraid, but then we knew this was a risk."

"What is it?"

"His Majesty's ship is right off our bow and he's coming aboard."

"Now?"

"Now. He was close enough to shout so I can hardly pretend to misunderstand and sail off into the sunset with you. He probably wants a good look at the vessel so it would be insane to hide you aboard. Roger Payne is waiting in the skiff for you on the shoreside. You'll have to hurry now."

"Yes, of course. But my clothes."

"I'll get them back to you later. You'll have to go back like that. It's probably better."

"Yes, it probably is . . ." she echoed, her voice trailing off. Tears blinded her eyes and her keen regret at not having more private time with him frightened her. As he reached for her in a rough, possessive embrace, a man's voice from up above shouted his name.

She scrambled up the cabin steps ahead of him but before they emerged on deck, he turned her to face him again. "I'm sorry it's ending so quickly and this way, sweetheart, and I dare to believe you are too. No time for even kisses—"

He pulled her hastily against him again, and his mouth covered hers, lingered. Then he pushed her on ahead and helped her down over the side into the little waiting skiff. Roger had them quickly to the bank and only then did she turn back to wave. But no one now stood on the shoreside rail. The clouds of sails were furled to bare masts and spider webs of rigging as she hurried away with Roger toward the horses in the woods that would take them to the barge landing.

He would never know of it, she prayed, but King Charles had won his victory of sorts today too. How much she had liked being with Richmond today, touching him, kissing him, but now it was all ruined—like when Aberdeen shattered the precious Chinese vase. If she and Richmond had managed some intimate time in the stateroom today, who could tell what might have been their celebration of the victory—and she was ready for whatever befell

357

with him! She walked beside Roger Payne without speaking, lengthening her strides to keep up with his.

Because one of their horses had thrown a shoe, they were much later than Roger Payne had planned, and he was very nervous. She moved mechanically now as dusk set in at Whitehall. She was tired, hungry, and still disappointed because the king had cheated her of the crew's victory celebration and of time with Richmond.

Worse, the courtiers were returned, and she had to hide in Richmond's rooms in the Bowling Green while Roger, following her directions, went to her suite to bring a gown and cloak. She was jumpy now too, her stomach tied in knots like ship's rigging from fear the king would seek her out immediately upon his return to see how her head pain was. She looked curiously around the duke's bachelor quarters while Roger was gone for what seemed an interminable time; then she changed and scurried back to her suite in a trice, with hardly a backward look or wave.

A white-faced Gillie met her in the foyer. "Laws, laws, milady," she whispered, "the king's here waiting."

"No! But he wasn't here when the man came for the clothes."

"No, milady, but he is now."

"I want you to go try to fetch some people, Gillie. Invite them here for dinner or to talk about the yacht race or something; then send someone for plenty of food. The Duke of York, Susan Warmestry, even Buckingham—anyone and don't be gone long."

The king loomed tall and dark behind them in the entry to the drawing room as Gillie went out through the still-open door and Frances closed it quietly after her.

"Where the hell have you been, Frances? I've been frantic today about your being left sick here and I find you're not even in," he rapped out.

"I am sorry, sire." Her voice sounded shaky and quiet next to his. This trembling wouldn't do. She fought to keep calm. "Didn't my maid tell you?"

"Only some sort of gibberish about a walk."

"Yes, exactly. I thought to clear my head today with a walk."

He moved forward to take her elbow, his grip uncharacteristically harsh. He pulled her into the drawing room, then toward the bedroom.

"Please let me go, sire. You're hurting my arm."

"I'm afraid I've been entirely too gentle, love, too damned gentle and permissive and stupidly patient."

"I do not wish to go in there with you," she managed but her voice still trembled.

"Out walking when you should have been at Greenwich with the others. Od's fish, I'd have won if you'd been there," he plunged on ignoring her refusal.

He pulled her hard against him in the entrance to her bedroom and stared, frowning, down at her.

"I'm sorry you lost, sire."

"Damned Scottish-hearted Richmond won and dared to flaunt the hellish bagpipes in my face too!"

"Oh. He played them?"

"Evidently. No one else I found on board could."

She felt her knees go weak as he held her in a viselike grip against him studying her face. Her pulse began to pound: he knew. Someone had told him or he'd guessed. He knew and he'd come to make her confess—to make her pay. If only Gillie would get back with the others!

"Your hair's all blown," he said suddenly, "and your face is pink."

"It's windy and sunny on the Thames. I walked along the river."

"For how long? Alone? Without even a maid? 'Sdeath, I think I shall start chaining you to my bed next week."

"Your bed? Next week?"

"I told you I'm done with patience. By next week at this time you will be my mistress—my lover—and thank me for it too, Frances."

His jaw went taut; his dark eyes glittered down at her in challenge as he waited for her reaction.

"I am sorry, Your Majesty, but I shall have to refuse that honor."

"You're not being asked, Frances. You're being told."

"Then I must leave court."

"And go where? You'll do nothing of the sort."

"Then you plan to imprison me—and rape me—repeatedly."

"Od's fish, Frances! I love you, I'm starved for your touch, for you moaning and moving underneath me. It won't be rape, love, not at all. I swear to you on all I hold sacred you will thank me for this later."

His eyes dropped from her face to the cloak still

wrapped about her, and he finally lowered his hard hands from her arms to divest her of it. She tingled where he'd held her as blood rushed back.

"You're hastily dressed too," he observed and his eyes grew coldly accusing again. "It's not like you."

"I vow, I didn't know I was dressing for the king when I went out or I should have taken more time. Or maybe after what you've announced just now I should have gone stark naked!" She felt trapped, harassed, but she was angry too and determined to fight back.

"I didn't come to argue or trade insults with you, Frances. Heaven knows, I get enough of that from Barbara. And she only gets away with it at all because she's willing to please me in bed, something I fear you have yet to learn."

"I shall never, never learn to be a whore like Madame Palmer! But she gave me very good advice once, I realize that now if a bit too late!"

"Such as?" he asked as his hands darted to seize both her wrists.

"She told me you would expect to be paid by my lifting my skirts for all you have done for me."

"Damn you, Frances! All love is an exchange. You have no right to put it that way!"

"But I cannot love you *that* way, sire, at least not now. So if you mean what you say about this ultimatum, it surely must be rape."

He backed her into the wall, pressing his hard body against her to still her protests. "Frances, little, naïve virgin Frances with the tart tongue. Do you really believe if I had you in my bed it would be rape when it came to it? Do you really?"

"Yes. Let me go."

"No. I'm afraid you have a little lesson coming and a long overdue one at that. I hope your dangerous little river walk cleared your head pain because I want you to remember all of this."

His hard arms lifted her so suddenly that she had been plopped down on her bed before she even started to struggle. Then she fought him silently, desperately, writhing and kicking, but one big heavy leg held hers still while one hand pinioned her wrists over her head. Deftly, he unlaced her bodice and corset and reached to her waist to loose petticoat strings she had so hastily tied.

"Stop it. No!"

"I'm going to ignore tears and pleas for a few moments, so don't exhaust yourself with them. Relax and pay attention."

"No. You can't, you can't. I've sent for others."

"Really? Od's fish, half the court thinks me a fool who has danced too long to your tune anyway."

He lifted her up against him, still holding her wrists, and pulled her gown and petticoats off in one bulky mass clear to her ankles, where he roughly yanked them away. His eyes went almost black as he raised his big hand to the neckline of her thin chemise and slowly tore it down the front.

"Please, sire. I'll hate you if you do this. I swear I will!"

"My beautiful little Frances, you have no inkling what I'm going to do. You may have your precious virginity for another week, I said, unless of course you react as I expect you to and ask me to care for that too."

She writhed under his iron grasp but he pressed her down. He hadn't undressed, hadn't done a thing to his own garments, she thought wildly. Where was that damned Gillie and everyone else!

His hot mouth descended over a breast to tease a nipple taut. She moaned, and he lifted his head trailing long black hair across her breasts.

"I know you like this, Frances. You have before, though you won't admit it. Can you imagine hours of this, of this all over your body? Do you really think you'd tell me 'no, no' then? And there's more, much more."

His free hand dipped between her thighs while his mouth tantalized her other nipple which he suckled greedily. She pressed her thighs tightly together trapping his hand. He loosed her wrists long enough to spread her legs and insert a knee. She hit at him, scratched, but he pushed her back down and had her hands over her head again.

"I know a man's never touched you like this, has he?"

"Don't!"

She tried to make her mind a blank, tried to think of sailing today, of Richmond's smile and gentle words. She tried desperately to wriggle her hips sideways but his fingers were skilled and firmly insistent, making her go all hot and shaky.

His voice had changed now into a passionate moan. "Frances. Damn, Frances, what you do to me! Just touching you like this, I get so wild I can hardly stand not to just take you. No one else has ever done this to me, Frances!"

She tossed her head and bit her lower lip as his hot

caresses spread through her lower belly and prickled her spread thighs. Richmond—she wanted Richmond like this against her, not this deceitful, powerful, demanding body. Richmond kissed her peaked-tipped nipples tenderly and she writhed under his flaming caress. She wanted him to lie with her, to possess her. She ran her tongue along her lips to moisten them for the next assault of his delicious warmth. She lifted her hips up to meet his thrust which surely must begin the rapture of their inevitable union. Stretching her long legs luxuriously, she pointed her toes and moved to ignite his passions even further until he would never dare deny their consuming love.

A huge cramp seized the calf of her left leg, and she cried out. Tears coursed down her cheeks and she heard herself screaming at the man pressed tightly to her. Men! She had seen it time and time again. They all lied! Men! She hated them all as fiercely as this leg cramp hurt her.

"I hate you! I hate you! Let me go!" she shrilled.

Richmond's face became the king's, contorted to a mask of shocked fury. His fingers stopped. He stood abruptly and, when he saw her reach for the bulge on her calf, he leaned forward to swiftly rub the terrible cramp.

She collapsed in shivering sobs while he touched her leg. Then he set her back and moved away when he was certain the cramp had ceased.

"Listen to me, Frances! Look at me!"

Grasping a pillow before her to cover her from hip to breast, she complied. "You are never to wander out alone again from here. Do you understand? 'Sdeath, do you?"

"Yes, sire."

"If every man I can think of hadn't been at Greenwich today, I'd almost think you'd been out to meet someone, but no more of that now. Do you really hate me, Frances?"

"I—no. No, I would never hate you."

"You mean that?"

"Yes. Just please leave me now."

"If you do mean that, then you will let me love you. And the way a grown man loves a grown woman, Frances, is not what we've had."

"I like and I value what we've had, and I do not want to change."

"So beautiful and so unwilling, my little angel who brings me hell on earth. Curse you, Frances Stewart," he ground out low. "I only hope I live long enough to see you ugly and willing someday."

He turned on his heel and stalked out, slamming the door with a violence that shredded the silence. Later, when Gillie came in, Frances dressed and went out to join her guests. She smiled carefully through the chatter of yachting and of bagpipes and of the king's unexplained absence at this lovely, impromptu soirée.

Part III

That Torrent

Song

Give me more love, or more disdain;
The torrid or the frozen zone
Bring equal ease unto my pain;
The temperate affords me none:
Either extreme, of love or hate,
Is sweeter than a calm estate.

Give me a storm; if it be love,
Like Danaë* in that golden shower,
I swim in pleasure; if it prove
Disdain, that torrent will devour
My vulture hopes; and he's possessed
Of heaven that's but from hell released.
Then crown my joys, or cure my pain;
Give me more love or more disdain.

—Thomas Carew

*Beautiful woman in mythology, wooed by Zeus in the form of a golden shower.

Chapter Thirteen

"I sometimes feel we having no home now because of this most terrible plague, my dear Frances," Queen Catherine told her in her broken, accented English. Her Majesty had sent the other ladies inside, but had indicated Frances should stay. Although Frances as maid of honor was often in attendance on the queen even in these difficult times when the court had fled London, it was most rare she spoke with her alone.

"I believe this July heat here at Salisbury has made us all bored and nervous, Your Majesty," Frances said and plied her fan a little harder though they sat in the shade of tall elms and there was a breeze.

"Bored and nervous," the queen repeated. "I thinking—my dear husband does say—that it all beginning from the night that comet flew across the sky over London, the comet with long, fiery tail at midnight bringing signs from the heavens," the queen intoned dramatically and swept her hand in a lofty arc for effect.

"I remember. It was the night of that yacht race from Greenwich."

"Yes, yes, and the king so furious that night and nothing ever been the same since."

It was true, Frances thought, though the queen hardly knew all that had changed the king that day. The loss in the yacht race was hardly the cause of his brooding moodiness, his deepening cynicism, even depression at times. Nor was the cause the declaration of war with the Dutch last spring, for that conflict had been coming for years. Besides, the war was popular with the masses and Parliament, which had opened their usually tight purse strings for one million two hundred fifty pounds to wage it. Not even the dread pestilence which had devastated London and the southern coast and was now marching inland had worried him so, though many wagered it was the cause of his ennui. Though Frances Stewart hoped no one else knew it, it was still His Majesty's failure to possess her that had greatly changed him.

"You frowning in your face, Frances. You not feeling so well?"

"I am fine, Your Majesty. I was only thinking of all the troubles starting, as you say, the day the comet fell."

"Do you believing it all—all things they say of that sign from heaven?"

Frances shook her head as her eyes studied the queen's kind face. "No, Your Majesty. As the king says, however clever the scientists are in these modern times, they can hardly be certain a comet means war, fire, pestilence and famine, though we've had the war and pestilence clearly enough. And, as His Majesty says, 'Od's fish, but they're a bunch of damned ninnies to claim it means the end of the world next year in 1666!'"

Queen Catherine's musical laughter joined her own as Her Majesty characteristically covered her protruding front teeth with her hand. Still, the queen's limpid brown eyes regarded Frances seriously despite their little joke.

"You missing the king now too, dear Frances, or you so happy for the time he is away from us?" the queen asked directly.

Frances gazed out across the valley of the River Avon stretched below the Tudor inn on Exeter Street where they sat and then lifted her eyes to the serenity of the spire of Salisbury Cathedral behind the trees to the northwest. "I would have to say both, Your Majesty. I miss him yet I am glad, as you say, for the—change. Is this— Did you wish to ask that of me here today?"

"Do not be unhappy, so nervous talking alone with me, Frances. You see, not like so many of the others who think Castlemaine so powerful with him, I know it is you."

Frances stared down at her fan and felt herself blush. "My Queen, I beg you to understand that I have not—"

"I know. I believe you. The others whispering what is not true. The king—our king—I know was not lying with you. And for that we are friends, you and I—allies in war, no?"

"Yes. I would like to be your friend and ally, Your Majesty."

That was evidently what the queen had wanted to say, to know, Frances thought, as she watched her fan herself contentedly, almost smugly. The huge dark eyes were not so guarded now, and a tiny smile lifted the perpetually pouted lips.

Frances chose her words carefully in the silence. "Your Majesty, it has been very difficult for me—for all of us, I know—that I live so closely to the king and admire him and so do not wish to anger him."

"Yes, yes. It set him back so, shaking him deep inside that you resisting his power. Yes, dear Frances, I know him so well you see, and love him still even like you loving someone else, no?"

"I? No, Your Majesty!"

"No? There no man you love, no man touching your heart? Shall you be a little nun until the world ending next year, Frances Stewart?"

They shared another brief laugh, and Frances' thoughts darted to Richmond. How she would love to speak of him to the queen, to someone she could trust to listen and not tell, but of course, that was entirely impossible. After the king's fury at finding she had been out that day of the yacht race, she had tried desperately to hold Richmond off again. Each time she had done that since she'd known him—refusing to see him alone, returning his gifts—he had become more bitter and she had become more confused. She wanted to be with him, to see him, but since the king had not made good his impassioned threat to force her to be his royal mistress and had even stiffly apologized for his rough behavior the night of the comet, she owed him not to see Richmond—didn't she? Why could Richmond not be patient and understand?

Frances started as the queen's long-fingered hand touched her own and then drew away. "There truly is a someone, my friend Frances, no? I see you wanting to cry. Listen, please to your queen. Be careful and be wise. The ones hating me hating you also, like Castlemaine and her Buckingham. And if you ever wishing my help to get a man you loving, my friend, you come to me and I help."

"I thank you, Your Majesty. I shall not forget that nor the kindness you have always shown me."

"So then," the queen said and stood, "we are good friends, good allies and we telling nothing of this talk to anyone, especially not to the king, no?"

"No." Frances agreed and stood to shake out her pale green linen skirts. "And you are right about us having no home right now, Your Majesty," Frances said as they went into the back door of the huge inn where the queen's party was temporarily housed. "First we fled London for Hampton Court, then to Farnham Castle, now Salisbury, and next month to Oxford. If only we could move out to Lord Pembroke's seat at Wilton, the whole court could reassemble there."

"Yes, yes, but Castlemaine saying no and so we stay here. I would like so to be rid of her, dear Frances, but she pleasing him still. Only, I think a son from me or from you would rid us of that woman! But I cannot give him this son and you will not give him such, no?"

Frances marveled again at the cleverness and control she had foolishly not recognized before in this little Portuguese woman. Shunted aside at times, ridiculed, the woman nonetheless knew her man and read aright the confusing threads of court intrigue.

Lady Scroope bustled up to them the minute they were in the hall by the queen's rooms. She dropped Her Majesty a quick curtsy and eyed Frances askance even as she spoke. "The Duke of Richmond has ridden in from Cobham, Your Majesty, to see the king but, of course, I told him His Majesty was feeling despondent and went for a week or so into Dorsetshire and thence to visit Oxford." Lady Scroope paused to take a sharp breath. "So, I told him you were with Mrs. Stewart and he asked to be presented to you, Your Majesty. He's awaiting in the front parlor."

Queen Catherine had nodded through the entire recital, her dark liquid eyes on Frances and not Lady Scroope. "Tell him, Lady Anne, we shall be there soon."

"We?" Frances echoed as Anne Scroope curtsied again and hurried off. "But he hardly came to see me, Your Majesty," she floundered. Her heart had thudded since Anne Scroope had said his name; surely, her alarm wasn't written all over her face for them all to read so easily, not right after the queen had tried to pry from her the name of a man she favored.

"Dear Frances, tell your queen nothing if you wishing, but remember, I been observing you as others too."

"Yes, but you will excuse me now?" Frances pleaded and took a step away.

"Yes. But wait for me a moment out where we sitting, no? There is one thing I am wishing you to do

374

for me today."

"Fine, of course. And give the duke my best wishes," she said feeling every bit a coward and an exposed one under the queen's steady perusal.

Frances watched Her Majesty go down the long, dim corridor past the others waiting for her. The queen waved them off and went into the front parlor where Richmond and Anne Scroope evidently awaited, Frances turned and strolled slowly back out the way she had come in.

Today, she thought, had been a revelation. The queen was hardly the foreign dolt many assumed: she was both aware and astute. She knew the king had not possessed Frances Stewart when most court rumors said he had; and, she must have guessed about Richmond and her. But if they'd been that obvious, others must know. Still, it had been months since she'd let him see her alone and now he was here, just a few walls away. Her pulse pounded and she prayed the queen's errand for her would send her far away because if she faced him he would clearly see her tormented desire.

She strolled along the garden path near where she and the queen had sat and stared out over the hedge toward old Salisbury Cathedral again. Its slender steeple almost snagged the rushing clouds blown by the warm July breezes. She would like to walk over to see the big medieval church, but they were nearly cloistered here in fear of plague, and stringent rules banned all strangers or unnecessary travelers from the town. Richmond, she mused, must have convinced them he was necessary.

She had turned to walk among the rosebeds when

she heard quick feet behind her. She spun around. She wanted to flee, but she wanted to throw herself into his arms so much more!

"Richmond. Hello."

"Frances, as beautiful and untouchable as ever." He hesitated. His eyes studied her face intently. "I first met you among the roses at Saint-Germain. Do you remember?"

He did not take her hand nor bow, though perhaps she did not deserve it. Instead, he drew a small dagger from his belt and cut a long-stemmed red rose bud for her.

"I remember, my lord. That rose was white."

"Was it, lass? Then I can only say things have changed since then."

"Yes." But his green eyes still reflected shifting gold shards in the slant of sun, she thought erratically, and his mere presence still disarmed her.

"You came to see the king," she said to break the silence. They moved into the shade where she had sat with the queen. She slowly twirled the long rose in her fingers to try to calm herself.

"It's war business, I'm afraid. I've been appointed Lord Lieutenant of Dorset to guard the coasts there and will be in charge of outfitting privateers to harass the Dutch."

"Privateers—like pirates?"

"Not exactly, Frances, but the French and Spanish as well as the Dutch seem to be getting in on it and we have to do all we can. If His Majesty had not sold Dunkirk to the tricky French, it wouldn't be such a safe harbor for our enemies to dart out from and raid our ships in the Channel. King Louis' France pretends to be fence-sitting, but they'd just as soon aid the Dutch and see us lose our sea power. In short, lass, I was summoned to report to the king, but it seems he's wandered off, so it's only you and I until he gets back."

"You and I and two hundred other courtiers scattered about Salisbury, though the Duke and Duchess of York's retinue has gone on a tour north," she protested quickly.

"Lucky duke to have a duchess to take with him wherever he goes so they don't have to be parted for weeks and weeks," he rasped low.

She turned away and gazed down into the Avon Valley to escape the intensity of his eyes. He always did this to her so effortlessly, made her go all jumpy and shaky inside like this.

"They say the pestilence is terrible in London, my lord."

"Yes, though some government workers have loyally stayed and there are quite a few still at the Naval Office to run the war. I'll probably go back to Westminster after I see His Majesty here."

"Heavens, you can't! It isn't safe! Mother's gone clear out to Oxford to wait for me there. You mustn't go back to London now!"

His face was serious as he turned her to him by her shoulders and then lifted the hand not holding the rose. "I appreciate the sincere concern. Why don't you give me a reason to stay then, come with me to Cobham or we'll go clear up north to Lennox and let king's business care for itself?"

She blushed hot under his gaze. "I vow, you don't mean it," she said low.

"If I knew how you felt, I might."

She lifted her eyes to his: the impact nearly staggered her. Her fingers tightened around his as she took one step toward him, drawn by some frightening, unfathomable power.

"There you two are!" the queen's distinctly musical voice jolted them from their enchantment. "Not setting out yet? Dear me, but I thinking the duke better than this for following pretty royal commands."

Richmond's face broke into a sly grin as Frances pulled her hand free.

"Pretty royal commands. What is she speaking of, my lord?"

While the queen stood beaming at them from a few feet away so obviously pleased with herself she even forgot to cover her protruding front teeth, he told her. "Her Majesty has commanded me to take one certain maid of honor—which one was it now again, Your Majesty?—on an afternoon's jaunt."

"Oh," Frances managed while the queen's silver laughter danced on the warm breeze.

"The lady, my Duke of Richmond, is this lady, Frances Stewart. Go, then, both of you. You two needing to go away, I think." Her Majesty started away before Frances could protest. "Take care of her, my dear Duke," she trilled over her shoulder.

"Richmond, did you put her up to that?"

"No, but I was pleased to think you had."

"Certainly not!"

"Then you refuse?"

"I didn't say that. We—she does seem to think she's done something quite wonderful."

"I would have asked you to go out with me anyway, Frances, but I'm done with pushing and pleading. I'm done with being hugged and kissed one week and ignored the next. If you do not wish to go with me, I will tell the queen so and not bother you again."

"Where will we go? You don't have the yacht hidden around some bend in the Avon, do you?"

He grinned and sighed. She saw all the tautness unwind in his face and stance. "I wish I did. But I can have two horses and some food in a quarter of an hour. We'll ride out to ancient Stonehenge and have a look around. It's only about nine miles, I hear. I'll meet you right here then. We can hardly disappoint the queen of England, you know."

"All right. And shall I come garbed as a lad or a girl?" she teased as she turned away. Her heart soared; her pulse was pounding like hoofbeats already, very fast.

His green-gold eyes went briefly, thoroughly, over her. "Come garbed anyway you want as long as you act like a woman."

At noon they rode out through the city's north gate on Castle Road and left the soaring spire of the cathedral far behind. They followed the river past the ancient ruins of Old Sarum two miles north and crossed it finally at a wooden bridge at Amesbury set amidst the rolling plains of southern Wiltshire. On both sides of the narrow, hedged lane, sheep grazed like puffy clouds in a green sea of grass.

They came up over a swelling crest of hill and there it was beneath their view, like gray stone blocks all set in a fairy circle—Stonehenge.

"The sky and land look so vast from here it doesn't seem very big," she observed.

"The huge central pillars are though," he told her. "Five or six times as high as a man, I'd wager."

"Have you not seen Stonehenge before, my lord?"

He dismounted, then led his horse and hers under a shady cluster of blue-green trees. "Never, lass, though my grandfather Howard, Earl of Suffolk, told me of it, but then he had a hundred half-true stories. Let's eat here in the shade and then go down and see for ourselves."

"Is that the grandfather who reared you when your father and mother died?" she asked as he lifted her down and his hands lingered on her waist. "Is that the same Howard family as Henry VIII's poor beheaded Queen Catherine Howard?"

"Questions, questions. Yes, the same family though that was four or five generations back. My mother was even named for Catherine Howard. My father was killed fighting for King Charles I's lost royalist cause at the Battle of Edgehill in 1642, so I cannot remember him. And when my mother died of smallpox in exile in the Hague in 1650, my sister Catherine and I were reared first by my grandfather, then by cousins at Cobham, though I spent two years in Paris with my uncle, Lord Aubigny by whom I hold title to the fief of Aubigny. And that, sweet lass, is the uneventful history of my life until Bonnie Prince Charlie became King Charles II and got asked home to England to rule."

"And if you were reared at Cobham, that's why you love it there so?"

"True. I fell in love with sweet, gentle Cobham a

long time ago and though she's hardly a pence to her name, I care desperately for her and I'll never let her go."

Frances pursed her lips as if to say "oh," but no words came. He stood, holding the reins of both horses, just staring at her before he tore his eyes away. "Come on then, lass. I hear a little brook down there so I'll water the horses while you set out the food."

They ate and drank warm wine which he decided to cool for later in the brook. They talked and threw gray, round stones into the shallow, rippling water while the lazy breeze fitfully stirred leaves over their heads.

"Let's go down and have a look at Stonehenge, then come back to finish the wine," he said at last.

"All right."

He hadn't touched her though they sat with their backs against the same tree trunk, but he helped her to her feet now.

"It's so peaceful here," she said low.

"I find the country always so, the country and the sea. The sun is beating down so hot today, we won't be gone long."

As they rode closer, the monoliths of Stonehenge rose up before them like protruding giants' fingers from the green earth. Two men were there but they headed away southward as the pair approached so Frances and Charles suddenly had the whole place to themselves. They held hands and walked silently into the circular embrace of barren stones.

"It's awesome," she breathed. "Heavens, whyever did thy build it and what does it mean?"

"And who is 'they'? As with a lot of things,

sweetheart, it's hard to understand, but there it is, undeniable and unmovable."

She eyed him sideways and caught him studying her again. As other times today, she was certain he spoke of the two of them and not what he apparently alluded to.

They examined the larger circle and half-ruined inner horseshoe of massive stones and placed around the outer, nearly hidden circle of regular holes. Finally, they sat inside on a central, rounded boulder, back to back, and just stared.

"They certainly didn't hew these massive pillars and lintels from the flat chalk downs around here," he observed at last. "They must have worshiped here or else the circle of stones told solar time or something, just as the rotation of stars can help sailors steer on the seas."

"And if they could do all this," she said, "what happened to them? I wonder if they believed some night-shooting comet would bring them war or plague or the end of their world."

He gave a short laugh. "If so, lass, I hope they had sense enough to enjoy life while they lived it. Come on, it's warm here. Let's ride back up to our little stream and go wading."

They drank cooled wine from the flask he had propped between stones in the running brook while she sat on a rock and dabbled her bare feet and he waded. The sun blazed down, and she felt her nose and cheeks turn pink, but she made no move to replace her bonnet. He stood facing her, ankle-deep in the clear rush of water.

"So, tell me, Mrs. Stewart," he said, his voice quiet,

"how do you reckon Her Majesty knew we were once friends?"

"Once friends? Are we not now?"

"I'd like to think so. I'd like to think a great deal more, but I've been burned before, you see, and I've grown cautious and cowardly in my old age."

She shrugged her shoulders slightly. "I suppose she just figured it out watching us at dances or dinners, or maybe Susan Warmestry told her. I don't know."

"And I know *you* didn't tell her," he said almost accusingly. "But if she knows, it means others might: Buckingham, Castlemaine, the king even. Your obvious confusion lately—since we were once growing so close—has Royal Charles guessed or said something to you? I know he's watched you like a hawk ever since the yacht, but then you've fully complied with his restrictions, haven't you?"

"I didn't come out here to be scolded, you know! I don't want to talk about it."

"We damn well will talk about it!"

"Maybe I just got tired of sneaking out in disguises, making up lies to see you."

"Fine. Let's have it all out in the open then, and I'll court you publicly. You are an unmarried, eligible woman and, unless you've decided you belong to King Charles, you have a clear right to make your own decisions."

"I do make them."

"I see. That's all I needed to know. Then the fact you put me off when the whim takes you means you do not care for my attentions."

"That's not true. I came today."

383

"That's not enough. Explain it to me."

She pulled her feet from the water intending to scamper back to talk to him from farther away. The sun, his eyes were too hot on her. But he stepped forward and had a slender, wet ankle in a firm grasp.

"Don't. I want to go up in the shade."

"My dear, that's exactly where we are going."

He picked her up as though she weighed nothing and strode noisily out of the water with her. His arms were iron bands and warmth emanated from his bare neck where her cheek was pressed. He put her down on her back on his spread waistcoat in an enclosed bower of shade where she stared up at his intent face, so close. With one big arm imprisoning both elbows at her waist, he gazed down at her.

"No struggles, no insults?" he asked low. "I'm going to kiss you, Frances, and I hope to be kissed back. And I want you to mean it. The first time I hear 'no' from you, you'd better mean that too, because I'll take you back and it will be long months again with the plague and war on top of your stubbornness to keep us apart. I want to be clear and forthright about what I want from you so you can understand and think about it. I want your very beautiful body, but I want much, much more. I love you, Frances, I have for a long time—forever, it seems. I want you to marry me and live with me at Cobham or on the *Francis*, in London, or wherever I am. I want you to be my duchess and bear my heirs and love me, Frances, love me."

Her gasp was stifled by his fervent kiss. He wanted her to think—how could she think when he did this? Her lips opened under the circular friction of his mouth slanted across hers. His hands were on her waist, her ribs, her hips while the sky and swaying tree limbs overhead spun them both around, around. She arched up slightly against him as he moved over her touching her everywhere.

Marriage, he'd said, and Cobham, children, duchess, love. But they couldn't, couldn't; the king would never let them, and she'd have to surrender to Richmond every night in this pool of passion—like this, every night, like this.

He pulled her upright against him and began to kiss her eyelids, her nose, her cheeks, even her throat arched back away from him in luxurious surrender. Her arms went wildly around his strong neck as she felt him begin to unlace her bodice in back.

Dizzily, she kissed him too, fluttering little touches of pouted lips along his hard jawline and in his ear. She nibbled on his neck and licked tiny circles at the pulsating base of his warm throat. "Frances, Frances . . ." he moaned, but she didn't stop.

He bared her to her waist and peeled off his shirt in an answering motion while she watched him through half-closed eyelids. He divested himself of his breeches while she sat among the ruffled waves of her own garments, half naked while shifting shade played over their bodies. She blushed hot as he brazenly lifted one knee to let her study him. Black curly chest hair tapered to a V over his flat stomach as if to point to his blatant desire for her. She could not hide, could not help the way she stared down at his obvious passion as if transfixed.

"You remember how wonderful it was the other times for us, my sweetheart?" he rasped. "Even an hour away from you—one moment—is too damned long, and I won't wait anymore.''

He moved toward her again, his mouth and hands doing wicked, wonderful things to her breasts and taut, pink nipples while he pulled her loosened skirts and petticoats away and she helped him. Completely naked, they clung together, and he moved over her again, parting her legs easily.

"This whole afternoon is ours, my love," he was whispering. "This whole afternoon and a lifetime of others if only you'd let me . . ."

His lips were on hers again, his tongue wildly darting to ravish her mouth. How thrilling it was when he did all this to her, so much different than it was with the king. She felt Richmond's desire probe between her thighs, enter her slightly, almost tenderly. The king—this is what the king wanted from her and what she would never give him.

She lifted her head to look at him as Richmond rained little kisses along one shoulder and slid heavily, deeply into her. Her white legs were spread wide on both sides of his hips and buttocks. His body looked so big as he began to rise and fall against her, while she let him—she wanted him—she loved him.

"No. No, I can't!" a woman's voice startled her.

He lifted to pull almost completely out of her and gazed down aghast, his face gone to chiseled stone.

"Hell's gate, Frances. You can. You are! Damn it, I told you one little 'no' and that was that!"

She gasped as his weight went suddenly off her, and he sat on the ground with his muscled, curved back to her, his big arms encircling his knees. He cursed low, his head slightly down. Tears blurred her eyes and made him look like two formidable, bronze-backed, men. She bit her lower lip hard in the deafening silence.

"I didn't mean it like that, my Lord Charles," she said shakily.

"Get dressed, damn it. I won't look. I'll have you back safe and sound to your little royal cloister in an hour."

She sat unmoving, desperately wiping away tears with her fingers. She ached from wanting to touch him, wanting him back against her, in her. Oh, damn, but she wanted him so terribly, she thought she would break into a thousand pieces like some broken jar if he didn't love her again. A torrent of feelings swirled around her, threatening to drown her.

Sitting on her haunches, she reached out a hand to touch his shoulder. His skin was warm, his body so hard. He didn't move.

"Charles, please don't be angry."

"All right, I'm not. Just disappointed. Get dressed."

She touched him gingerly with the palm of her other hand, lower on his other side along his ribs. "I don't want to. You said the afternoon was ours and I want to stay. I—I want you."

His big head lifted and he turned slightly to rake her with a dark, brooding look. "Say that again, so I'll believe you," he ground out low.

"Please make love to me. I—I want to love you."

His hands were ungentle as he hauled her across his lap. "You little witch," he threatened. "So help me, you'd better mean it!"

387

He cradled her head against him for a moment, but when he moved to lie down beside her again, she saw his manhood stood not so ready as before.

"Oh!" she breathed before she could stop herself.

"You hurt me, Frances, really hurt me, but now we're going to make up for that. Put your hand there and then kiss me back and just see what happens."

He pressed her hand down and took her willing lips while he swelled readily beneath her touch. It all began again then, only it was even more wild because she wanted so to please him, to love him. Mindlessly, she moved against him when he entered her waiting warmth. She clung to his neck and wrapped her legs around his hips when he asked her to. She kissed him back and lifted up to meet him and—and heard herself cry out. "Oh! Oh, I cannot bear it!"

"Let it happen, sweetheart! Let me love you—let me—ah!"

He collapsed against her while delicious torrents of flowing brook and soaring sky washed over her, through her. She almost thought she fainted, but then she could feel his hard, warm body over her still until he rolled them both on their sides facing each other with their limbs still entwined and him still gently in her. His muscular forearm was a warm pillow against which her cheek rested.

"I didn't mean to hurt you—ever," she said after a minute of silent mutual enchantment.

"I know. I understand that after everything you've been through, loving someone, trusting him takes some getting used to. And you've just made me so happy, I've rescinded all of that vast, longstanding debt you've owed me for over three years."

"But you said once only if I would become a member of your family." She stretched and shifted slightly against him. Already he was growing in her again, and the sensation was so disturbingly wonderful she couldn't think. She closed her eyes tightly.

"What if someone comes along?" she asked faintly when he didn't answer. His hand had moved to her breast again and she felt dizzy.

"Then they'll be treated to a damned good show, you little coward," he laughed and flipped her on her back, effectively pinning her under his hips while he continued to move slowly, tormentingly within her. She opened her eyes and her gaze collided with his intense stare only inches above.

"I like watching you," he said low and grinned brazenly. "I like watching all the walls and defenses tumble down and my beautiful Frances emerge from inside to love me back. I don't think I'll ever make love to you in the dark."

"If you want to have a discussion, you'll have— mm—to stop moving like that," she managed. "I can't think."

"Good. Fabulous. Then why don't you just concentrate on loving me like you did a few minutes ago and see what happens."

"I know what happens."

"Do you? Such vast experience, Frances Stewart," he teased but his voice had gone ragged and breathless from his own exertions.

He pressed closer and his mouth plundered hers again while she reveled in it until neither of them could breathe. Their love-making went on and on this time like a plunging, pulling ship, so wonderful, so unquenchable, so shattering. She cried out and clung to him at the last even as he surged into her. Had she even cried out that she loved him, desired him always? she mused as she held him and spiraled back down to earth.

She did love him and someday maybe, when she could escape them all—maybe she would decide to marry him. But then his Cobham needed money even as the king had in his marriage and she had none. She would explain later so he wouldn't be angry. He would understand now; he would—wait.

Curled up tightly against him in the delicious afternoon shade, she slept.

Chapter Fourteen

The next day after Frances' and Richmond's jaunt to Stonehenge, the king arrived back at court sooner than expected and with two French ambassadors in tow. The Dutch War was heating up, and King Louis XIV was most adamant about playing peacemaker although the English were not overly anxious for French tampering after the Duke of York's naval victory over the Hollanders in the Battle of South-wold Bay in June. Still, one of the ambassadors was the Duc de Verneuil, illegitimate son of the deceased King Henri IV of France, and therefore the *duc* was half uncle to both Charles and Louis. The other diplomat was the witty, little Honoré de Courtin who amused King Charles with his clever repartee. But, no doubt, His Majesty would not have even let the Frenchmen on the premises had he guessed their tactical plans for accomplishing their mission.

"The heart and soul of *le roi* Charles's court is playing at bowls out there on the back lawn again," Courtin whispered to the Duc de Verneuil, who listened avidly while polishing his monocle with a lace-edged handkerchief. "I just looked out in back. Castlemaine has that damned Spanish Molina on a leash, and the rest—*sacre-bleu*, the queen, Buckingham, York, Richmond. The country is at war and they're all at bowls on the lawn!"

"And *la petite belle* Stewart?" Verneuil asked. "I assume she's where the king can watch her. They say he's in perpetual whirls over her even though she's obviously his mistress and, therefore, our best bet for a liaison, *oui*?"

"I fear some of that information is debatable, *mon Duc*. My sources, though I grant you rather inexpensive ones compared to what we're used to, think the *petite belle* does not lie with him." Courtin laughed soundlessly at some amusing thought, a habit which greatly annoyed Verneuil.

"*Impossible*! You've seen her—utterly fetching. She's lived under his aegis for over three years now, my dear Courtin."

"I know, and I do not question the fact we should approach her to help us. She spent a year at grand Louis' court, though I was abroad and never met her there, so we may hope she favors the French cause. She was nearly a sister to the Princess Henriette-Anne, they say. Frances Stewart obviously holds a sway that Castlemaine does not. Let that expensive, breeding whore take the Duque de Molina's bribes and side with the Spanish in this mess—*la petite belle* Stewart is our hope whether she beds with the royal Stuart stallion or not."

"Why do you say she may not be the *mistresse du roi*? What did your so-called sources tell you?"

Verneuil pursued, suddenly intrigued by a young girl he had never met.

"*Un*—that she rode away unchaperoned for half the day with the Duke of Richmond yesterday. *Deux*—the little maid manages to be greatly favored by the queen who detests Castlemaine for the obvious reason. And, *trois*—the lady insists she is not his mistress."

The Duc de Verneuil's tiny silver mustache slanted up as he smiled. "*Certainment*—there it is! What lady in her right mind would deny such an honor, *oui*, and the prestige, power, and revenue accruing to that position if it were not true she beds not with him?"

"Exactly, *mon grand Duc*," Courtin said, laughing soundlessly again. "Still, let's fight our way through the lady's other admirers and see what it profits us. It is obvious the queen has no influence on the king and Castlemaine is in league with the damned, meddling Spanish."

Courtin and Verneuil both took a pinch of snuff as they went out into the humid afternoon breeze. "*Sacre-bleu*," Courtin observed, then cleared his head with a resounding sneeze. "It's always windy here but ever hot."

"*Oui*, and likely to be hotter for us yet in Paris if we do not manage to gain this king's promise to allow our King Louis to act as arbitrator in this Anglo-Dutch mess. France cannot afford to have either naval power win and rule the seas, or it will go ill for mother France. Look, Courtin. *Le belle* Stewart has the four most powerful men here cheering her on at bowls and her form is terrible."

"Ah—but only her form at bowls, *mon Duc*. Such pert breasts and tiny waist and such a stunning face. The Duke of York and even Buckingham seem ready to be ravished on the spot while His Majesty smolders. And that other watchful man, the tall, rugged one, that is Richmond, her apparent paramour from wherever they disappeared to yesterday, evidently with the queen's blessing and the king's ignorance, I might add."

The two Frenchmen strolled leisurely past the voluptuously pregnant and vibrantly gowned Barbara, Countess of Castlemaine, whose admirers next to Frances Stewart's were paltry: their diplomatic rival the unctuous Spanish Duque de Molina and two other young men they did not know surrounded her.

Courtin noted silently how the stances of the men clustered about the tall, slender Frances Stewart gave their feelings away—the serious, stodgy Duke of York looked doggishly fond; the king wretchedly moody, disturbed; Buckingham, cynical and objective; and Richmond, avid yet controlled.

Frances' next wooden ball rolled down the close-cropped grass alley and stopped far short of its mark. "You see, sire, I told you I would lose for you. Richmond and York have bested us for certain now," she muttered, hands on hips and disgust.

"York and Richmond only best us in naval maneuvers right now, Frances, and not bowls or aught else. Don't fuss so. It's my turn again and then we'll see."

"Zounds," Buckingham said as the two Frenchmen joined them, "but York and Richmond will soon be wishing they'd bet Frances for kisses they're so far ahead, Your Majesty."

"Od's fish, George," the king groused as his roll went awry too, "I don't need your cute remarks right as I'm bowling! If the king doesn't get Frances' kisses neither does anyone else, right, my dear?"

The quick look which darted between the frowning Richmond and Frances Stewart was not lost on Courtin or Verneuil. Then the woman gazed directly at the elegant, silver-haired Duc de Verneuil. Her sky-blue gaze and pout of annoyed lips stabbed him sweetly. *Sacré Marie*, he thought, no wonder the randy Stuart king is smitten by this one when he could have anyone else.

"Your Majesty," she was saying, evidently choosing not to answer her sovereign's rather pointed question about the kisses, "I vow, I have not been introduced to your friends."

"*Mon Duc*, Courtin, sneaking up on our little games eh?" King Charles said, neither smiling nor nodding. "Od's fish, I thought you two were in audience with the queen."

"Indeed, Your Majesty, we were until a moment ago," Courtin replied.

"Fine, fine. Frances, these are the honored ambassadors I have told you of—my uncle, the Duc de Verneuil and the clever, ubiquitous Honoré de Courtin. You know the others, I believe, gentlemen."

Frances swept them a graceful curtsy. She eyed the handsome, middle-aged Duke and then the much younger, shorter Courtin. "Welcome to our little court in exile, *mon Duc* and *Chevalier* Courtin," she welcomed them in charming, perfect French. "The

395

luxuries of Whitehall would, no doubt, be more to your liking, but the times are very dangerous with the dreadful plague sweeping London and carrying into the surrounding shires."

"*Sacre-bleu*, Mademoiselle Frances," Courtin replied, "so true, so true. But we are honored to be here despite"—he sniffed—"the company Madame Castlemaine insists on keeping."

"De Molina?" the Duke of York asked. "I'd not fret for that it I were you, uncle. They're birds of a feather, I'm afraid, parties 'til all hours and such expensive gifts for her that—"

"I really don't think you need to tell your uncle about the Spaniard Molina's actions, James," the king interrupted, switching the conversation pointedly to English. "He probably knows as much of Molina's goings-on as we do, and I have the strangest feeling he came over here not to uncle us or to chat with Buckingham or Richmond."

"Astute as ever, Your Majesty," Verneuil admitted. "And you would trust your dear old uncle to stroll about the roses with *mademoiselle*, then, would you not? I shall leave you my clever compatriot Courtin for company if you don't mind."

The king nodded in apparent acquiescence, but the Duc de Verneuil looked unpleasantly surprised. Buckingham leaned, insolently at ease, one foot up on a wooden bench while Richmond's eyes had narrowed to green slits, and York looked actually hurt. *Sacré Marie*, what a tangled web he'd walked into here, he mused, but was the elegant, lovely woman the spider or the fly?

She strolled away at his side, her pale yellow skirts

swishing slightly in the sudden silence. "You are hardly His Majesty's *old* uncle, my Lord Duke."

"How sweet of you, my dear. And you seemed pleased enough to be rescued from that group, eh?"

"Indeed, my bowling was wretched today," she replied.

He wondered if she had misunderstood or had cleverly avoided his subtle probe. She seemed young and yet she must be cunning if indeed she had avoided the king's bed, as all her welfare and success must surely depend on him.

"You no doubt recall your days at the French court with great affection," he began on a new tack, and smiled at her as they strolled among the riot of leggy, multihued roses. He knew he was handsome still, enchantingly so, his mistresses said, and perhaps this one would be a little susceptible to his long-practiced charms.

"My year at King Louis' court is an experience I shall never forget," she parried.

"Ah. Indeed. And you were very dear to the Stuart princess, the Grand Duc Philippe's Madame Duchesse, I believe."

"Yes, my Lord Duke. I miss her terribly even after all this time here. I vow, she was—is as dear to me as my own sister Sophia."

"Poor Duchess Henriette-Anne," he drawled and sighed sadly for effect.

Frances' elegant head turned, and she focused her intent eyes on him. "You have not come to say she is ill, my Lord Duke?"

"No, no, my dear. I referred only to her most unnatural, sad marriage situation, but of course, you know of that."

"Everyone does, I believe. I pray she finds joy in other things . . ." Her words drifted off, and she frowned as memories assailed her. Lovely, sweet Minette sitting with her years ago in a rose garden at Saint-Germain, hoping for love—love in her own marriage. Minette at the Louvre, her husband's prisoner while he dallied with his slender, blond Duke of Lorraine! Damn that foppish Philippe and all his boy lovers! Men—one way or the other they were deceivers and tormentors, except perhaps not Richmond, she fumed silently.

"My dear, I meant not to distress you. There is something we can all do to help the Princess Henriette-Anne—your Minette. Will you give me leave to speak of it?"

She let him take her hand in both of his. "Heavens, for the dear princess, anything."

"You know how desperately she wishes her two beloved nations, England and France, to be perpetual friends, then."

"Of course," she said carefully, her blue, blue eyes studying his face. "We would all wish for that but it may not be possible. The war is very popular here now."

"*Certainment*, it is, as your naval forces have tasted victory, but the Dutch are strong and clever. So, if your king could only be persuaded to take the advice of our king—"

"And that advice is, *mon Duc*?" she asked adroitly, challenging him in his own language which she spoke beautifully.

He hesitated. She looked so young; she had seemed

so frivolous at first—merely lighthearted. But she was deceptively clever, a carefully controlled woman and in control lay power.

"*Le Roi* Louis' advice, *ma chérie*, quite frankly, would be to let Louis be peacemaker in this wretched war for naval supremacy."

"I am sorry, but as I said, even with the Parliament, the war is very popular and we shall no doubt win. The Duke of York's fine victory at Southwold Bay indicates that clearly enough," she insisted.

"One victory makes not a war, *ma chérie*."

"Of course, but neither can a foreign king make victory in a war for us. It must be earned by us—ourselves."

"*Sacré Marie*, but you've been listening to generals, little one—or to great dukes like York and Richmond."

She colored slightly and gently tugged her hand away as if surprised to note he still held it. "I do not understand, *mon Duc*," she said. "Why do you speak to me of all this—this foreign policy?"

"Because, *ma chérie*, to put it flat, you can help your dear princess' beloved France in this, as well as your own dear England. After all, you have King Charles's ear."

She moved slightly away, and he made haste to follow. "But so does King Charles's dear sister the princess have his ear—and so does Castlemaine," she protested, "and she seems to favor the Spanish as peacemakers."

"He listens not to them and he does you, I believe," Verneuil insisted and his voice rose though he meant not to show his frustration. "*Sacré Marie*, shall the poor princess be disappointed again, then?"

"*Mon Duc*, unlike the Countess of Castlemaine, I prefer not to dabble in plots and subterfuge or in foreign or domestic machinations. And, unlike Castlemaine, I do not serve His Majesty, King Charles, in any capacity but as lady to his wife, our queen—and as his friend."

"Amazing!" he breathed.

"I am sorry if you have been misled."

"But aiding France, *ma chérie*, and the Princess Henriette-Anne would be so simple," he protested. "A few words to king Charles, a little invitation to Courtin and me to attend when you entertain him—"

"At bowls, *mon Duc*?" she shrilled, her flawless brow wrinkling in obvious dismay. "Believe me, I am in no position to aid you. Excuse me, please."

"*Un moment s'il vous plaît*! I believe you might do it for the Duke of Richmond if he asked, is not that true?"

She whirled back to face him, her eyes wide. "Richmond? What has he to do with all this?"

The deep brown eyes under silvered brows narrowed. "I thought perhaps, *ma belle* Frances, you could tell me."

"I—heavens, has Richmond spoken to you of the war? He lived briefly in France, I know."

"No—no, *mademoiselle*. I thought only since you spent all of yesterday afternoon off somewhere alone with him, you might have spoken to him of it."

She blanched, then blushed. That lucky bastard Richmond, Verneuil thought. Lucky, and probably loved while the poor King of England seemed more an impoverished, wretched suitor out on his royal ear and hardly loved at all—not the way he so obviously desires.

"I do not know what you imply, *mon Duc*," she said low at last.

"Nonsense, *ma belle petite*. You're a big girl now. You help our cause—only by allowing us to be close to you and thus the king, that is all—and Courtin and I do not tell him what we know about you and Richmond, and your lovely privy afternoon together."

"Mere surmisings," she challenged but her voice and lower lip trembled so fetchingly she made him want to embrace her.

"Shall I tell His Majesty what I know and let him decide?" he demanded.

"And what do you know?"

"Enough to make me so envious of Richmond I should like to run him through with my sword—but, *Sacré Marie*, my lips are sealed if you will but help."

"But—we go to Oxford in only a few weeks and if he has not budged by then, surely you will say the bargain is cleared."

"You will aid us, then?"

"Until Oxford and only to keep you in His Majesty's presence. I shall never be another Castlemaine, I vow!"

"No, *ma chérie*, you never shall."

Her eyes went once over his face; then she moved swiftly away. Though they both knew protocol dictated she should have been dismissed first, he let her go, entirely pleased. The clever, wily Courtin himself could not have done better. Tomorrow he would send her a note to remind her of her vow to help—and tonight, he would dream of being that fortunate scoundrel Richmond in her sweet, white arms.

Frances skirted far around the roses and strolled in front of the inn rather than rejoining the courtiers or going in through the back. Today had taken a terrible turn after the fanciful escape with Richmond yesterday. Foreign intrigue, political maneuverings, extortion. She and Richmond had obviously been watched, spied upon. But by whom, where, and for how long? Surely the Duc de Verneuil or his clever, little ally Courtin had not ridden out to Stonehenge themselves or had them followed. Oh heavens, they had made love twice in broad daylight in that little woods near the stream, and she had slept naked in his arms a good hour before they had headed back!

She glanced nervously up and down Exeter Street, the lane which ran north and south in front of the sprawling Tudor inn where the royal family and the women closest to the queen were housed in single, crowded rooms—with the exception of Castlemaine who had two fine, large adjoining rooms on the first floor because she was pregnant again and had insisted she could not climb stairs.

Frances entered the inn through the deserted public room with the massive hearth and low-beamed ceiling. She would go upstairs and claim a head pain or some such to give herself time to think. The last things she needed right now were the king's questions, York's fawning, or Richmond's unsettling gaze. She didn't dare be seen talking to him alone after what Verneuil had told her he knew; she'd merely write him a note telling him the meeting she'd promised him this evening before he left tomorrow was impossible.

She had one silk slippered foot on the stairs up to her room when Castlemaine's distinctive voice cut the quiet of the empty inn.

"Running off from that veritable raft of rabid admirers including the two Frenchies, dear Frances? That's always been your policy, hasn't it? Give them nothing, yet leave them panting for more?"

Two steps up, Frances spun to face Castlemaine who had come so close, she had one pearl-braceleted arm on the newel of the staircase handrail. "But, dear Barbara, who are you to scold me for leaving the party out back? Of course, your policy has always been to give them everything until they want nothing."

"You pious, little bitch. So pure, so damned virginal still, but I carry his son again and his affections, too!"

"If you are referring to His Majesty, I suppose this child could be his—or it could be several others', I don't know. But his affections, madame? Heavens, be serious. He was with me out there and not you, I believe."

"You do realize you've gone too far in your silly games, don't you, Stewart? You've ruined his admiration and awe, you know. He is furious at you. It won't be long now before he doesn't give a royal damn if James, Duke of York, has you or not!"

"Are you trying to recommend the duke to me? Is he some other poor castoff, who no longer suits you, from among the myriads you've entertained in your busy bed? I vow, I shall never, never take leavings from you, Madame Palmer!"

Frances stood her ground as Barbara came up one step to face her. Her hands tingled to slap the glowering woman's smug face, to tear her hair.

"You snide, little slut," Barbara exploded, her voice a shrill shriek. "You wretched, pious little whore—"

Barbara's hands came at her like claws but Frances shoved her back into the wall. Barbara's hand caught in her tresses and she yanked Frances' head back hard. As Frances spun around, she caught Barbara's chin with her elbow. Frances feared they would topple the few steps down to the floor, and she grabbed at Barbara to stop her fall.

Suddenly an arm was around her, a strong arm: a big hand appeared to pull the two of them apart. She darted a look and blinked tears away. Richmond!

"Stop it, you two! Fighting like alley cats! Stop it. Let loose, Barbara!"

"She insulted me, you bastard! Get off!" Barbara ground out at him.

"And you, of course, did nothing," he said low as he finally disengaged Barbara's hand from Frances' loosened hair and put Frances behind him at the bottom of the steps.

Barbara snorted and vigorously brushed off her arms and gown. "Pooh! I suppose she's got you following her around like a little lap dog or some such to protect her, Richmond. You did see her walk off back there with the king's bastard uncle, Verneuil, and that worried you, I suppose. Verneuil's kept a veritable stable of mistresses happy over the years, of course, and probably still has a bit of the *roué* in him yet, but I doubt if he favors icy vestal virgins. Now, if you two will excuse me, I merely came in to piss and I'd much rather tend to that than this!"

Richmond moved his foot from the step to let her flounce down and waited until he heard a door slam down the hall. "Are you all right, lass? I saw Verneuil come back alone."

"I'm fine, my lord. I was just going up to my room when she appeared."

"The king's engrossed with his little friend Courtin. Now where can you meet me tonight? I'd best go back out before I'm missed."

"Actually, I'm not sure I can manage it."

His rakish brows crashed instantly down over his green eyes, and one hand moved to the wall beside her to block her in. "You promised. You know I leave at dawn for London and then go to outfit the privateers soon after."

"I'm sorry, but it's obvious we're being watched."

"By whom? And so what? I told you we've got to get out in the open with this and yesterday, I believe, I heard you agree."

"I did not say so."

"No," he said, his voice deceptively low considering how angry he was getting, "you didn't say so. More to the point, you acted so."

She stared down at the little hollow at the base of his brown throat. A tiny pulse flickered there, the same one that had fascinated her yesterday when he had moved so close over her and moved up and down

405

repeatedly in her. . . .

"Frances, look at me." Woodenly, she complied, dragging her gaze up to lock with his piercing stare. "Did Barbara or Verneuil say aught of yesterday? Did the queen or king?"

"The queen," she said low, realizing she had not the time or strength to tell him of her bargain with Verneuil when he glared at her like that. It would be just like him to approach Verneuil himself to warn him off and then Verneuil would tell the king what he knew. She dropped her eyes.

"Look at me, I said. I love you, Frances, and you promised me time alone to say goodbye tonight. I have to go back out as I left York practically talking to himself and he's as likely to come in here after you as the king if I don't hurry back. Where will you meet me and what time?"

"I don't know—I can't say."

"Listen then. An hour after everyone goes to bed, come down the back servants' stairs and I'll be waiting there. We'll walk out in back."

"It might be dangerous."

He seized her shoulders and shook her once. "It will only be dangerous for you if you don't come, Frances. Yesterday you loved me in the sun and now you balk at a little walk in the dark. I'll be waiting, Frances."

He strode away out the front even as she heard other voices coming in from the back. Quickly, she turned and ran upstairs. Her room was a small quaint one with a slanted outer wall where a thatch-covered gable began to slope outside and with a large window she could set ajar to catch breezes in the warm nights. Her view was of the side gardens and the cathedral spire beyond. Heavy ivy climbed the wall outside, and birds nested in it, their song wakening her at dawn before she had become accustomed to her new surroundings.

A soft, feather bed, a table, and two chairs crowded the narrow space of floor, further eaten up by the two large coffers which stood open in the corner displaying her things. The queen's retinue in these cramped quarters made do with sharing two ladies' maids so Frances did many tasks Gillie and Jane, who were still at Hampton Court with her pets, ordinarily cared for. Still, here in this rustic simplicity, in these terrible plague and war time, it seemed natural and right that she live alone, alone without all the trappings of luxurious Stuart courts—alone without Richmond.

She sighed and tears filled her eyes as she leaned back to close her bedroom door firmly. Before Richmond, she had never cried like this, had hardly ever cried at all, but he always made her so confused, so wretchedly emotional. He was so different from all the others probably because she'd let him seduce her, or he'd been the first to ever dare to ask her to wed with him while the king kept everyone else at bay.

Only yesterday, she'd lain with him—twice and willingly. She'd let him speak love words to her and said them in return. She'd let him spill out all those plans for them—Cobham and children. Worse, she'd done exactly what she had sworn she'd never do. She'd lost much, much more than her virginity and control to him—she'd lost her heart.

She lay down heavily on the bed and stared upward

at the black-beamed, white plaster ceiling. "No," she said clearly aloud. "No, it cannot be. Men—don't trust them, don't love them or they will only hurt you." Mother's words, those are mother's words, she thought, and they were true.

It was warm, very warm in here, and she was mussing her skirts but she didn't care. Escape. She would love to escape, to run away in the dark but not to meet Richmond. She closed her heavy eyelids and welcomed the dark. She was so tired, so tired of this all and somehow the court could ruin even this lovely, rural sanctuary with plots, intrigues, and whisperings.

Whisperings, she heard them in the tree and ivy leaves outside her window, heard the voices down the steps. His beloved Cobham, that would be the place to go but then he would be there every night to make her love him, to make her touch his smooth, bronze shoulder to say, "I want you. Please love me."

She drifted slowly, wading in the erotic, rushing stream of his love. He held her, caressed her with his eyes and voice and hands. She moaned low and shifted her legs in anticipation. She drifted deeper, softer. Now she was in bed with him—no, there were more in this bed: Verneuil and the little Courtin chattering away at her in French. The king was watching, nodding, and Castlemaine was shrieking, and Richmond was nowhere here, and—

She sat up in bed, astounded to see her little, deserted room lit by the dimming light of late afternoon. A dream—it was a silly dream. "Oh," she moaned and put her head in her hands, "he's even in my sleep."

She washed her face and hands and repinned her tousled tresses letting them fall in curling tendrils at her temples and nape in *la négligence* style. She painted her lips with a rosy cochineal and powdered her shiny nose. She changed her gown to one of soft-hued pink satin with a single ivory underskirt, and she went down for supper. Unfortunately, Richmond sat just down the table by the queen where he could easily watch Frances as she sat between the king and the Duc de Verneuil.

Her heart beat very fast at Richmond's frequent stares as Verneuil and the king kept involving her in their wide-ranging conversations. It is so hot in here, she thought, even this late in the day. Whyever had they come to Salisbury to escape the pestilence when many other country places would do? How she'd love to slap Richmond's avid-eyed gaze. Did he think he owned her now?

She laughed with the others at Courtin's witticisms or the king's funny stories of life in exile at the stodgy Hague. The partridge pies, the side of lamb, and even the array of vibrantly hued fruit all tasted like dust though she drank a great deal of cool white wine to wash it all down. She'd have to whisper to Richmond that their meeting tonight was impossible. He would simply have to understand!

The long evening of playing various dice games began, but Frances was relieved to just stand and watch. At least Richmond looked involved, playing in-and-in across the room with the Duke of York, his watchful duchess, and the smiling queen.

She started at the king's deep voice so close. "Did you have a nice chat with Verneuil today, Frances, or does the fact he came back alone mean he said something to unsettle you?"

"No, sire, not exactly. Only that he spoke of Minette being unhappy, but we knew that."

"Indeed we did. And is not your tender woman's heart moved by the fact I am unhappy and it would be so easy to please me?" he asked low.

"Could we not have this discussion later, sire?" she countered and twirled a loose curl on one nearly bare shoulder.

"Indeed we can. I shall come to your room after midnight and knock once."

"No, I did not mean that."

His dark expression barely changed. "I realize that, Frances," he sighed and frowned. "I also realize it would be easier to win the Dutch War and halt the blasted pestilence overnight than expect loving from you. Ah, dear Uncle, join us," His Majesty raised his voice and his upper lip to smile at Verneuil's approach. "Frances and I were just chatting about foolish dreams, were we not, my dear?"

The Duc de Verneuil, elegantly attired in silver brocade despite the warmth of the evening, bowed grandly. "Foolish dreams, but how amusing." He laughed fully, reading Frances' surprised look which showed they had been discussing nothing of the kind, but she cleverly recovered her momentarily lost aplomb.

"Foolish dreams, yes we were, sire," Frances said. "To tell true, my Lord Verneuil, both you and the Chevalier Courtin were in the silly dream I had while napping this afternoon."

"Really, *ma belle* Frances, and will you not tell of

it?" Verneuil inquired smoothly, summoning Courtin from another group nearby with a flick of lace-encircled wrist.

"I dare not, for fear it might be misinterpreted," she laughed and plied her fan. She shouldn't have brought it up, she knew, but the king had deliberately goaded her. Besides, she was too warm and too dizzy in here. If she did tell it, at least it might warn Verneuil that she didn't fear him.

"I dreamed," she said, unaware both the dukes of York and Richmond had come up behind with Courtin, "that I was in bed with both the Duc de Verneuil and his little friend Courtin, though I vow I was fully dressed."

"But, *Sacré Marie*, what an honor!" Verneuil exploded while the king only glared.

"And I, Frances?" the king demanded.

"You—you were just watching, sire," she finished honestly, and wished at once she had not at all embarked on the telling of the dream.

"Od's fish, it figures, but then it was a mere dream," the king muttered. His dark eyes raked her despite the little crowd which had collected, including Castlemaine whose fan flipped so fast her bracelets jangled. "Just watching," he repeated. "But, Frances, I had a dream once I would never be king, and look at me!" He forced a loud laugh as everyone joined in raucously.

It is like the end of a very bad theatrical, Frances thought, as from then on the curtain slowly closed on their evening. Everyone whispered of the dream and she turned about too late and realized Richmond had heard. Soon he disappeared. The king was sullen and

Verneuil and Courtin merely amused. A disaster, a tragedy of an evening, she mused, as she freed herself from the queen's chatter at last and asked His Majesty for permission to go upstairs.

"Good night, sire."

"Good night, my Frances," he said low. "And you'd better work on getting your dreams straight, or I'll do it for you."

"I am sorry. I only told the truth."

"Then I shall change the truth. Damn the truth! Go on now. We're all tired and wretched depressed, all but the queen and Verneuil, it seems. I almost wonder sometimes if that blasted, hellish comet last autumn did not foretell destruction. Go on to bed, Frances. I simply couldn't abide accusing tears from you tonight."

She went slowly up alone. Richmond would have to understand. She couldn't take a chance on being seen trying to meet him tonight. She was too tired. Heaven help her—she was too certain of how she felt about him now.

She locked her door, undressed and sponged her warm skin in cool rose water a maid had left, then brushed her hair for a long while to pass the time. She straightened out her jewelry box and laid out clothes for tomorrow. At last when the inn quieted, she blew out her candles and fanned herself in the slightly stirring breeze at her window.

Cricket calls were unutterably sweet and someone's laugh darted out a window. An owl called disconsolately from the trees. She stopped her fan and leaned far out a moment reveling in the breeze which lifted her loosened hair. A clean quarter moon sailed above the trees, while winking fireflies studded the velvet lawns below. It was all so lovely, and she felt so wretched.

She pulled her head back in, leaving the window wide ajar and lay down in her lace and linen chemise hoping to sleep. She would be asleep and tomorrow would be here and Richmond—her Charles—would be gone. She would send him a note to Cobham when they returned to London as she could never send him one tonight. She would explain she cared for him, maybe loved him, but of course marriage plans were impossible. He would understand—he would have to understand.

She tossed fitfully, achingly on the narrow, warm bed. Surely now he was below to meet her, or maybe he, too, had been angered by her foolish telling of the dream and would not come anyway. But how she would love to know if he had come! And if she had met him there, and they had strolled out among the crickets and fireflies, what then?

She drifted in and out of leaden slumber. A scraping sound, a soft thud pulled at her floating thoughts. She moaned and pulled her eyelids open. She turned over on her side even as a big, black form blotted out the little rectangle of dim moonlight that had been the window. A hard hand pressed down across her gasping mouth before she could scream.

"You forgot your promise, lass. I waited over an hour. So I had to come to you," the deep voice hissed in the warm darkness.

She murmured his name against his imprisoning hand. She could not move as he quickly lay full length against her on the bed pressing her down on

413

her back. His breath rasped very hot against her ear and temple as he whispered. Her heart pounded in wild rhythm against his muscular chest which nearly crushed the breath from her.

"You're either a cowards or a liar, Frances Stewart, and I don't value either as a wife, even though I try to understand. And yet I want you, want you so. No pretty dreams to tell them all about going to be with me, my love?" The edge to his voice became sharp, and she tried to shift away, to loosen her mouth so she might explain about Verneuil, about how things she'd said to him would have to wait. "Let me give you a waking dream you can tell them all about tomorrow then, sweet, deceitful little Frances," he went on. "Tomorrow when I'm gone from you for who knows how long with the plague in London and the war at sea, think about this. If you would have come down to me, you see, I'd have known you really cared and were ready for what I have to offer. But if you only think you love me when I give you this, then this it is, my tempting, tormenting, little witch."

He peeled the thin chemise down off her shoulders stretching it across her waist and elbows to immobilize her arms and bare her breasts. Stunned at first, she began to writhe under him as she grasped his intent. In the dim moonlight, one hand still over her mouth, he divested himself of his breeches and pulled her chemise hem roughly up from knees to waist. But for the little rolled belt of her single garment around her middle and elbows, she lay competely nude beneath him.

Her words were smothered against his hand as he stopped her squirming to kneel between her warm, bare thighs. He intentionally spread his legs to force hers wide apart. His hot mouth lowered to her nipples which went instantly hard against his lips and tongue. Again and again he teased and caressed each wet peak in the silence of the dark room until she thought she would faint with desire.

"I don't really think you'd scream for help, my dear little tease, and I would like to take your mouth with mine, but this will have to do. You see, I couldn't bear any more sweet love words you don't mean later when I'm not touching you. I don't want to hear so much as another moaned 'maybe' to torment me later when we're not together. I've lived too long on my foolish delusions, so I'll only give you what you evidently want from me as a parting gift and be off for good."

He moved his free hand heavily under her derrière to lift her hips up toward him. She couldn't free her arms against the tautness of the rolled chemise. He pressed against her ready warmth which shamed her as much as it evidently delighted him. He drove slowly, deeply in. She went weak and hot and wild as he moved in a deliberately controlled way within her. She kicked finally, futilely at his legs but one smart spank against the side of her flank stilled her.

A rampant, flowing, drowning rapture swept through her as it always did when he touched her like this. He was forcing her, insulting her, shaming her, but she loved it—she loved him. His breathing became ragged, irregular against her left ear where he pressed his face into her rumpled pillow. Still the delicious caresses went on and on. In fierce abandon, she moved against his thrusts, welcoming him, wanting to be part of him like this forever. She loved him—she loved him desperately but his hard hand wouldn't let her tell him. A rolling wave of ecstasy swept over her spinning her around and around deeper into love with him. He said—he was—going away and he could so easily do all this to her.

He groaned and pulled away, cursing softly, his head down a moment. But she was certain, certain he hadn't reached his own sweeping release. She lay as if drugged, spent, and utterly satisfied as he moved to sit heavily on the edge of the bed and loosed her mouth at last. He swore low again as he stood to tug on his breeches and tried to lace them.

"Please, Charles—"

"Quiet!" he hissed. "I want nothing else from you you'll just take back later. And I only stopped just now because I intend to do no more to give you my babe as you evidently have no intention of becoming my wife. Goodbye, Frances. And if you do dream of me, don't worry about it ever being real again."

He was across the room and out the window before she even grasped his last words. No! He was going, leaving her like this! No!

Her legs were jelly when she tried to stand, tugging the wrapped chemise up and down from binding her arms at the elbows. He had—he had come and taken her and he was leaving. The room spun crazily and she almost fell.

She ran to the window and stuck her head out. He was gone, gone already. He must have dropped part way; she could not even see the white blotch of his shirt anywhere in the black and gray night. It was as if she had dreamed he had said that—dreamed him—and now he had disappeared into the darkness of memory.

She fell heavily to her knees, her wild hair against the window sill. Curled up tightly against the hard wall in the warm blackness, she wept.

Chapter Fifteen

Although the plague had finally glutted itself on
English lives and dwindled away, the war with the
Dutch had now spread to war with France. Frances'
favoritism with King Charles kept her from any
implications in the failed political maneuverings of
Verneuil and Courtin, but she had never done more
than invite the two ambassadors to attend her in the
evenings at Salisbury when the king was there. And
anyway, their threats of blackmail did not matter to
her now: she had not seen the Duke of Richmond in
the six months since Salisbury and, she told herself
grimly, would never be close to him again. The
desperate longing she felt for him became an empty
ache and then subsided to familiar, bitter anger at
how a man always hurt a woman who loved.

Loved—that was the word she always used to
herself about Richmond as the court returned to
Whitehall in March and fell back into its usual
routines as though the bubonic pestilence had never
ravished the town. She had really come to love him

for a golden while, but now it was over and served as a clear lesson to her.

She heard he was in Dorset or in Scotland or at sea. Her heart would hammer treacherously each time someone spoke of his exploits or when the queen brought up his name as if she were his champion. Frances pictured him here at Whitehall—in a coach which rumbled by in the park, on the stairs, on the dance floor, in her rooms half sprawled at ease on her settee. But he was gone and that was that; whatever had been between them was as dead as the foolish past. She imagined him at sea at the helm of the *Francis*, windblown, laughing, and utterly pleased to be rid of her. He would never speak low, raspy love words to her, so what did any of that matter now?

The same characters in much the same poses fell back into place in the drama of her life, speaking their lines in the same proper scenes, but she was not the same, and try as she might to be gay and aloof, in her heart she knew she had changed.

"Dear, sweet Frances," the Duke of York's sonorous voice broke into her reverie, "what sort of host do you think this makes me?"

She whirled around to face him at the window of St. James's Palace where she had been gazing out over the park though little could be seen in the dimming light. She had not realized anyone had seen her leave the dancing or had followed her. "Forgive me, my Lord Duke, what did you say?"

"I said, sweet lady," he murmured lower and took one hand in his, "you make me feel a terrible host when you wander off like this alone. Are you feeling indisposed?"

"No, I am fine, my lord. The music and the food are wonderful. I just felt like walking." She realized too late she should have said "walking alone" because he tucked her arm against his brocaded ribs and pulled her gently along the stretch of windows in this dim drawing room several chambers from where everyone was dancing.

"Melancholy over the king's behavior?" he asked.

"No, Your Grace." She wanted to pull her arm away, but he held it so firmly and looked so smugly pleased, she couldn't bear to hurt him. He tried so carefully, so desperately to please her, and at least here was one man who had demanded naught but smiles and kindness.

"But I know his black moods, his temper, wear on you," he pursued.

"He has much on his mind, my Lord Duke—the war, the plague's devastation of the populace, the fickleness of public opinion—"

"—and Frances Stewart," he finished for her.

She tugged her hand back and turned to face him in the frame of the next tall window which reflected their wan images in the growing dark. "That is as it has been since I came to Whitehall, Your Grace. I cannot help that."

"I theorize that you have caught His Majesty's moodiness, his pained, distant expressions of late as one catches a winter chill."

"I?" she asked, suddenly wary. Had his uncle, that crafty Duc de Verneuil, or the queen told him of Richmond's desertion of her?

"I thought—I feared—perhaps you'd come at last to love His Majesty a bit," he said hesitantly.

"I do a bit, Your Grace. I told you once before, I admire him and—"

"*I mean*," he ground out and his lower lip quivered, "as a woman loves a man—desire, the way he's desired you. I thought that now he shows marked favoritism to Castlemaine again and has paid her gambling debts of thirty thousand pounds at Yule and since she bore him this third son at Oxford you've felt the bite of jealousy as the rest of us mortals do and your heart toward him had changed," he finished in a rush.

She breathed a sigh of relief. He knew nothing of Richmond and had been foolishly jealous only of the king she could not really love.

"My Lord Duke of York," she began slowly, "think what you will but, I vow, I care not if His Majesty reconciles with Barbara. Truly. I think his perpetual kindness to her is rooted in his love for his children. Besides, he has offered much to me I have chosen not to accept as my ties to him are of fondness and not—not . . ." she faltered looking for the proper word.

"Not the passion of the heart," he concluded for her almost poetically and smiled.

A line from the little poem the king had sent her over two years ago at Tunbridge Wells jangled in her mind: "O then, 'tis O then, that I think there's no hell like loving, like loving too well." How different, she mused, was that fantastically impassioned poetic effort from Richmond's curt note she had found thrust under her door the morning after he had come through her window to make her his only in cruel parting: "Forgive me if I have hurt you, but like begets like. So why could not love beget love? Your servant ever, C."

"Frances,"—the Duke's earnest voice pierced her thoughts—"he would detest me for this, but I am glad you cannot love him that way."

She stared blankly up at James, Duke of York, for a moment while her mind grasped his train of thought again—the king; he spoke incessantly of that other Charles Stuart, the one who did not haunt her thoughts and torment her dreams.

He watched her azure eyes mist over, and his pulse beat very fast beneath his lace shirt cuffs. She must care for him a little, he thought, and for now, a little was enough. Afraid his royal brother would guess his tormented love, he'd been so careful, so circumspect around Frances for so long. Quickly, while she stared dazedly somewhere in the area of his cravat, he leaned forward and kissed her cheek. His arms swept around her; his heart soared. In the one second she was in his embrace, he exulted so that he thought at first the deep, rumbling explosion in his ears must be his own galloping passions.

She shoved him away and squealed even as the king's livid face came out of somewhere mouthing oaths. The duke stepped back even as the king shoved him hard into the stretch of satin drapery at the tall windows.

"Damn it, brother! Damn you both! Od's fish, but I turn my back a moment and what do I find?" His Majesty shouted.

The king held Frances by one slender wrist, but his wrath was definitely aimed at the Duke of York. "Sire," the duke began, "don't blame Frances. It's been a long while coming, sire, and it just happened."

"Did it, James? Hell's gates, I do blame Frances for being indiscreet enough to get off alone with a hungry fox like you! A long while coming? Pray, James, enlighten me on that!"

"Gads, sire, I've admired her for a long while, that is all, and as she's not attached—"

"Not attached! Now you listen to me, you damn fool! She's mine! Mine—has been and will be!"

"I beg to differ, sire," James began, but his voice shook now, and he sweated profusely under his curled periwig and elegant garments though this was a chill March evening.

"I beg to differ also, Your Majesty," Frances spoke at last and dared to pull her braceleted wrist free of the king's grasp. Her voice resonated with an oddly controlled fury. "I do not belong to you, sire—not to either of you!"

"'Sdeath! I spare you both my wrath by choosing to believe that I only just now happened here to see the duke's first wretched and clumsy attempt to tamper with your affections. Is that not true, Frances?"

"His Grace has never kissed me before, sire."

"Or held you—grabbed you?" he insisted. Each time he turned his head toward her such a demonic glint crackled from his black eyes that her surprise ebbed to awe at the livid display.

"Never, sire," she said and glared back at his piercing stare as boldly as she could. "Now, if you will both excuse me please, I am returning to the dancing."

"Not until you have my leave," the king retorted and seized her wrist again. "Go into the next room and wait for me. 'Sdeath, go on, mistress, or you'll be very sorry."

He pointed and she went in a swish of skirts feeling both very furious and a little afraid. She had never seen him like this, but heavens, she was not his property like the damned crown jewels and it had only been a foolish little embrace and kiss. Surely he had seen her surprise and outrage!

The room she entered was a small, elegant salon even more dimly lit than the drawing room. She had begun to light three more big candles in glass chimneys when she realized she was going to hear every word of their discussion despite the walls and closed oaken door.

"'Sblood, I swear, James, this from you! If I cannot trust you in these terrible times, then whom am I to trust?"

"You have Castlemaine to content you, sire!"

"You stupid ass! I am hardly content with Castlemaine! It's Frances I want, man—Frances I desire—Frances who refuses my gifts of land grants and jewels."

"She took the emerald necklace she wears even now for Valentine's," the Duke of York shot back. Frozen in the little side room, Frances lifted her hands to the warm, square-cut gems at her throat. She felt as though she stood between them now, and they both stared at, pulled at, her.

"Hell's gates, she'd take a Valentine present from any poor dolt. I swear, brother, but you've let me down. Never—never touch her again. Damn you. I

425

think you'd best get your own house in order and stop your duchess from brazenly chasing her new master of the horse—what's-his-name—Harry Sidney."

"That is unfair, sire. You know Castlemaine beds others, has for years."

"Od's fish, James, Castlemaine is not my wife! Now get the hell back to your blasted party you've deserted and plan to be at sea for the war eternally if I ever see you alone with Frances Stewart again!"

Frances stood rooted to the floor in the sudden hush after all the shouting. Her heart began to thud rhythmically as she heard the duke stalk off loudly without another word. A distant door slammed.

She pulled her hands from the emerald necklace and smoothed her pale pink skirts. A clock ticked loudly on the marble mantelpiece. She waited. The door latch clicked, moved upward. The gray light of the open door revealed his swarthy face, raven hair, and broad shoulders. The door closed quietly behind his tall form; the candleglow glinted white from his eyes and teeth as he spoke in a low, barely controlled voice.

"Come here to me, Frances."

She moved closer slowly, about halfway across the Brussels carpet.

"Here, I said!"

She stood two feet away and stared up at him, but her defiance fled and in the way his eyes swept her, he knew it.

"I believe you said out there, Frances, you do not belong to me. Shall I prove otherwise? The carpet looks soft enough for what I have in mind."

426

"Please do not shame or insult me, sire. I do not deserve that."

"Do you not? And what of shaming or insulting me—with my own brother?" he yelled suddenly losing his grasp on his obviously hard-won calm.

"I regret that!" She was shouting now too, when she had meant to be so aloof. "I vow, it never happened before and won't again. He surprised me."

"I know, I know," he groaned and pulled her into a crushing embrace against his hard body. "But why did you go off like that, love? Why do you do this to me?"

She stood stiffly in his arms and did not speak while his huge hands roamed her shoulders, waist, and back to finally cup her soft rounded bottom through her skirts.

"Please don't, sire."

"Hush. I thought you at least had enough sense to try to soothe me when I'm angry. Soothe the savage beast," he murmured enticingly. "Soothe me just a little, my Frances."

His mouth dipped to cover hers in a fervent kiss. She relaxed against him responding simply to his warmth and gentleness until his hands again grasped her derrière tightly, lifting her against his strong thighs and loins.

"No. No, sire," she managed.

"Hush, I said." His mouth imprisoned hers again even as a hand moved to squeeze a breast through the satin bodice, then lifted to dart wild fingers under the lacy décolletage to flick a nipple taut.

"They'll all miss us in there," she protested and pushed hard against his iron chest.

His lips pressed hot kisses to her throat arched back away from him as his hips and blatant manhood thrust against her. "You should have thought of that before prancing off alone, Frances, off with James. 'Sdeath, if you're out to get a new reputation for yourself at court parties, it is certain as hell going to be with me!"

He forced her lips to his again with one hand on the back of her head. His free hand lifted her skirts and petticoats at the side, creeping higher up her thigh above her gartered stocking to grasp her soft cheek again.

"Stop it!"

He bent her backward in his arms and squeezed her so tightly for a moment, she couldn't breathe. "Now, you listen to me, you little tease. We're going back out there, arm in arm, smiling, and I'm going to send you back to Whitehall ahead of me and the queen. And tonight, when I am ready, you may expect in private, a very eager male visitor. There will be no maids and no other fond admirers hanging about and no damned white cats or chattering parrots—and don't bother to be dressed. Do you understand me?"

"You're hurting me!"

"Do you understand?"

"Yes!"

He loosed her, then steadied her as she stood back away from him to straighten her bodice and skirts. Then, arm in arm as he had said, he took her back out as if they had been for the most amusing stroll. Though she refused to even look at him as he entrusted her to Lord Arlington and his wife and went off to talk to some others, soon enough he was back, amiably taking her arm again.

"I know you won't like this, but Barbara's coach is leaving now and you're going with her," he told her out of the side of his mustached mouth as he led her away.

"I shall walk first."

His hand tightened painfully on her upper arm. "I believe Barbara said the same, but both of you will do as I say and with no sniping. At least I know you detest each other so much that there will be no plotting. It's a mere ten-minute ride and you will both cooperate."

In the lofty, grand entry hall, footmen appeared with her high-necked blue velvet cloak; a silent, fuming Castlemaine stood ready with her maid Sarah. Frances refused to look at the king as he personally swirled her cloak around her shoulders. Suddenly, the Duke of Buckingham appeared, and as if in a silent pantomime, the king and Buckingham took them out and handed them up into the big, painted and gilt Castlemaine coach.

The door slammed. Sarah, Barbara's maid, huddled in the dark corner as though afraid for her life as Barbara and Frances sat staring at each other. The coach jolted away across St. James's Park toward Whitehall.

"I suppose you've misbehaved too," Barbara drawled and pretended to stifle a yawn.

"I suppose," Frances returned, trying to sound equally bored. "But, I vow, I thought you were in favor lately."

"Pooh! Henry Jermyn's finally been allowed back from France, you know, and His jealous Majesty is merely afraid if I stay at St. James's Palace, I'll let Jermyn have me in an upstairs room or some such." She studied her long elegantly tapered nails, then thrust them into her black velvet muff for warmth. "I did that once at a party before with Jermyn and the king was furious for days when someone tattled, you see."

"Yes, I do see."

"And you, Frances? Hoping still to be decorated for sainthood someday as the oldest living virgin?"

"Please do not commence that discussion again, Barbara. I wearied of it long ago. You start to sound like my parrot Joli who knows only seven different phrases which he repeats at all hours."

"Of course, you *were* missing with James, Duke of York for a good fifteen minutes before the duke came stalking back all green at the gills with his doggish tongue hanging out," Barbara goaded as though she hadn't heard Frances' insult. "Gads, I daresay, that's long enough for all kinds of mischief."

Frances was tempted to restart the wrestling match they had begun in the old Tudor inn in humid Salisbury almost seven months ago, but the carriage halted throwing Barbara against her knees.

"Uh!" Barbara grunted. "Damn that drunken driver. Dolts! Jackasses up there! What is it?"

Thuds and shouts sounded from above. A horse whinnied and men's rough voices rumbled very close. Almost simultaneously, the carriage doors on both sides were yanked open. Chill air shot in. Barbara gasped and her maid Sarah screamed. Wide-eyed, Frances dug her knuckles into her lips. There were three horsemen, maybe four and all were masked!

"That's a good bit a vile language for such a fine lady," one man said as he peered in, then clambered through the door. He turned in Frances' direction, but swiveled his masked, hatted head immediately back to the white-faced Barbara. "We are in the presence of the king's illustrious, fancy whore Barbara, Countess of Castlemaine, are we not?"

"How dare you, you vile bastard!" Barbara screeched, but her voice quavered when she saw the dagger in his hand glint in the torch someone held at the door.

"My pleasure, whore," the man laughed with a mocking bow. "We got what we want here, men! Drive it off a ways!"

"How dare you!" Barbara repeated. "We are indeed from the king's court. You will swing from Tyburn for this robbery!"

The man snickered and lifted the dagger toward Barbara's throat while she pulled her black velvet cape closer around her. "Think royal Charles'll save you like he done afore, slut? We know you spends his privy purse like it was water'n gets involved in all sorts of foreign Catholic plots. But don't be afraid. We hardly have robbery in mind, lady whore. Tonight, for all five of us, you'll get to do what you do best."

Frances found her voice at last as Barbara's wild gaze darted to her. "Please, sir, you've said what you wanted. Please let us go," Frances pleaded.

The carriage had jerked to a halt again and the

doors were reopened by three masked, staring men with torches.

"I'd keep a real tight lip, mistress," the man with the knife warned Frances. "We have no quarrel with a couple of lady's maids however pretty faced. The 'prentices are pulling down the brothels in Moorfield tonight, and we'd thought to come pull down the great brothel of Whitehall the king keeps only we'd get kilt for sure. So we come to teach a lesson to the greatest whore in the kingdom. Climb down here, you sluttish Catholic bitch," he finished grandly and motioned to Barbara.

Sarah screamed as Barbara clung wildly to her. Frances jumped forward to pommel the man's head and shoulders but another man climbed in and rough hands dragged her back. Barbara was pulled screaming past until the man stuffed something in her mouth and lifted her out the door. Her black cape was tugged away, pulled, then disappeared out the door.

Another man climbed in the coach with a drawn pistol. Frances' captor shoved her across the seat nearly on top of the wailing Sarah and climbed out. "Watch 'em close and keep 'em quiet, man. I'll trade with you when it's your turn on the whore."

Frances' heart pounded in her throat. "Shush, Sarah, just hush up!" she hissed. "Look, sir—please put a stop to all this," Frances asked the masked guard with the pointed gun. "People will find out. We also are ladies of the court. There are other carriages right behind."

"Shut up. You're both pretty enough to get all spread out too if'n you don't just shut up. Shut up or

I'll tell Ben!"

"Please call Ben. Please make him stop all this. The king's guard will be along any minute," she heard herself say as she fought to keep her voice calm.

"Not where we are. Not behind the Ice House," he brazened. "Now shut up!"

Frances wept silent tears while Sarah huddled against her, quivering. Outside, the men's crude comments and laughter were all too discernible. They had evidently not carried Barbara far from the coach.

"She likes it. I knew she would!" one voice cawed.

"His Majesty that good to you, whore?" Several men laughed.

"Come on, another one of you, come on. She's hot and ready and look at those sweet tits! Take a taste there—she likes it, I says!"

"Please make them stop!" Frances begged, her hands clasped imploringly. "Please!"

"You're a pretty one tears and all," the man told her. "Might consider it for a little roll with you, mistress. What's your name again?" His voice was uneducated, rough; and his hands looked like a laborers' hands. This was a nightmare; this could not be happening here and so near the palace!

Frances covered her face with her hands when their original captor climbed back in still shoving his shirt in his breeks. He took their guard's gun. "Have a go at her, my lad. Someday you can tell your grand-children you lay where a king did!" He guffawed raucously as the guard scrambled out. The man with the gun put both muddy feet on the seat next to Frances. "Be sure to tell the king he's picked a real

433

hot whore, my girls. Can't say I can fault his logic. Too damned bad he don't toss her out with all the other intriguers what saps his purse in this hellfire war though."

Frances thought she was going to be sick, but she stared down at her hands holding Sarah's. She concentrated on her white knuckles, on blocking out the terrible obscenities from outside the carriage. Then it was evidently over. There was a sudden silence. They wouldn't kill Barbara after— No, Frances thought, and lunged forward toward the door. The man yanked her back even as Barbara was handed roughly up, a crude gag still in her mouth. She was gowned but her cloak was gone, her skirts torn and muddied, and her bodice shredded to the waist.

"Good night, ladies—and king's whore. Tell him to get his queen with Protestant child and win this damned Dutch War and forget about whores. They's for what you just got, fancy lady—'prentices and randy tinsmiths. Your fine footmen will be back in a trice, once we unties 'em."

The doors slammed. Hoofbeats thundered, faded.

"Oh, madam, madam!" Sarah shrieked repeatedly.

Barbara held her torn bodice up with one muddy hand and pulled out the gag with the other. "Shut up, Sarah. Just shut up," she moaned. She looked up, surprised, as Frances bent over her to wrap her own cloak around her shoulders and tuck it carefully in.

"Crying for me, Frances, or yourself?" she asked low. "You owe me now. I could have told the bastards who you were."

"I tried."

"You little fool. But they were just men, Frances, excited men. Gads, where are those damned lackey footmen? I need a bath."

Frances stared at Barbara in awe. Her eyes were glazed, her face ashen and drawn, her hair, skin, and ripped garments muddy. Yet she sat erect, uncrying, seemingly in control.

"I'll get out and drive us, Barbara," Frances said and made a move to the door.

"Wait! Sarah, stop that infernal sniveling. Listen, if the footmen were left behind and know nothing of what really happened, I want you two to swear those men just insulted us and left. They've dumped the footmen and driver somewhere. I didn't see them outside."

"Barbara, we can't. They—they committed a heinous crime. The king will find them out, punish them," Frances protested.

"No. No! Please, Frances, I've never asked you for another favor. Please—I-I took it all and didn't turn them on you."

Frances frowned. Had she forgotten she had been gagged? But what did it matter after all this horrible torture, this cruelty? Why didn't Barbara faint or dissolve in horrified tears?

"Frances. Sarah. Swear it, please. Gads, I'm begging you, Frances. I could not live if they all knew. Please."

"Yes, I swear it."

"Sarah?"

"Oh, madam, madam, oh, I'm so sorry."

"Damn you, girl! Promise me or I'll strangle you!"

"Yes, madam, yes M'lady Countess."

435

"All right. Frances, drive back if you can and both of you had best agree to the story they just stopped us to insult me. We'll all claim they called me king's whore and let it go at that. I'll burn these clothes before the rest get back to court and no one will know."

"I pray not, Barbara," Frances said.

Barbara's eyes narrowed to menacing slits. "I'm sending Sarah to my uncle's house at dawn until she gets hold of herself so if anyone does know, I'll deal with you, Frances Stewart. Now just get me back—get me back."

By hiking her skirts up, Frances managed to clamber up on the high driver's seat and unwrap the eight reins from where the blackguards had tied them. She had never driven a big coach and four, and she felt the chill bite at her cloakless form and lick the wet tears from her cheeks. The horses moved off easily, evidently grateful to be heading for their stables. The lights of sprawling Whitehall eventually emerged from the budding trees as Barbara's displaced footmen and driver came running and yelling from the darkness. A little crowd of servants had gathered, but Frances pulled up at the Holbein Gate to avoid them.

She skinned her knee and ripped a stocking climbing down as Sarah helped Barbara out. The servants ran to them; the footmen were out of breath. "Madam! Madam, the men had guns!" one footman shouted. "Are you all right then?"

"Yes, no thanks to you bastards!" Barbara ground out. Frances took her other arm as the three women moved quickly inside.

"Madam, madam, did they rob you? Are you hurt?

Leonard has gone for the king!" her driver said.

"Zounds!" Barbara swore low. "The fools. That's all I need, Frances."

"Look, all of you," Frances turned to tell the growing crowd of servants even as she hurried Barbara inside, "we were not robbed but those ruffians insulted us, insulted the Countess of Castlemaine, and she's so upset she's like to have the vapors. Go see to the horses now. Go on, all of you!"

"Should I stay, Barbara? I could help fend off the king's questions or whatever," she offered when they had Barbara in her rooms.

"No. No, go on, Frances. And thank you. It's too much tonight—too much—and I don't need your pity on top of it all." Barbara looked away, tears in her eyes at last, and Frances went. As she closed the door the final thing she saw was Barbara throwing her best velvet cloak to the floor and ripping away her ruined bodice vehemently.

With Gillie and Jane's help, Frances bathed, donned her plain green, watered silk gown and waited. She played with Joli and the cats half-heartedly and tried to shut out the terrible echoes of the crude things those men had said to Barbara as they had raped her. Surely, she hadn't liked it as they had boasted to each other. These were just more men's lies, excusing the cruel way they used women.

It was almost an hour before Frances heard voices. She had long sent her maids away, but not to capitulate to His Majesty's earlier threats. After all, this surely would distract him and she was not certain she could ever let any man touch her again. . . .

"Frances!" The door to the hall resounded at the

rapping of a walking stick. Then he was not on the privy staircase and probably not coming alone, she rejoiced, She opened the door to find the king looking entirely distraught and Buckingham merely looking. The king swept her into his embrace before he was even inside while Buckingham stared and nodded stiffly.

"I thank God you're all right!" His Majesty said as they went into her drawing room. "Barbara will hardly talk of it. Buckingham says her maid's hysterical and Barbara won't let me see her at all. I thought you could tell us exactly what the wretches said. You actually drove the coach back in your pink evening gown, everyone says."

"I—yes, I had to. They had forced off the driver and footmen with guns, sire. They wanted to terrorize us and they said horrible things to Barbara."

"Things no doubt half the kingdom's saying," Buckingham murmured under his breath.

"Quiet, George," the king rapped out. "At least Frances is coherent and makes it easier to understand."

Frances lifted her eyes from her lap, and her gaze snagged on the king's narrow, slaty stare. "Heavens, of course, Barbara's upset, sire. She screamed back at them for a while," Frances rushed on when it occurred to her that if they didn't believe the story Barbara might blame her.

"And why, pray, did she stop screaming back?" His Majesty probed. "It is hardly like her to fold up like this at mere insults or even in the face of guns."

"I think their masks frightened her too," Frances answered.

"Hm. I suppose. My darling, you'll simply have to forgive me for rushing away tonight but Barbara's so shaken I'd best go down to comfort her again as George seems dour and entirely unsympathetic. Apprentices at Moorfield, wretched anti-Catholics—whoever—they will pay for insults to the Stuart crown," the king finished grandly.

He was leaving, Frances thought. She was temporarily off the hook as she had been so many times before when she had nearly met disaster with him. She certainly did not begrudge poor Barbara his presence: in fact, unknowingly, Barbara had already returned the favor of Frances' covering her with her cloak and her lies.

"Of course, I understand, sire. Actually, it was an awful experience for all of us and I'm exhausted. I'll see you tomorrow then." She forced a wan smile.

"Certainly, my dearest, and don't think I am forgetting our earlier talk. I am only grateful they hurt neither of you, but they shall pay the utmost forfeit if they are apprehended anyway." He leaned swiftly forward to kiss Frances under Buckingham's stony perusal. "George, let's go," he concluded sharply as if Buckingham were some heel-trotting spaniel.

She walked them to the foyer, but they hardly looked back. She closed the door and leaned her shoulder against it, then jumped away seconds later as it rattled sharply again.

"Sire?" she asked before she realized her own foolishness in case it was someone else.

"Do you really wish it were your king, Frances? It's Buckingham. I need a word with you."

"Tomorrow then," she called through the door.

"Zounds, Frances, come on. Let's say Barbara sent me."

She opened the door a crack; impatiently, he pushed it with both hands to slowly move her back.

"Tell your message and then be gone," she clipped out.

"Don't worry. *He* won't be back to see us together. He's all avid lover when Barbara's truly distraught, you see. Besides, I have no intention of getting too intimate with a certain blue-eyed lady made of solid ice on such a chill night. However did you stand the ride back without the cloak you left St. James's in?"

She stood her ground in the middle of her little foyer. "What?"

"I said, Frances, it was kind of you to lend Barbara your cloak after she somehow lost hers. That was your blue velvet cloak in her rooms on the floor, wasn't it? Hers, I believe, was black and not among the tattered remnants of a gown she sent that little chit Sarah out to bury."

"To bury?"

"Yes, clever, wasn't it? After all, she could hardly burn a fine satin gown like that in the grate with His Majesty and me looking on."

Ignoring Buckingham's presence, Frances sank in the single tapestried chair in the foyer. "Then he knows?"

"Knows what, Frances? Tell me."

"Ask your dear cousin. I told you what happened already."

"Horse manure! I assume they raped her, or at least one of them did," he plunged on, leaning closer over

440

her. "I also assume they didn't touch my favorite vestal virgin or she wouldn't be sitting here so primly right now, covering for whatever Barbara's afraid of."

"Get out of here," Frances managed still stunned by his clever deductions. "Why do you make such foul claims—accusations against your own cousin? I vow, whose side are you on, my Lord Duke?"

She shoved his arm away and darted up, but he caught her easily to swing her around, his big hands on her shoulders. His blond periwig came slightly askew as he shook her once and she almost laughed at the sight. She felt dizzy, tired. She wasn't sure suddenly exactly what she had told him already.

"Ask Barbara," she repeated quietly.

"Oh, I shall, I shall. And she'll eventually tell me as I have so much on her that I almost own her."

"I warrant she wouldn't agree."

"Just listen and carefully, little Stewart. Your sudden unholy alliance with Barbara is amusing and touching, but I didn't come to laugh or cry. Now listen to me because I'm only going to say this once."

His voice was cold, she thought, cold and metallic like the glint of the rapists' knife and pistol. Little flickers of fear feathered up her spine as he held her in his hard grasp.

"Barbara has some very intimate letters His Majesty sent her early in their liaison, some before she even lay with him at the Hague the first time. Very intimate, very explicit, erotic letters which would greatly embarrass him now should they be made public."

"Why do you tell me this?"

"Listen, I said. Occasionally, when she is feeling especially foolish or afraid, she wants to use those letters to blackmail him—for revenues, lands, grants for the children . . . for creating her a duchess or some such tripe."

"But I don't want her to attempt that sort of crazy trick," he went on. "I know him. He'd ruin her, ruin all the family's hopes to stay near him."

"Ruin your hopes, you mean."

"Ruin one hell of a lot. And now with these damn sons of bitches coming out of the rotting woodwork of society to harm her like this—to defy their king enough to attack her—it would be absolute lunacy to let such letters out. The bastards might get drunk enough to tear down anything with the Villiers name on it, and after a certain point, even this king protects his royal good name. We'd be out on our ears, bastard offspring in the family or not."

"I see."

"Not quite. I intend to hold this incident tonight over Barbara's head to keep her from making good her threat to release the letters. I really don't think even lusty Barbara would like it boasted far and wide that she entertained a pack of rowdy scum between her busy thighs—though she probably could have handled half of London with a smile."

"Let me go! You disgust me!"

"Stop squirming, Frances. You see, Barbara can be very vindictive when she's crossed. That poor little Sarah blubbered all over me how she's being sent to exile at our uncle's house until all this flap is over."

"I cannot help it that you have made your own wild assumptions about what happened tonight or

442

have gotten some mixed-up story from an emotional servant girl."

"Ah! Now you've seen my point, Frances, and even cleverly jumped one step beyond to try to ward me off. Yes, indeed. If you don't behave and help me out on this, Barbara might believe you told me—told others and what would she do then? Surely you have a little skeleton or two in your little closets hereabouts? A phantom lover perhaps like the Duke of York or of Richmond—"

"Let me go, you monster! I hate you! Let me go!"

She yanked away from him only to slap his smug face with a stinging glow. She gasped, amazed at her own action, but he only grinned and his eyes went lecherously to her heaving breasts.

"Ah, little Frances, if you only knew how I'd like a night with you to teach you a thing or two to answer that little slap. I warrant you'd profit from being turned over a man's knee, angel, and taught some manners, taught who's master in a man's bed. There would be tears and begging, Frances, and in the end, an ecstasy of pleasure for both of us. When His Majesty tires of your little games, I'll be there to take you in. Then you'll do things my way, but until then—never, never strike me again."

He moved closer, his fists clenched but a strange smile on his rapt face. She pressed back against the wall behind her, mesmerized, horrified. "Until then, pretty Frances, be a good little girl and I'll try to protect you from Barbara's insane wrath. You'll owe me. Then we shall see."

Her skin crawled with loathing. If he came nearer, she'd rake that lascivious face with her nails. "Stay back. You disgust me," she managed.

"So you've said. Just don't cross me, that's all." He put out a hand to touch her breast. She hit his arm away stiffly. He laughed and went out, leaving the door ajar.

Her legs shook and her back ached as she moved to close the door. She latched it, then sat again in the single foyer chair and stared at her clasped hands resting in her lap as she had stared at them in the coach when the men had dragged Barbara out. She shuddered and a big tear plopped onto her green silk lap followed by another.

What a tangled web it all was—the king's quicksilver affections, her tenuous reputation, Castlemaine's shame, Buckingham's filth, the Duke of York's foolishness—and Richmond. Richmond far away somewhere and hating her. A phantom lover in a closet, Buckingham had goaded—Richmond, Richmond. If only, if only he were here, how much better and simpler it would be just to tell him and ask his advice. Perhaps he would promise to take her to Cobham, to Scotland—the world beyond—as he had once, but he cursed her now and her life was so empty.

Her white cat Perth sashayed out to rub against her legs and Frances picked the poor thing up to smother it with hugs and tears until it squirmed to be set down.

Here she was at the Stuart court beloved of the king, fashionable, clever, beautiful—everyone said so. Yet she felt empty and wretched and hardly young at all anymore. What will you be doing when you are thirty? Richmond had asked her once. She had no idea, but she didn't want it to be this.

Resolutely, she stood and wiped the streaming tears from her cheeks. She had to get hold of herself. Nothing—especially no man—was worth all this. She squared her shoulders and went straight into her bedroom to write a happy letter to Minette.

Chapter Sixteen

The Duke of Richmond's pulse pounded with exertion and excitement as he mounted the steps two at a time from the barge landing to the terrace at Somerset House. His long absence from London outfitting privateers for the war made the familiar London sights seem strange and foreign now, and that unsettled him. Worse, an apparently as-yet-uncontained fire burned downriver in the old, walled city; he could see the flames and smell the smoke from here in the clear, hot sky of this Sunday midmorning, September 1, 1666. But mostly, his blood pumped and his emotions churned because in a few moments he would see Frances Stewart after a separation that had been much too long. He'd tried to put her out of his mind and could not; he'd tried to stop loving her, but that was as futile as stemming the scarlet flow of that raging fire.

Pensioners and minor nobles, housed at the expense of the Crown at Somerset House, lined the terrace gazing eastward into the sun at the gray smoke and ruddy blaze. Even this far from the spreading conflagration, soot and cinders sifted down, carried on the capricious northeast wind. An old man decked out in military garb grabbed Richmond's arm as he hurried by. "What caused the fire, m'lord? It's for a certain heading this way. Any real news?"

"I've just come from Whitehall," Richmond told him, "but the news is sketchy there too." People surrounded him immediately, pressing in to hear his words. He scanned the crowd for Frances or her mother.

"Tell us, my lord, pray tell us!" an elderly woman implored, her clawlike fingers touching his arm. Black charred fleck dotted her silver hair and dusted her frail shoulders.

"The king has been informed this morning that a fire began near two of the clock in a baker's shop in Pudding Lane down by London Bridge," he told them in a loud, calm voice. "The king's baker, Thomas Farymor from Thames Street, escaped from his burning house over the roof to a neighbor's house and with others has reported to His Majesty. The wind has spread the fire up Thames Street, you see, and to the warehouses—the goods we need to win the war like cloth, hemp, leather, and tallow are going up in flames." His voice became more strident as he realized his last year's efforts to help win the Dutch War might literally be going up in smoke in one short day. "All this ash and this strange smell—it's our precious war supply reserves burning like a damned torch!"

"It's out on the bridge itself now! Look!" someone

shrieked and the crowd shifted away from him to gaze down the sweep of river to the stack of gabled buildings on the bridge's north end now obscured by belching smoke as the tinderbox of plaster, wood, and thatch that was old London flamed and died.

"Sir, wait!" Richmond seized the old man's arm as he too moved away to look. "I'm here to see Lady Sophia Stewart and her daughter, Frances, who's visiting today. Have you seen them? Do you know them?"

"Stewart? Surely. The king's Frances Stewart, you mean. The mother—she was on the terrace earlier. Don't see her now or the pretty daughter."

"Sophia Stewart's rooms—are they first or second floor?"

"Can't say I know, m'lord. Lady Stewart has a few women friends, I warrant, but no gentlemen about."

"No, of course," Richmond murmured, more to himself than the old officer, as he hurried into the riverfront entrance of the Tudor brick-and-marble Somerset House built by the Lord Protector Edward Seymour back in the boy King Edward IV's reign.

Dim corridors stood silent and deserted; on the first floor he knocked on two doors before Sophia Stewart's distinctive clipped voice with a mere hint of Scottish accent answered.

"Who's there? The fire's still a long way off, and I won't leave!"

"Lady Stewart, it's Charles Stuart, duke of Richmond. May I speak with you, please?"

"Oh, dear. Well, yes, I suppose."

The face had aged since he had seen her last, the hair grayed slightly. He had forgotten how her eyes were Frances' cerulean blue color. Sophia Stewart's gaze was guarded, and her hands gave away her nervousness.

"Lady Stewart, I understand Frances is here. I apologize for just dropping in like this when everyone's so worried about the fire, but I have come to see Frances. Her maid Gillie says she's here for the day." His eyes swept the small, elegant drawing room behind Sophia Stewart as he spoke. Somehow he knew Frances was not here: he would have felt her presence.

"Does the king wish her to come back?" the woman replied warily. "Surely he can't concern himself with Frances when the city's burning."

"No, I do not come for the king. I realize this looks impulsive, my lady, as Frances didn't know I was coming, but I haven't seen her for a good long while and wish to speak with her. If she is not here, could you please tell me where I might find her?"

"No, she is not here as you can see. She was, but she took a horse from here and will be gone—for a while yet. You could no doubt see her at Whitehall when she returns, my Lord Duke."

He cursed silently for the way his heart fell to his feet. You stupid, overly fond dolt, he told himself, you hardly expected her to be waiting with bated breath when she didn't even know you were coming to London or would want to see her. And here, glaring at him, stood the woman who had evidently soured Frances on him, poisoned her against men in general. He just knew it!

"I am sorry to bother you, Lady Stewart, but quite frankly, I would rather wait for Frances here than at

Whitehall. I realize it would be a great imposition to ask that I could wait here though. You say she took a horse from Somerset stables? Can you not tell me for where?"

"No. I—" She faltered and her eyes jumped away from his cold perusal of him, then back. "The fire, my Lord Duke, I can see from my window it's burning London Bridge. I really don't know the city down that way as I seldom venture out up toward East Cheap, but I was just wondering if it could be close to Cannon Street."

His heart thudded, and he shouted loudly enough to make her jump. "Cannon Street? Why? Is that where she's gone?"

"No, no. Of course not. I have—acquaintances there and I just wondered if their house—"

"I hope to hell it's not where she's gone as in calmer times it's in the heart of shoddy Cheapside, let alone now," he ground out low. "It's a mere stone's throw from where the fire started and is probably charred rubble by now."

"Oh, no! Cannon Street?"

Richmond seized the woman by her thin upper arms. Other than the eyes she didn't really look like Frances at all; he could not imagine the vibrant warmth Frances was capable of flickering to life here. "Tell me! If she's gone that way today, it may be too late!"

"Please don't. I—I promised I wouldn't tell. I swore it. I only really know because I found one of the horrid letters. Oh, she was furious, so distraught. I told her, you see, never to trust her reputation to a man, any man, and now she'll pay—"

He shook her hard. He was hot with fear and frustration as though he stood already within raging flames where he surely must go now. "Where on Cannon Street? What letters? Tell me!" he roared.

Her face contorted as if she would cry, but no tears came. "A man—a vile wretch—has written her some letters threatening to spread all sorts of lies about Frances—Frances and the king."

"Who is the man? Where? Cannon Street?"

Her head bobbed like a linen doll's. "Yes, yes. She lied to me about why she went off in boy's garb, but I saw the letter with her things. It's with her gown she left in the bedroom."

He loosed her and shoved past into the drawing room. He ran into the bedroom.

"You can't go in there!" she shrieked as she followed him in.

He ransacked the pile of her petticoats and gown on the bed. A folded parchment fell from the lavender bodice to the crimson brocade bed coverlet. As she came up sniveling behind him, he read in crude, angular script

Friday

To Frances Stewart. I told you in the first letter not to go ignore me or you'll be sorry. I know of all your sinful doings and if I don't get what I want, all others will too. Item the first: You naked in the king's bed and later carried naked to your rooms. Item the second: You lets him put you to bed alone. That is for starters. I know much, much more and soon everyone will or else you come. Come alone, Sunday morning

452

and ask for one John Davis at Two Swans Court, Cannon Street, hard by Walbrook.

He stuffed the note up his shirt sleeve and ran. Behind him, Sophia Stewart was shouting, screaming other words he ignored.

On the Somerset steps, the boatman he'd paid to wait for him had rowed out a little way with two others to see the conflagration of the bridge better.

"Get the hell in here, man, and now!" Richmond bellowed, motioning broadly with one arm. He scanned the letter again as he waited. One John Davis at Two Swans Court, Cannon Street, hard by Walbrook. At least, thank God, that was the far end of Cannon Street, away from the flames. Damn her! Dressed like a boy, going alone to see some bastard blackmailer in the midst of London's great fire!

As he nearly yanked his boatman's passengers to the steps and clambered in himself, he remembered the other note that had fallen from her garments once—the love poem from the king she had hidden there. Damn, damn, damn! She brought him nothing but heartache and trouble and he still loved her desperately beyond reason. Time and again he had tried to rid his mind and soul of her, but she haunted him yet. Haunted— Who knows but he might be too late even now if some devil had her in hell's fire on Cannon Street.

"Move over, man," he ordered the surprised boatman. "You take one oar and I'll use the other. Then row—*row*! Bend your back like Satan was after us!"

The nearer they got to the fire, the more the broad

river was clogged with fleeing boats burdened with people and piled with goods. Whole households went by on barges nearly weighted under. Along the riverbanks, people shouted, begging for any river-craft which would stop. Boatmen screamed exorbitant prices to those lining the shore and yet plenty clambered on board anything that would float while the wretched poor sat on their bundles, held their children, and wailed.

"Here, put in here—along that wharf," Richmond shouted over the din. A haggard woman and three small, ragged children, their white eyes staring dumbly from soot-blackened faces, huddled against a scorched single tree trunk before a burned-out shell of a warehouse. The boat bumped the steps. Richmond handed the boatman one of his two pouches of gold guineas, an outrageous amount.

"Woman," he said to the mute, stunned mother, "get your children in here and this man will take you across to Southwark." He lifted the smallest boy into the boat beyond him as he stepped out, then scooped up a scrawny puppy the lad had dropped and put it in the boat. "Listen to me, man. Take them over and come back here directly. I'll be here at this spot with one other person and I want room for us both. I'll pay you that again—double."

He did not look back as he ran up Queen Street toward Cannon Street. Instantly, he regretted not soaking his handkerchief and himself in Thames water. Breathing through the damp handkerchief would have lessened the effect of the cinders and of the acrid smoke that singed his throat and lungs; his eyes stung from the gray fog of fumes engulfing

454

burning warehouses nearby. This block still stood but riot reigned rampant. Everywhere people loaded goods on carts, barrows, or their own backs. Already up ahead, at a shoemaker's shop sporting a frayed sign of a dirty wooden boat, the thatch roof crackled demonically.

Running headlong, out of breath, he wound his way through the traffic heading either south to the Thames or northwest away from the flames toward Moorfields. He tripped over a long firehook someone had evidently meant to use to pull down these flimsy, old medieval structures to halt the fire. A few men tried vainly to topple a building with ropes. He was off his knees in one fluid motion and tearing down the crowded, chaotic cobbled street again.

Just ahead, at Cannon Street where Walbrook would come in, a narrow rickety shop, with two stories leaning outward above it to block the smoky patch of sky, creaked, rumbled, then crashed crazily into the street. Watching the cluster of cheering men who had tumbled the building hoping to stop the relentless path of the fire, Richmond recognized the Lord Mayor of London, the fat, unscrupulous Sir Thomas Bludworth.

"Damn it, Bludworth, the fire's already caught these roofs! Pull them down a few more blocks over!" Richmond shouted despite the searing slash of air in his scorched throat. He coughed and ran another block to get through as Bludworth turned, cursed, and shrieked maledictions at whomever had dared insult his honored office.

This narrow lane one block closer to the devouring devastation was nearly deserted, but was much more dangerous—a quickening inferno. He could hear his feet pounding on the cobbles, feel the tearing ache in his side as he ran mechanically on. Sweat poured from him as the increasing incandescent flames on both sides rolled at him. In a building nearby, timbers, rafters—an entire upper story—shuddered and fell, bathing the street behind him in sparks and belching smoke. He held his breath. His eyes ran so he could hardly see. Frances. Frances up here just a little ways farther. Frances—the Two Swans—on Cannon Street.

When Frances pulled herself from the realms of murky blackness, she was immediately aware of heat and the dull roar of encroaching flames. Despite the pain in her head, she jolted instantly conscious. A gray shroud of acrid smoke hung in the room where the man called John Davis had struck, tied, and left her. Coming back with friends, he had said—coming back to force her to pay him everything he asked. A wracking cough scraped her parched throat despite the crude gag that filled her mouth and made her want to vomit. How long had she been here after he hit her on the head with the handle of his pistol? The flames, which were at least three blocks down Cannon Street, must be causing that roar, like a storm, just outside.

She squirmed onto her belly to lift her face to study her hands tied to the ugly iron bedstead above her head in this squat, little room under the eaves in the Two Swans tiny courtyard off Cannon Street. Now, she wished that loathesome man would come back.

Even his outrageous demands for money and his ludicrous comments about her relationship with the king were better than this. But maybe the fire had stopped him and the friends he had gone to fetch, or maybe he had thought it better to just let her die. No. No! Not roasted in some seething holocaust, not alone and young and tied like this!

She moved quickly to her knees and got her mouth close enough to her tied hands to pull the gag out. The hemp was tied about her wrists in big knots which reminded her irrationally of those along the rigging of Richmond's yacht. Richmond—Richmond, a distant, impossible dream. She coughed and gasped in more strangling gray smoke as her teeth bit at, pulled at the knots.

Her head pulsated; her teeth hurt in perfect rhythm with her throbbing wrists. The room was hotter than the sun. Maybe the fire was beneath or beside her now. The doomed house, bereft of occupants, only waited to be engulfed. It almost seemed the roar of flames and the crackle of timber had devouring music in them now, music accompanied by a bass chorus of deep men's voices calling, calling her name. His voice, Richmond's, calling to her in the inferno of their love.

"Frances! Frances! Are you anywhere here? Frances!"

Richmond. No, no, it could not be real.

Her mind snapped back to the defiance she had shown her would-be blackmailer, John Davis. He was despicable. He infuriated her, and she had told him so. He was all the vile men she'd ever known: he was hypocritical Philippe who tried to control

457

Minette; King Louis of France who cared for no one's reputation but his own; Buckingham with his snide implications; King Charles, the master manipulator of her life.

"I'd never pay you to stop lies—just lies!" she could hear herself shout at John Davis in this dingy, little room. The man's unshaven jaw had dropped in shock at her fury. "Leave me alone!" she had shrieked as years of being repressed and dominated boiled up inside her. She raised her fist in his face. At the moment he struck, she wasn't even afraid, only outraged at any man who threatened any woman!

"Frances! Frances!" the familiar, thrilling voice yanked her from her feverish reverie. It could be real—Richmond. Richmond, here . . .

"Richmond! I'm here! Here!" A fit of jagged coughing wracked her as she stared hard at her wrist bonds through the mist of swimming smoke. Distinctly, she felt heat on the shoulder she pressed to the filthy wall. She sucked in a wrenching breath, lifted her head, and screamed from the very backbone of her being.

"Richmond! I'm here! Here!"

Reality faded, whirled in gray fog. She had imagined him, of course. At the last, her heart had reached for him and recreated his love anew, not in this horrible, fiery apocalypse of the world's end but in the sweet garden of his arms.

A voice roared close to her. Arms lifted her, shook her. Her wrists were instantly freed. "Frances. Frances! Wake up. The stairs and below are ablaze. We're going up to the roof."

Up? He had said "up." "Up?" she echoed as she

fought to clear her head, fought to move her feet. It was Richmond, demonically black but heaven to her eyes. He dragged her to the window but the air was little better here. Still they filled their lungs with it in huge gasps. He thrust his head out and swore violently. She leaned against him, irrationally content, her sopping shirt sticking to his.

"What is it?" she managed.

"We'll never make it to the roof from here. We could have jumped across. Here, I'm going to hold you out the window as you'd never manage me. There's a fire hook outside on the wall. Get it. Don't drop it, and we can slide part way down on it."

He half held, half dangled her out before she could react or fear. The ten-foot wooden pole ending in an iron hook was barely within reach. One hand on the back waist of her breeches and one around her thigh, he steadied her. She looked down the three stories and thought she would faint. Angry flames clearly chewed at the first floor already. She lifted the hook. It was very heavy. Her back and head screamed at her as did the flames hovering below and flickering on the house beside them. Smoke roiled in the rectangle of the tiny square of the Two Swans Court which was surrounded by old buildings.

He pulled her back slowly, even as the waist of the breeches dug into her soft belly. His hand met hers on the wooden length of pole. He set her down inside and leaned out. Turning the pole hook end up, he sank the forked teeth of the sharp hook over the wooden sill.

"I'll go first, so you can drop to me. It only takes us halfway down, but I will catch you. Don't look at the flames below. All right?"

Her eyes swam. His big, dark image wavered like the sea. "Yes," she coughed. "Yes."

He squeezed her shoulder and went heavily over the sill avoiding the hook. She heard him hack, gasp, and grunt as he went down hand over hand, his legs around the pole. Then he dropped an interminable distance to the street.

"Come on! Hold tight. I'll catch you!"

She edged carefully over. Her weight dragged her hands down the wood, despite how hard her thighs gripped at the thin pole. Halfway down she clasped it hard. Flames clutched at her legs from a window below. She went down farther into the drifting heat; then, there was no more wooden pole for her legs to grasp.

"Drop, Frances! Drop, lass!"

Lass! She let go into gray vastness, but hard hands had her, broke her fall. She leaned her face gratefully into his soot-covered chest.

"Are you all right?" he asked. "Are your legs all right?"

She nodded wildly. "Yes, I think so."

"Then I'll have to lean on you some. I think I sprained my ankle dropping."

His face contorted at each step; his weight, despite his good foot, was tremendous on her. They went out the only way they could, through a narrow passageway filled with deserted stacks of household goods and dead, upturned, roasted pigeons. One block over, pitch ran in runnels down the sewer conduits and refuse boiled in a stench that staggered them worse than the acrid smoke.

"My horse," she gasped out. "I had a horse back there."

"Long gone. Everybody's fled," he said. "I have a boat on the river but we'll never get back to it from here. Over there, come on."

They hobbled for three blocks amidst the rubble of still-smoldering warehouse foundations, then turned toward the river near St. Paul's Wharf. Here, the random, undisciplined wrecking crews had evidently gone before in their mad effort to pull down enough houses to halt the flames. Some doorways still standing bore the sad, crude plague crosses from the pestilence last year and the words *Lord Have Mercy*. Near the river, homeless people huddled, some stunned to mute awe at the sweeping destruction of their city. Others ranted and screeched, their huge white eyes wild in blackened faces.

"The Dutch, the Dutch done it!" someone in the crowd they joined screamed. "They done it to win the war, burnt all our war goods, I heard. There's nothing 'cept brick chimneys and foundations on my whole street and Wilt seen the cobbles heated like coals and the conduits cooking! Churches is the only safe place, I says!"

Despite his wrenching pain at every step, Richmond pulled her away to shove them into a place at the river's edge. She leaned wearily, crazily content against his hard, panting chest as another empty barge edged in on one of its numerous trips from Bank Side safely across the Thames.

In the shoving, screaming press of people, Richmond flashed a handful of gold guineas at the burly boatman, and they pushed onto the barge to stand wedged in with the refugees of burned East Cheap. He had one hand on the back of her waist; he steadied them with the other on a railing. She stood pressed to him beside two crying women, her arms linked behind his waist, her head perfectly under his chin. The barge lurched, swayed, then rocked eternally as the orange and gray vista of burning London grew smaller.

"Damn bastards on these boats are charging the poor wretches exorbitant fees," he murmured low, but she only held to his strength and did not respond.

Damn bastards and exorbitant fees, she thought—that blackmailer John Davis. She hoped he was dead in the flames with the roasted pigeons and she'd never hear from him again. Richmond couldn't know of the man, of course, but somehow he had rescued her so perhaps mother had found the paper in her dress and sent for him. It had been ages since she'd seen him, held him like this. From this burning hellish nightmare had come a little taste of heaven.

"We're almost there, lass. Damn, but my ankle's killing me. At least I didn't break it."

She looked up at him for the first time. Her blue eyes linked to his, so green and gold and intent in his grimy face, eyes more hot and devouring than the flames. "You were lucky then," she heard herself say. "I too. You saved my life. I thank you, my Lord Charles—thank you."

He moaned in a deep sigh. "I didn't mean to ask this now, Frances, but John Davis obviously hit you on the head as you've got a huge bump turning blue. He didn't—harm you otherwise, did he?"

Somewhere close by a baby squawled. "No, my

lord, truly."

"Thank God. Then where was he?"

"I don't know. He said he went to get friends and he'd return. He hit me on my head and I think I fell too. Then I woke up and you were there."

He sighed again, and she jolted hard into him when the barge ground ashore.

Exhausted, they lay on their backs in a grassy field at Paris Gardens along Bank Side amid the homeless of London. By afternoon, the orange and gray devourer across the river had left a huge semicircle of devastation reaching west and north toward old Baynard's Castle. Still the river barges and anything that would float plied their lucrative trade back and forth while the growing ranks of displaced citizens, their remaining possessions on their backs, huddled and watched.

Richmond and Frances lay on the grass close together, her head on his upper arm. They had both fallen asleep for a while, she thought, even amidst the shouting of adults and the cries of children. She stirred slightly, aware of an unfamiliar jumble of physical aches and pains as she moved. When he spoke, she started, digging her shoulder slightly into his upper ribs.

"Frances. We'll have to go down to the bank and bribe one of those fee-crazed ferrymen to row us to Somerset House. Your mother is probably beside herself with grief and worry."

"Yes. All right." She sat up, crossed her legs and gingerly flexed her arms. "How is your ankle?"

"A bad sprain, but I'll make it that far. I'm starved too. You see, I only went to Somerset House to find you and take you out—your mother too, if I had to—out for dinner. But I figured I'd have to go help the king see to firefighting and here I did it all the other way around."

"Thank heavens you came, my lord. I didn't even know you were back."

His eyes in his grimy, streaked face were very serious. "If you would have known, would you have waited, hoping I'd come?"

Her heart accelerated to the same rapid rhythm that had pushed her on as they had fled the flames. "I—it has been a very long while. The queen and others have spoken of your duties along the coastline, but I hardly knew—for myself, that is—what you were doing or . . . thinking."

He sat up at last and leaned heavily over his knees, his big hands crossed over his shins. "I was doing my duty for His Majesty in this damned Dutch War—and trying to forget I love you!"

She sucked in a gasp of air as if he'd struck her. Before she could stop it, her hand lifted to touch the little hollow of his smudged cheek, then drop, as if guilty, to his hand. He turned his big head and his eyes caressed her. Slowly, rapt in their steady, intense mutual gaze, he lifted her hand to his lips and kissed the inside of her wrist. Her blood thundered, raced, as impulses dashed up her arm to her breasts and backbone to feather clear down to her stomach, loins, and thighs. Still holding her wrist against his mouth, he whispered, "And you, sweet lass?"

"I? Heavens, since you've been gone, I've been

very busy."

His green-gold eyes went instantly guarded at her careful reply, and he loosed her hand. "Busy getting into trouble as usual," he said evenly, and leaned back on his stiff arms, apparently at ease all of a sudden.

Her breathing quieted. The aching in her body softened as she forced herself to relax. "I know it may not seem so to you, my lord, but I vow, I have been taking care of myself very well."

"Then it appears to be all my problem that everytime I quite literally run into you I end up torn and bruised from rose bushes, tall trees, raging fires, or some such. No, lass, if I sound lighthearted, don't believe it. You could have easily been killed today, along with the other stupid pigeons who didn't realize they could get burned by fires."

Anger flared up in her a moment at his insulting comparison, but she knew he was right. She should never have even dignified those blackmail letters by responding, but she was so afraid John Davis would tell her mother or put what he evidently knew in the *Spectator* or *Tatler* newspapers or some such. Then, like Castlemaine, she, too, would be a target for angered men as king's whore even though she had never lain with His Majesty and never would!

"Frances? Are you going to tell me about it? I can't help you if I don't know. I had the letter from your things though it's fallen out of my cuff somewhere and has probably burned to a crisp as well you could have by now."

Copying his posture, she embraced her knees with her arms. It felt comforting to sit this masculine way, as if she were protecting herself against his power to make her go all soft and yearning with a mere glance.

"I received the first letter a little over a fortnight ago," she began, her cheek on her knees, her head turned away from his stare. "It was quite filthy, lies blown out of proportion but founded on truths about the night Buckingham and Barbara drugged me over two years ago. I burned the letter, but that's how I knew it had to be the Villiers behind this John Davis who signed it.

"The illustrious, power-hungry Barbara and Buckingham. Hell's gates, I don't doubt it. Did you speak to them of it?"

"No. I didn't want to give her the satisfaction of thinking it had rattled me, and I never speak to him anymore unless he addresses me directly in front of the king about something as innocuous as the weather."

"What has he done to you?" he asked sharply.

"Nothing. He just said some insulting things last March about what he'd like to do when the king threw me out someday."

"Such as?"

"Please, my lord, I don't want to speak of him. I am handling it just fine."

"Oh, yes, yes, I can certainly tell that," he retorted, his voice dripping sarcasm. "So you decided when you got the second note to do what? Dress like a lad and go all by yourself to talk a filthy-mouthed blackmailer out of bothering you? In East Cheap during a roaring fire, no less!"

"The fire was blocks away when I got there, and I didn't intend to stay long!" she shouted back. "I didn't know it was going to be such a vast fire! I thought he wouldn't dare hurt me since the Villiers wouldn't possibly go that far. I was going to threaten him by saying I'd tell the king."

"How clever! The most you should have done is tell Barbara off and let the king handle it. I daresay, there's enough dirt on Barbara to settle her down, but never—never—take on scum like this Davis evidently was yourself. If he outlived this fire, we'll have him in the Clink Prison or the Tower for libel in a week!"

"But that will make it all public!"

"And show his claims are therefore not true. I swear, Frances, it's a rare miracle your ice-thin reputation hasn't gone the way of Castlemaine's long ago. If you had an ounce of sense, you'd have plucked up your courage and gotten out of that nest of Whitehall spiders when you had the chance."

She felt herself blush hot and her nipples beneath the linen chemise and shirt point enlarge to hard, tingling nubs. He must be referring to his offers to marry her, but surely after this last separation, he couldn't mean to imply that again.

"Of course," he went on, his voice suddenly cold and taunting, "if you want to end up like Barbara, barely hanging on through all sorts of filthy, little games, I suppose you'd do at least as well, only don't expect me to play your Buckingham."

"He isn't always on her side, you know," she challenged, anxious to shift the subject. "They fight with each other, and he loves to find things to hold over her."

"I realize that. So she doesn't even really have him,

you see. I used to think you'd never be like her, lass, but sometimes you try so very hard to be."

"That's not fair!" she shouted until she saw people nearby staring, listening, and lowered her voice and put her head to her knees again. She told him then the story of Barbara's brutal rape by the men who had halted their carriage and of her pact with Barbara not to tell the king. Actually, she had vowed, she remembered, not to tell anyone, but Richmond was different. He had to understand she was nothing like Barbara, but when she finished the recital she had thought would placate him, he sounded more furious than ever.

"I see. Hell's gates, but you are taking care of yourself indeed, Frances. You're not only in danger of being raped daily by the king, but probably by Buckingham from what you've said. And I've heard about Jamie, the Duke of York's obsession with you. Now half the ruffians in London could just stop your carriage and take their turn with you on the ground! For all you know, John Davis and his cronies might have had you on that iron bedstead when you were unconscious!"

"He—they did not!" she yelled oblivious to nearby curious eyes. "You, damn it, are the only one who's ever forced me!"

"Forced you?" he ground out. His jaw was stiff; his cheeks flushed beneath the soot. "I assume you refer to that last night in Salisbury when you'd led me on, then refused to even come down for a farewell kiss. I came to you, Frances, granted and I silenced your mouth; but your very sweet body was all too willing and I distinctly recall how you even began to meet my every thrust with some very willing movements of your own. I almost think you'd been lying there wishing I'd come up to force you, as you so piously put it!"

She went prickly hot all over at the shared memory. It was all too true. She had tried to tell herself otherwise, tried to forget that night, to hate him or forget him, but she couldn't.

"I apologize," she said low after a little silence and dared to lift her head to face him. "I didn't mean to accuse you like that. Yes, you're right. I did—I did want you to and I've admitted that to myself since."

His lower lip dropped slightly, and his green eyes, now in shadow under his thick brows, widened. "Then," he asked very low, "you don't—didn't—just want me when I began to touch you, but even, a little, when we were apart?"

"Yes. Sometimes."

"And still?"

"Maybe."

"Maybe is not good enough, Frances. Maybe will never be good enough."

A baby's squalls nearby shattered the aching, tenuous moment. A boy walked among the huddles of people hawking "Bread and cheese—real fresh," and a plump woman behind him called out "Plenty ale fer a shillin'."

Richmond summoned the vendors over with a shout while his challenge echoed in Frances' ears. Gratefully, she drank the ladle of warm ale straight down as did Richmond his. He bought them both a second drink despite the ridiculous price, and when the lad and woman had wandered off among the others, they

469

wolfed down their bread and cheese. After, Frances went over into a clump of bushes the women seemed to have appropriated as their privy area, while Richmond gave a big lout with a large family a guinea to help him off where the men were going. Then Frances returned and sat for a while alone on their little plot of grass wondering what could be taking Richmond so long. When he hobbled back, leaning on the same man, he had washed his face and arms, even stuck his head in water evidently as his wild hair was plastered closely to his head.

"Miss me?" he teased and her heart soared foolishly at his light tone. "There's a stream over there but it's full of half naked men, so I brought my handkerchief wet for you. Your tawny hair looks speckled with ash and your face is a blackamoor's— here." He moved closer on the ground and grasped her chin with one big hand while he dabbed at her cheeks and forehead. "I think you're right that you fell after the bastard hit you. Does this bruise on your forehead hurt?"

"Yes. Thank you, but I'll do it."

He loosed her chin and offered the sopping handkerchief immediately. "Fine. Far be it from me to touch a lady who doesn't like it."

Slowly, after she had cleansed her face, neck, and hands and had shaken her head to cast off the flecks of soot and ash, they stood and made their way amidst the refugees down to the river bank. Across the broad stretch of gray-green Thames the city still burned, smearing the hot September sky in scarlet and gray. Behind the perimeter of fire lay the skeleton of seething devastation; ahead of it was more city, virgin, untouched, just waiting to be despoiled.

"It can't reach Somerset House, can it, my lord? Or Whitehall?" she asked.

"Not for a day or so even if that wind keeps up. By then, who knows. There may be rain or the idiots, like Lord Mayor Bludworth, fighting the fire may pull down the right combination of houses."

"It's been a horribly dry, hot spring and summer. Sometimes I almost wonder," she said, "if that comet everyone worried so about didn't foretell disaster indeed. We've had pestilence and fire and war. . . ." Her voice trailed off as the arm he had placed around her shoulders for support hugged her close.

"All I can say is, if the end of the world is coming, lass, you'd better give some serious thought to what you'd like to be doing when it does."

Flaunting the last of his coins, he hailed a man in a boat who had just discharged a motley array of burdened passengers, and they climbed carefully in.

"Sure ya want ta go back across this way, m'lord," the gap-toothed oarsman demanded.

"Yes—but up to Somerset House past Whitefriars Stairs, at least to Temple Stairs. Here, I'll make it very worth your while."

They sat together in the stern of the boat while the man bent to his task, cursing low under his breath at having to row upriver when he was exhausted. He swore repeatedly as he had to maneuver to avoid thick oncoming traffic, but soon Frances and Richmond heard none of his imprecations. They had become lost in the intoxication of their mutual closeness.

"You can hardly help to fight the fire now, not

with that ankle," she said, her eyes snagged with his.

"I know. It hurts like the very devil, but I should at least report in. The only person I talked to at Whitehall was your maid. Joli and the cats wouldn't even give me the time of day. Now if I only had something to distract me from this terrible pain I got rescuing a certain lady . . ."

She smiled at the impudent tease: then, as if a willful stranger possessed her body, she leaned forward to kiss his cheek. She was surprised but thrilled at his instant reaction: his hands lifted to her back to press her close and she half slid across his spread knees as his mouth covered hers with a fervor that took her breath away.

She met each moving, deepening caress of his lips and tongue wildly, while her hands fluttered up his back, pressing, kneading his powerful muscles, pulling him closer. His tongue darted in the velvet depths of her mouth, tracing the inner curve of her teeth and soft lips. Mindlessly, she answered, matching each demanding thrust of his tongue with hers.

Her bottom, clad in thin boy's summer breeches, felt the unmistakable hardness of his immediate desire for her. Unheeding of the boatman or the stares of others moving past, their own fires threatened to consume their very sanity.

"By Gemini, m'lord, almost there. We're past Whitefriars now," the man's shout shattered their trance. "These stairs good 'nough?" he yelled as Richmond reluctantly set Frances back on the seat beside him.

"Yes, fine," Richmond told him. Suddenly, he didn't care if Frances' mother was beside herself with worry or if he had to walk another quarter-mile farther on his throbbing ankle. He had to have more time with her alone before he took her back to that smothering, condemning mother of hers again.

They got out at the foot of Exeter Street near old Exeter House which the pandemonium of fire and refugees had not yet reached. Slowly, they moved off a little way down the bank until the eastern façade of Somerset House loomed into view beyond some poplar trees whose leaves rattled in the hot breeze.

"Frances, wait a minute," he said almost gruffly. They had not spoken, had hardly looked at each other since they'd awkwardly scrambled apart at the boatman's words.

"Your leg?" she said hastily. "I can go ahead to fetch some men to carry you."

"No, not that. We'll be going in the servants' entrance to avoid unnecessary stares. You don't need rumors you were caught in the Great Fire dressed like a boy to add to all the others."

Her legs still felt wobbly from the boat ride, from the dreadful day, but mostly from the touch of his hard body against hers. The warm river breeze lifted and rustled the leaves overhead and sounds from the river seemed to fade away. She took two quick steps back into his arms even as he reached for her.

"Frances. Frances, lass," he moaned, his lips caressing her temple and his face softly lashed by her windblown hair. Oblivious to where they were, she clung to him, tears of joy blinding her. She stared up raptly into his face; two images, then one of his earnest face stared at her as he moved to take her face between his big hands.

"I'm so damned grateful you're all right, my lass, and still care about me after these wretched months he sent me away. Sometimes I almost think he must know how much I want you."

The king—impatient, sardonic, driven, even threatening, she thought, but that did not matter now. "Yes," she told him so breathlessly, her words mingled with the moan of poplar leaves, "and today when I thought I might die, I thought of you."

Her words of endearment were smothered with a devouring kiss she returned fervently. She pressed up against him reveling in the feel of him, holding tightly to his strong neck while his hands caressed her back, her waist, and soft, pliant buttocks.

"I've dreamed of you so many nights in my ship's cabin, my lass—dreamed you might still want me."

Her hands, as if they had a will of their own, stroked, kneaded his powerful back muscles, then dropped to hook in his broad belt to stop the whirling and spinning of the riverbank. She fluttered beseeching, silken kisses across his square jaw line and nibbled at his lower lip. She had meant to just thank him for saving her life today and go inside across the wooded green behind them, she told herself. But she hadn't known there'd be a fire inside her too, threatening to ignite anew all her repressed passions for him. . . .

Despite his painful ankle, he tugged her back onto the little wooded bank behind a thick clump of trees. She knelt willingly beside him on the cool grass hidden from view. He rolled them over once and began to divest her of her belt, breeches, stockings, ruined linen shirt, and thin bodice.

"I ought to use this belt to tie you to my bed

forever," he rasped and he bent over a ready nipple.

"Mm, but this isn't your bed. Oh, I'd forgotten how that feels. I can't think."

But her hands were sure on him, loosening his wide leather belt and unlacing his tight breeches. He held himself in check, letting her unshirt him, the little telltale pulse racing at the base of his throat while the skin over his cheekbones went taut with barely leashed passion. He threw off his stockings and boots himself and came hard against her soft, supple body again.

The impact of his muscular frame shot her wide awake with a jolt of energy she had forgotten existed. She molded her breasts flat against his dark-haired chest, rasping female to male nipple, reveling in the sensual scrape of his curly, resilient hair on her smooth skin.

His hard hands cupped her soft buttocks, and she boldly moved to do the same. His lifted knee and leg caressed her inner thighs, separating them as their lips locked, merged in mingled passion. Then, to her surprise and trembling fear at first, he lifted her and moved her legs apart on either side of his hips so adroitly that she sat across him looking down. She saw instantly his brazen intent; her head cleared. Even as the crack of thunder broke so close, she cried out, "I do love you so, my Charles!"

"Yes, love me, Frances. Here—let me lift you up again. Will you? I want you to ride me."

Any sane reply she could have made caught in her throat, awed to silence by the crowning rapture of her ecstasy. "Yes, I want to—I know your leg hurts."

She meant to say more, to tell him how her life had been since she'd met him—about the sudden, overwhelming deluge of emotion that drowned her fears and hesitations, about the desire to do as he asked whatever voices echoed of encroaching danger nearby.

Eagerly, he lifted, then settled her on him even as she glimpsed the roaring inferno against the distant sky. Vibrant and seething, dangerous and scarlet hot, their rapid motions consumed them until they both collapsed together on the cool, soft grass. The sweep of river brought urgent voices drifting to them, but they did not budge for endless moments as they clung together.

"Frances, my love, are you asleep?" his voice came to her, normal and sane at last.

"No. I have to go in. Mother will be beside herself with grief."

"And I have to go to Whitehall somehow. The whole city's going up in flames and here we are. . . ."

"I know. We just manage to find ourselves together at the strangest times."

He chuckled low in his throat. "But I do accept this lovely gesture today as a very appropriate thank you for the fact you have cost me a good suit of clothes again, lass."

She smiled almost shyly at him as she gathered and pulled on her scattered clothes in the growing dusk. His eyes were on her even now as she distinctly felt a thrilling tickle along the breasts and thighs he had so expertly ravished. Although, he probably did not mean to have it so, his next quiet question broke her mood: "The king, Frances—things are still as they have been with him for you, are they not?"

She jammed her mussed, filthy shirt in at her

belted waist and sat back on her haunches. "You mean, I take it, have I lain with him. How could you ask me such a thing after—after we just—"

"I didn't mean it that way, lass, but I have to know."

"I see. You go off for months without a word after the way we parted last time and so you think wild, little Frances must have just caved in to him after all my careful work to hold him at bay all this time. Without your fine advice and attentions, I would be his for the taking, is that it?" Her voice rose shrilly and she hated herself for that, but she couldn't help it. All the worry over keeping out of the king's clutches crashed back on her like a leaden weight.

"No, that's not it at all. Come here."

"No, I don't think well when you touch me. That's obvious." She scrambled to her feet. "You think I've been wretched and lonely just pining for you, don't you?"

"Do you realize, lass, we always end up arguing? Come over here, I said!"

"As you also said, you need to go to Whitehall, so maybe you can just ask the king yourself."

"You are exhausted, Frances. Either that or you need a good thrashing." She moved farther off while he looked darts at her and began to put his own clothes on. He stood awkwardly, leaning against a tree to pull on his besmirched boothose, and she knew he would come after her in a moment. Then she'd go all pliant and willing in his arms; he could make her say and do anything he wanted!

"Pray, sit and rest one moment, my Lord Duke, and I shall fetch someone to help you. I'll ask for help to get you back safely to your rooms at Whitehall.''

Like a coward, she turned and ran. She felt tears coming, tears of longing and relief and anger all confused, and she couldn't bear for him to see. If he touched her just once more, she'd break into a thousand jagged pieces and scream her love for him—beg him to marry her as he had once mentioned doing so long ago.

She did not dare to look back or she would turn around and be lost to herself forever. Then someone else, a dangerous powerful man would control her emotions even as he did now when she was near him. She owed him for her life and she would find some way to repay him, perhaps get money for his impecunious Cobham or even tell the king about John Davis' plot, like he had said and ask the king to reward Richmond for his help. But then the king would know the Duke of Richmond had come looking for her and wonder why.

She pulled open the heavy oak door of the side entrance to Somerset House, the one through which the vendors came and went, and hurried through the deserted, vast kitchens. No fire burned here in the huge, empty hearth, no fire at all for the first time in hours. Then why did this low-burning fire in her loins have to torment her whenever she ran away from him?

She hurried up the servants' narrow, crooked steps to the floor above to find some men to go out and help him. Even here, this far away, she thought she smelled the char of burning dreams, and then she realized the odor was in her own clothes and hair as well as her deepest memory.

Chapter Seventeen

From the week of the Great Fire of London onward, Frances detested her own weakness in controlling her emotions where the Duke of Richmond was concerned. He was impeccably polite and studiously friendly to her whenever they met at court once or twice a week when he was in town on leave from his naval war duties or after his hasty visits to his Cobham estate. But she, despite the outwardly calm demeanor she struggled to maintain both near and away from him, was tormented by longing and haunted by memories she could not control.

She told herself it was mere infatuation, but soon she stopped pretending that to herself. Or, perhaps it could be profound gratitude just built up over the four years she had known him. He had taken her places to widen her narrow, controlled world; he had sent her gifts; he had shown her the depths and heights of rapture's joy; and he had saved both her pet parrot's life and her own from looming destruction. He could be gentle and so utterly charming that with him she often forgot not to trust him. And once, he had asked her to be his wife and duchess, the mother of his heirs, but she'd best not think of that now. To her utter frustration and dismay, he remained warmly charming—merely that, as if he were awaiting something from her. In the three months since the Great Fire had been vanquished from London, the great fire in her body and heart for Charles, duke of Richmond, had never gone out at all.

Frances followed Queen Catherine down the broad sweep of staircase with many of her other ladies. Though the court was still in mourning for the death of the queen's Portuguese mother, this was Her Majesty's twenty-sixth birthday and for the masquerade ball celebration this evening, the myriad formal accoutrements of funereal piety had been set aside. For one fabulous evening of revelry, there were no somber hues or severe coiffures, nor were there subdued cosmetics of traditional grief.

Unlike many of the others including the eternally carping Castlemaine, Frances hadn't minded the imposed period of mourning at all: it suited her changed mood, and it was a definite relief not to have to constantly display and arbitrate style, especially in this time of war with Minette's France from which all fashion flowed. The king had even tried to set a new style of elaborate Persian fashions, but everyone had only pretended to be amused; when King Louis XIV mockingly decked his footmen in the same, exotic garb, the Stuart court went quickly, quietly back to their Francophilic tastes, war or not.

"I say, dear Frances," Queen Catherine was calling

back over her shoulder as the bevy of beautifully costumed and masked ladies swept down the tiled corridor toward the Great Hall, "are you feeling good this night?"

"Oh, indeed, Your Majesty," Frances replied and moved closer to the queen in a little spot Lady Anne Scroope made begrudgingly for her at the royal elbow. "Do I not look all right?"

"Pale—too quiet too, my dear Frances. Still, as everybody always saying, Frances Stewart looking pretty even in the black clothes and in the plain hair of mourning, no?"

"Do they say so, my Queen? That is kind."

Catherine of Braganza's musical voice chimed in a brief laugh, then she lowered her voice. "Kind—here, Frances, do not believe it. But, my dear, I have not told you what our Castlemaine said of how you looking."

They laughed together huddled over the queen's ornately painted fan which matched her shepherdess gown so outrageously ruffled and decked with tinkling bells that the sheep and shepherd too would be frightened away. Oblivious to the narrowed eyes and snide remarks of the others jostling for favorable positions as they approached their grand entrance to the ballroom, Frances whispered her thanks to the queen. Already, the lilting strains of mingled instruments, even the new imported violins the king so favored, filled the air.

Frances wondered whether Richmond would be here, and, if he was behind a velvet half mask as everyone was supposed to be, whether she would know him instantly. Surely, she would recognize the square chin, the firm mouth with enticing, full lower lip, and if she were to be close enough, the emerald eyes with sun shards would give him away for certain.

She started at the queen's final whispered words, annoyed at herself for daring to gaze off into nothingness when she stood so near her queen. "Frances, you be smiling and enjoy all this whenever your queen sees you tonight, yes? I will be smiling too, whatever does happen."

With a forced smile of her own, Frances returned the characteristic half-smile with which Her Majesty hid her protruding teeth. "Yes, I will, Your Majesty. Thank you again."

These last weeks, finally, Frances thought, the queen has given up inquiring about Richmond or mentioning his name at any excuse; now Her Majesty contented herself with concerned looks and circuitous benevolences. For that and for the queen's courage and concern when she continually grieved over her mother's death and for her native land which she would probably never see again, Frances admired her. For the cheer and unflagging kindness she displayed despite the lack of royal heirs and of a devoted husband, Frances dared to admire King Charles's queen as her friend.

The women paused, fluffing gowns, patting tresses, and adjusting the rainbow-hued velvet masks. The orchestra inside halted, the double doors swept open, the king appeared. He was all dazzling smile for his queen under his green mask and white silk turban, but his eyes were unreadable shadowy slits as the women entered. A romping coronto spilled from the orchestra as everyone applauded.

It took Frances only half the distance of the room to realize Richmond was indeed here and to pick him out. He stood towering over almost everyone in the first row of courtiers who'd passed close to the royal entry of the Stuart monarchs. He was rakishly attired as some sort of buccaneer or pirate, even to a silk cloth tied askew around his head and a curved scimitar stuck in his broad leather belt. His breeches were black velvet and a gold silk shirt opened in a daring V halfway down his dark-haired chest.

How apropos, Frances thought grimly, careful not to turn her head one whit so he could tell she noted him. But it probably would not have mattered anyway: her heart lurched as she saw the buxom maid of honor, Annette La Garde, dressed as a milkmaid, leaning heavily, breathlessly, against him, gazing up. Her full bosoms pressed into his upper arm and he hardly flinched away. Rather, his deep, annoying laugh floated to Frances distinctly among the jumble of voices and soaring music as she swept past to stand beside the queen's chair on the dais.

A stream of courtiers hurried forward immediately toward the queen, offering congratulations and gifts. Soon Frances' arms were full of scented boxes and nosegays with jewels nestled in the petals while Lady Scroope already held an enamel box and tiny clock.

"Od's fish," the king's voice cut in above the hubbub, "somebody fetch some footmen with trays. These maids of honor are not beasts of burden, you know." He stood up and moved behind the queen's chair, seemingly to organize the confusion. Frances hoped he'd send them away from their station: she could see the Duke of Richmond with that plumpish Annette still draped on his arm moving ever closer in the line of courtiers.

Then the king's unmistakable, long-fingered hand was on her upper arm from behind; his breath rustled her curls beside the mask. "Here, Frances, step down and put those things on a tray," he ordered brusquely, but when she took the three stairs down to obey, he followed her. "You look stunning, of course, love, but 'sdeath, isn't that silk shirt rather tight and it's cut up the sides to your knees. I don't mind looking at the contours and legs it reveals but I don't need the others gaping."

"It's Oriental style, sire—a Chinese lady's dress from imported gifts the queen has never worn, and it's slit up the sides so I can walk and dance. Do you wish me to leave and change to something else?"

"No—no, of course not. It's just rather daring, that's all and you have not been that lately. I'm supposed to be a desert sultan or some such, but I wish now I'd come as the Chinese khan. Od's fish, their word is law I hear, and then with one little crook of a finger, you'd be waiting where I want you, I warrant."

"I like your costume, sire, especially that silk wrapped thing on your head, but please don't tease me here. I need to get back to Her Majesty and obviously you do too."

His full mouth under the narrow, ebony mustache twitched down at some wry thought. "Yes, obviously, my dear. How sweet of you to remind me of my husbandly duties. Just you remember though,

484

your legs always did inflame parts of me I dare not mention here."

Furious, she nearly pushed past him, so close she could smell the sweet wine on his breath. Stolidly, she rejoined the smiling, chatting queen at the carved arm of her chair, unfortunately just in time to see Richmond and Annette la Garde move up one step on the dais. Queen Catherine's head swiveled to Frances, then back to Richmond but her eyes were in shadow behind the mask.

"My dear Duke of Richmond, no?" Her Majesty was saying. "I can tell almost everyone. I am very good at this," she said and laughed, carefully hiding her mouth with the edge of spread fan.

"Indeed you are, Your Majesty," Richmond replied. "Your shepherdess gown is lovely and I'm beginning to wish I had come as a lost sheep." His teeth flashed white under his black mask as the queen giggled at his gibe.

"No, no, my lord—a pirate for you, that is good. Pirates love sailing, I know."

"And stealing milk maids' hearts, Your Majesty," Annette La Garde crooned and curtsied at his side.

Frances' backbone stiffened as she watched the little scene. Despite the mask, she was certain Richmond had just frowned, but she could not fathom where his eyes might be looking, and wild little butterfly wings feathered in her lower stomach.

"A pirate, eh, Richmond?" the king's strong voice cut in as he sat back down at the queen's side. Frances noted Castlemaine had appeared from somewhere, garbed brazenly—rumor had reported all week that she would be—as the Queen of Sheba as though that could get her back in this Stuart Solomon's good graces.

"The scimitar, sire," Richmond was saying, "is from a captured enemy vessel and I mean to give it to you, but I needed it for this wild display tonight."

"From that Dutch merchantman you spoke of which put up the all-night battle with guns blazing?" King Charles asked.

"Yes, the very one, sire, the one with the Oriental porcelain when we needed war goods."

Richmond and the king shared a laugh, though Frances could not see anything amusing about what he had said. Battles and blazing guns? No one, including Richmond, had told her a thing about his doing more than supplying and outfitting privateer ships to harass the Dutch and French vessels menacing the English Channel!

"Your Majesty," the duke addressed the queen again, "upon this occasion of your birthday, I should like to present you with a carved gold brooch that is very precious to me and has been in my mother's family, that of the Dukes of Norfolk, for years since the days of King Henry VIII. My mother said once it was a gift only for a true love, and as I regretfully have none, I hope His Majesty will not mind if I offer it to you."

Frances gasped as he extended the gift to the queen. In the green velvet box he held open nestled the filigreed oval brooch he had offered to her her first Christmas in England and which she had returned to him. A sharp stab of jealousy and regret twisted in her. Tears flooded her eyes behind the mask. Why had he not told her all of that family tradition about the brooch? But then, of course, she had never given him a chance.

"No true love for you, my dear Richmond?" the queen was asking. "But I think, there must be one somewhere, someday, no? I thank you for the lovely gift."

Better Her Majesty's cloaks and gowns display the beautiful, ornate piece than that simpering, bosomy Annette La Garde's, Frances fumed. Two tears traced jagged paths down under her velvet mask. The greetings and gift giving went on and on. The velvet box which held the brooch disappeared on some hovering footman's tray. Frances' legs began to ache, even to tremble before it was over.

When the queen and king descended the dais at last to begin to circulate among the revelers, Frances joined old Chancellor Clarendon's little group knowing his stodgy presence would keep away most of the court gallants who would otherwise ask her to dance. For the first time she would remember, she couldn't bear to take the floor, or to see Richmond's elegant dance style mingled with that of the gushy, top-heavy Annette's.

"My dear Mrs. Stewart," Chancellor Clarendon boomed when he saw her, and he instantly made a place for her among his cronies and supporters. "We've been speaking of the King's Committee investigating the fire. Mrs. Stewart saw the Great Fire from close up, didn't you, my dear?"

Frances' head snapped up. But no one knew, she thought, of the horrible day she had been nearly trapped by that blackmailer John Davis in the fire— no one but Richmond.

"You were at Somerset House with your mother the entire day, I heard," Clarendon was saying and his goatee bobbed as he talked under the mask and hood that represented the black-robed judge, Daniel, from the Old Testament.

Frances relaxed instantly. "Yes, yes, I was at Somerset and certainly much closer than those of you who were out at your country homes that day. We were absolutely deluged with ash and cinders even there."

"They drifted as far as Windsor even," Lord Ormonde said. "All the statistics are appalling—more than thirty-two thousand homes destroyed, four hundred thirty-six acres leveled, one hundred thousand people homeless, and four-fifths of the old walled city gone."

"I can tell you've been reading the transcripts of the investigation into it, my lord," Chancellor Clarendon said still nodding as he had to punctuate each statistic. "But the king's been wonderful through this and it's obvious a finer, grander, and safer London shall rise again Phoenixlike from the tragic pyre."

Frances smiled, stifling an outright grin. King Charles was right—the old man was a born politician, always lecturing, always talking as though he spoke before the rows of woolsacks in the Houses of Parliament. But the king had done well indeed—at least in this fire mess: he had gone out among the fire fighters to offer encouragement and incentives, he had addressed the homeless masses at Moorfields on the fourth day when the fire was over at last; and now he had commissioned the long-faced Dr. Christopher Wren, whom she could see even now across the room dressed as some sort of astrologer, to rebuild ruined London along his grand, neoclassic plans.

Chancellor Clarendon took Frances aside, assuming his usual fatherly pose with her. He lifted a goblet of champagne for her off the steward's tray and even took one himself as if to deny his myriad court enemies' criticism that he was all work and no frivolity.

"You're smiling under that mask, Frances," he observed. "Let's speak clearly, dear girl, in the few minutes we may have alone until the king or someone else descends on us. Everyone says you haven't been your usual happy self lately. Forgive an old man for asking, but is it this silly John Davis imprisonment in The Clink or is His Majesty getting uncontrollable again?"

"And do you think the John Davis blackmail scheme is silly, my Lord Chancellor?" she asked to avoid his probe about the king.

"Pish—the man's a lunatic and you did exactly right to tell His Majesty and have him locked up."

"But you see, my Lord Chancellor, it worries me that Castlemaine has had the same sort of— detractors, and things like this John Davis problem put me in her category now."

"Nonsense, my girl. Only idiots or enemies would even breathe a word that would place you in the same category with that woman. *You* have kept your honor, and I daresay, your own bed. She is no better than a fancy slattern despite the continued rewards he heaps on her for the bastard children's sakes. Spaniel dogs and children—he's always been soft there."

"I heard—the queen hopes—that now that His Majesty has actually had Buckingham thrown in the Tower for his latest machinations, it may weaken Castlemaine even more," she said.

The old man sighed and downed the rest of his champagne. His pudgy cheeks puffed out under his black mask, and she saw through the eye slits his intense stare fastened on her. "I would give half my household if that could only be the case, Frances, but I've seen Buckingham rise again above His Majesty's royal wrath and disfavor far too many times—the lady too. I can only be grateful that His Majesty thought enough of his queen's honor to imprison Buckingham for promoting a plan that the king should set aside his barren wife to find his royal Stuart heirs elsewhere. Of course, the blackguard Buckingham can just envision Castlemaine's bastard brood being legitimatized with their Uncle George as their guardians. Pish!"

"And so," she observed quietly, "that's made a much worse rift between your allies and the Castlemaine camp."

"Worse, Frances? Not really. It couldn't be worse. The Villiers-Castlemaine crew has always published far and wide that I intentionally got him a barren queen to assure my own grandchildren by his heir, the Duke of York, would someday mount the throne. And what do you say of all this, Frances?"

"More and more, my Lord Chancellor, I say I wish I weren't even here to see it all, but I despair he'll ever let me go."

He patted her hand so that her unfinished champagne sloshed, but she ignored it. "And I say, my dear girl, you've always been wiser than the cleverest of us learned, wily politicians scampering about to accomplish the king's mercurial desires. You've seen when to concede or retreat, but you have never capitulated to his obviously amorous warfare. You've kept yourself out of dangerous foreign entanglements even when sly foxes like Verneuil of France wanted to control you. You've refused bribes and held up your reputation which easily could have gone the way of that whorish, plotting Castlemaine —right into the mire and mud. I'm proud of you, dear girl—you've always been the wise and clever one in this nest of jackals indeed!"

He patted her hand again, and after she politely refused the opportunity to accompany him, he bowed and shuffled off to join his son-in-law, the Duke of York. That was all she needed tonight on top of flashing her legs at the king; if His Majesty saw her chatting with York, his raging jealous streak might precipitate more threats, more uncontrollable passion.

Jealousy. Passion. Oh heavens, but she had felt both tonight when Richmond had presented to Her Majesty the brooch he had offered her once, but she surely knew not to be jealous of the poor, dear queen. It was that pudgy Annette La Garde draped all over him that had really set her off, but for what? For what?

The stubborn tears she so detested blurred her gaze again and she slipped out the side door to the hall running parallel to the length of the old Great Hall. It was cooler here; it cleared her head. She walked toward the stone terrace along the Thames and removed her awkward mask at last to carefully lift clinging tears from her thick lashes with the back of a finger. Ahead, the door to the terrace stood slightly ajar and cool, night air swept down the wooden floor to creep up her stockinged legs where the Chinese skirt was slit. She would step out for just a moment to calm herself before she went back in. It had been mild for mid-November and the terrace was lighted.

Wavering flames from wall sconces lit the long stone walk in great blotches of white interspersed with pools of shadow. She leaned on the wide stone balustrade and inhaled the damp river wind. She felt her carefully coiled and curled tresses dance loose as she breathed in the invigorating, fitful gusts.

Clarendon thought she was wise and clever, but what did he really know of her beneath her real mask? she thought. She had made a terrible mess of things here in the Stuart court, things that both she and Minette had spoken of, planned for in that long, last year they had spent together in France. "Love him for me," Minette had pleaded, and she had tried, but now it was all a tangled snare. She saw clearly what clever Clarendon did not: soon, she must either bed with the king or be his enemy for life.

And Richmond—oh, damn Richmond with his strong, comforting arms, his promises, and pleas. She had hurt him repeatedly in her twistings and turnings to escape her wretched feelings for him. If only her body hadn't always betrayed her when he touched her or gazed on her that special, fiery way. If only her heart didn't rule her head whenever he was near.

She spun around at the clank of metal on metal, hoping nonetheless it was he.

"I didn't mean to startle you, lass," the tall pirate standing there told her. A distant torch lit his big-shouldered silhouette in a strange halo and gilded the curved blade in his belt along its crescent edge. She could discern the V-shape where his daringly cut shirt exposed his dark-haired, muscled chest and she could so well picture the rest of his lean, angular body despite the dimness. He did not wear or seem to have his black mask anywhere.

"You didn't startle me, my lord. I just stepped out for a little breath of air," she managed.

"Then, as far as you know, His Majesty is not coming out to meet you?"

She should have retorted flippantly at that, she told herself, but she was so happy to see him—and alone. "No, my lord. And whatever have you done with little Annette?"

He joined her at the stone balustrade, his hands beside hers before he answered low. "I didn't come with her or ask her to join me in there this evening, Frances. Besides, she is hardly 'little Annette.' You ought to know by now I prefer a more slender type and one that is not such a clinger."

"Yes," she responded. "I remember you said that a long time ago about Amanda Wells."

"I suppose I could tell myself that's why you've hardly been a clinger, hoping to please me, but I know better," he said.

Her voice was as soft as a sigh. "Do you?"

"Look, sweetheart, I'm leaving again on king's war business tomorrow, and I don't know how long we might have this blessed privacy before someone else walks out here. I do know better than to ask you to come down to kiss me farewell after everyone's gone to bed, and I can hardly climb in your third-story windows at Whitehall, so I'll make this quick and blunt."

A gibe about pirates taking what they want came to her mind but it never got past her lips. He pulled her swiftly against him as his mouth crushed hers. Her head spun, her blood raced and here on the sweep of broad terrace where anyone could see, she surrendered ecstatically. Her arms lifted to pull him to her; her lips and tongue danced intricately with his. Her breasts pressed to him flattening out despite the thrust of her nipples through the Chinese silk; her soft belly and thighs molded to his hard, angular lines with compelling force.

"Oh, hell, Frances," he groaned as they held to each other, gasping for air at last. "Damn, damn, why do you do this to me just when I think I've got myself under control?"

She stood on tiptoe against him to feather little kisses down his jawline until he groaned again and stood her away, his hands hard on her shoulders. "Frances, I don't know how long I'll be gone this time. I just meant to kiss you goodbye." His voice was raspy, broken as if he'd run a long distance. Her voice was shaken too.

"I see," she said. "I didn't know. I never know when you're going or coming anymore. I didn't know you'd been to sea to fight."

"Just once when a Dutch merchantman surprised my supply forces for my privateers near Harwich. We only meant to defend our position and ended up capturing the ship. It wasn't much of a battle really. I'd like to think you've been worrying about me though."

"Yes," she admitted, amazing herself evidently as much as him. "I do."

"Frances—"

"Wait, my lord—Charles. I know I've made a mess of things and ruined it all."

"You've tried, my sweet lass, but as you can see by my rather avid presence here and by the way you can so easily tear me apart, you've hardly succeeded. These last few months I've waited for you to come to me—waited for you to understand how I feel."

Her heart threatened to thunder out of her chest. She couldn't breathe, couldn't think, could only feel. "I love you, Charles, I admire you and—I love you."

His head jerked to a slight tilt and torchlight caught the sunny shards in his green eyes. "You do?" he managed, his voice almost a low croak. "You do?"

"Yes, I do." She nodded wildly and began to cry even as he swept her into an iron embrace to spin them both around. He was chuckling crazily in her ear even as he still gasped for breath. He stopped the tumultuous display at last, and they leaned in mutual embrace against the reality of the hard stone balustrade.

"I had thought, Frances—I had despaired you'd ever say that or ever admit it to yourself. All those years of being taught not to trust men, to hate me—it has been like that, hasn't it?"

"From my mother, you mean? Yes, but I think for myself, you know. I've looked around here and in France. I've seen how it is."

"All right, all right. Hell's gates, let's not argue now. At least, finally you've seen how it is with me, lass, that's all that matters. I've never loved anyone as completely as I've loved you these years and never shall again. Will you marry me now?"

There was a tiny, aching silence while river sounds and the lilt of a distant minuet drifted to them to recall a world outside their embrace. "Now?" she faltered.

"I mean now that you know you love me too, now that you understand. Tonight, I admit I can't manage it, but I'll cut my duties short to come back for you soon."

"He won't let us."

"We won't tell him until it's done."

"But Cobham. You've admitted you need money for Cobham and the Scottish estate. I have nothing but a few jewels and I'd be honor-bound to leave those behind."

"Hell, there's no honor-bound around here, Frances. You've seen that. I am only grateful for the miracle the king has been so patient with you. And as for Cobham, she's a good Kentish crop and livestock estate and she'll earn her way out eventually. Let me worry about that. The dowry you bring me is you."

"But if Cobham is in debt, the Crown could claim it and he would probably rescind your offices."

"Look, sweet, if you love me, marry me and get out of this maze of masks and disguises that you've seen in there tonight. I expect he will take my office of

Lord Chamberlain away soon enough as he basically distrusts my Scottish heritage—and he knows, unlike the others, I'd rather be away from him. The navy duties he could not rescind until after the war as I'm needed too much if he's serious about a victory. Don't fret for all that."

He sighed. "You know, I'm starting to sense the onset of Frances panic again, the same disease that's made you back off everytime we've been intimate or honest with each other before. I won't again go through the hell you've put me through off and on these last four years, Frances. You say you love me. Then say you'll marry me or I won't ask again."

"Why must you be so demanding about it? Surely, I can consider it and then we'll talk about it when—"

"You have considered it," he insisted, his voice gone sharp and cold as the sword at his waist. "We have said all there is to say just now, and I see by your set jaw and trembling lower lip I'm just where I was when you sent back that brooch I gave the queen tonight. 'I might marry you, maybe, perhaps, my lord'—it's not enough, surely I've made that clear before. Good night, Frances. Thank you for your words of love. Goodbye."

He dropped a hard, quick kiss on her forehead and whirled away. The heels of his shoes made forlorn scraping sounds as he strode away down the terrace to be drowned in each separate pool of light then swallowed by the darkness while she just stared.

She thought of running after him, of shouting his name, of begging him to marry her, but motion and words would not come. She was really doing it for him, she told herself, protecting him from all the anger that would surely befall his precious estates if she wed him. Cobham—damn it! She was even, wretchedly jealous of Cobham.

She realized she was cold suddenly and the wind she had fancied as mild had gone chill to lick at the jagged trails of tears on her cheeks. She blotted them carefully with her perfumed handkerchief, hoping her belladonna eye color had not smeared. She ached to just go off alone to bed, but then she would be missed and would make herself even more miserable by sobbing into her pillow.

Straightening her wind-blown coiffure, she started back inside at a good pace. She would put her mask back on to hide the tears and laugh and drink and dance. She would exhaust herself with revelry and then tomorrow, soon enough, she would redon her mourning garb for the death of a precious love.

By two of the clock Frances was abed but not asleep. In a rolling, repetitive blur, Richmond's impassioned words—his parting words—chanted in her brain. Both cats slept at the foot of her bed as if to comfort her, but she tossed and turned so much they soon thudded off to go elsewhere. There was a muted knocking, knocking somewhere far away—like the sad sounds of Richmond's heels as he stalked away. She had danced and had downed a great deal of champagne, and yet, annoyingly, she felt stone sober. She had luxuriated for half an hour in a hot bath, still she couldn't sleep. Heavens, at least that wretched tapping somewhere had stopped, and she heard Gillie get up off the settee where she had asked her to sleep tonight.

"M'lady. You awake, m'lady?" the girl's gentle voice came at the door.

"I am now, Gillie. What is it? What was that knocking sound?"

Gillie padded soundlessly into the room, and Frances squinted to make out her white face and nightshift in the dimness. "Pardon the lateness, he says, m'lady, but the king's man, Mister Prodgers, be in the privy staircase and he says you're to come quick to His Majesty."

"What? Is he ill?"

"No, m'lady. To talk, he says, and to take the privy staircase. Mister Prodgers is standing in the doorway now."

"Heavens! Something's wrong. Here, get out a gown. I cannot go there and by privy staircase undressed!"

She wiggled into a plain blue silk daydress and left her hair loose. Whoever was with the king would just have to understand. She tugged on only one petticoat and shoved her feet into velvet mules while Gillie laced her and tied her long, loose tawny hair back with a ribbon. Edward Prodgers, in the privy stairwell, gave an audible sigh of relief when he saw her.

"Is he ill, Prodgers?" she asked as he indicated he would light her way down the steps and went ahead.

"Ill? No. Disturbed, I'd say. I realize it's a surprise—so late. Come along, please, Mrs. Stewart." Their feet on wooden stairs echoed hollowly to nearly drown their whispered words.

Prodgers opened the door to the king's rooms for

499

her. She saw His Majesty immediately, sitting in a brocade chair before a low-burning fire. Prodgers followed her in, then hurried off and closed the door to the small, intimate drawing room behind him. The big, coal black head swiveled. She saw then he wore a silk dressing gown and his feet were bare.

"It pleases me you come and quickly, Frances," he said in almost a monotone. "It would really have put me even more out of my humor than I already am to have to fetch you."

She stood her ground near the door. "I don't understand. Are you all right? What has happened? It's the queen's birthday. I thought you'd be with the queen."

"My little moral conscience speaks, as always. Od's fish, I've been with the queen until an hour ago and it didn't assuage this need I have for you. I could go down to Barbara as I've done countless times before when you've denied me, but that wouldn't help either—not past morning's light."

He stood, dropping the goblet he held, with a hissing splash, on the hearth. He came at her around the table and slammed the door as she opened it to flee. The sharp crack of wood on frame echoed in the stillness broken only by their breathing and the fire.

"No, you see, I'm not all right at all, my sweet. I haven't been ever since you've been underfoot here at Whitehall or anywhere else I've been." He leaned close, his hands flat on the wall on both sides of her head. "Surely you've noticed how you effect me— bother me—Frances. 'Sblood, my darling, beautiful little tease, it's gotten to the point where I have to do something about it for the good of the realm.

You distract me from business, you see, royal business. A few drinks at that damned birthday ball, a glimpse of those legs while you were dancing with all the others and I can't even concentate on making my wife content on her birthday or sign a few wretched documents or write coherently to Minette. It's got to end."

Her heart thudded. She had to convince him to send her away. She could have Gillie take a note to Richmond saying she'd marry him and live at Cobham away from here. Mother could come to visit, and Minette would have to understand. "You're sending me away?" she dared, turning her head slightly to the side to avoid his wine-laden breath and desperate, glassy gaze.

"'Sdeath, never. I'm taking you to bed the way I should have done years ago and slaking my thirst for you once and for all!"

"No, sire, you can—" was all she got out before his mouth descended hard to force her soft lips apart. His hands, treacherously skilled, imprisoned her arms at her sides, then lifted her. She kicked, squirmed, but he did not break stride as he moved swiftly with her to the door, opened it somehow, then went, pressing her against his bare chest where his robe had pulled awry, down the hall to his huge bedroom.

"No! No, I'll scream!" she threatened as he dropped her in the middle of the vast bed and knelt beside her. His face looked demonic just before he rolled her over onto her stomach.

"Scream all you want," he ground out. "Now that would really give blackmailers like that bastard I've imprisoned for you plenty to write about. I'm willing

501

to keep this private—let the gossipers think I've never had you. I've offered you lands, grants, titles, I've done everything to woo you, Frances—now, damn you, hold still!"

Her bodice, she foolishly had not bothered to put a chemise under, gaped as he pulled her up and roughly peeled her skirt and petticoat away. A scream caught in her throat as he threw his robe off and they faced each other naked across the width of bed.

"Think about it, Frances. The time has come for us, and it is now. No escaping, no denying. Not only am I king, but I am one hell of a lot stronger and bigger, so why not submit to the inevitable? If not, you'll make me be rough and just do things anyway I can, which is not the way I'd like to handle a beautiful, frightened virgin."

She gasped. Virgin! He expected a virgin! And worse, a frightened one and all she felt was boiling fury!

He pulled her flat on her back under him and held her down with his weight while his hands and mouth roamed over her soft flesh. His hands were treacherous; his words erotic. Her nipples pointed under his deliberately sensual assault. She tried to shift away; she tried to make her mind a blank, but Richmond's words, Richmond's face, Richmond's body and love tormented her. Damn this king however patient and kind he'd been before. She wanted Richmond like this. She loved only him!

"Mm, my darling, you've wanted me too all this time. I've known that. I understand your hesitation, your fears. Just hold still now and let me take you— let me give to you. I'll make you so happy, a wealthy woman, anything you desire if you'll only desire me."

"No. I cannot. Cannot!"

He pressed into her harder and spread her legs under him. "You will in an hour, damn it, you will," he insisted as he positioned himself heavily over her, pinning both wrists above her head with one big hand.

Hard fingers nudged her soft core. "No! Don't," her own cry surprised her as she tried to squirm aside. Her soft thighs only grazed muscular, unmovable hips. Skilled fingers stroked, darted.

"Oh, Frances," he rasped. "My, easier than I thought and readier. You please me, love, always did. You must have broken your virgin's spot with all that riding. Hell, so much the better."

He relaxed one moment to prepare to thrust into her. Wildly desperate, she managed to free one arm. Her lifted elbow caught his chin. He grunted, then swore.

"This is exactly like what happened to Barbara, sire—exactly," she said, trying to control her words. "I guess I'm to be your whore now. She was hauled off, forced down, and raped brutally that night from the carriage after we'd been at the Duke of York's party. And now you're treating me the same, like a whore, a victim to just force and rape like those horrible men did—"

His face lifted close over hers. "'Sdeath, what?"

"Barbara and I lied about what those apprentices did in the carriage that night," she said levelly, grasping at a tiny flicker of hope when he drew back slightly from impaling her.

"They didn't rape you? Is that what happened so that—"

"No, they raped Barbara—all of them cruelly because she was your whore. And now, you are treating me the same!"

Fury, shock, disappointment ran riot across the swarthy, taut face so close over her. "How could you ever—ever—compare me with lawless criminals and rebels like those, you little witch?" he rapped out and pulled away from her instantly. He sat heavily on the side of the bed, his head in his hands. His words were muffled. "And Barbara survived that and then took me that night when I was comforting her. She did all that and you can't even love me a little."

"I do, sire, only not the way you've wanted."

"I don't understand it," he murmured low as she scrambled off the other side of the bed to pull on her rumpled gown. "You're not cold, Frances, that isn't it. Even tonight you were ready when I—oh, hell, get out of here before I finish what I started just to prove to you I'm the terrible bastard you evidently think I am. Go on! And stay out of my way until I decide what I'm going to do with you!"

She scooped up her shoes and ran, half dressed. There were no words to say, there was no way back to friendship or the delight she had felt once with him. She groped her way up the dark stairwell to her room and shoved the drop-leaf buffet table in front of the door.

In her bedroom, she lit a huge tallow candle immediately and, disheveled and shaken to her very core, sat at her desk overlooking the black Thames. She took a piece of parchment, dipped her quill in the inkwell and wrote,

My dear Lord Richmond,

I realize you said you would never ask me again to wed with you, but I would gratefully and willingly accept should you ever change your mind.

You were so right that I must go away from here, and I am certain I would love your Cobham as much as I do your yacht the *Francis*.

Please call on me or send for me at your earliest convenience as I swear these words to be true, as were the others that I finally said to you upon the terrace.

Forgive me please, and I certainly shall you if you reject this heartfelt desire. Please, my Charles, I do not want it to be too late for us.

Yours,
F.

She read it twice, then folded and sealed it with hot wax which she spilled on her wrist in her haste. She sat at the window holding the note until dawn, then woke Gillie and sent her, with a lantern, out to the Bowling Green where Richmond had his suite at Whitehall. She paced the floor in circles while her cats grabbed lazily at her swishing skirt. Her pulse pounded; she felt as invigorated as if she had slept all night rather than not at all.

She would stay out of the king's way indeed. She might even move to rooms at Somerset House for a while, saying she needed to be near her mother. She whirled and paced, making her plans.

If Richmond agreed, she could leave for Cobham immediately to await his return from sea to be wed, or she could sneak away as he had suggested only tonight—no, that was last night now and the new day was golden in the sky outside over the river.

"M'lady, I'm back."

"Well? What did he say? Have you a note?"

"He had gone, m'lady. Only his Scottish steward from his Kent estates was there and he said the duke's gone to sea out of Dover somewheres."

"But he was here only last night! He cannot be gone already! Where is my note?"

"Mister Payne, his man, m'lady, he promised to get it to the duke soon as he comes back to his estate or when he knows for sure where he is. That was all right—to leave him the note, m'lady?"

Frances sank on the edge of the chair. "Yes. Roger Payne—I'm sure he's trustworthy. But the duke said he wasn't leaving until today. . . ."

She rose and leaned her flushed cheek on the cool window pane, gazing out over the busy morning river traffic darting freely here and there. He was gone and she was here, stuck here in close proximity to people she distrusted and even feared now. How long, how long before that impassioned letter reached him—and what would he say? Heavens, it would serve her right if he tore it to shreds on the bow of his ship and cast it to the Channel winds.

"M'lady, is there anything else I can do?"

"I want a hot bath, Gillie, if you'd send for water, please. Hot tell them. And then lay out some riding clothes as I'm going to see my mother. Right now,

I'm tired and I just want to be alone, you see—"

"Another hot bath?" Gillie began, then checked herself. "Oh, yes, m'lady. I won't even uncover Joli's cage a bit so it will be real quite here for you."

Gillie closed the door softly as she went out. And even after the bath water came, Frances stood at the window a very long time just watching the river flow toward the sea.

Part IV

The Sea

Song

Love still has something of the sea,
From whence Venus arose;
No time his slaves from doubt can free,
Nor give their thoughts repose.

They are becalmed in clearest days,
And in rough weather tossed;
They wither under cold delays,
Or are in tempests lost.

One while they seem to touch the port,
Then straight into the main
Some angry wind in cruel sport
The vessel drives again.

At first disdain and pride they fear,
Which if they chance to 'scape,
Rivals and falsehood soon appear
In a more dreadful shape.

By such degrees to joy they come
And are so long withstood,
So slowly they receive the sum
It hardly does them good.

'Tis cruel to prolong a pain;
And to defer a joy,
Believe me, gentle Celemene,*
Offends the winged boy.**

An hundred thousand oaths your fears
Perhaps would not remove;
And if I gazed a thousand years,
I could no deeper love.

—Sir Charles Sedley

*a pastoral name given affectionately to the lady addressed

**Cupid, god of love

Chapter Eighteen

The tennis courts King Charles had installed in 1662 at Whitehall always attracted a large gallery when the king played at any reasonable hour. Too often the slug-abed courtiers, exhausted after an evening's revels, were noticeably absent from His Majesty's daily six-in-the-morning bouts. But today, perhaps to flaunt his still-marvelous physique at thirty-eight when others of his age had gone pudgy soft, the king had challenged the recently freed Duke of Buckingham in a nine-of-the-clock invitation match.

Frances sat wedged between two other maids of honor in the second row of wooden galleries while the leather ball thwacked repetitively onto the wooden strips of the floor. It was always warm in the enclosed court; everyone knew the king preferred it so and boasted he often lost as much as four pounds a game when he ceremoniously weighed in afterward and compared that figure to his prematch weight.

Susan Warmestry leaned over to say something,

and Frances met her halfway so Amanda Wells on her other side, who'd never yet forgiven her for supposedly robbing her of Richmond, could not hear. "It's obvious those weeks in the Tower have sapped Buckingham's usual vigor," Susan mouthed.

"Perhaps that's why His Majesty insisted they play," Frances whispered back. "Buckingham is temporarily eager to please after his last downfall, but soon enough he'll be riding high as usual."

"I doubt if he'd even have been recalled now if His Majesty hadn't gone back to Castlemaine these last two months," Susan said. "He may call her a jade who meddles with things that are no concern of hers, but when she dared say he was a fool for allowing his most loyal subjects to be imprisoned, he took the abuse from her without the slightest remonstrance. And he's given her a gift of silver plate worth at least five thousand pounds. I've seen her flaunt it at her supper table, the witch."

Frances nodded absently. Her eyes went back to following the to-and-fro path of the flying leather ball. Castlemaine, a witch. That was what the king had called his mistress that night he had tried to force Frances into his bed—the night of the queen's masquerade birthday ball when she had last seen Richmond over two months ago.

She sighed, then applauded mechanically with the others as Buckingham missed the king's volley by several yards and barely saved himself from sprawling on his annoyed face. Heavens, she thought grimly, but the king could punish one well when he chose.

Oddly, he had not really taken revenge on her for

her desperate refusal last November, even at the final moment he had worked for so long. Even after her adamant rejection of him as he had moved to totally possess her open, vulnerable body that night, he had protected her.

She had feared royal retaliation for weeks, planned for it in those first long days she did not hear any reply from Richmond to her impassioned letter. But, not only did the king remain kind and polite to her, he evidently had not told Castlemaine what Frances had blurted out to him about the brutal, secret rape. Perhaps his own attack on Frances had shamed him to silence, or else he knew the depths of Barbara's vindictiveness and wanted no bickering or plotting at court. Instead of cruelty to Frances these last months, he had shown his vile-tempered mistress Barbara, Countess of Castlemaine, a marked favoritism she had not enjoyed for years.

Instinctively, Frances shrugged before she realized how foolish it could look to Susan, the ever-frowning Amanda Wells, or the others if they noticed. She couldn't begrudge Barbara anything; on the other hand, she couldn't be much more than civil to her either. Lately—since her long, tormented wait for Richmond to answer had begun, she hardly cared about anything here at the court, none of the things which used to mean so much to her. Lately, fear had begun to grow in her like a cold, gray mushroom, fear that she had totally overstepped the bounds with Charles Stuart, duke of Richmond. He might have received the letter long ago, laughed, and trodden it underfoot. Minutes, hours, weeks—interminable, like this wretched tennis game.

"I said, Frances, isn't that your girl down there in the doorway motioning to you?" Susan was asking.

Frances swiveled her head which, as if to cheer her, was all coiffed with yellow silk ribbons set amidst her dangling tawny curls. "Yes, it's Gillie, but I can't imagine what she'd want. Perhaps my mother is here. Excuse me, Susan. Excuse me, Amanda."

Amanda ruffled her skirts unnecessarily and let Frances pass. Frances hoped the king wouldn't notice her departure in the middle of a match he was so obviously winning; but then, what did it matter if he did? He had his poor, faithful queen here, all eyes and smiles for him although he'd ignore her after the match; and Castlemaine, appropriately decked out in flaming scarlet satin, stood fanning herself, leaning haughtily on a pillar at the very edge of the far observation area. Whatever foolishness Gillie had to offer, she was glad to be escaping. It was like a steamy summer day at Salisbury in here—how the opponents could stand to dash about and sweat in full periwigs and brocaded regalia she'd never fathom.

Gillie's eyes were wide; she even danced from foot to foot as if she would explode with her news. Frances' heart thundered in perfect counterpoint with the riotous applause they left behind as Gillie produced a large, buff square of parchment sealed with an imprinted oval of red wax. For one instant Frances stared at the missive held in the girl's slender fingers before she grabbed it.

"It's the ducal seal of Richmond, m'lady! His man brought it to your room, that Scottish man, you remember."

Frances ripped it open, slowly now, afraid of what

the large, black, slanted letters would say. She leaned on the brick wall outside the tennis courts near the Privy Garden in the cold, late February sun and read words which strangely echoed her own:

My dear Frances,

I realize I said I would never ask you again to wed with me, but I would willingly discuss it should you be of the same mind.

Please call on me in my rooms in the Bowling Green at your earliest convenience as I have just returned from the sea and Cobham. If your intent is still firm, time has long passed for secrecy and hesitations.

Your,
C

"Heavens, he's here!" she said and skimmed the controlled, noncommittal words again.

"Here? Where?"

"Sh. Come on. We're going for a walk."

"Here? Where?"

"Gillie, I vow, you are beginning to sound like Joli. I am going for a walk, I mean. You go on back up to the rooms to finish whatever you were doing and if anyone comes looking for me, I don't care what you tell them as long as it's not where I am!"

Frances lifted her pale yellow satin skirts to avoid soiling her hems on the scuffed gravel along the path in the Privy Garden.

"But where *are* you going to be?" Gillie's exasperated voice called after her as Frances hurried past the king's sundial and the big mounted tube he used to study the stars. She hurried across a grassy square and cut behind a tall, clipped yew hedge at the west end of the gardens before she remembered she'd left her velvet cloak draped across her seat in the tennis gallery. She didn't care; surely Susan would rescue it.

Her pulse raced with her feet. Escape, she thought. From the tennis courts, from Whitehall and all the intricacies of the maze in which she had managed to entangle herself. If only Richmond still cared, still wanted her. Escape to a rural, quiet Cobham she had never seen, escape to forgetfulness in Richmond's arms.

She paused, out of breath and warm from her running, near the wing of apartments fronting the old Tudor and Stuart Bowling Green. She had been to his rooms once before, the day she had dressed like a boy to ride the yacht *Francis* to victory against the king.

Against the king—that's what this was and there would be no escaping the royal wrath if Richmond did agree to have her. Despite it all, she didn't want to hurt His Majesty, or her mother. She'd never meant to hurt anyone, especially not Charles, Duke of Richmond.

Forgetting to even look to see if anyone was watching, Frances, clutching the letter to her pale yellow lacy bodice, knocked twice on the door. Someone moved inside to answer—a man's heavy tread. The oak door swung inward to reveal the burly, red-haired Roger Payne. Cradled in one arm like a baby was a sprawling set of bagpipes.

"Mrs. Stewart," his richly burred voice said,

"won't you please step in? Happy to see you again, mistress."

"The duke, Mister Payne. He is here?"

The man nodded and his pipes whined a bit as Richmond's deep voice floated to her from within. "Frances, come in and welcome. I am definitely here."

She stepped in, aware of Roger Payne's broad grin as he stood in the open doorway watching them. Richmond sat at a huge, littered table in his white shirt sleeves. He had evidently been writing or figuring on an abacus at his elbow. He stood and moved around the table toward her. They stopped five feet apart. Their eyes snagged and held.

"My Lord Richmond," Roger Payne's voice came from across the room, "you don't still favor a tune, do you?"

Richmond's eyes did not waver from hers. "No, man. Maybe later."

"Aye, milord. I'll be off then."

The door closed. Behind the table where Richmond had sat, flagrant sunlight flooded the room to make her blink as she stared.

"Then you did get my letter?" she said low. "I wasn't certain."

"I returned from sea to Cobham but a week ago and there it was. The wartime naval duties have been wretched. I've been north to Aberdeen and Edinburgh for a month, and it's been damned cold there."

"Oh."

"You wrote the letter the very night you last sent me away," he said, his voice carefully avoiding the accusing tone the words promised.

"I didn't send you away—but, yes, that very night."

He took one big stride closer, but evidently changed his mind. He halted and indicated with a stiffly raised hand she should sit on one of the two upholstered, tall-backed wing chairs near the low burning hearth. He sat in the other directly across from her, scooting it closer so she could have touched his feet if she but stretched hers out.

"You want me to explain?" she asked. She gripped her hands tightly together in her lap until her fingers went numb.

"You've no cloak," he said suddenly, then, "Yes, I want you to explain why you changed your mind at last."

"It's rather simple really, my Lord Charles. I realized you were right."

"About what, Frances?" he parried. "I swear, I've said so many things to you over the years that evidently didn't mean a damn."

"That's not true," she insisted quietly. She felt her cheeks, even her ear tips, blush hot pink. "I just wasn't ready."

"For?" he prompted.

She remembered his wild, ecstatic reaction last time she had told him she loved him. She swallowed hard and her voice shook. "I do love you, my lord. And as I—as the letter said, I would choose to wed with you if you will still have me."

His intent, serious expression did not change. "Agreed. I've brought a legal marriage contract from Rochester in my home shire that we will sign later. But I still want you to tell me the rest of it."

Her mouth fell open until she thought to close it. Had she heard aright? He had agreed instantly to wed her, but he sat like a stone statue, an accusing, all-knowing deity demanding a full confession fo some wretched sin!

She broke the magnetic intensity of their mutual gaze by looking jerkily down at her hands. Her knuckles had turned very white in her silken lap, the hue of springtime narcissus.

"After you walked away on the terrace that night," she began slowly, "I went back in to dance."

"I know. I heard. Go ahead, lass, I've agreed to wed you and I meant it." He hesitated, biting his lower lip as she looked up. His face flushed then, and she jumped as he yelled, "The royal stallion has had you, hasn't he, the bastard!"

His words were choked out in a strangled cry. Wild-eyed, she started again, but he still sat un-moving where he was, his big hands clasping the arms of his chair.

"Promise me you won't do anything foolish, my lord!" she cried. "He didn't—not really, and he's been kind since."

"Has he? Kind?" he mocked. He leaned quickly forward and his long arms shot out to lift her and pull her to him as he stood. "All these years, damn it," he ground out, "and the thing I feared most sends you to me!"

"He didn't—he didn't finish. Let me explain. He tried—he sent for me at two of the clock—"

"That night? That's about when I rode away—imagine—in the dark. I couldn't stand to be near you after you had said no again. Go on, then."

519

"He was very angry. He said the time had come and he couldn't even see to business, didn't care about the queen or Castlemaine if he couldn't have me. He said I'd thank him later and that I'd always been underfoot to tempt him."

"And then he forced you? Hell's gates, did he?"

"He tried, I said. He—he carried me to his bed, he—we were both there and undressed and he was on me—"

He loosed her so suddenly to spin away that she almost fell. His chair slid heavily partway across the hearth. She moved behind her chair, steadying herself against its high back. "No, I swear, my lord, he didn't! Just as he moved to—to—"

"I assume he duly noted you were not a virgin."

"I—yes."

"Explain to me then, please, Frances, how you managed to stop a rampaging bull from taking what he desperately wanted and what he had, all prepared, there under him for the mere taking."

"You don't believe—"

"You couldn't stop me in the carriage the first time, could you?" he challenged, and his voice actually quivered.

Awareness jolted her like a slap: he was jealous, desperately so, and she'd hurt him again. She'd always put him off, always prevaricated, but she would do neither now. "I am telling you God's truth whether you believe me or not, my Lord Charles," she declared. "It wasn't that I couldn't stop you as much as I didn't want to."

She came out from behind the chair and faced him, her arms at her sides, her hands grasping wrinkled

520

handfuls of her yellow skirt. "I screamed at him about Barbara's rape by those men who stopped the carriage. I told him he was treating me exactly the same as they had her—like a whore, a victim. He was furious. But he stopped before he took me, my lord, I swear he did!"

He nodded. His piercing green eyes were hooded, but she knew he studied her intently from head to silk slippers. "If he had—possessed me, Charles," she asked low, "then would you have changed your mind?"

"No, though I'd probably have gotten myself into a deeper dungeon than even that son-of-a-bitch Buckingham when I challenged the king to one of those damned duels he forbids."

"You wouldn't have!"

He sighed. "No, sweet, wayward lass, I wouldn't have. I've invested far too much time, grief, and energy in you to lose you now."

"Then am I some sort of challenge to you?" she heard herself ask foolishly. For the first time, she noted the hint of a smile that wryly lifted one corner of his mouth.

"Look who's asking all the questions now," he retorted, his voice almost gone light. "And am I not some sort of amusing ah, challenge, as you put it, to you?"

"Certainly not. If I didn't love you, I would never—"

He came to her in two huge strides and lifted her high against his chest. Her arms clasped his neck; their lips met in a careful, then crushing kiss. Even when it ceased, she held to him while he murmured,

"I want to believe it at last, my sweetheart, I want to. Show me."

Her head snapped up, but he obviously did not mean what she had thought. Instead, he carried her across to the table and put her down in the chair he had vacated when she'd entered. "Here," he said and spread a rolled document open before her.

It was a marriage contract declared in the shire of Kent, the seat of the Bishop of Rochester, four days ago, February 20, 1667. Unhesitating despite her trembling hand, she dipped the proffered quill in the ink well. But his big hand covered her wrist warmly to stay her.

"If you sign, Frances, there's no going back ever. I'm heading for Cobham in a week to make wedding plans, and we'll have to elope to make certain we can get you away. By the end of March we'll be living at Cobham, probably in disgrace, and you'll be my wife. And I will expect a wife in every sense of the word. I love you with all my heart, Frances, but I want to make certain you mean it. And I also intend to invoke my marriage contract right for us to bed together after we've both signed here today."

She gripped the pen so tightly she felt the quill bend in her hand. Contract rights—she'd heard they existed, in rural shires, of course, but they were so old-fashioned no one required or expected them anymore. And why had he become so ruthless now as if to scare her off? Her mother's words, more than two decades of stern warnings, jangled in her ears.

She bit her lower lip and signed her name on the lower line in large script.

She heard his sigh of relief. His left arm pressed her

shoulder lightly as he leaned forward over her to sign his name and both his titles: Duke of Richmond, Duke of Lennox. Next month then, she thought, I'll be duchess of both.

He straightened and sanded the signatures, then let the parchment roll closed without shaking it off. He pulled her chair back for her; she rose and turned to face him.

"A deed well done at last, my sweet lass," he said. "And now, if I'm to be your lord, you need a little loving to make up for a great deal of lost time."

"Right now, you mean? But it's scarcely ten in the morning. Tonight—"

He laughed and the sound tingled up and down her backbone thrillingly. "I forgot how much you've yet to learn of me, lass, how much I have to teach you, and maybe the other way around too, I warrant."

He led her into the small bedroom by her wrist, and she went willingly, struck mute by an overwhelming shyness. The heavy draperies were drawn, the coverlet turned down. "I arrived very late last night and was barely up when you came," he said, as if in guilty explanation.

He seemed suddenly in a hurry. That excited her, and she helped him as he undressed her, though a nervous trembling shook her now. He gazed at her as if awestruck when she stood nude before him on the soft rug next to the high, wide bed. His eyes caressed her and she drew her soft belly in as if his gaze were a blatant, physical caress. She distinctly felt her nipples leap to pointed nubs as he merely looked at them.

"Please, Charles—" she said before she knew she

would speak.

"What, my sweetheart? What do you want? Tell me."

His voice was a velvet rasp, the flow of words enticing, luring. She took a step toward him.

"Aren't you going to—undress?"

"Do you want me to, Frances?"

"But aren't you?"

"Then you want me to?" he crooned, his green gaze mesmerizing. "Yes, yes, I will," he said and moved quickly as if tired of some ploy she could not fully grasp.

He stripped off his garments so rapidly she almost panicked at the breadth and length of his hard, naked body. Already, already, plainly, he desired her; she could not tear her eyes away.

"Tell me what you want now, Frances. I want to please you."

Her limbs felt languid as if she drifted in warm, rushing water. "Love me, Charles."

"How? Tell me how. Let me love you every way," he murmured.

She lifted his hands to her breasts to still the aching tenseness of each bursting, pink nipple. His thumbs stroked torturingly, wonderfully across each, around each; then his lips and fierce tongue followed to kiss and lick and pull each rosebud taut until she thought she would scream with desire. Hesitation and uncertainty fled.

She ran her hands up his arms, over his shoulders and onto his chest all covered with crisp, curly dark hair. Then her fingers fastened on his thick, brown head. As if another woman possessed her, she stretched up to kiss him, to rub her body full-length against him; she lowered her hands to the angular slant of his hips to knead and caress him there, to fondle his hard buttocks, while his hands and mouth moved so wonderfully over her that her knees buckled and they fell entwined onto the bed.

"What now, my Frances? Tell me, what you want," he whispered in her ear when his tongue was not plundering there.

"Oh, please. I can't bear it—I'm burning—" she faltered.

"For what? I saved you from the fire once before. Don't you like this one, my sweetheart? Damn, but you helped to light it, to fan it. You have for years. Tell me what you want."

"Love me, take me—in me please!"

She didn't need to ask again. He rolled her under him while she separated and lifted her knees in blatant invitation. They both cried out in the joy of fierce union as he pierced her sweet, willing warmth and as great crescent waves of passion, like heavy seas rolled over them, through them.

She lifted her hips to meet his every movement, his aching withdrawals, his deeper, demanding, thrusts —again, again, again. They whirled, they rose as the final surging wave engulfed them, crashing together, then swimming slowly up into a sunlit pool. Court, fashion, power, king, she thought—nothing mattered now, nothing but this man, this union, and this rapturous crown of love.

"Really, Barbara, you've overstepped and badly

this time. A rope dancer in your bed!" King Charles scolded as he leaned his hands on the balcony of her drawing room overlooking the Privy Garden.

"That's a foul lie!" she exploded. She joined him at the railing to glance quickly down to be certain no one in the gardens would hear what years of experience told her would be a very loud discussion. "I suppose Clarendon's friends told you that? Or Frances Stewart. Pooh! It is a pack of lies!"

"My dear Barbara," he replied in his infuriatingly calm voice, "I hardly care but for the children—and the fact I rather thought I had treated you well of late. I know it's true about him—Joseph Hall, a rope dancer! And neither the old Chancellor's cronies, however much they detest you and George, nor Frances told me. Od's fish," he said so low she barely caught the words, "Frances hardly gives a tinker's damn what you or I do anymore."

"Pooh, I said. She was green with envy when you took me back—I mean since we've been so close of late as you say." She moved her graceful hand to his wrist under the lace cuff and stroked up his arm. With a bored sigh, he pulled gently away. She looked stunned for a moment, as if he had struck her. Anything, she thought, anger, hatred—anything was better than this indifference, as though he had never desired her, never even cared for her at all.

"All right, I admit it about Joseph Hall, sire. Gads, so what if he's a public entertainer? He's terribly clever and wild for me!" she brazened.

"No doubt," His Majesty observed wryly and folded his arms across his chest. "It's no doubt great fun and marvelous free publicity for a guttersnipe to bed with the king's long-acknowledged mistress, and maybe earn some coins on the side for not even doing that ridiculous dance back and forth on a tightrope. Oh, I'm certain it all excites the hell out of him."

"I don't pay him! Besides, the same could be said of Nell Gwynne, Moll Davis, and your other theater whores! They're gold diggers too."

"'Sblood, Barbara, don't summon a crowd with that screeching. Granted, the same can be said of the pretty little actresses who've climbed out of the pit with sheer pluck, a little talent, and lots of verve in bed. I never said otherwise. But then, Nell Gwynne has a heart of gold, and I never could say the same for you, my dear. Yet somehow," he said and sighed heartily again, "I had hoped for more from you. How foolish of me not to have learned by now. Good day, Barbara. I have much to do and only stopped to tell you to, at least, be a whit more discreet about your rope dancer."

She ran after him, nearly tripping over her most seductive robe in the velvet mules she had donned thinking he would want to lie with her when she'd heard he had suddenly appeared. In her mirrored entry hall, she caught his arm and he turned to face her, an almost stoic look on his usually sardonic face. "Gads, please, sire, don't go off in a huff after how well we've gotten on these last months."

"I am king of this—this royal circus, Barbara, something you seem unable to assimilate at times judging by the way you treat me. Od's fish, I don't begrudge you your tumbles in other beds, I haven't for years. But then—a tightrope dancer!" He laughed gruffly while she frowned. "I think I've always been a

527

sort of tightrope dancer too, to get my kingdom back and keep it through these wretched times; so perhaps in the end, I don't mind even him." His hand moved to her door latch.

"Wait! If you can be so *blasé* about it, then why did you come back to my bed after chasing little Stewart for so long? Could it be you had the ice virgin at last and were disappointed?"

Black eyebrows crashed over slaty eyes. "I don't want to speak of Frances, Barbara. It's none of your business. 'Sdeath, suffice it to say that for a while I admired you for something best left unsaid, and it drew me back, that's all."

She shot around him to block his exit. Her rounded silken buttocks pressed against his hand still on the latch as she put her arms out. "Tell me, please. Tell me why. I want to know!"

He stared down at her impassioned face, the face that used to excite him so he could hardly wait to get her alone, to bed her, to hold her. What had gone wrong? Had his wretched, incurable love for Frances Stewart been the cause or had he and Barbara changed so? Now, he hardly cared what she did at all, even when it shamed him by implication as various ruffians passed through her bed to titillate her jaded senses.

"Let's just say, Barbara dear, I was proud of you for bravery under duress. I didn't even mind the duplicity for once."

"What? What are you speaking of? Something that happened—wh-when?" she floundered.

"It hardly matters, but, Od's fish, you might as well have a sincere compliment when you can. I thought it very brave how you bore up to protect your reputation and my feelings when you were dragged from your carriage and raped by those common blackguards. And I felt sorry for you, that's all."

For once, Barbara Palmer, Countess of Castlemaine, was speechless.

"I'm certain you did it partly to save yourself, of course, my dear, but it really touched me as rather noble," he mused aloud.

"Noble? No-ble?" she sputtered. "Gads, my reputation would have been shredded by Clarendon for certain if he'd found out!" She knew better than to try to deny the rapes if he'd found out somehow. Her eyes narrowed, her hands fastened on his waistcoat. "Who told you and why so long after it happened? My maid? Stewart?" she coaxed, her voice as soft as she could manage in her shocked fury.

"Let's only say, Barbara, I learned it from evidence which came to light at that time. Somehow, it touched my heart for a while. It really doesn't matter anymore now, does it?" he added as if consoling a petulant child.

He moved her away from the door and went out into the hall where she could hear the familiar cacophony of spaniel yelps and courtiers' voices awaiting. At least, she thought, he's been in here long enough that everyone will think he's lain with me in midafternoon.

Damn, but the informer must have been Frances Stewart despite the fact that the little slut hardly paid any heed to her and never rose to her taunts anymore. Her maid Sarah, who'd been a witness, had never been fetched back from her uncle's house where she'd sent her; still, one of the ruffians themselves could have been captured and confessed—new evidence, he'd said.

"Gads, what a hell of a mess!" she moaned aloud and smacked her hands on her silken thighs. If only George weren't temporarily on his best behavior after being released from the Tower for sedition and libel against the queen, he'd know who had told and what to do. But George himself had cruelly used the knowledge of the rape he'd garnered from her maid to keep her in line more than once, so she daren't tell him this. Besides, more than the king, he'd surely degrade her for sleeping with a common entertainer like a rope dancer, whatever Joseph Hall's well-endowed attributes for entertaining in the boudoir!

From mere frustration, Barbara picked up a glass chimney that sat over a candle and heaved it at the papered wall of the foyer. It shattered to slivers and tinkled to the tiled floor. She felt like a rope dancer now, carefully balancing, caught between the king's tenuous good will and her desire for revenge against Stewart if she'd told him.

She glared in disgust at her image facing her in the mirror. She looked old—old at twenty-seven and plump, terribly plump compared to slender Stewart. She should have broken this damned mirror instead of a glass lamp! For now—for now, she'd just bide her time until she knew the way to be revenged for good on that lying, prissy slut Stewart!

She felt the vibrations of the knock on her door even as she heard it. The king certainly wouldn't come back after that exit, and Buckingham had gone off until later, tavern hopping with his cronies as if to celebrate his pitiful showing against the king on the tennis court earlier today.

"Yes, who is it?" she called through the door. "My maids are out."

"Countess, I am sorry to bother you, but may I not speak with you? It's Amanda Wells and everyone's gone off."

Amanda Wells, Barbara mused. She'd never had much business with the flighty, little, red-headed maid of honor, never could really abide her since she had once been so tight with Stewart. But then that had been years ago when they both first came to court to serve the queen, and they obviously hadn't been friends since.

She opened the door a crack. "Amanda. Well, well, come in then."

The girl looked nervous. Her pale, milky skin dotted by freckles almond powder could not hide was flushed, almost mottled with color as though she'd run a long way; her eyes were almost feverishly bright.

"I knew not whom to come to, but I warrant you can help," Amanda gushed before Barbara even led her into the drawing room.

"Gads, girl, what is it? If you've managed to get yourself with bastard child, I've no nostrums to give to rid yourself of it."

"No, no, Countess, not that, but I know we have a common goal."

One of Barbara's elegant auburn brows arched, and her crimson lips pouted. "Do we now? Pray enlighten me, Mistress Wells."

"Frances Stewart!" the girl said and smiled

531

triumphantly as if the mere disclosure of the name had said it all. "Frances Stewart. Oh, I warrant, we both want her brought down because she'd taken—tried to take—the man we love."

"*We*," Barbara squawked. "You and—the king?"

"No, no, Countess," Amanda said and leaned forward to hit her fist on knees covered by the black velvet cloak she carried. "The king for you. The Duke of Richmond for me!"

"Richmond! Gads! I had often wondered about him and Stewart, but there was no evidence, no real sign. Hell, girl, are you certain? He hasn't even been here for most of this year!"

"I know, but he's back now and she's been with him in his rooms since she left halfway through the tennis match until just ten minutes ago, Countess. She ran out so fast to see him when her maid fetched her she even left her cloak. I followed her and waited. Four hours alone in his rooms with him the moment he returned to Whitehall, you see."

Barbara expelled a hissing breath between clenched teeth. "Gads, I do see, Amanda. How clever of you. And has she been off with him other times?"

The girl's red head bobbed. "They left the queen's birthday ball and met sub rosa on the terrace. I saw them kiss. And once I know they went off for the day last year at Salisbury when the court was there to avoid the plague—and with the queen's blessings. I got that fact, Countess, from a French ambassador at Salisbury who had had a bit too much to drink one night," the girl crowed, obviously proud of herself.

Barbara smiled and stretched her arms along the back of her settee, suddenly happy and relaxed. "I'm in absolute awe of you, my dearest girl," she said. "Quite frankly, you've made my day. I swear, I had greatly underestimated the little slut, thinking she was angling for the king and then I believed she was too cold to care for men in general. Well, well, well. Gads!"

"You see, Countess, I didn't know what to do as *I* could scarcely tell the king, and no one would pay the slightest heed if *I* merely started a rumor. Frances Stewart's reputation is permanently white as snow, I'm afraid, and you know His Majesty had that one man locked up in the Clink Prison for trying to blackmail her."

"You were right, my dear, to come to me. I will take care of it all if you'll just keep what you told me a secret for a little longer. And of course," she added with a wink, "come see me with any future proof you have of their little trysts."

"Oh, thank you, Countess. You will tell His Majesty then?"

"You know, dear Amanda, what is really needed here is for His Majesty not to be told—but to find them together himself." She threw her head back and laughed. "Gads! Now, wouldn't that be the absolutely perfect solution to all our troubles!"

Amanda heard her own laugh join the Countess' shrill voice. Yes, that would be perfect. This way, if there were repercussions, the fiery mistress of the king would take them all. It wasn't that Amanda wanted Richmond back for herself—that pain had dissipated long ago—but Frances deserved this and had for years. Frances had told her that night Richmond had refused to lie with her that she did not love the Duke of Richmond when, obviously, she did. This would balance the slate between them and maybe send that selfish bastard Richmond away in disgrace once and for all so she wouldn't have to look at them together.

"Amanda, are you listening?" the Countess of Castlemaine was saying. She tapped Amanda's knee sharply with an index finger. "Just remember to keep mum, and I promise, His Majesty shall know of it at the first and most opportune time for us. You're a gift from heaven today, dear Amanda, you just don't know. Will you have a drink or two with me to toast the occasion? I am absolutely parched after privily entertaining the king so long in the middle of the day."

Amanda looked properly awed, Barbara thought, as she rose to fetch a bottle of wine. Just as well all her cooks and maids were out as she didn't need them hovering behind doors to hear what either of her unexpected visitors had to say this afternoon. She selected a fine Louis XIV champagne and hurried back to the little Amanda who was unabashedly admiring the way she'd recently redecorated the elegant room in chinoiserie.

"Here, my dear. Gads, you and Richmond were once a duo, you say, and Stewart ruined it all? Don't fret for that. Oh, you'd have been a darling duchess, I am sure, but there are many other landed and titled fish in the noble sea of England, I warrant. I'll introduce you to young Jermyn. Don't worry a bit over the Duke of Richmond now that they're both going to get their well-deserved comeuppance. I swear, I had several chances years ago to bed with

534

Richmond, but I just turned him down. I always was a bit curious to know how well he was—you know—built to please a woman. Perhaps, you could tell me. I just know His Majesty would have flown into an absolute pique if I'd ventured to find out myself, as he always says Richmond's Scottish at heart, and he's beat him at yacht racing too. Here, my dear, more wine?"

"Yes, a bit. It's lovely."

"Look, why don't you just stay for supper, then, and we'll talk more?" Barbara chattered. Her heart soared: years of problems with that little whore Stewart ruining her plans were almost ended. "My cousin Buckingham will be back later with some friends, Amanda, and we'll make up a bit of a party. I say, have you ever met a rope dancer?"

"Oh no, Countess, never."

"Marvelous. Just call me Barbara, my dear. Just Barbara. Here, a toast to Richmond and Frances Stewart. May they get together soon again—preferably all the way together, even as the king walks in, stares and . . . explodes!"

Their laughter mingled with the clink of their crystal champagne goblets as Amanda listened and Barbara talked on and on.

Chapter Nineteen

Frances munched on a piece of oven-warm, gilt gingerbread while her mother popped chocolate bonbons, the new confectionary rage from France, in her mouth as they strolled among the stalls and shops of the Royal Exchange newly built since the Great Fire. Lady Stewart's maid and both of Frances' girls, Gillie and Jane, followed along, laden with varied parcels wrapped in tissue or stiff paper while their mistresses peered at counter and hanging displays of household goods or ladies' apparel. Gold, jewelry, and silver shops surrounded them in this central section of the vast, pillared great gallery of stores all decorated with hangings and illumined with wax torches in numerous sconces: everywhere the eye could see, shoppers bustled, fops paraded, and lovers strolled. Anyone who was anyone thought the Royal Exchange in Gresham College, London, was a most wonderful place to be seen.

Frances especially was thrilled. Not only was she out of the constricting walls of Whitehall, but for the first time in her life, she had her own money to spend. Heavens, not exactly her own money, she chided herself, but her Richmond had insisted she take four hundred pounds from him to buy herself things she needed for a lengthy stay in rural Kent. Always before, except for the use of her yearly honorarium as maid of honor, such needs had been provided through gifts of the royal household—first from the Queen Mother, Henrietta Maria, then Minette, and then Queen Catherine.

But now in just a few weeks she would be a married woman, a duchess in her own right, however tenuous the finances of the Duke of Richmond's landed possessions were said to be. The heady jolt of being liberated from reliance on the royal Stuarts assailed her brain again.

They walked past glittering jewelry displays toward counters of perfumes and women's accessories. Frances gazed at a beautiful array of cut-glass bottles filled with imported, scented waters. How sweet everything was now, she told herself. Her life had changed this last week, and she was bursting with excitement. Yet she could not say a word to anyone yet—especially mother.

"Mm, Frances, try one of these, my dear. These bonbons are wonderful," Sophia Stewart managed despite a mouth full of chocolate.

"No thank you, Mother. I warrant they are, but I'm watching my complexion and I fear they'd do the most wretched things to my face."

"Piffle! They couldn't harm a face like yours, and you could stand to put some weight on too. I'd have thought by your early twenties you'd have put on a little more and not be so slender still. I say, are you going to buy French perfume too? You are simply made of money today, aren't you?"

"Don't scold. Here, sniff the stoppers of some of those nearest you and tell me what you like. Something light—something like a country garden."

"A country garden?" The familiar cold tone of her words carried a subtle protest, but her mother obliged by following her lead and smelling the array of luscious odors.

"I still think I favor frangipani though I've worn it for years," Frances said. "Oh, this one's orangery, Mother, the kind all the women at Louis' court wore as he couldn't abide anything stronger. No, definitely not orangery. I might even try to distill my own from rose petals and other blooms, you know," she blurted out before she could check herself.

"Distill you own? Where? In His Majesty's much touted science laboratories? I hardly think you've time or need for that at court, Frances, and just look over there! Those two dandies ogling you from behind that pillar by the glove booth! How crude!"

"Who, them? Heavens, that's one of the Duke of Lauderdale's sons with some hanger-on he's picked up, I warrant. Just ignore them. I do."

"Saints preserve us, I should hope so. I shall never get used to the way young men flaunt themselves, or just begin to mince and chatter without proper introduction these days—or show up unannounced as your friend Richmond did yesterday when we were walking in St. James's Park."

"Or that time he arrived the day of the fire and

ended up saving my life, Mother?" Frances shot back. It amused her that she had nearly launched into a defense of Richmond to her mother, but she let it go at that one comment. It wouldn't do a bit of good to have an argument over her mother's proverbial topic of not trusting men. No, it wouldn't do at all to open up that Pandora's box by admitting she had told her dear Charles where to find them in the park, not when she was enjoying herself today so immensely.

"I'd like that tall bottle of the frangipani scent, please," she told the watchful, smiling merchant and ignored her mother's "hmph" because she had ordered the largest size.

"What else then?" Sophia Stewart asked and groaned dramatically as if to signal a precipitous end to this shopping jaunt.

"Some long, perfumed leather gloves for autumn, I think," Frances threw back over her shoulder as she hurried on with Gillie and Jane hovering close behind.

"For autumn?" her mother remonstrated. "But it's only mid-March, silly girl."

"I know, but—but I like the scent to be very faint, and it takes a while to wear off. Anyway, I get so busy sometimes I don't get shopping much. Just the gloves, a lace stomacher for a candlelight ivory dress I'm having made and I'm done." Frances pulled on the various elbow gloves to test their length and softness until she glanced up and caught her mother's sour look.

"What's the matter, Mother? Don't you like what I've chosen?" she asked, dangling a buff pair of soft Spanish leather gloves from her fingers.

540

"What? They're fine, I warrant, dear. Just fine. I was thinking of something else—one time a great while ago when my mother and I went shopping."

"Oh, but you were frowning. Here, Gillie," she called to her hovering maid, "take these crowns and pay for these; then come down the way to the shop with stomachers and laces under the glass. Lady Stewart's feeling tired so we'll go ahead."

She put her arm through her mother's to humor her, and they strolled past cluttered counters boasting boxes of the pungent Virginia tobacco for men's pipes. Her Charles loved the stuff, she mused. Though he seldom smoked in her presence, the sweet tang of it clung to his clothes at times. How she'd like to buy him some as well, and a lovely wedding gift like a clock or some wonderful, new navigation instrument for the yacht. But he'd made her promise to spend this money on her own trousseau, and besides, mother would have a raving fit if she bought even a small gift for a man.

In the narrow, high-shelved lace shop, she stared for a long while at the ribboned, lace-decorated stomachers which tied over a plain satin bodice to give added elegance and formality. I need something beautiful but not too sophisticated, she mused, as the shopkeeper displayed yet another one before her critical eye. She wanted this to be the finishing touch on a perfect bridal gown for a rural wedding.

"Just a little too ornate up the middle with those pearl buttons," she told the man. "Something with only lace and ribbons perhaps and all in candlelight ivory hues."

"Perhaps something like these," he said. "I sell a

great many of these for bridals, you know."

Afraid her mother would read her thoughts, Frances flicked a look sideways at her. But Sophia Stewart seemed not to hear; her face looked grayish and she swayed slightly into the slanted glass window which displayed the fine wares.

"Mother! Are you all right? Oh, heavens, I'm sorry I've kept you dashing about and standing on your feet all afternoon. Here, I'll take that one with the little ruffles and bows and we'll go sit down."

"I'm fine, Frances, just fine. Don't fuss so in front of this poor, busy man."

They sat amidst the late afternoon bustle on a marble bench surrounded by piles of packages while the maids went to fetch two hired hackneys. She should have used Charles's coach whatever mother said about it, Frances thought, but then going off from Whitehall in it might have been noted by Castlemaine or someone, and they didn't need that after they had been so careful this week he had been back. They had only seen each other in fairly public circumstances after that first day she'd gone to him. But tomorrow he'd be going back to Cobham to arrange everything and tonight, he vowed, he'd come to her rooms to bid her a proper adoring lover's farewell. And then, very soon they'd find a way to get her to join him there for the wedding—a wedding in a home she had never seen, a new mistress amidst people she had never met.

Her mother looked more herself now as their maids went off in one hackney with the packages and Frances and her mother took the other.

"Perhaps it was just too many chocolate bonbons," Frances observed when they were settled.

"What? Nonsense. I'm fine. It just bothers me to see all those loose-footed dandies gawking, that's all. And you really should have asked the king or queen for a coach from their mews like those we've used before."

Frances sighed. "Mother, we only saw two loose-footed, gawking dandies, as you call them, and they didn't bother us one whit. As for the coach, I don't like to ask for special favors."

"Favors? He's let you have it before—remember—when you first came to court, and no harm was done. Besides, the king knows we've all served his royal family well at great personal expense."

Frances' head snapped around as she studied her mother's face. For one minute she had thought some sort of lecture or warning was imminent but she looked lost in pensive thought again, her face crushed by such a frown of concentration that Frances feared a return of the spell she'd had inside the lacer's shop.

"Mother," she ventured, her voice soft and low. Sophia Stewart's head turned to her; the blue eyes she had so clearly inherited shone alarmingly bright in the dimness of the jolting hackney with its leather window flaps nearly down. "Were you thinking of how father served the Stuarts and then died in their service? I think about him a great deal even though we never speak of him."

"Your father, Walter Stewart, bless his soul, Frances, was happy in what he was doing at the last," her mother replied, in a voice even more shrill and strident than usual. "He was happy, ecstatic even,

543

working himself to death that way for them—for her—in the terrible conditions at Saint-Germain. Nothing else mattered, and I'd best not think of that at all."

"Nothing else mattered? But he had you—all of us there," Frances faltered. Her mind dashed, raced into the deepest reaches of her memory. Somewhere, way back, of course, she'd known her mother hadn't been happy with her father; she had lied to Minette about that once, lied to herself even. Despite the cold, sharp expression on her mother's face, she had an overwhelming urge to defend the long-dead father she could scarcely recall.

"Oh, yes, he had his family," her mother's vitriolic voice went on. "For the love of the saints, he'd have given me a babe a year to leave me with if I had let him. His love, Frances, was not me or his family, never was."

"I don't believe that, mother. You can't mean it. I have memories of him, you know. I was six when he died."

"Piffle! A child's view of an adult world. You weren't there when it all started. You couldn't know."

Their shoulders lurched together as the hackney rattled around a sharp turn. Outside, someone cursed their driver in gutter talk, and he shouted back.

"When what all started, mother? Tell me."

"It's my business, Frances, and best unspoken."

"Mother, please go on. Tell me about father. I want to know and understand. Is it—does it explain why you detest men?"

"Don't be impertinent! I detest men—yes, I admit

544

it—but because they are despicable, the whole lot of them, not to be trusted with love and the pure faith only a woman is capable of."

Her voice quivered, crackled, stopped. Frances watched fascinated as her mother, who never cried, dabbed at her flowing eyes and began to speak in a rush of words there was no way to halt after all the years.

"It's not your father, really not your father Walter at all as he helped—at first—after all the trouble. It was Michael Buchanen, you see. Your father took me on after Michael Buchanen and only loved the Queen Henrietta Maria afterward when I disappointed him and was so ill, I suppose."

"Who is Michael Buchanen?" Frances dared, her eyes wide. "In Scotland? He loved the queen?"

"No, your father loved the queen. I don't know, maybe after he saw I was so devastated and could not love him—not after Michael Buchanen."

"Oh, no. I see."

"No—no, you can't. You can't understand. I was eighteen and I should have been married. My sisters were. I was an old maid, they said, but then there was Michael Buchanen and I loved him instantly the very day he pulled my spaniel Bonnie out of a rushing burn where she'd have drowned for certain."

"But then you married father instead?" Frances asked in the silence while her mother stared at her knees and wiped her tear-streaked cheeks.

"It was a terrible disgrace. Your father was willing and my parents thought it best—a doctor educated in Padua and Paris and called to the exiled Stuart court—away from all the shame of my . . . my losing

Michael Buchanen even after the church banns for our marriage had already been read twice. I married your father right away."

"I'm so sorry, mother, so sorry you were hurt."

"Hurt?" the shaky voice shrilled. "Michael Buchanen just changed his mind, changed it for someone else, I say. Everyone told me I was blessed to have Walter Stewart willing—but I had loved, really loved and trusted beyond all caution, Michael's vows to me. I should never have believed him—and I have believed no man since!"

Frances trembled as though she had no control over her muscles, no control over the rash question she had to ask. "Mother—if you loved and trusted Michael Buchanen so much then—did you, I mean, how long before I was born then—when you married father?"

Frances' eyes met and locked with her mother's glassy, drowning stare. Just as Richmond had asked for the right to bed her when they'd signed the marriage contract—a right she'd freely bestowed— had mother too bedded with Michael Buchanen and conceived a child?

The carriage jolted and lumbered on somewhere through London on the way back to Somerset House. "Frances, my dear girl"—The voice came strangled, guttural, no longer the sharp, high tones of her mother familiar to Frances over the years—"it all was so jumbled, so close and so very confused, and I moved as if in a daze. One minute I had Michael and then the joy was ruined and I was wed to Walter. I was devastated still despite his kindness. You came then. I was so ill, so very depressed, you see, and we went to France soon after."

"But I have to know. When were you wed? I am so sorry, mother, but tell me when!"

"In January, at New Year in Aberdeen. They made me wed him in the same church where they'd read the banns for Michael and me."

"But I was born in September, September sixth, nine months after. Did you— Mother, when in January? Tell me! Am I Michael Buchanen's or Walter Stewart's child?"

Her mother's white palm flashed at her but the slap was feeble. Still, it stung, deep into the core of her trembling being. "How dare you ask me thus, Frances! How dare you! Don't you think I'd have told you, that your father Walter would have loved you less?"

"But he didn't love me less," Frances crooned as her tears flowed too, from the rent emotions and jagged hopes. "I was his own. He loved me. I remember that."

"Of course, of course, and it's all so confused and terrible in my own mind, you see. Of course you're Walter Stewart's daughter as clearly as I was his wife."

Frances nodded wildly through blinding tears as the hackney lurched to a stop. As clearly as I was his wife, she'd said—as clearly as you might be a faceless, cursed Michael Buchanen's child, she could have said. As clearly as I've always taught you to hate men, she should have said.

"Frances, I'm sorry we had this foolish discussion. I suppose I could have told you years ago, but I usually never think of it now, truly, and you mustn't either. If I hadn't been reminded today of shopping with my mother once when I was first betrothed, I would never have thought on it at all, I assure you. Frances, whatever is the matter now?''

She almost blurted it out—Richmond, the coming marriage, her love and trust for him sustaining her at last. But now, in light of this new and terrible knowledge of her parents' harsh beginnings and of their thwarted happiness which she had so clearly sensed since childhood, she just couldn't. All the fears, the distrust her mother had taught her crystallized to a hard, rocklike clarity. She saw it, understood it, and found the strength and love to cast it aside for the first time in her life. Richmond, she thought—his love and trust has done this wonderful thing for me.

"Frances, are you all right? I'm sorry, my dearest, sorry I upset you.''

"It was a shock—to hear it all from you, but you mustn't worry for me, mother. I am better than I've been for years, better than you know. I'll go upstairs with you to get you settled.''

"No. My maid's waiting right here. Dry your eyes, my Frances. Don't let anyone know we cried.''

"No. I won't. Thank you for going with me. I'll see you Sunday if the queen decides not to go to Hampton Court.''

"Yes. Fine. And I am so sorry.''

"I'm all right. Everything's all right now.''

"Goodbye for now, then. Just think of all the pretty things you bought.''

The hackney driver and her maid helped Sophia Stewart down in the curved west drive of Somerset

House and the front door swallowed her up as she went in. Gillie climbed in with a few packages Jane had not taken on ahead. The hackney door slammed as Gillie's light voice chattered about their purchases and what she intended to do now that she and Jane were to have the evening on their own away from duties.

Frances jolted upright. She had arranged for Gillie and Jane to be away when Richmond came for his adoring lover's farewell, as he put it. Soon, in two hours, she'd face him, after all this today, face him and want to tell it all to him. Maybe she shouldn't fully trust him—love him—after what she'd heard today. But he was different, not like the others she'd known—that list of cruel others whose names had now all been blotted out by some long-lost Michael Buchanen who could very well be her own father!

"M'lady? Are you cryin'?"

"I vow, it's nothing, Gillie. Nothing. Just a wretched head pain. Before you leave, I'd like you to go to Lady Scroope and tell her to inform Her Majesty I won't be down for supper."

"Yes, m'lady, so much excitement with the shopping and all. And then you can cover Joli's cage and lie down in the quiet and get a peaceful night's sleep."

"Yes. Yes, of course," Frances' voice trailed off devoured by the rattle of hoofs and wheels on cobbles as the hackney swung up to the Holbein Gate of vast Whitehall.

"How delighted I am to have you here this

evening, my dear lord," Queen Catherine murmured to King Charles, and she smiled at him so very genuinely she quite forgot to cover her mouth with hand or fan.

His Majesty shuffled his big feet as if he were a guilty schoolboy while the four spaniels clustered about him shifted and whined before resettling. "We should spend more pleasant evenings like this, my Catherine," he said, "now that spring is almost here."

And now, Queen Catherine thought, hoping her face looked merely pleased, that Castlemaine is out of favor once again and Frances Stewart has gone to bed early with a head pain after shopping with her mother all afternoon at the Royal Exchange.

"Catherine, my dear," he began in such a sonorous tone it pulled her attention from her musings immediately, "I do want you to know I still believe we can have children."

The dark, languid eyes he had always admired, widened in surprise. "Do you, my dearest lord? I pray for it daily, yes," she said low.

"Od's fish, yes, I think we can, only perhaps we— I—have not concentrated on it long enough. Long enough at one time, I mean," he floundered, his black brows nearly obscuring his obsidian eyes.

It amazed her that he, the clever, glib, debonair cynic, should stumble for his meaning—for his very words—as she, Portuguese Catherine, had for years in this adopted foreign land of hers. She nodded as if to encourage him. "The Holy Virgin knows we have tried, my lord, no?"

"Yes, but perhaps too regularly—you know, my

dear, twice a week for years like clockwork."

Her melodious voice had an edge to it now. "Like clockwork, my dear Lord? It was never like clockwork to me—never!"

"I didn't mean it was mechanical, Catherine!" His big hand moved across the inlaid fruitwood tabletop to cover her braceleted wrist. "And I certainly wasn't censuring you, not in any way. 'Sblood, my Catherine, it's I who have set—well, set the pace, and I swear, a change would do us good, perhaps mean success where an heir is concerned. You've been healthy enough ever since that wretched bout with spotted fever, I dare say."

"Oh, yes, yes. Healthy enough, so there should be a child, no? Despite distractions, you have hardly ignored my bed these years, my Lord King, this I admit."

He stood, towering over her as always and tugged her gently to her feet. Distractions, she had termed them, his innumerable nights with the others they'd assiduously avoided discussing ever since she'd given him his way over Castlemaine five years ago. Catherine's dark curled and ribboned head came barely to his chin. "So, my beloved wife, to put it bluntly, I would have us spend more time in company—different time at least."

Her voice was almost inaudible despite the sudden muffled racket in the corridors somewhere. "My dearest Charles, I am your wife and queen and subject. You have only to command."

He spoke louder to lift his words over the approaching hubbub—loud voices, women's voices, and running footsteps. "I am only a man in this, my

dear, and I wish not to command nor to beg, but—
Od's fish, what is that noise? Don't your damn
women know when to stay away?" he groused. He
quickly loosed Catherine's hands which he had just
considered lifting to his lips as a final contrite,
courtly gesture, and strode across the drawing room.
He yanked the carved door inward as Barbara, with
Lady Scroope and Susan Warmestry clinging to her,
fell inward.

"Oh, sire, sire, I must speak with you," Barbara
gushed, making a hasty half curtsy in the queen's
direction.

"Damn it, Barbara, I'm in privy audience with Her
Majesty. Get away, all of you!"

Lady Scroope and Susan backed quickly away
while the red-brown spaniels at his feet cavorted and
yapped. Barbara held to his arm, not budging. "It's
absolutely essential, sire—treason, plotting, call it
what you will," she hissed. "Gads, sire, you must
come!"

Annoyed beyond reason at her rude, ill-timed
intrusion, he plucked her hand off and shoved her
back. Damn the jade! This wild display had
obviously blown his pretty speech to Catherine all to
hell, and she'd pay for it. He had the door half closed
against her when he caught her next desperate words.
"Stewart! Frances Stewart is plotting against you
right this moment and I can prove it!"

He loosed the door suddenly aware the queen had
come closer. The spaniels still barked so loudly, he
wondered if he'd heard aright. "You silly shrew," he
cursed, his narrowed eyes gone to glittering slits.
"'Sdeath, this time you've gone too far. Frances was

ill and went to bed!''

"She did indeed, sire, and with a man!" Barbara announced grandly and dared to smile.

"My Lord King, what is it?" Queen Catherine's voice rose to challenge Barbara's strident tones. "A plot, a plot, she says, no? Is our Frances hurt?"

He swiveled his coal black head from Barbara to Catherine and then back again, suddenly more furious than he could ever recall being. "No. Stay here. It is your lady of the bedchamber, Castlemaine, who'll be hurt when I look into his hellish lie!"

He strode into the hall and down its length so fast that Barbara could scarcely keep up with him even running. He heard one of her shoes fall off as he stared up the main stairs to the third floor. Courtiers eternally waiting for a favor fell away as he passed. His yeomen guards, taken utterly by surprise, hoisted their pikes and ceremonial lances and jogged along in his wake. He thundered up the steps, spaniels and a screaming Barbara at his heels.

"She's been doing this for weeks—years, sire, you'll see. I've tried—tried to warn you before what a deceiver she is, but you would not listen and—"

He slammed the door to the stairwell behind him so hard the walls and floors shuddered. The door to the little suite of rooms he'd so carefully chosen for Frances five years ago looked peaceful, normal. It was another Castlemaine-Villiers plot, a pack of lies, of course, as foul as any they'd concocted yet.

He put his hand to the door, lifted the latch, shoved the door inward. Guards, spaniels, Castlemaine were all on his heels but silent now, and even others followed curiously down the dim stretch of hall. Od's fish, why had he lost his head like this? He should have used the privy staircase and apologized to Catherine before dashing off like a raving lunatic.

"Keep the Countess of Castlemaine out here," he said curtly and yanked Barbara's hand off his brocade sleeve. He shoved the panting spaniels back with one big foot and stepped into Frances's familiar black-and-white tiled foyer and closed the door on them all.

The room was calm, quiet; there was hardly any plot or any man in here. The door hadn't even been latched and a chair stood near it as though a maid who'd been here had just stepped out. He'd surprise Frances and tuck her in just as he had years ago. He wouldn't stay long, or she'd fret for her eternally precious virgin reputation. Od's fish, but Castlemaine would be banished this time for good!

He heard it then as well as sensed it, and he wanted to flee rather than know what lay beyond the closed bedroom door. A man's deep voice, her answering laughter, a clink of glasses.

Stealthily, swift as a huge black leopard, he crossed the chamber to the bedroom door. He pushed it open, fearstruck, but he need not have been so silent: neither person on the huge, mussed bed heard him. Frances half sat, half reclined against the Duke of Richmond, nestled cosily, intimately there while his free hand stroked a firm, white, pointed breast. As far as he could see, both were completely naked, and Frances held a wine goblet to his lips.

The scene swam, darkened, merged before his eyes. Blood coursed through his veins, pounded against skin and skull. Everything went crazily crimson as he vaulted into the room screaming he knew not what.

Frances shrieked. The goblet flew; blood-red wine splattered the sheets and Richmond's bare chest as he half rose, thrusting her behind him. Richmond stood, facing the king in a wary crouch as if ready to spring. At least, it registered on the king's stunned brain, the man wore breeches. But Frances was completely nude, scrambling off the other side of the bed and wrapping her soft, alluring nakedness with a sheet. It was all too obvious the bastard had just had her. Damn, but the little witch looked more angry than afraid!

"Hell's gates, Frances!" King Charles heard himself roar. It couldn't be his voice; he never lost his temper like this. Never, even when he'd heard his father's head had been taken by the rebels had he wanted to kill as he did now.

Rage ebbed to disbelief, then drowned him in exquisite pain. "I'll have your head for this, Richmond," he shouted, "your head, your lands! I'll even take your pretty little whore here! Frances, damn it! 'Sdeath, tell me he forced you! Tell me he forced you!"

She came around the end of the bed when he was sure she would cower and cry. He didn't know her, this tawny-maned, tousled woman, wrapped like an Egyptian princess he'd seen once in a painting. Whatever had happened, she was no longer young, nor vulnerable.

"I am sorry, sire, sorry that you are hurt, sorry you have to come in here like this to find out," he heard her say. "I know it is a shock, but you must surely realize His Grace did not force me."

"Sire, I really think you—" Richmond put in as he

555

moved forward.

"Quiet, Richmond!" Charles screamed, then looked back to the woman as though the man did not exist. "'His Grace,' is it, Frances? And what other names do you have for him—your secret paramour? Has there been a string of others? 'Sblood, you're as bad as Barbara!"

She faced him boldly, her hands holding the sheet over her high, heaving breasts. "I am not anything like Barbara, sire, and you know very well there has been no string of others!"

"Do I, my dear Frances? Do I? How many times has this rebel, treasonous Scottish duke had you then these years I've been your royal footstool, yearning for a kiss, sighing for a few moments alone with you? A virgin, indeed, you little slut. I believe I'll just send Richmond to the Tower and even the score with you for five damn, hellish years of fawning like a jackass at your heels while you scorned me!"

"No, I didn't! I admired you, I appreciated you, but I love him!" she shrieked as Richmond moved to pull her away and dared to thrust his big body between Frances and the king.

"We're to be married, sire," Richmond said low, a controlled voice in the room at last. "I wish to marry Frances and she has agreed. We love each other, sire, and hope for your blessing."

The two tall men glared eye to eye: neither flinched, neither blinked. "Be damned to you, Richmond. Never. And get your blackguard hands off her. Guards!"

Frances clung to Richmond begging him not to fight, pulling at his raised fists. The room exploded

556

with yeomen guards, six of them in their scarlet and black livery, flaunting their ceremonial pikes, the filigreed CR II on their broad chests.

"Arrest this man. Hold him downstairs until I decide his fate," the king clipped out coldly, his eyes still on Frances. He wanted to hurt her, see her beg and plead. His fury and hatred frightened even him.

"Please no, please—no," she was murmuring to Richmond, not to him as he had wished. "Don't fight, my dearest, all will be well. Heavens," she brazened, her gaze now on the king in open defiance, "we've done nothing illegal and this is a reasonable king."

King Charles watched her face as he nodded to the guards, and four of the six dragged Richmond off none too gently. The other two scooped up his boots and the other garments he'd strewn next to the bed, and followed hastily.

King Charles faced her across the yawning space of six feet. He tried desperately to manage a controlled voice. "You, Frances. All we have had, all I've done for you and you do this." Her face looked dazed, distant despite the unflinching way she met his stare. Then, her lovely brow cleared; it seemed she summoned her thoughts from wherever they had fled.

"I am an unwed woman, sire. I wish to marry."

"Not to some impoverished traitor!"

"He's not impoverished and you know he's served you loyally—loyally at Westminster and in this Dutch war, in Scotland—"

"Loyally in my woman's bed, Frances?" he shouted. He sprang at her before she could dart back, he shook her until her head bobbed and the sheet came loose to taunt him with her proud breasts and the glorious rosebud peaks she'd let another man ravish.

"Stop it, sire! No! Stop it! I am not your property! No!"

He threw her across the bed and stood over her like a dark, avenging god. "You'll never marry him! Never. If you want to wed, I'll select someone proper later."

She sat up on her haunches, defiant again, not his gentle Frances. Her hair was tumbled wildly over her shoulders; her blue eyes flashed icy fire. "I will wed with Richmond, my King, or I'll leave court for good. I'll enter a nunnery—if you take his lands I'll go to Scotland with him if need be, or to sea!"

He stepped back aghast. The furies of Barbara all these years, the civil war, years of Clarendon's scolding—nothing had prepared him to face this brutal defeat at the hands of one he loved, yes, loved!

"You're quite distraught Frances," he managed, his voice controlled, low for the first time in what seemed like hours. "I ought to just have what I've foolishly longed for all these years, on this bed with no whit of emotion or concern as if I merely took what was owed me by some street strumpet, but I cannot so I—" He shook his head to clear it. He was adrift again in drowning emotions. "I intend to send for your mother so she can—nurse you. I'll warrant Lady Stewart will grasp the import of this situation if you do not. Until then, there will be guards in the hall and at the Privy Staircase."

He spun on his heel and rushed from the

constricting atmosphere of the room as though demons were at his heels. In the hall, Barbara, her crimson smile triumphant, reached for him. "Get out of my sight and stay there," he spit at her as he strode away.

He heard the guttural whispers, the gossiping murmurs of his courtiers—his supposed friends—as he stormed downstairs. Two of his guards stood like stodgy sentinels at the door to his own suite.

"Where is Richmond?" he asked.

"Inside, Your Majesty."

Charles Stuart, duke of Richmond, faced Charles Stuart, king of England, across the stretch of floor in his privy Vane Room. Four guards stood near the pacing duke, not touching him now.

"Leave us," the king ordered.

"All of us, sire?" one scarlet-suited buffoon dared to ask as if nowhere in this vast palace tonight were his royal wishes law.

"Yes, damn it! Get out!"

The door closed. His breathing stilled, but he could hear his heart and pulse racing in pained pattern in the silence.

"I'm replacing you as Lord Chamberlain, Richmond."

"As you wish, sire."

"I'm sparing you your wretched Kentish and Scottish inheritance lands on the condition you stay away from Frances."

Their eyes met, held as surely as if a duel were being waged with swords instead of nerves. "I am sorry, sire, but it would be dishonest of me to agree to that. I cannot stay away from Frances."

"Did you not hear me, man? Your heritage, those pasture and garden lands you run off to see whenever you can. Your Scottish lands too!"

"I understand the threat, sire. I have done nothing to deserve the loss of my estates, and I trust you will not mean that later. I have served you well and hope to yet. As a matter of fact, I am leaving to help outfit the fleet of privateers tomorrow, as difficult as that's getting with snared and broken supply lines—or am I relieved of my naval duties too?"

"No. The sea's a good place for you. It spares you Buckingham's recently vacated Tower of London cell, and I intend to launch a full investigation into your finances while you're gone."

"As you wish, sire. I'll send my man over with my ledgers; though, I must admit, he's a proud Scotsman and you probably won't abide him."

"You overconfident bastard. I also banish you from the precincts of Whitehall—from the City of London until I send for you. Do your duty at sea and stay well quit of here. Do you understand?"

"Yes, sire."

"Get out of here then. Send for your things later. Just get out of my sight."

"Please, sire, I wish for leave to say one thing."

"No. No! You're not saying goodbye to her. You've already obviously done that this night and grandly."

"No, sire—no farewells. Only this—her mother has reared her to hate and distrust men. I love her. It's changed her. You can see she's changed, become stronger, more confident. As you've cared for her too, don't take that from her, sire."

"Take that from her? Are you daft as well as brazen, man? I've never had a damn thing from her, I see that now. Minette and Frances—the only two women I've ever trusted and really loved and now there is only Minette. Odd," he said low as if to himself, "I've loved the only two women I never could possess."

"I will stay away from Whitehall and London, sire, as you command," Richmond said low and edged toward the door. "But in King Charles's great England, sire, it cannot be a sin to love."

"Wait! Don't ever tell her I asked, but I just wondered—is she—can she indeed be warm and loving when—"

Their sharp glances clashed across the room, but then the king's gaze became softly beseeching before it hardened to metallic black again.

Richmond frowned, his lips compressed into a firm line. He nodded jerkily.

"Then how long—tell me how long has it been thus between you," the king managed.

"Blame me, sire. I've loved her for as long as I've known her, that first summer she came to England. I believe you can understand and forgive that. For Frances—she has loved me, if she loves me, only a little while."

Richmond bowed stiffly and yanked the door open. For one instant the guards blocked his exit, and the king had a fierce urge to rescind his reasonable punishment, to order him imprisoned, hanged, or sent to the farthest barbarian island of the Americas in eternal exile.

"Let him go," he said instead and lifted one ringed hand. Then, even before the guards closed the door, he sank down in his chair and put his head in his hands.

No one dared disturb him until someone summoned his brother near midnight. But James's voice too eventually ceased, while the eight well-tuned clocks in the room chattered their ticks and rattled their chimes as though nothing had happened at all.

Chapter Twenty

In the two weeks since the king had discovered them together and Richmond had been banished, Frances had heard from her betrothed only once until she received the note her maid Gillie had just handed her. Frances stood by Joli's cage and opened the stiff parchment with trembling hands while her cats rubbed against her legs as if to comfort her. The penmanship was bold and hurried: one glance and she saw she must be too.

My own Frances,

I have been briefly to sea at war. As I am forbidden the palace and city, you and I must wage our own war.

Tonight and tomorrow night anytime after nightfall, I shall be waiting with a carriage and your new life at the Bear at Bridgefoot where we supped once. Come at all costs and we shall retrieve your goods after.

Be courageous but cautious.

My Love Eternally,
C.

Yes! Yes—courageous and cautious . . . a carriage . . . a new life awaiting, away from here, from censoring looks and constricting walls. Away from here to become mistress of her own house, her own life at long last. Heavens, it was long overdue and she was ready. Tonight—she would go tonight.

"Keep a smile. Aawwk! Keep your distance!" Joli's squawk jolted her.

"Yes, my Joli," she smiled as she fed him a piece of biscuit to quiet him. "A smile to hide my plans today, a smile for the future tomorrow, a good long distance from here."

She absently fed the bird more broken bits of food as her mind raced. She'd wait until the very dead of night and not dare to take Gillie or Jane as they'd be undeservedly scolded or worse if they were caught. The king had questioned them both and warned them about their mistress' staying on the Whitehall premises for her own safety. Her mother, too, had even had her say when His Majesty had summoned her, but their intimate talk in the carriage after shopping two weeks ago had evidently made a difference. Her mother's lectures about the evils of marriage had been half-hearted; Frances suspected she even favored Scottish Richmond if it had to be anyone at all, and fortunately, the king had failed to tell Sophia Stewart he had discovered her daughter naked in bed with the duke.

She reached a finger into Joli's cage and stroked the bird's chartreuse wing feathers while he preened. She would go alone but for her pets. She could hardly desert innocent creatures, leaving them to face the king's rage. He's always hated the cats, and the maids did not love the animals as she did. She would have to manage Perth and Aberdeen in some sort of sack in which they could breathe. Joli's cage she could carry. Other than that, only her wedding clothes and a few accessories would go for now. But she needed help, needed to have a carriage or hackney waiting, and she needed to assure protection for her and Richmond even at distant Cobham when all hell broke loose again here. And for help of any kind here at hostile Whitehall, there was only one source—the long frustrated Queen Catherine.

Frances rummaged through her folded petticoats until she found what she wanted—a summer one of wide-weave linen she could see through when it was held to the light. On the floor she pulled her cats together over the petticoat, gathered its edges and lifted them to make a huge, loose sack. They meowed twice, squirming for positions, then quieted as she held them to her and crooned their names. She loosed them and shoved the petticoat under the bed until later.

She took out her best satin petticoat and spread it on the bed to make another sack. The skirt of her wedding gown, her bodice, the new lace stomacher, slippers, stockings, and gloves made a luxurious, soft pile. She added her ruffled silk pink bedgown and nightsmock for the formal bride's bedding. She threw three daydresses on the pile, then took two away as the parcel became too bulky. She would simply have to follow the duke's suggestion and send for her things. She would ask the queen to oversee that too. Surely, there were seamstresses at Cobham to tide her over.

She took a few cosmetics, but left all her jewels with a brief note of thanks to the king that requested they be returned to their givers as she was being forced to make him unhappy which she'd never wished. The huge pearls he had given her the first year she'd come to court slid heavily through her fingers and clicked back into her jewel box. Amazingly, she didn't regret leaving any of this.

She hid all her prepared booty under the bed; then she stood, pondering whether to go dressed as a lad or merely cloaked and masked. Boy's garb might be safer, but she couldn't resist having at least another set of garments; and if she were seen in the palace, lady's garb would seem less suspicious.

She did not go down to the formal supper in the Great Hall. The Duke of Monmouth and his wife Anne had returned from a trip to the northern shires, and no one would miss her while being regaled with the lively, nervous Monmouth's stories and antics. Besides, she had not appeared at table on some other nights lately, and no one had scolded her for that.

As if to say a silent goodbye, she paced the perimeter of her suite of rooms while the evening wore on. Gillie and Jane would be up soon. She'd let them undress and bathe her; then she'd send them away. But first, she had to chance seeing Queen Catherine. The queen only could she trust in this dangerous endeavor: of all the people she had known here at court these years, but for her maidservants, the dear queen alone would wish her good fortune and dare to help her too.

When she judged supper would be over, Frances went to the queen's rooms. Her Majesty would come upstairs without the king to prepare for his later arrival as she had the last two weeks since Castlemaine had ruined both Frances Stewart's position, and ironically, her own. The king sought his wife's company almost nightly while Frances kept to herself gladly and Castlemaine kept to herself in a towering fury.

Luck, it seemed, was with her so far this evening. Queen Catherine with only four other ladies swept in chatting and laughing.

The light voices quieted; elegant eyebrows lifted. "Frances, my dear," Her Majesty said and poised her fan to cover her mouth as she smiled, "how wonderful to have you back with us, yes, ladies?"

"Indeed," Anne Scroope murmured unconvincingly as the others chimed in with forced smiles and mute nods.

"Thank you, Your Majesty, for your continued kindness and understanding," Frances said, her eyes on the queen. "I realize you probably have only a few moments, but might I have a privy word with you?"

"Of course, yes! His Majesty is coming up soon, but you can assist me while the others wait just outside, yes, my ladies?"

Everyone shuffled and swished off with curious or haughty glances. When they were alone, the queen smiled openly, not covering her mouth. Then she crossed immediately to Frances and rested her delicate hands on the younger woman's shoulders.

"I knew my Frances would be coming back from her exile upstairs. I scolded him, told him if he banished you to your rooms, I be going to visit you, but he vowed he only banished Richmond. I am so sorry for the pain, Frances, but so happy in hearing you loving my friend Richmond after all this time he was loving you, no?"

"No—I mean, yes, Your Majesty. It is for that I have come to ask a great favor."

"Poor Frances. I already asked the king can Richmond come back to court, and he said no."

"If he said no, it doesn't matter, my Queen. You see, I plan to go to him."

"*Santa María!* To run away?"

"Yes—to elope—to be married. Please, you will keep my secret, will you not? I felt—I thought—I could trust you for help."

The queen clasped Frances to her tightly, then released her as if uncertain she should have allowed such an emotional display. "Oh, Frances, yes, yes. May the Virgin forgive me and my dear husband too if he finds out ever, but yes. Now what shall I be doing?"

"The duke's waiting for me tonight. I'd best not tell you where so you could honestly say you don't know if anyone asks. I need my possessions and maidservants sent to me later. And any good words you can have for us when the king hears would be appreciated. It's the only way. I need a conveyance of some sort waiting after midnight tonight in the park or outside the gates. I would send it back within the hour. But no one must know."

"Yes, dear Frances, I shall help. This very night. Oh, blessed María!"

The queen's large, limpid eyes glowed with unshed tears as she clasped her hands tightly together. "Here, Frances, come here and then you must hurry away to not meet the king. Come over here."

Queen Catherine bustled into her bedroom and Frances followed curiously. Her Majesty went over to a large marble table under a gilt-framed mirror and bent over her huge, multitiered jewelry box. She pulled out the small enameled drawers and rummaged about loudly.

"Something for you for a wedding gift since I will not be there," she murmured.

"Your Majesty, you are too kind. I take your friendship and loving patronage with me, please, nothing of your jewelry."

"No, this is yours, my dear. See? Here!"

Framed by the queen's delicate fingers was the carved, gold brooch Richmond had offered to her so long ago and to the queen last year.

"Here," the queen repeated, and summoned Frances closer with a flick of her other wrist. "Remember his words the night of my birthday ball when we were all in masks, Frances? I knew that under your mask you cried. Here, it was always being yours, yes. Here."

Tears filled Frances' eyes as the queen stepped close to pin the brooch to the low neckline of her gown. "My mother said once it was a gift only for a true love," Richmond had said that night. Now the brooch and all it meant had come full circuit to crown the rapture of their love.

"Go, go now, my dear, loyal Frances, before he comes. A carriage will be awaiting you at the Holbein Gate after the palace falls silent. It will wait until you come. Go with my love and wedding good wishes, and I pray we shall meet soon and happy again, yes."

Frances curtsied, her brimming eyes on the queen's clasped hands. "I shall never forget your kindness, or the love you have shown me despite your right to hate me, Your Majesty. I shall never forget—" Her voice caught in her throat.

Oblivious to the fact she was nearly running, she hurried out ignoring the cluster of whispering, waiting queen's women. In the stretch of corridor she heard too late the warning yelps of spaniels, the approaching buzz of men's voices. Hastily, she dashed tears from her eyelashes and curtsied to the inevitable.

"Od's fish, Frances," the king's deep voice rang out, then quieted for his next words as everyone hushed and gazed at the wayward miscreant they had gossiped of but hardly seen for two weeks. "Just leaving the queen? You should have come down to supper. I hope all is well."

Her blue eyes lifted to collide with his stare of slaty black. She forced a taut smile. "Yes, all is well, sire. Thank you for your kind invitation to supper and your concern. I shall remember that."

"Indeed, you keep too much to your rooms," he scolded lightly, his coal black eyebrows nearly meeting for a moment as his frowning gaze went over her. "You really must promise me you will get out more."

Her heart nearly pounded behind the satin bodice his gaze dared to caress even now. "I promise, I shall, Your Majesty," she said low and moved backward on a quick curtsy to avoid further probes of eyes or questions. She knew he stood momentarily watching her retreat: no sound floated to her, not even the barks of fretful dogs.

She breathed a sigh in her own rooms as her quick brain dashed repeatedly over every aspect of her plan. Minutes dragged while Gillie and Jane fussed over her and finally tucked her in. After they left, she rose and wrote them and her mother brief notes, then stood by her window glazed in moonlight. When, at last, the palace went dark and silent, she dressed, pinning the Richmond brooch to her gown, and paced her rooms one last time while her cats' curious eyes glowed luminous at their mistress' unusual behavior.

She fed the animals, then hauled her petticoat sacks out from under the bed. She rounded up the cats and tied them in, holding their warm bodies against her cloak as a precious burden. She lifted Joli's covered cage and the bundle of her garments. Laden so heavily that she walked with a swaying gait, she gazed once around the familiar, elegant little suite, whispered a prayer, and went out.

She took the servants' stairs down, precariously holding a low-burning torch aloft for light while the cats mewed and squirmed.

"Sh, sh, stop it. Good kitties!" her whispers hissed back at her in the silent staircase. She heard someone running several floors below her and froze against

571

the wall, hoping they did not see her light. But a door banged and all fell to muteness again.

On the first floor, she darted across the end of the corridor which led to Castlemaine's rooms and accidentally bumped Joli's brass cage on the frame of the door leading outside. She managed to lift the nearly spent torch into a metal wall sconce. As she jostled the cats to get a better grip, a sound came from down the hall, and she dashed out. She'd be doubly blessed to escape from here if she never saw or heard anything from Castlemaine's direction again!

Her right arm already ached from holding the cage as the crisp night air enveloped her, stirring her hair and cloak. The gravel of the Privy Garden path crunched underfoot. One of the cats meowed terribly loud. In the moonshade of a tall fruit tree, she gazed back, awestruck, at the royal wing of the sleeping palace. It was suddenly as if she'd never belonged there at all. Silver windows glittered coldly; the edifice's ponderous vastness loomed over her under scudding, low, moon-gilded clouds. How long, how long before she'd ever be back—perhaps never with a civil welcome after this final affront to the powerful man she had not meant to hurt. She couldn't hate him—never—only she loved her own Charles Stuart so.

She turned her back and hurried out of the high-arched Holbein Gate, free at last of the embracing brick arms of Whitehall. Never, never, never, her feet whispered on the sliding gravel walk once so familiar and now so foreign. A black box of a carriage and a pair of snorting horses rose directly before her. Tears crowded her eyes in silent gratitude to the dear queen.

She moved slowly closer to it, expecting a coachman to appear, but she froze at the sound of voices—a man's, a woman's. Castlemaine's. Before she could shift away into the gloom, the carriage door cracked open, barely missing her face. Silks rustled; a wave of heady perfume preceded the unmistakable laugh. "Good night then, Jermyn, my sweet, sweet, randy stud," Barbara, Countess of Castlemaine called back into the carriage even as she stepped down to jolt into Joli's wire cage.

"Gads, what the hell!" she hissed, but not before the clatter of hoofs and the rumble of carriage wheels evidently drowned out her cries in Jermyn's ears. The coach rolled away into darkness. "Who in blazes—Stewart! You!"

Frances stood transfixed, so furious at this chance twist of fate she could not speak. The birdcage swung heavily in her hand; the cats writhed in her hard grip.

Barbara's surprised face pushed closer through the gloom, her eyes wide and the flash of her teeth stark white. "I swear—I do swear if it isn't the pious, little Stewart who turned out to be a whore after all, only with Richmond and not my king."

"Just go inside, Barbara," Frances managed at last, hoping her voice sounded calm when her heart was thudding out of her chest. "Jermyn's gone and who knows who will be breathlessly awaiting your arrival in your bed."

"So high and mighty, Stewart, always were," Barbara shot back, hands on her voluptuous hips. "And may I be so bold as to inquire why you're prancing about after dark out here alone? Did Richmond just let you out from some delicious, little tryst? The king removes his guards from your suite but two days and willful, spoiled Frances is out on her own again."

"Get out of my way, Barbara! The last thing on earth I want to do is argue with you—or ever see you again either. I'm leaving to see my mother."

"Pooh! More like running off to Richmond's bed if you are indeed going instead of coming," she crowed, then clapped her hands crazily and jumped up and down. "That's it, that's it, isn't it, little Stewart? Gads, it's too perfect, too lovely. George will just adore this!"

Frances could hear another carriage in the dark, rolling closer up the cobbled street from the direction of the royal mews. She must shake Barbara off and get away. The woman's long-tended hatred was capable of ruining everything.

"Look, Barbara, you've wanted me gone for years. You've threatened it, wished for it," Frances' voice rose more stridently than she'd meant it to. "Wherever I'm going, just walk away and let me be. The king is yours now, so—"

"No! No, he isn't. You've ruined that, you and this sickly lust he harbors for his queen lately. You've ruined it all one way or the other. He was happy with me once but you were younger, finer—better, damn your pious little soul! You won't have Richmond's love while I rot here alone, and the king looks elsewhere—no! Never!"

Even though Frances darted back, Barbara threw herself against her. The cage jolted to the cobbles; the sack of cats dropped, squirming, down Frances' skirts into the street. Barbara's fist thudded once, twice into Frances' shoulders; a clawlike hand seized her hair beneath the hood of her cloak and tugged her backward.

Blind with rage, Frances grabbed desperately at Barbara's skirts, at her arm as she dragged her along toward the sleeping palace. Their scuffling feet sounded terribly loud on the paths of the Privy Garden as Barbara hauled her under the arched gate. Pain tore Frances' scalp, and doubled over, she moved helplessly along.

"You'll never be free and happy now, Stewart," Barbara gasped out. "Just like me—he'll lock you in—you'll never get away to Richmond now to be all cosy and loved."

Anger and panic exploded to sheer strength in Frances. Somehow, despite the blinding pain along her scalp, she tore her hair free of Barbara's grasp. Both of Frances' hands lifted, struck upward at Barbara's face etched white in the vivid moonlight.

Barbara flew backward several steps. She raised her hands to protect her face even as Frances' fist connected one good blow on her chin. The carriage! Frances could hear the carriage at the gate. Grinding gravel scattered underfoot; a garden fountain chattered somewhere very near. Richmond, Richmond! Nothing must ever keep them apart now.

Wildly, Barbara swung at her, and Frances ducked. The woman was heavier, a raving fury energized by her own panic and pain. Swift as lightning, Frances lifted and shoved Barbara back with all her strength. She'd make her sprawl in the roses or fall on the grass so she could flee this place forever!

Barbara, Countess of Castlemaine, grunted,

shrieked once, and tripped backward with a great slosh into a Privy Garden fountain.

Frances stared one instant, panting for breath. The black fountain water rolled once over the woman. Barbara thrashed, sputtered, then sat up sodden on her haunches. Her face glistened in the wan moonglow, a mask of agony, bereft of all else that had ever lit those once lovely features.

"I am sorry—it has always been so between us, Barbara," Frances rasped out, and fled.

The cage and cats were shrouded blurs on the dark cobbles near the halted carriage. Her blood pounded, pounded in her ears. She gasped for air. It would be just like Barbara to rouse all Whitehall, to tell the king to set up a hue and cry to stop her, only back there, at last, Barbara had looked so wretchedly beaten.

"You Her Majesty's passenger, mistress?" a husky voice behind said. She jumped and the cage rattled.

"Yes. Yes, I am. I need to go across London Bridge right now."

"Jupiter, an' what's all that you be cartin', mistress? Here, let me help you in and we'll be off right fast. An' it looks like you fell or got all windblown. Here, up you go only we can't go clear across the bridge as they be fixin' fire damage on it. I can get you clear to the river there though."

"Yes, fine. Let's be off. We need to go as quickly as possible."

It was velvet ebony in the carriage but she didn't care. She fumbled to put on her mask while the cats wriggled for new positions in their makeshift sack. They lurched away. Frances tried to imagine where the carriage was now: on the edge of beautiful St. James's Park; somewhere along the route where Richmond had taken her that very first day in London?

The ride seemed endless; her pulse began to thud apprehensively. She should have arranged for a password with this driver. The last time she'd gone off alone a blackmailer had almost killed her, and Castlemaine had been dragged from a carriage that time in the Park and—

They halted. The door yanked open. "Mistress, somebody sure will steal this carriage an' I leave it settin' down here to escort you clear across. Somebody be meetin' you near here?"

"Yes, yes, don't worry. Here, take this cage and help me down. The cats are driving me to distraction."

"What's in the cage? Cats? Where?" he asked gruffly as he complied.

Her arm muscles trembled as she lifted Perth and Aberdeen in their petticoat sack and reclaimed the cage. "Thank you, sir. Tell Her Majesty I am forever in her debt."

"Wait, mistress! You can't just walk off. Where's the folks meetin' you? The queen will have my head, she will."

"They're just on the bridge. Go on now, so no one wonders."

She turned away, surprised to be enveloped almost instantly by drifting river fog that smothered all reality. The muffled clatter of the retreating carriage was swallowed by shifting silence. She held the cats so closely to her one hissed. Yes, here above her

577

swimming in mist was the entry to the bridge, still being rebuilt after the ruin of the Great Fire. Scaffolding slanted crazily overhead peering at her from the mute cloud of fog; ladders dipped at her from above. Cold and clinging, the gray swirling mist embraced her eagerly.

Footsteps shuffled nearby, and she pressed her back against a half-erected wall, her eyes wide to pierce the fog and night. A sharp bell made her shriek involuntarily, but the man's voice gave her the comfort of reality as it approached, then passed: "Bellman Reams says past two of the clock, and a chill, foggy night!"

She heard water lapping at the massive stone footers of the bridge as she edged her way onward. She was afraid to just stride out, irrationally terrified the bridge would just end in the deep unknown, even as her life had. No, no, what was wrong with her? She was going toward her new life, holding to her dear friends, her animals. Ahead was light and warmth and the strength of Richmond's arms.

Interminably, she moved into the fog. Now she was on that old section of bridge the fire had not burned. With the river wind in her ears, she could almost fathom she heard the encroaching crackle of devastating flames again.

She broke into a shaky little run over uneven cobblestones. She turned her heel, nearly stumbled. Heavens, why had she not demanded the carriage driver escort her across?

Lights, lights in lower windows, little golden squares in the foggy gloom of dangerous Southwark. What if he wasn't here? Oh please, dearest God, let him be here! Let this wretched escape be over or, at least, safely begun.

The melancholy, drifting strains of a muted bagpipe reached her ears. The crude inn sign of the black bear dangled suddenly overhead emerging from the ghostly mist: the Bear at the Bridgefoot. She was here—here to Richmond—and no one had stopped her, not even the specter of Castlemaine.

She fumbled with the heavy iron door latch, so exhausted and burdened with her cradled load that she couldn't budge it. At last she shoved the door open and the dimly burning fireplace in the room nearly blinded her at first. The melody of sad pipe music swirled around her to mingle with the fog.

The music ceased as she took a wary step inward and bent over to tug off her mask. "My Lord Duke! Look!" a man's voice barked.

From near the huge fireplace, a tall, dark form vaulted toward her, arms spread wide. "Frances, my sweet lass, my sweet lass, you came!"

She set the cage down and they pressed the squealing cats between them in a fierce hug. Behind them Roger Payne closed the door.

"Frances—the cats!" Richmond shouted in surprise and lifted the writhing sack from her arms.

"Yes, yes. I couldn't leave them there to face all that."

"Where are your maids?"

"I couldn't even tell them of this or they might have been implicated. It was hard enough for them before when the king questioned them. I sneaked out, you see, and told no one but the queen who helped me and I had to walk—"

"The queen? The queen helped!" Both men roared in exuberant laughter to drown her explanation, and Richmond pounded the red-haired Roger on the back. Tears filled Richmond's eyes even as they fell from hers, the result of their almost hysterical joy. At last the men untied the sack and produced two ruffled, annoyed white felines.

In the warm circle of Richmond's long arm, Frances walked to the hearth to sit beside him on a wooden settle and to sip warmed, spiced wine. His face was sober now, intent, as his eyes went thoroughly over her to be certain she was indeed unharmed and really here.

"My sweetheart, this beautiful woman I will wed is not the Frances I first knew and fell in love with, for that enticing Frances was a young, vacillating girl. Now I find a courageous, strong woman I could love no deeper than I do now, but tomorrow, I think, I will love her even more."

Their eyes met and held in that second of staggering, breathless impact that always leapt like wildfire between them. They leaned together to kiss lingeringly over her cup.

"I vow, I've been a bit mixed up at times, only I do know one thing for certain," she said low. "Though I told no one my destination here, I think we should set out at least at dawn."

"Dawn," he said, and grinned as he stroked the slant of her cheek with curled fingers. "If we don't set out within the hour, we're like to face royal roadblocks on the way to Cobham. Roger's gone around to fetch the carriage now so we have at least a few hours at Cobham before we're wed tomorrow."

"Tomorrow? But you can't mean— It's almost tomorrow already!"

"Do I detect bridal jitters," he laughed. "Yes, Frances, wed tomorrow in Cobham's church because then we'll be beyond royal reach, no matter how terrible his immediate reaction. Everything is being prepared for us there, my love."

She swiveled her head to gaze into the low-burning hearth flames. Gold and reddish hues danced along a single massive log. Tomorrow then, by this time she would be wed—his wife at unfamiliar Cobham, a new and unknown world begun.

"Frances, sweet lass. Are you— You're not sorry? I've seen you pull back so many times from the inevitability of our love, I couldn't bear it again."

She heard the carriage rumble up in front. Exhaustion rippled through her; she reached out to seize his big hand from his knee.

"No, not sorry, my Charles, and not pulling back either. Only tired and a little bit afraid—"

His other hand lifted to her lips to still them. "Sh, love. I won't let anything harm you that I can control, ever again. Come on now. There's food in the carriage and warm tartan blankets."

He lifted her effortlessly and she clung to him, closing her eyes and pressing her face to his warm neck. Here was safety; here was love.

She leaned back on the carriage seat and tucked her weary legs under her as Roger handed in the cage and both disgruntled cats. When Richmond climbed up and they jolted away, he pulled her onto his lap, cuddled her, and wrapped her legs in a blanket. The bouncing, bone crunching, lantern-lit ride southeast through Southwark to the Great Kent Road might be almost comfortable this way, she mused.

Utter exhaustion assailed her as she nestled closer in his arms, her head on his shoulder. He began to speak of the wedding, how thrilled the villagers and house servants were, of all the improvements she would see in progress at Cobham. She murmured a reply and settled closer, warm against his strength. His heart thudded rhythmically against her ear; the coach clattered away from court and king and mother and London and all she had known—but now she was not afraid. Soon, floating in his sheltering embrace, drifting in a fog of feelings, outward, outward she moved over the bridge of her life.

As the clear blush of dawn melded to eggshell blue in the eastern sky, Frances Stewart first beheld her new home at Cobham Hall in England's garden land of Kent.

"It's lovely—and so much grander than I had pictured it!" she exclaimed as she leaned out the carriage window to gaze, wide-eyed, across the plush green grass and patterned flowerbeds sweeping to the red stony skirts of Cobham. Richmond had held her tenderly in his arms during the hours of their jolting ride these thirty miles, and now he pressed eagerly behind her to study her face as she met the other love of his life for the first time.

They rolled past tender-leafed apple and cherry orchards, some even hinting of blossom color on this final day of March. The vast, manicured lawns lapped like an emerald sea along the curved gravel lane that led to a three-storied, rose-hued brick mansion built in expansive Tudor style during the great Elizabeth's reign. A veritable miniature Hampton Court, Frances marveled, with its fine, protruding bay windows; clusters of ornately twisted chimneys; gray slate roof; and four octagonal, turreted towers crowned with elaborate weather vanes which seemed to guard the farthest reaches of the edifice. As they swept by one wing of the house and approached the front façade, Frances noted the house was laid out in a vast H-shape with the main entrance in the central cross piece of the H.

"It's not as expansive as some dukes' country houses, Frances," Richmond was saying, "but with the home in Scotland, it's plenty for a growing family."

She laughed delightedly, suddenly overwhelmed by a heady sense of freedom. A new energy suffused her weary limbs, and her heart beat very fast with nervous anticipation. "I vow, my dearest lord, how you do presume! We're not even wed and you're speaking of a growing family!"

He grinned like a delighted boy who'd just been given a Yuletide gift, and his brows lifted rakishly. "You do realize, Frances, some others will speak of it if I do not. After all, to everyone but those select thousands of scandalized Londoners who will know the truth of our sudden elopement, this marriage today may look slightly precipitous and rural Kentish tongues will wag."

"You teasing rogue! And since I've always been so zealous for my reputation, you mean, we shall not bed together for a month or so to be certain their worst suspicions are not satisfied by a Richmond heir a mere nine months or less after today!"

She grinned to see she had temporarily bested him as he caught her shoulders to pull her back inside and turn her to him. "Heir or not, growing family or not, my own sweet lass, I now have everything already I'll ever need to content me—never doubt that."

Their lips hesitated inches apart as the carriage slowed; she nearly drowned in the green and gold dappled depths of his eyes waiting for his mouth to touch hers. "I'm so glad, my Charles," she breathed. "I want to make you very happy for having saved me like this."

He moved slightly away and tilted his rugged face in that surprised look of his. "Saved you? Is that the way you see it? I did it for love of you, Frances, but still I am receiving much in return, you see."

"Yes, I know. I vow, I didn't mean it like it— Oh, what is all that noise?"

Cheers and raucous "Hurrahs" greeted them as the carriage slowed to a halt. A crowd of people who had gathered on the front brick terrace under the stone Richmond coat of arms cheered and waved. Thirty, maybe forty people, Frances thought dazedly, servants and workers, and— Oh, heavens, her hair must look like a haystack and her eyes were bleary with tears and sleep. Hastily, she smoothed her tousled coiffure while Richmond fluffed her skirts out for her like the best lady's maid.

"I really wish you'd have told me this," she murmured, pinching her cheeks for color. "A passel of pets, a bundle of clothes—I probably look like some milkmaid you took pity on along the road."

"Not you, Frances, never. You look every whit the elegant, charming Duchess of Richmond and Lennox already. Just smile that fabulous smile and you'll dazzle them all. Besides I had no idea they'd turn out like this. As a matter of fact, they're supposed to be preparing a bridal feast for a hundred, and riders were to set out immediately when they saw us to summon the neighbors. As Joli says, keep a smile. Here, I'll get down and hand you out."

Roger Payne's grinning face appeared behind Richmond's proud one as she lifted her skirts with one hand and held his proffered hand to step down. Ragged "Hallos" and "Hurrahs" rang in her ears, and someone repeatedly clanged a tinny cow bell. She held tightly to Richmond's arm, nodding, smiling, waving, and repeating the string of names the master of Richmond recited as he introduced her to the more important house and estate servants and farmers.

They stood now on the single raised step of the huge double-doored entryway. The cacophony of kindly cheers quieted as a small, blond girl stepped forward from the crowd. From her trembling fist sprouted a small bouquet of violets and lilies of the valley. An adult hand emerged from the crowd to urge the child another step forward. Her blue eyes stared up at Frances as if awestruck.

"Lady Stewart," the duke announced, "this is Amanda, the blacksmith's youngest girl."

Frances moved down from the step to stand before the solemn-faced girl. She knelt down to her. Tears flooded Frances' eyes, and she silently cursed the exhaustion that made her so weepy; it could not be only that these simple folk had touched her heart so deeply already.

"Amanda," she said low, as if only to the girl, "what a pretty name and what a lovely girl you are. The posies—are they for me?"

Amanda nodded grandly and thrust them at her. Their hands touched and impulsively Frances kissed the child's cheek. The little girl started, then threw her arms around her new mistress while Frances hugged her back. If only it were this easy to love and be loved, Frances thought, as the crowd surrounded them, all cheers and shouts again.

The duke sent his people back to work with hearty thanks and orders for the wedding at four and the meal at six. Roger Payne, one white cat under each arm, followed by a freckled boy toting Joli's cage, came behind them into the high ceilinged entry way. Brushing clinging tears away, Frances tried to take it all in.

"The linen-fold paneling is very fine, my lord. I haven't seen its like since France," she heard herself chatter on. "And these tiles look very fashionable."

"Some of Cobham is, but most of it isn't yet, my love. It's a grand home with more old Tudor than modern Stuart to it yet, but I've been working on it bit by bit for years and now that I have the most fashionable woman in England here to live, I warrant, I can have some advice on how to do it well at last. I am excited to show you all of it—the gardens, outbuildings, and orchards too, but I think if you don't get some real rest in a bed before this afternoon, I'll have my bride nodding off at the altar as well as fighting tears."

"I'm fine. I want to see it all right now. Surely there is time to see it all."

"It will take two days for you to see it *all*, my love. Come on now. We will have time to do it *all* later. But for now, humor me a little. Maybe just to make me think there's a little promise for the obedient wife in you the last few hours before we're sealed and bonded."

He grinned and swept her up in his arms even as she tried to pull open a big oak door to examine another room. He went quickly up the curving staircase with her two steps at a time and did not stop until he had strode down a long corridor to lay her on her back on a large, red canopied bed in a high-ceilinged bedroom.

He sat down, leaning over her, while she left her hands loosely clasped about his neck. "Is this our room, my lord?" she ventured in the awkward silence.

"No, love. Just one where I thought you could rest and be gowned later as the housemaids are decking our master suite with traditional gilded rosemary and myrtle boughs."

Her face went instantly serious. "I can't believe it's happening. I can't believe it's today."

"I'll make you as happy as I can—as happy as you'll let me make you, Frances."

"I know—I believe you. How can I ever thank you enough?"

"Don't think of it that way—as if you owe me something. You've got to realize it isn't like that at all. But, right now, I want you to sleep and I'll have a lovely young maid named Glenda wake you for a bath and gowning at two. And I'll send some food and wine up then. Promise me you'll eat something before you're sent for.''

She struggled bolt upright, despite his restraining hands. "My gown and all my things! They're tied up in that petticoat in the carriage. I swear, they'll be a mass of wrinkles!''

"All taken care of. Trust me. Everything will be done and waiting.''

"Oh. Are Joli and the cats all right?''

"Everything, I said. Now lie back and get some rest. I don't intend to introduce the guests at Cobham tonight to a duchess who can't last through a good Scottish reel or rant.''

He stood and moved away across the room as if he hesitated to touch her again. Was he daft? she thought. She couldn't possibly sleep here in a strange house with her own wedding plans going on all about! And she couldn't bear to have him go out and leave her here like this, though he didn't look as if he even had time to kiss her goodbye after all they'd been through!

"My Lord Duke of Richmond,'' she called as he reached the door. "Are you—aren't you going to rest somewhere too?''

"Certainly not there next to you, my sweetheart, though the temptation to do so vexes me sorely, so sorely in fact, I'm afraid if I did so much as kiss you, I'd lose control and neither of us would have the strength later to make a showing let alone dance. Please try to rest, Frances, as I promise it will be a long, long night. Just ring that little bell on the side table if you want Glenda before two. Sleep, love . . .''

his last words drifted to her as he went out and quietly closed the door.

She heard his footsteps fade. Was he actually whistling? She stared up at the gathered underside of the brocade canopy. This room would be fine for mother when she visited—or for her sister Sophia. She closed her eyes for just a moment to rest them and stretched her limbs, sore from cuddling close to him in the carriage she could still almost feel rocking and swaying beneath her.

This room swam in fog just like London. No, her tired eyes were closing. This room must overlook the back of the house; she would get up in just a minute and gaze out through those heavy draperies to see the view from here.

The view from here—all those eager faces down below, country faces without cosmetics, with none of Castlemaine's fashionable black velvet beauty patches, and certainly no stylish masks. Richmond's people, her own now, staring at the strange woman come to be their new duchess and wondering what she would be like.

The bed was soft, soft as sailing his boat the *Francis* on a gentle river. Her yacht flew out of the fog and crested free on the rolling waves of the sea. She turned over once, ever so gently, and she was no longer afraid.

"I was afraid of something like this, but I didn't think she would dare!" King Charles roared to his distraught brother, the Duke of York. "I should have been more careful, more watchful, but I thought if I let her pout a bit, she'd come around. You know what the last thing I said to her was, James? Can you imagine?"

The Duke of York stood on the other side of the vast table in His Majesty's science laboratory in St. James's Park in utter dread the king would begin to throw glassware or his damned latest acid experiments his way. The king had already cleared a cluttered bench of blown glass tubes which now crunched underfoot as he continued to pace furiously.

"No, sire, how could I know?" the duke said fidgeting from foot to foot. "What did you say to her?"

"I told her she kept too much to her rooms and she should get out more! Od's fish, how prophetic! Out of her rooms, out of Whitehall, out of London—out of my life for good, damn her!"

"You don't mean that, sire. She'll want to come back, our fashionable Frances, and having a married lady about has never been a hindrance to you, I daresay. Just how long do you think a stylish girl reared in cousin Louis' French court, who has lived in yours, will like flower picking at boring Cobham? Granted, Richmond's enticing to her now, I suppose, but, I swear, he's a country squire at heart and she'll tire of that."

"Will she? Will she!" the king muttered as he ground shattered glass under his big feet with each stride. "She's changed, I tell you, changed. Of course, she's been stubborn before where my wishes were concerned, that's been consistent enough behavior. 'Sblood, I grant you that, but I always felt it was a certain distrust or dislike for men in general. Now, I'll never forgive this. Never! She's not coming back while I am monarch of this wretched, joyless realm! What's that look for, damn it—that pious look that reminds me so much of mother's just before some ranting lecture?"

"Nothing, sire, only—zounds, it appears all this upheaval has been engendered by the same thing as what you scolded me for when I foolishly got myself embroiled with Anne and had to marry her. Don't you remember?"

"What? This hardly smacks of that ludicrous predicament. You deserved that, getting her pregnant. I wish to hell that's exactly what I'd done with Frances Stewart, but it isn't."

"No, sire, I'm referring to the charge you gave me to reprimand you if you ever lost your head for a woman. Never get tangled with a woman you really care for; I believe those were your words. Let them have your body and your brain but never your heart you said and—"

"Get out of here, James! Just get out. I said I didn't want to see anyone today and that included you. I can hardly expect you to understand."

"That's not true, sire," he protested stodgily, giving his heavily curled periwig a furious shake. "I do understand, only— Oh, hell, enough of arguing with you today. I'll be off then. As I said, I'd be willing to put my name on an order to send the Duke of Richmond to sea again immediately. This *is* war after all."

"Yes, James, it is indeed, but I'll not show a weakness by panicking to attack before it's time. Let them be off at Cobham billing and cooing. I don't give a damn about either of them anymore—they've both defied me. Send him back to his naval duties when the war needs him, not before."

The duke's smooth eyebrows lifted in obvious surprise. "As you wish, of course, sire. Forgiveness is a grand and noble tactic."

"Hogwash to the grand and noble. Be damned to them both, I said. But I will find out who here helped her. Someone else still living on my largesse and good will has defied me too, and I won't have vipers in my nest. Castlemaine, Buckingham, even the rumors say, your father-in-law old Chancellor Clarendon. I'll root out whomever it is here. They shall feel my displeasure. And tell someone as you go out to sweep up this mess. I hate disorder. I didn't mean to throw things. I'm going for a walk!"

James, Duke of York, jumped quickly away from the doorway as his older brother clapped his broad-brimmed hat on his full, ebony periwig and strode past him without another glance or word. The duke stood quietly, blessing the silence as the outer door slammed.

He gazed back into the tall-window room in which King Charles satisfied his scientific thirst for new knowledge: glassware, lanterns, tubes, prisms, scales, microscopes, all breakable, all of it.

He sighed. If he ever became king he would not fuss and tinker off here alone like this. He'd rule and command and never let a woman's disobedience ruin his day. He was certain he could have bedded Frances Stewart months ago if he'd ever been allowed full rein with her.

Now, all the courtiers would suffer because of one stunning woman's tenacity and pluck all these years, and her daring denial of her king at the last. Damn, but some of Castlemaine's camp who'd been looking for an excuse for years to topple Chancellor Clarendon had even seized on this disaster to spread the word Clarendon had arranged it to be certain Frances Stewart could never be queen and bear an heir for England while the queen could not. Ludicrous, of course, when one knew the iron-clad, almost puritanical honor by which the old man had always lived his life, but the king was so lividly irrational, anything could happen in these times of stress and war.

James, Duke of York, sighed loudly and headed outside to rejoin his little entourage who no doubt wondered by now what had befallen him. He smiled tautly. He hoped the little Stewart and her Richmond enjoyed themselves while they could. That damned fortunetelling comet had preceded pestilence, war, fire—and now a broken royal heart, over a woman! He shouted a sharp laugh in the narrow hall as he went out to join his men.

Chapter Twenty-One

Frances felt she had been born into a new world orchestrated by some fantastical, unseen hand. As if by a mere turn of imagination, her beautifully prepared wedding garments appeared after her scented bath, and when the smiling slip of a young maid named Glenda had helped her dress and brush out her hair, Frances gazed awestruck at the lovely bride in the gilded mirror her other two ladies' maids held for her.

The tawny-haired woman in the glass looked so calm and serene, so certain, yet Frances felt butterflies flutter inside as servants flitted swiftly by on ephemeral wings of time. She wore her hair long and brushed out as any fashionable Restoration bride would, the thick tresses were held back by the traditional circlet of aromatic myrtle leaves. Loosely sewn knots of colored ribbons, for the young men at the ceremony to pull off and wear in their hats as bridal favors, dotted her gown of French candlelight satin, the low-cut bodice, and lace sleeves. Her heavily fringed bride's gloves too, traditionally purchased by the groom, would go to the bride-men who led her to the church.

Glenda seemed not at all in awe at dressing the about-to-be Duchess of Richmond as she laced on the beautiful new stomacher Frances had purchased with her mother that day at the Royal Exchange two weeks ago. At least, she thought, having a down-to-earth girl like Glenda about to help Gillie and Jane when they came would make all of this dream world seem real.

"It's not too tight, Yer Grace?" the sweet-faced, brunette maid asked.

"It's fine, Glenda. You and the others have done a marvelous job, and I thank you. And I'm not Your Grace yet, you know."

"Glory, I know, Yer Ladyship, but the duke was just reminding all of us to call you that after and I'm just practicing."

"The duke was down overseeing the servants, then?" Frances probed, still slightly annoyed at herself for sleeping until Glenda had awakened her at two.

"Oh, 'course, Yer Ladyship, like he always does. He's here so seldom, you see, he goes about just doing everything even though, 'course, Master Roger Payne's a wonderful steward and all."

They all jumped at the knock on the door, and one of the older maids named Lindsey opened it. A short, squat man filled the doorway and several others crowded close behind him.

"Time to head down, Your Ladyship, if you're ready, I mean. Allow me to present myself and your bride-men. I am Henry Flaxney, the duke's wardrobe keeper and this is the house steward Roger Payne, whom I've heard you know, and the head bride's-man is Squire Randall Courtney from the next estate toward Gravesend.''

All three men literally gaped at Frances' appearance during the introductions, and she recalled the many times gallants at Louis' or Charles's courts had done the same. But this was so happily different: these were honest-faced friends of her Charles, about to escort a bride, not leering fops hoping for a chance of their own. She felt the tightly wound coil of tension in her breast begin to unwind ever so slightly.

"I thank you. Yes, I am quite ready, Mister Flaxney and gentlemen.''

They were hardly gentlemen, of course, but for Squire Courtney, and everyone grinned broadly. The portly Flaxney stepped aside then, and as if on cue, Roger Payne and Squire Courtney stepped forward with laden arms: in a basket Roger held Perth and Aberdeen, both sporting silken neck bows and Squire Courtney lifted Joli's beribboned brass cage up to her surprised face.

"His Grace just wanted you to know," Roger repeated slowly as if reciting a memorized speech, "that your growing family is all ready for today and you're not to worry about a thing. Tell my lass that, he said.''

She laughed delightedly and pulled off her gloves to caress the animals before she led her small bride's contingent downstairs. As she left the animals behind, reality rushed back: last night she'd fled the only life she'd ever known and had hurt, no doubt, two people she cared for who might never forgive her now. All of this lovely, rural sanctuary of Cobham, this quaint and charming day—her mother and her king would never forgive her now!

Slowly, she traipsed downstairs the rest of the way on Roger Payne's strong arm while the others followed. At least no one seemed to whisper at her back, not here at Cobham as they did at court. Frances looked straight ahead, her curiosity about the house smothered by her nervous concentration. They stepped outside into the vibrant, late afternoon sun to face a gathered crowd waiting to strew her path to the church with flowers and rushes. She started momentarily, jerking Roger's arm.

"Roger," she whispered, turning to him. "I don't even know where the church is here. Is it far?"

The ruddy-faced man shook his head, his face serious. "No, Lady Stewart, just back around the last wing—the chapel, as the duke decided all of a sudden today not to go clear into the village where we'd be expected, you see. Not far, I warrant, after the long way you've already come."

Someone held out a bouquet of early spring flowers wafting the sweet scent of the bell-like lilies of the valley, and she took it as they started off. After the long way you've already come, Roger Payne had said. Yes, she'd come so very far to reach this day, so very far from the rose gardens along the terrace at Saint-Germain where she'd first beheld the young Duke of Richmond. So far in the two most elegant, sophisticated royal courts of the world to reach this rural path stretching before her to the distant brick and gray stone chapel. So far through distrust, confusion, fear, and disappointment to find one man, of all men, including whoever her father really was, who could be trusted.

On Roger's arm she walked, stiff-faced, between her other two solemn bride-men while, in contrast, country maids cavorted about laughing and casting flowers and rushes before their feet. As they neared the tiny chapel, Roger and Squire Courtney held aloft their gilded branches of rosemary, the flower of constancy and love.

Another cluster of unfamiliar, happy people awaited her at the doorway of the chapel; she squinted in the slant of warm March sun to scan the group for tall Richmond. He must be inside—that was traditional in court weddings she'd seen, but then who knew quite what to expect out here amidst trees, vast lawns, and open Kentish skies? She clasped her sweet bouquet tightly in gloved hands, a tiny, taut smile now on her face. Then, in the open doorway of the chapel, she saw him.

He was garbed in buff brocade and the impact of his charismatic elegance stunned her. Why was it she'd always pictured him windblown and casually dressed? This sophisticated, stylish man was an utter stranger despite the roguish wink of one green eye under the broad brim of his formal groom's hat. Her toe caught in her skirt, but Roger Payne had her elbow. Suddenly shy, she stared down at the bridesmen's gilded boughs of rosemary until Richmond's huge gloved hand appeared extended to her. Her bouquet trembled as she lifted her hand to his and stepped in at his side.

"Are you all right, sweetheart?" his words came

low. "You look ravishing—just a little shaky, perhaps."

She turned her head to look squarely at him, and the rush of mutual magnetic emotion nearly swept her under. Sweet surrender flowed from her wide gaze and from the touch of her hand as if she had no separate self anymore, as if she never wanted to be apart from him again. "I love you," his shadowed lips mouthed, and she nodded as if entranced by some unfathomable spell. He gave her hand a tiny tug, and they walked forward together.

The small, dim church lit mostly with long wax tapers and decked with the omnipresent myrtle and rosemary was a sea of faces. From somewhere behind them a small boy's choir sang in angelic voices. The priest's low words blurred by. Now a shining gold band glinting candlelight encircled her finger; she wondered what the inscription might read. It was bad luck to tell, and it might be bedtime before she could examine it—bedtime with her husband who stood so close still holding her hand.

After the final prayer and music, the married couple and the four witnesses partook of the ancient custom of drinking wine with sops from the silver gilt bride cup. Then it was over. The duke sighed, grinned, and kissed her soundly, his hands firm on her slim waist. It was considered good luck for the bride to cry, but she felt too dazed and happy for a tear, though the bridegroom's eyes looked misty enough for both she heard Roger Payne whisper to Squire Courtney.

From the solemn service, they recessed slowly to the chapel doorway where it seemed that at least half the English countryside had turned out to cheer and throw violets and frolic. Young girls called brides-maids fell in before and behind them now, carrying long garlands of flowers, gilded wheat for fertility, and hawthorne branches for hope. Already, young men snatched their ribboned bridal favors from Frances' gown and sported them on their hatbrims for good luck while everyone cheered and laughed. Frances began to giggle so at everyone's antics that Richmond exploded with laughter as he swept her up to carry her the rest of the way to Cobham Hall for the banquet.

It was a large Great Hall, Frances marveled, with lovely, tall windows, though the oak wainscoting looked old-fashioned, and the numerous, lofty pairs of mounted deer and stag antlers would have to go eventually. The bridal repast, set on long tables for a hundred guests, was glorious; the wines flowed freely amidst numerous kissing toasts to the duke and his new duchess.

"Duchess of Richmond," her new husband said, leaning so close to her she could catch his distinctive, disarming, manly scent in her flared nostrils. "The title duchess always suited you, and I cannot wait to convince you fully of that tonight. A wife in my bed, and the most beautiful woman I have ever seen— hell's gates, I hope this is a short banquet and festival!"

She felt her skin from her eartips to the tops of her rounded breasts suffuse with a hot blush as his eyes went thoroughly over her. "You tease," she man-aged, as her pulse raced and her stomach cartwheeled over at the mere remembrance of what his mouth and hands and body could do to her. The impact of his nearness, of his complete rights to her now, stunned her to stuttering confusion like some mere country girl.

After the final course of sweets, imported fruits, and thick, yellow Cobham cheese, Roger Payne and two other men began wailing on their bagpipes as the long tables were cleared and set back along the walls. The tall, burly Roger now wore a dark-hued kilt and stomped his foot to keep the other two pipers in time with his romping lead.

"Come on, sweet, bonny wife," Richmond grinned and seized her hand to pull her to her feet. The room exploded with applause as they rose to begin the dancing. "That's our rather obvious cue for the start of a wild Scottish reel!"

The two of them danced alone at first in the improvised steps to a sort of running coronto. Soon Frances began to giggle: after months of French dancing lessons in Paris and years of being the finest female dancer at King Charles's Restoration court, she hardly knew a step of Scottish reels or rants or jigs.

Everyone joined them now, crowding the wooden floor in reckless abandon as the pipes swirled from tune to tune. Frances and Richmond stood at the head of eight couples in a reel. Again and again they twirled, then wove down the moving line to meet and sweep under an arch of raised arms to begin again.

Though Frances caught onto the steps readily enough and felt real pride in soon executing them well, in the rolling sea of smiling, nodding, friendly faces, she recognized only a few and those she had met only today. She whirled around, secure in Richmond's grasp again. So much wild change, she thought, in so little time, so many new steps of a life to learn.

They sat out a tune to catch their breath and downed tall goblets of wine to cool themselves.

"Heavens, I'm so hot," she said, fanning herself with her hand, "but it's so much fun—a real test of strength."

"I have heard, my love, that wedding nights can be like that. I know I intend for ours to be," he said and winked at her over the rim of his lifted goblet.

"Do you, my Lord Charles?" she retorted, rising to his teasing double-edged meaning with both hands on her hips. "I vow, I'm not so sure my new husband won't just fall asleep after all this wine and exertion—besides, Glenda told me you were seeing to business all afternoon instead of resting."

"Glenda told too much." He grinned and refilled their glasses as they stood at the end of the table away from the loud musicians. "And did she tell you she's far gone in love with our Scottish steward, Roger Payne, and would love to get him to bed with her so he'd wed her?"

"Really, my lord! Of course, she didn't tell me that. I hardly know the girl."

"It's as true as country gossip can ever be, my lass. Roger's a strange one at men-women games—he's in love with her too, I warrant, but he knows if he beds her, he'll feel he has to marry her."

"But if he loves her—" she began. "Oh well, it's just that that's hardly the way it usually is with most men today, as they'd just as soon bed and never wed."

"True, in the fashionable, elegant worlds I hope we never have to live in again, Frances. But though the Duke of York has often dubbed me a country squire at heart, don't confuse what I said about Roger and Glenda with our situation. The fact we had bedded and I was desperate for you—that way—never could have coerced me to marry you if I hadn't loved you. I don't love or marry to help even beautiful ladies escape, as you put it, nor because I take pity on their precarious plights. I want you to understand that, to believe that."

The intensity of his emerald gaze pierced her with a sheer, alluring power that almost made her sway into him. She nodded and bit her lower lip, nearly staggered by the sensual pull of his devouring eyes, his deep voice, and nearly overwhelming presence.

"I do believe it," she managed, her voice raised over the pipes as they dashed into yet another jaunty tune. "And I do love you too."

He put his goblet down and nodded once as though they had sealed some unspoken bargain. He took her wine from her unresisting fingers and pulled her almost roughly into his arms, kissing her hungrily until finally the cheers and shouted jests around them pulled them apart.

They danced again as black velvet night fell outside the torch- and candle-lit Great Hall of old Cobham. In a lull of music, young men from the estate ran races for the bride's garters which the tipsy winners displayed grandly on the points of wooden spears. A piece of huge honey cake was broken above Frances' head and the whole cake distributed for favors.

Everyone came up sooner or later to greet the new Duchess of Richmond with a welcome and a curtsy or bow. As it grew later, Frances sat on Richmond's knee to watch the dancing, quite out of breath, her nearly ungartered stockings too loose now for her to rejoin the revelers.

"I say," he said low in her ear, his warm breath stirring her tumbled curls along her temples, "I believe I'll exercise my new husband's prerogative and send you up with the maids for bath and bedding to breathlessly await your new lord's arrival."

"But everyone's still here," she said, turning to him.

"Duchess, have you never been wed before or just what is the cause of this foolish protest? The wedding guests always see to the bedding and then return for more food and drink—and I think you'd best obey your new husband at least for a day or so. Besides, the dancers will get more and more rowdy from now on, and I don't intend to have other men handling you," he ended quite sternly.

"Oh," she said, her gaze fixated on the little throbbing pulse at the base of his bronze throat. His skin looked so very brown and healthy from all that sailing and overseeing here at Cobham, she thought as her mind darted about for a clever retort. All the men back home in London looked properly silken pale this time of year.

Home, in London. No, this was her home now. This was her husband now, his hooded eyes watching her face, his big hand casually along her hip and thigh.

"I'll go up now then, my Lord Charles. How long

will I have?" She rose to her feet and his embrace dropped slowly away to free her.

"I can hold these silly jackals back for at least an hour, but as for myself—is a half hour enough, my lass?"

"Yes—all right. A half hour." She curtsied to him and turned away. Instantly, Glenda was at her side, and they attracted a little contingent of others as they hurried upstairs.

The master bedchamber pleased her with its grandly frescoed ceiling of clouds and cupids and its soft blue Belgian carpets underfoot. Lovely aquamarine drapes echoed the brocade of the big bed with its curtains, canopy, and coverlet. Garlands of flowers were festooned everywhere, but there was no time to study the room now. With Glenda's help, behind a painted Chinese screen, Frances bathed hastily in tepid water scented with a sweet, rose perfume Glenda produced while other women put the final touches on the room. In her pink satin robe and ribboned French nightsmock, Frances emerged bravely from behind her private screen only to be swept up in the giggling enthusiasm of these dear, country squires' wives she hardly knew.

"Here, get her in on this side. Oh, Lillian, but this bed's vast."

"At my wedding, I sat smack in the middle and let *him* choose his side," someone said.

The satin sheets felt smooth and cool against her bare feet and ankles as Frances climbed obligingly in. On the underside of the canopy, the ornate Richmond family crest—her crest now—stared down at her.

"Oh my goodness, it's been scarcely a half hour," someone shouted. "I hear them! I hear them!"

Frances seized Glenda's slim wrist as the girl plumped her pillows, then moved to step away. "Glenda, wait. Thank you for all your help today—your support. I have two maids coming soon from London, but if you're willing, I'd like you to be in my personal service too."

"Oh, Yer Grace!" the girl crowed so shrilly that others turned to look despite the fact ten men were rushing in the door with Richmond in the lead wearing only open shirt and his breeches. "Glory, for a certain, if you want me, Yer Grace," Frances heard Glenda say.

Explosive laughter, guffaws, shouted good wishes assailed them both as Richmond climbed immediately in the near side of the bed as if to shield her from the avid stares however properly she was robed. Apparently in a hurry now, he took the traditional goblet of sack posset and downed a quick gulp. Frances drank as he held the cup; then it made its rounds.

"He's all ready and willing, my Lady Duchess!" a booming male voice shouted at last when the posset was gone.

"Teach her who's going to be lord here!" another roared.

Frances blushed anew at a shower of increasingly ribald remarks. At the door as they all filed out, someone turned back long enough to fling the traditional stocking of good fortune. Roger Payne was last out, with Glenda at his elbow. The girl waved, Roger nodded and closed the door.

Richmond dashed a quick kiss on her cheek and jumped up to run over to bolt the door. "You can't trust the rascals at country weddings, you know," he said and immediately pulled the shirt the men had evidently nearly torn from him up over his head in one fluid movement. He walked to the foot of the bed, then leaned forward to put his palms down on it. His stare moved over her, slowly down, then up again.

"My friends kept me drinking their bedding toasts and giving me some rather specific advice about how to handle things tonight, Frances, so I didn't get a quick bath as I wanted, and I don't intend for you to surrender yourself to someone who smells like a fieldhand, however eager he is. I'm just going to jump in your bath water and I'll be back straight-away. May I assume you'll be right there waiting?"

She felt awkward, very shy, and utterly undressed at his look despite her garb and the warm coverlet over her to her hips. "Yes, you know I will." She managed a wan smile.

"Two minutes," he said and turned away already unlacing his breeches. "Two minutes and I'm going to start making up for five years of wanting you and too seldom getting what I wanted!"

She heard him splashing the water. Despite the fact that she trembled with nervous anticipation, she refused to let him think she'd gone totally submissive and shy. "If you can't reach your probably dirty back or whatever, just let me know," she dared in her breeziest voice.

"Tomorrow for that sort of fooling. If you come over here, we'll never make it back to that nice, soft bed."

She heard him get out, the flap of a linen towel. He padded out barefoot, still half wet and moved around the room snuffing out most of the many candles. The lofty chamber dimmed to silver gray as she stared at his big, glistening body with only his lean hips covered by the white slash of towel. When she moved to blow out the candles on the bedside table, he said in a deep voice suddenly gone raspy, "No, love. Leave the ones by the bed. I want to see you."

The bed dipped as he sat on the edge of it, one bare, dark-haired leg bent along the coverlet. "Country weddings are a lot of fuss for so simple a thing. I hope you didn't mind all the foolishness there at the end. The rural folk think no one's legally wed without all that, I warrant."

Her eyes snagged with his, and she thought for a moment she'd forgotten how to speak or breathe. "No. It was lovely."

"So are you, my bride, so are you. And since everyone's gone at last, may I help you out of that pretty pink robe?"

Her hands lifted to the ribbon ties until she saw he meant to do it, so she put her hands down beside her hips and studied him at this intimate distance of inches. Now he looked like her roguish, seagoing Richmond again, all disheveled, his hair damp and curly along the nape of his neck where he'd splashed water in his haste. Despite the sweet scent of flowers permeating the room and wafting from her own skin, she wondered fleetingly if he realized he, too, smelled of ladies' rose-scented perfume from her bath water.

"How about that ruffled nightsmock too?" he asked low, one thick brown eyebrow quirking

609

upward. "I'm afraid you've got me at a great disadvantage as I've naught but this little piece of towel to cover me."

Without waiting for her answer, he swept the coverlet from her legs and lifted her across his lap. His embrace was undeniably strong and eager around the small of her back and under her knees. Her open mouth met his willingly, fiercely, as she lifted her face.

He moaned deep in his throat, shifting her closer, slanting his mouth wildly across her first one way and then the other as he felt her ready response. The tip of her slick tongue teased his as his big, warm hand slid slowly up her satin leg lifting the ruffled hem of her nightsmock in a huge cuff around his wrist.

"Sweetheart, sweetheart, my Frances, I'm wild for you, always, always have been. I love you so—I can't get enough of you."

They tumbled back and rolled over once, landing face-to-face in the middle of the big bed. She was not afraid now, suddenly not shy. Always, always he had done this to her when they touched or even gazed: she trembled with pure rapture under the firm caresses of his rampant hands and at the feel of his mouth along her skin. He lifted himself away from her and gently tugged her single garment up and over her head. The cool air whispered over her warm body, and a flaming chill raced to her nipples and to the very pit of her stomach—everywhere he looked or touched. He hesitated one tottering instant then, his green gaze darkening on his taut, passion-glazed face.

"You are so beautiful, my love—so beautiful,

outside and inside too, my Frances."

He bent low over her naked flesh to flicker molten paths of kisses from her ears to her throat to the pointed tips of her breasts and back again. Every kiss or stroke or look shot raging flames clear to her loins until she moved her hips in wild little circles of invitation. Her palms caressed his molded back muscles and grasped his shoulders to pull him down for another fiery kiss.

He began another tender, teasing assault on her nipples. Again his hands grasped the pert globes of her breasts to offer himself the pink-crested nubs while he licked and suckled them. Again and again the wet, hot tip of his tongue dashed icy circles around the pinkish aureoles until she thought she would drown with surging ecstasy.

"Oh, oh!" she murmured and tossed her rippling hair back and forth on the satin sheet. "Oh! Mm, oh heavens!"

"Yes, heavenly, my love," he rasped and changed his tactics instantly. His fingers now stroked her velvet thighs which she opened for him mindlessly. One knee, two knees knelt between to open her totally to him and she wanted it, loved it and him. She heard her breathing come in little, panting gasps as he lowered himself slowly into her caressing warmth. A woman's voice very close cried even as he sweetly pierced her, "I—oh, I love you so—I want you so!"

He whispered hot words she did not catch in her own frenzy to match the rhythm of his powerful body. One hand under her hips, he lifted her to meet him as their unbridled mutual rhythm went on and on. She clung to him, gasping for breath when he freed her mouth, as she felt the roaring fire consume her very core to shoot incredible showers of sparks through every limb. His hot thrusts pressed her down, down, down into the very depths of raging love, until he, too, exploded in the ultimate conflagration.

They clung together, dazed and damp and warm, yet suddenly awakened to the rush of the chill air in the dim room. He settled them on the still-rumpled pillows and pulled the coverlet up over their languid limbs.

"I'm so happy, my lass," he said so low when their breathing quieted she wasn't certain at first he had really spoken. "I meant to take it slow and gentle with my bride, but then—I just couldn't."

She lifted her head drowsily from his shoulder to study his earnest face. "Are you apologizing, my lord? I liked it, you know."

He chuckled low. "Yes, I do know, my sweetheart, but I really am going to have to begin all over again as soon as I catch my breath so you can see what I had planned originally."

"Mm," she smiled at him lazily. "But I'm very content and sleepy now."

"Still, I'd wager it wouldn't take much convincing to get you to let me try again."

"Heavens, but you're confident!"

"Heavens, but you're waking up and getting saucy for a lady who's about to be loved all over her enchanting body all over again."

Their eyes held in that teasing, little challenge, and she felt desire rise again from just looking on him and lying with her chin and hip and one breast against his warm, lean frame.

"I cannot believe we are really wed, my Charles. It seems surely we must be hiding out on the yacht or in my rooms—"

"Or in the royal mews or under a bush at Stonehenge," he finished for her. "I know, love, but it is true, and I want you to be so happy here and not think of—people you've left behind."

She saw a little crease of doubt cross his brow, the tiniest dulling of the sparks in his green eyes. "Oh no, I vow, I won't. Everyone's been so kind and there's so much to do."

"Granted, but being with new people in new surroundings and keeping busy doesn't always help if you're away from someone you care about. I know. I've tried it time and time again at sea or in Scotland, desperate to get you out of my mind and heart."

"But it isn't like that for me, as my mind and heart are hardly involved with anyone but you."

"I pray not, my love. I hope and pray not. 'Sweet lass, my eternal love,' the inscription inside your rings says, and I meant it."

Tears filled her eyes to blur his face so close. Everything had been busy, rushed—she hadn't even taken her ring off to read the inscription, but she imagined she felt it warm and secure along the curve of her finger.

"The ring," she managed, brushing away a tear, "this day, this night, everything has been so lovely— a rapturous day to crown my whole life."

"Don't cry, sweet. Not tonight. Damn, I almost forgot. Let me up a minute. I've got a special gift for you."

"A gift? Now? With everything else? But I don't want a gift. After all, I couldn't get one for you yet and you told me not to spend that money for—"

"I know," he said from across the room where his big naked body shone whitish as he fumbled with some crinkly paper object he produced from a drawer, "but this is a special gift for my new duchess." He thudded back across to her. "Here, just pull off the paper."

"All right, but get back in bed or you'll catch a chill."

He did as she asked, though his striding or standing about the room naked apparently did not bother him one whit whatever it did to her composure. The package was as big as an apple, wrapped in tissue paper. His hairy, bare leg pressed along her smooth hip and he leaned so close she could smell the rose scent on him again.

"Open it!"

"I am. I am. Oh, it's exquisite!"

A beautifully enameled watch top clicked open to reveal a painted scene on its face under the delicate hour and minute hands. At the foot of a tree in a flowery meadow, a naked lady with tawny tresses reclined on a couch of scattered blossoms. Hovering above her, winged Cupid poised his bow ready to let his arrow fly, but his aim looked so awry he could surely never strike the lady. And in the distance, a smiling gallant gentleman approached, but the look on his face was utterly unreadable.

"My Lord Charles, it's wonderful, and it tells a whole little story!"

"I know. And what does the story tell you?" he prodded, and dropped a quick kiss on her bare shoulder above where she held the coverlet over her breasts.

"The man, I would say, loves the lady, but if Cupid's arrow goes off target, she may not love him back."

"Alas, sad, but true, I'd say. But note how she is waiting to be found naked—even as you here."

She smiled at him and her slender, tapered fingers lightly stroked his arm. "I believe," she murmured, "that the lady doesn't even need Cupid's arrow. She is already awaiting him—like this—of her own accord. I believe she has done such for a good long time, only now she also knows she does it because she loves him."

"Do you think that's the way of it then?" he asked, utterly serious despite her attempts to lightly reassure him. She nodded and her eyes filled with crystal tears. She had never been more certain, more fulfilled: she would do it all again, brave anything to be here and his like this. The silence, broken only by their breathing and the rustle of tissue paper as she nestled the watch in it, stretched out between them. She reached behind her to place the gift on the bedside table.

"So," she dared, her voice intentionally slower than her racing pulse, "whatever do you suppose that gallant cavalier did when he arrived at her flowery couch?"

One corner of his firm mouth quirked up. "And what about the nude, tawny-haired beauty?" he parried.

"Probably she let him kiss her."

"Kiss her? Where?"

"On her lips, of course!"

"Is that all? But she obviously has sweet, firm breasts and satin thighs to taste. . . ."

She felt herself go prickly hot clear down between her legs. Why didn't he kiss her? Why had she ever started this crazy game?

"She—she probably liked that very much," she told him.

She leaned forward to press her pouted mouth to his seemingly passive one. But instantly, he responded, pulling at her lower lip, then running his slick tongue inside to taste her honeyed tongue. But when she pulled back slightly, he let her.

Oblivious to the satin sheet which dropped away to uncover her breasts, she kissed him again, pressing close so that her erect nipples grazed his thickly haired chest. The sensation was wildly stimulating, and she wrapped her arms about his neck.

His hands lifted her from behind, to stroke and cup her soft, resilient buttocks as he pulled her across his lap. Her tumbled hair flowed over her back like a warm curtain, and he tangled his fingers in its masses, tipping her head back and chin up until she was facing his impassioned, rugged face only inches above hers.

"You're mine, Frances—no one else's ever! In my own heart and mind you've belonged to me from that first moment I saw you!"

"It took me so long to find myself, my love, and now I've really found you too—forever."

The kiss that claimed her was determined, then

powerfully possessive. They slipped down into the soft depths of the warm bed, their limbs entangled, their caresses fierce, mutual. Desire swept them both away again like a great undertow of passionate sea tossed by sudden winds and surging over shoals they could not fathom. She clung to him, rolling, cresting—both plunging ships in a storm that ended in a mutual crash upon the beach—a final calm.

When he spoke warm words against the nape of her neck some time later, she stirred and stretched. "Frances, are you awake?"

"Mm. I guess I am."

"Tomorrow I'll show you all of Cobham—our home."

"Yes. I want to see it all, learn all about it, meet everyone again."

"You smell delicious, lass. You'd better go to sleep before I lose my head again over you."

"You smell delicious too, Charles, Duke of Richmond. There's nothing like a scented rose-water bath to make a man irresistible."

He nipped at her shoulder and pulled her closer until her back, hips, and thighs cupped perfectly into the curve of his hard body. "That damned stuff," he whispered. "I was so eager to get into bed I didn't think of that. If I ever do something that crazy again, I'll at least make certain you're in the perfumed water at the same time."

His warm hand grasped a knee, then slid treacherously higher to rest between her warm thighs. She could feel his growing desire for her again and she tensed.

"Relax, sweetheart, just relax against me. I want

you again, but I've learned to wait. Sleep now and then in an hour or so, we'll see."

Amazingly, he seemed to doze, his cheek against her shoulder, his hand still between her thighs. She went limp, comfortably safe in his embrace. Her limbs floated with weariness as if in languid water, but her brain raced.

She had done it—she was free of them all, free of the king and married to this man she surely must have loved for years. Their joy had blotted out the distant world today and had made all the past guilt, uncertainty, and heartache go away. Cupid's arrow must have found the lady, and surely she'd lived happily forever more.

Their cocoon of scented body warmth enveloped them even as essence of roses had wafted between them that first day in the gardens of Saint-Germain. She nestled closer, swirled in the soft arms of sleep. The naked lady slept amidst the flowers with her gallant gentleman, and rapture's love crowned all their dreams.

Author's Note

Frances Stewart and her Duke of Richmond lie side by side even today in London's famous Westminster Abbey among the great and beloved of Britain's past. Their resting place may be visited. It is a small chapel which forms the apse of King Henry VII's Chapel. Ironically, King Charles II's body also lies in a vault not far from the duke and duchess, a fact that might have greatly suited his sardonic view of life.

King Charles had, in fact, forgiven Frances but a year after her elopement, and she and Richmond spent some time at court when they were on their own estates. However, the king did blame the no-doubt-innocent Chancellor Clarendon for counseling Frances to marry, and royal decree sent the loyal, strict old man into permanent exile.

Frances herself died in 1702 shortly after attending the coronation of the Duke of York's youngest daughter, Queen Anne, the offspring of his "plain, unwanted" wife, Chancellor Clarendon's daughter, Anne Hyde. As Richmond's death had preceded hers,

Frances' will left behind her parrot which she had brought from France years before, some beloved cats, and a vast collection of art, some of which is in the royal collection of Her Majesty, Queen Elizabeth II, today. Her will also shows she became an excellent businesswoman as she donated a rich endowment (including her ceramic Cupid watch) for the upkeep of her Scottish lands, an estate she and the duke had renamed Lennoxlove and which she inherited through a special dispensation of King Charles upon her husband's death.

Many of the other personalities whose lives Frances touched fared not so happily as she in later years. Barbara, countess of Castlemaine, whom King Charles created Duchess of Cleveland when he sent her away at last, was married bigamously at age sixty-five to a much younger man who treated her abominably. A spendthrift to the last, she died destitute in Paris. It is through Henry, duke of Grafton, son of this Duchess of Cleveland and Charles II that Diana, Princess of Wales, wife of the man who will someday rule as King Charles III, traces her royal heritage.

King Charles II's impetuous, illegitimate son, the Duke of Monmouth, was beheaded for a treasonous rebellion against his uncle, the Duke of York, then King James II, a few months after King Charles's death. As King James II, King Charles's brother and heir ruled for only three years until a bloodless revolution overthrew him for his Catholicism and despotism and forced him to flee to France, replacing him with his Protestant daughter Mary and her Dutch husband William. Sadly, Minette, King

Charles's beloved sister and Frances' friend, died painfully of peritonitis after a single, joyous reunion with her brother Charles in 1670. Rumors at both French and English courts insisted she had been poisoned by her possessive, jealous husband, the homosexual Philippe, brother of King Louis XIV of France.

Only King Charles's patient, beleagered Queen Catherine of Braganza ended her days in a self-imposed, somewhat peaceful exile. Widowed by King Charles II's death in 1685, she moved for a while to Somerset House, then returned home to her beloved Portugal after thirty years as an English Queen. Her elaborate state funeral in Portugal was proof that her people admired her, much like Frances who observed her unwavering, sad dignity as King Charles's queen.

Although much court scandal of the Stuart era views Frances Stewart as either flighty or "cunning," as Samuel Pepys' famous diary calls her, my research makes me believe the truth is otherwise: Frances managed to hold off an avid, powerful king for years; she foiled treacherous plots by such perverse characters as George Villiers, Duke of Buckingham, and his rapacious cousin Castlemaine; and she avoided political embroilments, as with the French, which had swamped many another royal favorite's career. Frances' beauty and her sophisticated charm, which reign yet in Britannia's proud profile on British coins, attest to her timeless magnetism and allure.

Frances was her own woman in the face of nearly overwhelming odds, and she managed to escape unscathed to live honorably with the man she loved despite the eccentric, frivolous times. Frances' strong marriage with Richmond and the fact she never remarried or had her name linked with other men even after his death, though she returned frequently to reside at court, indicate that she did indeed find and cherish rapture's crown in her tumultuous life.

—Karen Harper

THE BEST IN HISTORICAL ROMANCE
by Penelope Neri

HEARTS ENCHANTED   (1432, $3.75)

When Lord Brian Fitzwarren saw the saucy, slender wench bathing in the river, her fresh, sun-warmed skin beckoned for his touch. That she was his enemy's daughter no longer mattered. The masterful lord vowed that somehow he would claim the irresistible beauty as his own . . .

BELOVED SCOUNDREL   (1259, $3.75)

When the handsome sea captain James Mallory was robbed by the scruffy street urchin, his fury flared into hot-blooded desire upon discovering the thief was really curvaceous Christianne. The golden-haired beauty fought off her captor with all of her strength—until her blows became caresses and her struggles an embrace . . .

PASSION'S RAPTURE   (1433, $3.75)

Through a series of misfortunes, an English beauty becomes the captive of the very man who ruined her life. By day she rages against her imprisonment—but by night, she's in passion's thrall!

JASMINE PARADISE   (1170, $3.75)

When Heath sets his eyes on the lovely Sarah, the beauty of the tropics pales in comparison. And he's soon intoxicated with the honeyed nectar of her full lips. Together, they explore the paradise . . . of love.

Available wherever paperbacks are sold, or order direct from the Publisher. Send cover price plus 50¢ per copy for mailing and handling to Zebra Books, 475 Park Avenue South, New York, N.Y. 10016. DO NOT SEND CASH.

THE BEST IN ROMANCE FROM ZEBRA

TENDER TORMENT (1550, $3.95)
by Joyce Myrus

Wide-eyed Caitlin could no more resist the black-haired Quinn than he could ignore her bewitching beauty. Risking danger and defying convention, together they'd steal away to his isolated Canadian castle. There, by the magic of the Northern lights, he would worship her luscious curves until she begged for more tantalizing TENDER TORMENT.

SWEET FIERCE FIRES (1401, $3.95)
by Joyce Myrus

Though handsome Slade had a reputation as an arrogant pirate with the soul of a shark, sensuous Brigida was determined to tame him. Knowing he longed to caress her luscious curves and silken thighs, she'd find a way to make him love her to madness — or he'd never have her at all!

DESIRE'S BLOSSOM (1536, $3.75)
by Cassie Edwards

Lovely and innocent Letitia would never be a proper demure Chinese maiden. From the moment she met the dashing, handsome American Timothy, her wide, honey-brown eyes filled with bold desires. Once she felt his burning kisses she knew she'd gladly sail to the other side of the world to be in his arms!

SAVAGE INNOCENCE (1486, $3.75)
by Cassie Edwards

Only moments before Gray Wolf had saved her life. Now, in the heat of his embrace, as he molded her to his body, she was consumed by wild forbidden ecstasy. She was his heart, his soul, and his woman from that rapturous moment!

PASSION'S WEB (1358, $3.50)
by Cassie Edwards

Natalie's flesh was a treasure chest of endless pleasure. Bryce took the gift of her innocence and made no promise of forever. But once he molded her body to his, he was lost in the depths of her and her soul. . . .

Available wherever paperbacks are sold, or order direct from the Publisher. Send cover price plus 50¢ per copy for mailing and handling to Zebra Books, 475 Park Avenue South, New York, N.Y. 10016. DO NOT SEND CASH.